Casual Now
Meghan French

MEGHAN FRENCH

Visit my website at www.meghanfrenchauthor.com

Cover design: Neil, https://www.masterpaintingnow.com/

This one is for the anxious girlies, the ones who have been told directly or indirectly that they're not enough.

JJ Jeffers and I both know that's BS.

Contents

Content Warnings

Some of the following content warnings may be viewed as spoilers. However, your mental health is important to me, so please take care.

Anxiety

Descriptions of cheating

Gambling/Addiction

Mentions of emotional abuse

Mentions of childhood neglect and trauma, off-page

Gun violence (no fatalities)

Prologue
Amy

Several months ago

Patrick

I can't stop thinking about you, Amy. You're distracting me at work!

Me

I'm sorry! If it makes you feel better, I can't stop thinking about last night either. It's making it hard to focus on all these emails I need to send at work.

Patrick

I love the way you are so dedicated to your work. You are so talented, so amazing at what you do. Proud of you baby.

Me

I'm proud of you too, Pat!

One week later

Patrick

Hi angel. Just thinking about your laugh. It gets me through my hard days.

I know you're bogged down with nonstop field trip groups at work today, but I just wanted to say that you are sexy and gorgeous and you make me a better man. That is all.

No wait, that's not all. You are perfect in every way and I am so lucky to be your boyfriend.

Okay, last one: Jerry just showed us pictures here at work of his new puppy. We should adopt a dog together.

Me

Adopt a dog together? We don't even live together yet! <laughing emoji>

Patrick

Not yet, but soon.

Me

<heart eyes emoji>

Really?

Patrick

Baby, I want your forever. I want your mornings, afternoons, and nights. I want you to be the only one I'm kissing from now till eternity.

Me

OMG who even are you? Can you just come over already?

Patrick

OMW.

Four days later

Me

Hey baby! I got a Save The Date for my coworker's wedding in July! Just thought I'd let you know so you could pencil it in your calendar.

Patrick

July? I don't know what I'm doing then, but I'll be there!

Me

Well, yeah, that's the point of a Save The Date. They send it far enough in advance so you put it on your calendar and then the real invitation comes closer to the event date.

Patrick

> Baby, anywhere you go, I go. I'm more than happy to be your +1!

One week later

Patrick

> Hey sexy. I'm just thinking about our first date. How did I get so lucky to have the perfect woman agree to not only a first date with me, but multiple dates, and then to be my girlfriend?

Me

> I feel like I'm the lucky one. You are the best. Thank you for the flowers you sent to work. Alicia told me to tell you to knock it off. It's making the rest of the girls jealous.

Patrick

> Only the best for my baby. Tell Alicia her boyfriend needs to step his game up.

Me

> Alicia doesn't have a boyfriend.

Patrick

> She should get one. Then we can double date.

Me

You'd do that? I didn't know guys were really into that or only went along if their gfs dragged them.

Patrick

Not sure about other guys, but I'd do anything for you, Ames. You're my #1 girl

Me

Thank you honey!

Patrick

I'm serious. I can't wait to wife you up!

Me

<heart eye emoji> <kissy face emoji> <pink heart emojis>

Two days later

Patrick

I miss you.

Me

I miss you too. I can't believe I haven't seen you in only three days. It feels so much longer!

Patrick

As soon as I get home from this work trip, I'm coming straight to you. Fuck going to my apartment. I need to see my girl. I love you.

Me

> I love you too! What time does your flight land?

Patrick

> 5:37 at O'Hare. I'm hoping to make it to your place by 7?

Me

> Can't wait!!

Four days later

Me

> Did you see there's a new tapas restaurant opening on Southport?

Patrick

> Let's go! Red wine, patatas bravas, paella…<drooling emoji>

Me

> I'll find out when it officially opens and make reservations!

Patrick

> This is why I love you.

The pounding in my head is relentless, timed perfectly with the pulsing beat from my downstairs neighbor. Dude does not know the meaning of quiet hours, although seeing as it is ten in the morning, I can't exactly claim he is violating the apartment's rules. Normally, I'm not home during the weekday, but this is little excuse for the asshole downstairs. Day and night he blasts his music, and often it is the same songs or movies on repeat, ad nauseam. He never answers the door when I knock in a neighborly attempt to ask him to turn his music down. Since I am home sick today, though, it seems I am stuck listening to Anaconda by Nicki Minaj on repeat for the foreseeable future. Lovely. The song itself isn't terrible, but by the fortieth time this morning, I have had enough. My headache, paired with an inability to breathe out of my left nostril and a scratchy throat, makes for a lousy day in bed.

Luckily, my phone ringing distracts me from the thumping beat coming up from my floor. I smile, seeing Patrick's name on the caller ID.

"Hi babe," I answer.

"How are you feeling, sweetheart? Is your head any better?" The concern in Patrick's voice bleeds through the phone. He's always been an attentive boyfriend. God, some of the texts this man sends me! The other day, after telling me how much he loved me once again, he sent me some property listings in the city in neighborhoods that were close to good schools. It threw me for a little bit of a loop–we haven't ever talked about marriage or kids explicitly before, but I wasn't freaked out. Instead, it made me fall for him a little harder. I have never been with a guy who talks so openly about the future, and a future with me.

I still am not sure how I feel about having children. Don't get me wrong, I love kids. My job as a museum educator revolves around them. But, I thoroughly enjoy the idea of sending children home at the end of the day, too, so I can do my own thing. And, if I do end up having kids, as much as I love Chicago, I'm not sure if raising them in the city is something I'm up for. Patrick and I have been together for three months, so we have plenty of time to figure out the details, but I love that he is considering the future and our lives together.

"It's not great," I admit. "Pete Peterson downstairs isn't helping either." Pete Peterson is not his real name. I actually don't know my neighbor's first name, but his mailbox says "P. Peterson," so my best friend Danny christened him Pete and the name has stuck ever since.

"Ah, shit, that sucks, I'm sorry, baby." Patrick croons. "I can bring you some medicine and tea on my way home from work?"

"That would be great. I'd love to see you, but I don't want to get you sick."

"I'm not scared of getting a little cold. I'll bring you some goodies and if you want to hang, we can. Or you can sleep; whatever would help you to feel better."

Seriously, how did I get this lucky?

After our call, I turn on trashy daytime television; I'm not going to be able to sleep with the rave going on below me anyway. Danny ended up ordering noodle soup delivery to my apartment, bless his soul. After a few hours, he sends me links to new murder shows I can watch on our shared streaming account. While Danny and I don't live together, we have been friends since we were fourteen, and in my mind, that qualifies us as family, therefore allowing us to fudge the rules of shared accounts on our streaming network. Besides, Danny only lives a ten minute walk away; that practically counts as a shared household anyway. I begin drifting off to the dulcet sounds of true crime and don't wake until several hours later.

Pete Peterson's at-home concert is still going strong by the time Patrick pops by a little after five. I've been doing a good job so far of tuning it out, and with both the medicine and the nap I took earlier, I feel significantly better than I did when Patrick and I talked earlier.

"You know, we really should have keys to each other's places. Then you won't have to get up to answer the door when I come over." Patrick says as soon as I open the door. *Swoon.*

"Oh, sure, we can exchange keys. Danny has my spare, so I'll have to get a duplicate made, but I can do that." Patrick sighs. I know what he's going to say before he says it.

"How long has Danny had a key? He just comes over whenever?" Patrick mutters. We've been through this before. I don't know what Patrick's hangup is with Danny, but I can only assume it's because Danny is a guy. Patrick doesn't have any issue with my friendship with Alicia, my next closest friend, who I hang out with almost as frequently as Danny. The three of us are together fairly regularly. And while Danny is pansexual, he's been in a committed relationship with his boyfriend, Tim, for more than a year. In fact, other than a childhood crush that lasted about a day and a half, I've never had feelings for Danny beyond a warm friendship. I shook myself of that (admittedly one-sided) crush almost immediately because I never wanted to risk our friendship, even when I was sixteen. Patrick knows all of this. In fact, Patrick knows everything; I've never kept my relationship with any of my friends a secret.

"Yes, Danny has a key. Yes, I suppose Danny could technically come over whenever he wanted, but seeing as he's a normal human, he only comes when I ask him to. It's not like he's hanging out here when no one's home," I say, rolling my eyes. Patrick is an amazing guy, but this one issue with Danny is starting to grate on me. Danny has been nothing but kind and supportive of my relationship with Patrick, so I'm not sure where Patrick's tension is coming from. I remind myself Patrick is feeling insecure and needs my reassurance, not my annoyance. I loop my arms around his neck. "Danny is a friend. Alicia is a friend. You, my amazing man, are my boyfriend, and I love you." I give him a peck on the cheek and pull back to assess his emotions.

This seems to quell some of Patrick's unease as he leans down to kiss me. "Prove it," he murmurs against my lips.

"I don't want to get you sick," I whisper hesitantly.

"I don't care if I get sick," he responds simply. And, because I'm feeling better, I pull him to my bedroom, intent on proving exactly how much I love my him.

Patrick turns us and walks me back to the room until the back of my legs hit my bed. Gently, he pushes me down and pulls the tie on my silk robe. He looks down hungrily and licks his lips, pushing my robe off my shoulders and getting onto his knees. My breath hitches in my throat; while Patrick is great at foreplay, he often does not offer to go down on me. It's clearly not his favorite form of foreplay, which is a damn shame, because it happens to be my favorite.

He swipes his thumb through my wet folds, groaning when he feels my slick entrance. He places his palms on my knees, sliding them up the tops of my thighs and back down my inner thighs, spreading them wider for him. He throws my legs over his shoulders. Slowly, torturously, he brings his mouth to my core and licks a long swipe up the center. I fall back on a moan as Patrick presses his mouth fully against my pussy and begins applying his magic tongue everywhere. He sucks on my clit, causing my back to bow and a loud gasp to escape my mouth. The man is truly gifted. Patrick chuckles against me before resuming his ministrations, spearing his tongue inside me. He then replaces his tongue with first one finger, then two, curling them slightly to hit the spot where I need him, while he resumes tonguing my clit. My moans increase in their frequency. And while all of this feels incredible, Patrick and I both know this isn't going to make me come. I've never been able to finish from oral sex, despite my enjoyment of it. So I'm not too disappointed when Patrick stops his efforts after only a few minutes, flopping onto the bed next to me, unbuckling his pants, and pulling out his swollen cock. He quickly sheaths himself inside a condom with the speed of an F1 driver.

"Come on, baby, get on top," he says, voice husky. It's not my preferred position tonight, given that I am still recovering from my cold from earlier today, but if Patrick wants me to do all the work, I'm willing to make the sacrifice for a night. After all, he did just give me an amazing, albeit short, oral session. I swing my leg across his body and he slides up the bed, propping himself slightly against my pillows. I have a momentary hesitation that we're having sex in my literal sick bed, but it doesn't seem to bother Patrick. He notches himself against my entrance and I begin my slow slide down. I place my hands on Patrick's chest while I'm bouncing up and down, grinding myself against him, and Patrick, hands on my hips, controls some of my motions. After a few minutes, my muscles slowly tighten the more my clit rubs against the base of his shaft. Patrick can tell I'm getting close. He presses his thumb to my clit hard and I fall apart, sighing his name, toes curling underneath me. He follows shortly after, stuttering his movements, coming with a grunt. I collapse on top of him and he rubs his hands slowly up and down my slightly sweaty back. It's then that I notice he's still fully dressed. Again, not my preferred way of doing things, but it does make me feel a little powerful that my boyfriend couldn't wait to get inside me long enough to fully undress.

I smile to myself as I roll to the side, allowing for Patrick to sit up. He goes into the bathroom and grabs a wet towel to clean me and lies back next to me. Pulling me close to him, he pets my hair and murmurs sweet nothings in my ear.

"I can't wait to marry you. You are the perfect girl for me." Life doesn't get much better than this.

Two days later

Patrick

Guess what? I got the promotion!!!!!

Me

I'm SO fucking proud of you, Pat! No one deserves it more than you! Let's go out to Gallagher's to celebrate tonight!

Patrick

I actually think some of the guys at the office want to go out with me instead. Rain check?

Me

Oh, sure, of course. Just let me know when!

The next morning

Me

Hey babe, I haven't heard from you in a bit. Just checking in. Are you hungover from your celebration last night?

Patrick

A little.

Me

Anything I can do to help you feel better? I can bring you Portillo's or ibuprofen if you want?

Patrick

Nah, I'm good. Thanks though.

Me

Okay. Well, did you want to do dinner tonight to celebrate?

Patrick

Sure. I'm gonna take a nap.

Me

Okay, sweet dreams! Just let me know what time you want to go out and where and I can get us a reservation.

Several hours later

Me

Hey sleepyhead. How are you feeling?

Two hours later

Me

Are you still sleeping? That must be some hangover!

One hour later

Me

Babe, I'm starting to get worried since you're not answering your calls. I hope you're feeling okay. Just wanted to know if you wanted to rain check dinner if you're still feeling miserable.

Another hour later

Me

Well, it's 8:00 and I still haven't heard from you so I'm guessing dinner is a no go? Hope you're doing okay. Hit me up when you get this.

The next morning

Patrick

Hey sorry about last night

Me

Is everything okay? You had me worried!

Patrick

Yeah, everything's fine.

Me

Ooookay. Should I be concerned that I'm getting the bare minimum of information from you? Or am I just reading too much into the tone via text?

Patrick

No, everything is good. Hey I'm gonna head to the driving range with Sawyer. I'll hit you up later.

Five hours later

Patrick

Do you have time to talk?

Me

I'm getting a manicure in about five min. What's up?

Patrick

Okay. Look, I hate to do this over text, but I don't think we're on the same page anymore. I just wanted a casual relationship. It seems like you want more.

Sorry, I just don't think this is working. I'm feeling a little suffocated here.

Me

You need to pick up your phone.

Are you seriously breaking up with me via text??!!?!

PATRICK.

Patrick

I'm sorry. I'm not ready for something big and serious.

Me

Are you fucking for real right now???

CHAPTER ONE

Amy

Present Day

"**A**nd this is one of our most popular exhibits: an interactive human body! You can walk around the different chambers of the heart. There's even a pathway from the nostrils to the lungs, so you can really see what happens when we breathe!" I tell the excited group of second graders as we come to my favorite exhibit in the Humanities Museum. I smile as the kids disperse, running through the giant replica of the human body.

I've always loved museums. As a kid growing up in the suburbs of Chicago, it was always a treat to come into the city and spend the day at a museum. Usually Tuesdays were free ticket days, and my mom and I would spend summer hours wandering the exhibits of the Field Museum, the aquarium, the planetarium, and the Humanities Museum. While all museums are fascinating, the Humanities Museum is my favorite. A few years ago, the museum had a traveling exhibit about Egyptian mummies and I geeked out so hard. My job as a museum educator has me planning field trips and summer camps for kids of all ages and to say I love my job is a huge understatement. My boss is pretty awesome and I met one of my best friends, Alicia, through this job. The best part of my job is that I work for the Chicago Museum Association, meaning that I am able to organize events at any of the city's museums at any given time. While today I am working with second graders from the western suburbs at the Humanities Museum, tomorrow I get to work with high school juniors who are considering careers in aerospace engineering at the planetarium. Most of my work centers around the Humanities Museum and the planetarium, but I occasionally host groups at the Field Museum when their coordinator, Gina, needs help. Every day my job has me doing something different, which keeps me from ever getting bored.

These days, I'm especially grateful for the distraction. Ever since Patrick and I broke up–or, more accurately, ever since I got dumped out of the blue *via text!*–I've been struggling to get back out into the dating world. I still don't understand what happened with Patrick. All he kept saying was that he wasn't ready for something more than casual. Excuse me? *I* wasn't the one seeking out housing properties near schools for *us* to move into together. *I* didn't propose we adopt a dog together. Hell, even Patrick was the one who suggested we exchange keys. Yes, I was along for the ride every step of the way. I loved him. I thought he loved me, and maybe he did. Until he didn't. And now I'm left reeling, with no sense of closure.

It's not like I still love him. I'm long over that relationship. I grieved the loss over many bitching brunches, as Danny, Alicia, and I call them. I cried enough tears to fill Lake Michigan. And then suddenly, I woke up one day realizing I was all cried out. I remember looking at myself in the mirror, wondering where it went wrong. My chocolate brown eyes were puffy from tears and lack of sleep, and my dirty blonde hair was just dirty. And in that moment, I decided that was enough; I allowed myself two weeks of heartbreak. That was more than enough. I was no longer going to grieve for a man with the audacity to break up with me via text, like a fucking coward. Then, even my anger dissipated over time.

I no longer feel any emotions toward Patrick. I guess that's not true; there is still lingering confusion. I don't know what spooked him, and to be honest, I don't really care anymore. But I learned my lesson: just because a man says pretty words and tells you he loves you, it can all come crashing down in an instant. It's best not to become attached.

I'm at the point in my life where I'm viewing the breakup as a blessing in disguise. Or, maybe now that I'm no longer wearing rose-colored glasses, maybe it's just a blessing. It gave me time to really think about what I want in a relationship and what I don't want. And what I know is that I don't ever want to be put in that position again. If all men are looking for is casual, then I can be casual. I can guard my heart while still allowing my vagina happiness. New rule: hookups, friends with benefits, and casual dating only. I'm not looking to get married. Maybe I was at one point, but it is not worth the heartache anymore. I'm older and wiser and not falling for that again.

Danny tells me I'm being ridiculous and thinks it's just the grief talking. But what he doesn't accept is that I'm no longer grieving that relationship. While both my best friends agree Patrick is an idiot, they're split on their opinions beyond that. Alicia, while maybe not outright agreeing with my "casual only" relationship outlook, takes the "it's your life" approach and is happy as long as I'm happy. Danny, god love him, is still trying to convince me to give love a shot.

High School Danny would be slapping Adult Danny against his head. High School Danny was a cynic. Adult Danny, now deeply in love with Tim, believes in fairy tales, and while I'm generally really happy for him, I need Adult Danny to take a back seat and bring in High School Danny right now. He'd say "fuck love!" right with me, striking the match for me, ready to burn down my love life and all potential romantic prospects with it. But being in love has made Danny soft, and mindful, and happy....which is really, really annoying when I'm choosing to be single. Which is not to say I'm choosing to be celibate. More power to those people, but I am not one of them. The batteries in my vibrator have never had such a good workout these days. I'm surprised my vagina hasn't skipped town out of disgust and neglect from real, non-silicone attention. But now that I'm twenty-seven, dating and meeting new people isn't as easy as it was in college. I know I have to get back out there. There are only so many nights I can take holed up in my apartment with a book as my only companion. I've already read half of my Kindle To Be Read list, and while my book boyfriends are charming and thoughtful, they don't exactly replace the prospect of finding a real one, something my vagina doesn't hesitate to remind me of all too frequently.

I'm dipping my toe back into the dating pool by trying online dating and it's been nothing short of exhausting. Someone needs to invent a better way of meeting people, because if I get one more generic "Hey" message without any sort of conversational follow up, I'm going to scream. If I wasn't so afraid of getting murdered or contracting a flesh-eating STD, I'd probably embrace online dating a bit more. But between sifting through profiles, wading through conversations to vet someone enough to guess that they're probably, maybe, not a serial killer enough to meet up in public with them, the long process just to get laid—not even to find a real connection!-- is slowly killing me.

Alicia offered to set me up with her brother's friends. Hard pass. I'm not looking for a relationship or anything serious; there seems like too much of a risk I'll run into the guy again if things go south when we have more than a tenuous connection to other people.

"Oof," I gasp as a second grader tumbles into me, shaking me from my thoughts. "Let's use walking feet so no one falls!" I use my best teacher voice. I've never been an educator because I could never decide on a specialty or an age-group I liked best. I couldn't decide if I wanted to do special education, general education, high school, elementary school, or preschool. Plus, with the state of public education funding these days, I wasn't sure I wanted to go all in on a classroom environment. My current job allows the best of all worlds, allowing me to work with all student populations, although there's still some risk of funding getting cut at any given moment.

By the time I wrap up with the field trip group I've got scheduled today, I have enough time to head to my office to prepare for tomorrow's activities. Because most of the museums in Chicago are clustered in the same area, my office isn't too far away. I grab my jacket from the coat check at the front of the museum and button up; March in Chicago is a crap shoot and today, the weather is gloomy and chilly. I snuggle in closer to my peacoat and jog across the street to the planetarium. My office is housed in the basement of this building, scattered amongst extra exhibit materials and a handful of other offices. My tiny broom closet of an office fits little more than a desk and a filing cabinet, but it's all I need. On days where I don't have groups coming into one of the museums, I work from home. Or, more accurately, I work mostly from home and partly from my favorite neighborhood coffee shop. Nothing like sipping a warm, dirty chai latte while working from a cozy chair in a hip spot with good vibes.

My phone dings with a notification from my newest dating app. I swipe it open to reveal a one word message: "Hey." I groan, dropping my forehead onto my desk, cursing the gods of shitty communication.

CHAPTER TWO

Amy

I'm actually looking forward to this date, so much so that I agreed to do it at my favorite coffee shop, Caffeine Kingdom. Normally, I wouldn't risk tainting my cozy home away from home in case the date goes sour, but Jared and I have been talking off and on for a couple weeks and he seems like a decent guy. We had originally planned to grab drinks after work last week, but he had to work late. When we both had last minute openings in our schedule this afternoon, we planned an impromptu meetup here.

Jared was funny and kind in our chats, so I am looking forward to meeting him in person. Surprisingly, he looks just like his picture on the app too; score one for an honest guy! He shows up looking handsome in blue slacks, a white button down, and brown shoes. His blonde hair is closely cropped and his thick-framed glasses are flattering without being overly hipster. I smooth my hair as I stand to greet him. He gives me a peck on the cheek and asks what he can get me. I hold up my dirty chai, letting him know I've already gotten my drink, but thank him nonetheless.

When Jared stands in line to order, I mentally run through things we can talk about when he comes back. I guess I'm more nervous for this date than I realized, if I'm planning conversations in my head already. I changed my outfit three times before settling on what I'm currently wearing; I guess that should have been my first indication of nerves. Jared looks like he came from work, so I am glad I settled on black cigarette pants and a baby pink sweater that shows off my curves. I'm not majorly blessed in the boob department, but I get by. While I still have yet to lose the extra weight I gained during COVID quarantine several years ago, I feel pretty in this outfit without looking like I'm trying too hard. Ugh, I hope I don't look like I'm trying too hard.

Jared returns with a smile and a paper coffee cup, interrupting my overthinking.

"This place is great; I'm going to have to come back here more often!" He reports. "Did you know Maisie, the barista, is getting an art degree? She was working on some sketches at the register and showed me them. They're incredible."

Jared's been at my go-to coffee shop for five minutes and already knows the staff better than I do. Should I have been asking Maisie personal questions this whole time? Small talk with people in the customer service field is not my forte. I always feel like I'm intruding on them or dragging out conversations with them unless they initiate social small talk first. They're busy people, I don't want to keep them from doing what they need to do.

"Wow, that's great! I'll have to ask her about it sometime. I sometimes work here instead of my apartment when I work from home. It's nice to get a change of scenery. When it's warmer, the patio is amazing," I gush.

Jared and I make conversation; thank god he's a gifted conversationalist and I don't have to worry too much about awkward silences. He grew up in a small town in central Illinois and has been in the city more than ten years. We chat about our favorite bars and restaurants and learn we don't live too far from each other, only four L stops away on the Brown Line.

Jared and I end up talking so long, we each get refills of our coffees. I offer to buy the next round, and after some coaxing, Jared allows it. I'm a strong believer in splitting costs; I have a great job and can pay my own way. When I stand to get in line, I realize we've been here longer than I planned. The sun is setting and the line at the register has grown longer. Evidently, this is the place to go for evening joe on the way home from work. I end up getting in line behind a man with an adorable, slobbery Rottweiler who eyes me intently but remains standing next to his owner. I love when places let dogs inside while their owners place to-go orders; I feel so bad if they have to leave their furry friends outside just for a quick visit.

"Well aren't you just gorgeous?" I say, as the dog's little stump of a tail goes crazy. The man in front of me turns around.

"Thanks, I did just get a haircut," he jokes. I give him a polite smile, but I only have eyes for his pooch. "This is Bruno; he's very friendly. You can pet him if you'd like."

My day has been made. I crouch down to Bruno's level and am immediately knocked over as the dog thrusts his butt up against me, apparently looking for scratches. I laugh and scramble back to my feet as the owner apologizes profusely.

"Oh my gosh, I'm so sorry! He's a leaner. He loves everyone and demands butt scratches immediately upon meeting you."

"Well, that I can do for you, Bruno!" I continue loving on the dog until it's time for the owner to place his order, and I place mine and Jared's shortly thereafter. Returning to Jared, I gush over the beauty of my new friend, Bruno.

Jared and I remain at Caffeine Kingdom for another half hour before agreeing to another date, this time promising to actually get drinks after work next week. As I walk back to my place alone, I'm starting to feel a little more optimistic about this online dating thing. I didn't quite get butterflies from Jared, but there's potential there, and that puts a smile on my face.

CHAPTER THREE

Amy

I sink into the couch next to Alicia and Danny at Danny's condo. Tim was called into work and will likely come home to the three of us drunk, shouting about god knows what. I hope he's ready to deal with our shenanigans.

Danny tops off our wine and places an order for Thai food. He's always in charge of ordering because he knows Alicia and I get too engrossed in conversation to remember to order until all three of us are starving. While we don't always get together for Saturday night wine and trashy television, Tim and Danny are heading to the suburbs tomorrow to visit Danny's grandmother, so our Sunday brunch plans shifted to Saturday night winedowns this weekend instead.

"How was the second date with Jared this week?" Alicia asks. She already asked this in our group chat, but I told them I'd give them all details in person.

"It was fine. No spark," I start.

"Hold up. You claim you want casual but now you want a spark? You don't need a spark to ride his dick, love." Danny has never held back on his opinions and I don't expect him to start now.

"Noted." I take a larger sip of wine than I intended and press my lips together.

"What aren't you telling us?" Alicia eyes me suspiciously. Danny, previously looking at his phone, whips his head up at me, a gleam in his eye telling me I'm not getting out of this one so easily.

I sigh, resigning myself to my fate. Danny in particular is like a dog with a bone when it comes to gossip, and if there's even a whiff of the sexy kind of gossip, he's relentless.

"Okay fine, we hooked up! Or we tried to at least." I throw my hands up in the air. I don't know why I'm acting guilty about this. I'm a grown woman; people hook up all the time.

"Nothing wrong with that, babe," Alicia soothes. "But you know you're gonna have to give us the details, right? And what does 'tried to hook up' mean, exactly? Technical difficulties?"

"No!" I cover my eyes with my hands. "I suppose…it was fine. No spark." I repeat, hoping it will get me out of having to explain more while at the same time knowing it won't. Danny and Alicia just wait. "Fine," I huff. "We went back to his place and were making out on his couch. Just as we approached second base, he got a phone call, apparently from his sister, and ended up talking to her for so long, I just left. I'm not sure he even noticed me leaving at the twenty minute mark of their phone call."

"Ooh, that's rough. Maybe there was an emergency?" Alicia supplies helpfully. My glare indicates otherwise.

"Not unless making small talk, making brunch plans, and planning to go to a baseball game next week constitutes an emergency," I grumble. "I don't know if I did something wrong or what. Or if that person on the line even was his sister; I mean, who plans two events in one week with a sister during the middle of your date?"

I habitually give people the benefit of the doubt, probably to a fault. So when Jared initially picked up the call during our date, I didn't think too much of it. Who am I to judge family dynamics? Maybe his sister was sick or new in town? However, after several minutes of awkwardly sitting on Jared's couch, smoothing my skirt and waiting for him to remember he was in the middle of a date, my benefit of the doubt mentality shifted to plain old doubt. I doubted my ability to keep Jared entertained—did I say or do something to turn him off? Did he feel pressured to invite me back to his place when he really didn't want to? Did I somehow misread the signs? Was *this* the sign that Jared was too polite to directly give me? After two instances of Jared holding up a finger and mouthing "one minute" while failing to wrap up his conversation with his alleged sister, I gave up. As much as I was doubting myself, I have enough self-respect to make up for the lack of it coming from Jared. So I waved goodbye, not stopping to see if he even noticed, and took my leave.

"I don't know," I continue hesitantly, casting my eyes away from Danny and Alicia. "Maybe I'm just too picky. Maybe there is no real, sweep-you-off-your-feet romance, and it's just made up to sell movies."

In college, I was in a long-term relationship that ended a year after we graduated and just couldn't make the distance work. Aside from Patrick, who was introduced to me through my old coworker, I am so far removed from the dating scene I apparently don't know how to pick them anymore.

"Don't say that. Tim is proof that kind of love exists; you just have to find it." Danny squeezes my hand reassuringly. "You're a catch. You look fantastic, you're hard working without being a workaholic, and you have the best personality. The right person is out there." He gives me a warm smile.

Maybe all relationships evolve the way Danny's and mine have, but when you know someone almost your whole life, the shift from childhood friendship to adult friendship is a magical thing. When we were younger, Danny would never have been so bold as to give me such straightforward compliments. Maybe it's the confidence that comes with age, or the security in a long standing friendship, but I find so much comfort in our relationship—and to think Patrick was threatened by it. A small niggle of worry works its way into my heart as I wonder if any man I date will ever accept our friendship at face value.

My anxiety is interrupted by the arrival of our pad Thai. For the rest of the night, I get lost in good food, good wine, and the laughter of my close friends.

CHAPTER FOUR
Jackson

"**S**ean, you know I love you, but I've got to go. I can't be late the first week of the season!"

My brother continues rambling, advising me to consider a new sponsorship deal with an energy drink company. I'm not opposed to the deal, I just don't have time to discuss it right now. I overslept this morning, so I didn't get a chance to connect with my brother until later than I typically would have, and it's been pushing my whole routine back this morning. I know I'm lucky to have my older brother serve as my agent; he's the best in baseball and, as of recently, the best in soccer, too, when he picked up a few new players from the Chicago Tornadoes this offseason. Sean keeps talking, but it's hard to tell if he's speaking to me or to his secretary, Kevin. He is constantly multitasking, so I'm not even sure he's heard what I've said. I hang up anyway. Another perk of my brother being my agent is that I can do things like hang up on him. I'll talk to him after the game, I think, as I lock my car and jog across the street to enter the lobby that leads down to the clubhouse.

There's a swarm of fans behind the steel barrier outside the players' parking lot. Normally, I would stop to sign autographs and take a few pictures with fans, but today I don't have time. I give the fans an apologetic smile and hustle off, swiping my ID badge to get me into the building and out of the public eye.

Opening Day was Wednesday, so I know the fans are eager for a strong start to the season. As today is Saturday, there are more fans than usual waiting outside the lot and a pang of guilt hits me. Fan relations is such an important part of this job to me. The Chicago Foxes have played in the same city, the same stadium, for nearly one hundred years. I'm well aware that without the fans, I wouldn't have a job. I'd still be playing baseball, but I wouldn't get a paycheck for it. Knowing that, I always make it a priority to give the fans the attention they deserve.

I head down to the clubhouse and change into my workout gear. April in Chicago is still cold, so I'm in my Foxes orange joggers and a blue sweatshirt. My schedule has me lifting and stretching in the first group before heading to the field to hit batting practice and do some light conditioning work. Once I'm finished, I'll grab food and work on mobility before heading out to the field for pregame stretch. I take a deep breath and grin at my best friend, Caleb Andrews, our second baseman and my old college roommate.

Caleb's locker is next to mine and he's got as goofy of a grin on his face as I do on mine. When you get down to it, all my teammates and I are just a bunch of kids excited to play baseball. We're living the dream, and between defensively manning the infield with my best friend, solidifying myself as the season's likely cleanup hitter, and all the other perks that come along with being a professional athlete in the best city in the world, I know I'm living a charmed life.

"Hey pretty boy, you're gonna be late to our meeting!" Caleb throws over his shoulder as he runs down the hallway toward the theater that also serves as a whole-team meeting room. We usually go over strategy on the opposing pitcher before starting our individual work for the day. I catch up to Caleb easily, giving him a shove. "Watch the goods!" He exclaims. "This body just inked a two year extension; I can't be getting injured the first week!"

I laugh. I'm truly happy for my teammate; he's been through a lot in the last year. His fiancee, Jenny, is battling breast cancer at twenty-eight years old. He needed that contract extension to stay in Chicago to allow her access to her current oncology team without having to move across the country and transfer her medical care.

When we all reported to spring training this past February, Caleb was a ghost of himself. I had never seen him so subdued, like he didn't even want to be there. A Caleb who was not enthusiastic about baseball was as foreign to me as Chicagoans putting ketchup on their hot dogs. Leaving Jenny, even for the six weeks we played in Arizona to prepare for the start of the regular season, took a toll on him. Caleb has always been devoted to Jenny, from the first moment he met her years ago, but ever since her treatment began, his dedication has reached a whole new level. Jenny has her family in Chicago, and they took her to all of her appointments while Caleb was out of town, but I know he felt guilty for not being physically present during that time.

Jenny pushed him to go, knowing he needed to be with the team, not just on a physical level, but for his own mental health, but Caleb didn't see it that way. Especially in the beginning of spring training, he was teary and sullen. He was constantly glued to his phone and luckily, team management was understanding of his needs and gave him a lot of leeway in their demands of him.

I made Caleb's wellbeing during this time my biggest priority. Seeing my friend suffer and being there for him was the least I could do for both him and Jenny. She was a rockstar with her treatments and keeping her spirits up. I texted with her almost as much as Caleb did.

When Caleb broke down crying in my arms after a game one night, a piece of me broke with him. He shared his powerlessness to help the love of his life when he was two thousand miles away from her. Jenny expressly forbid him from leaving spring training, but him staying away took a toll as well. Jenny is my friend, too, and I think I needed to feel helpful almost as much as Caleb did. As a result, throughout the time we were gone, I helped him create weekly gifts for her. It allowed us to feel like we were actually doing something to help. One week, we created a video diary of all the things Caleb loved about Jenny and all the things he would have liked to do with her in Scottsdale if she would have been able to make the trip. The next week, I helped him put together a self-care spa package complete with nail polish, body scrubs, and a hair mask. One week, we attempted to make cookies in Caleb's extended stay hotel room kitchenette; we almost burned down the hotel before settling on ordering cookie delivery from a local Chicago bakery instead. Keeping Caleb busy and feeling like he was doing something to help in Jenny's cancer journey helped his mental health immensely, which translated into improved performance on the field. Team management obviously noticed, and fans already loved Caleb, so the Foxes offering a contract extension to my best friend was a foregone conclusion. I couldn't be happier for him.

My brother, Sean, is also Caleb's agent and he worked tirelessly with the owners of the Foxes to hammer out a deal to allow him to stay with the team that originally drafted him. For the early part of my career, I hopped around to different teams, especially in the minor leagues. I was a hot commodity, which made me a valuable trade asset, and teams used me as such. Now that I've been in the majors for six years, I've found stability in Chicago after playing in Philadelphia for a few years. I've established roots here. I've made friends with my neighbors in my building; hell, my downstairs neighbor even watches my dog on road trips, which is a godsend. I'm in the middle of my career at twenty-nine years old, and I plan on playing as long as I can. For as laid back as my personality is,

I know when to buckle down and get the work in. Today is no exception.

Later in the morning, I watch my teammates take batting practice and tug my winter hat down tight over my ears. Someday, I will get used to Chicago springs. Today is not that day. But, like always, I make the best of it. The beats are bumping through the PA system and I'm dancing while I wait for my turn in the batter's box. I'll do anything to keep warm, but I also really love this song.

"Jeffers, are you coming out with us tonight?" Kyle Crawford, today's starting pitcher, yells at me from the dugout. He's one of my favorite pitchers, and because he's starting today, he got to pick the tunes. I knew I liked him for a reason. As someone who only has to play every five days, though, him going out tonight with a day game tomorrow does not have the same repercussions as me going out. Sure, he still has to show up to the ballpark and get his workouts in, but he can do that hungover since his presence is not actually required on the field. If I show up hungover, I'm likely to take a one-hop grounder to the face if I'm not paying attention. No thanks.

"I'll hit dinner with you, maybe a little dancing at the club, but it's lights' out at ten PM for me. You guys gonna be there longer than that?" I already know the answer. Crawford is a notorious playboy; if there are single women out, he'll stay out till he has to drag his ass into the ballpark the next morning.

"You know it. I haven't been out in the city since October; I've got a lot to make up for!" Crawford spends his offseason in Arizona, but Caleb and I make our homes here year-round. While I grew up moving frequently, my younger brother, Nate, settled in Milwaukee, so it makes sense for me to stay here. Sean is in New York, but he makes it out to visit me on the road or here in Chicago several times per year. Prior to last year, I had other reasons to stay in this city, too.

"Okay, count me in for a little bit. But then I'm going home to sleep." I used to be just as much of a playboy as Crawford in my early years. When women flock to you just because of the job you have, it's hard not to get caught up in that lifestyle. But a few years ago, I changed my ways. I had my reasons, and while those reasons no longer exist for me, I haven't had the heart to go back to my player roots. I guess that's what happens when your heart is ripped out of your chest and spat on.

I rub my hands together, willing the warmth into my fingertips before I step into the box. This offseason, I've been working on gratitude, positive thoughts, and visualizing success. I breathe in as my hitting coach tosses the first pitch. Breathing out, I swing, connecting with an instant homer. Yes, this is going to be a great season.

Last night, after we pulled out a resounding win, Crawford, Andrews, and Carter Perez, our left fielder, had dinner at our preferred steakhouse on the Chicago River. I stuck around for about an hour after to go to a rooftop bar. Luckily, this one was equipped with a heated, glass greenhouse-type structure on the roof so we got the outdoor vibe without experiencing the outdoor temperatures. As usual, women were drawn to our group, and Kyle Crawford in particular, like moths to a flame. Caleb and I engaged in polite conversation with them, but we both knew we were leaving the bar by ourselves. Caleb is so madly in love with his fiancee it's not even funny, and I find it's harder to muster up the energy for another meaningless connection followed by an awkward goodbye. As soon as the women who had approached us in the bar figured out Caleb and I weren't interested, they shifted their attention to Perez and Crawford; we heard no complaints from them.

I am taking Bruno for a long walk this morning to make up for the time I didn't spend at home last night. I stopped in after the game and before I went to dinner, but I still feel some dog-dad guilt when I don't spend as much time as possible with Bruno. Lisa, my downstairs neighbor, is always happy to spend extra time with him, so I hope he doesn't feel too lonely.

Bruno is enjoying every second of this walk. He believes he's a great hunter and squirrels quake in his presence. In reality, the squirrels just climb the nearest tree and chatter down at him. I swear, I even saw one shake their little squirrel fist at him for being a general menace to the limited wildlife in this area. My condo has a dog park that has both an indoor and outdoor section on it, which is great in a pinch, but whenever possible, I try to get him to the real outdoors on a walk. I have to head in early to the ballpark for another day game, so I don't have a ton of time to walk with Bruno, but there's enough time to hit Caffeine Kingdom, a new coffee shop I discovered about half a mile from my condo.

I don't have too many vices in the world. I try to limit my drinking during the season, or at least when I have day games the next day. I never got into chewing tobacco like some of my teammates, but even most of them who did dip quit with the league's push to eradicate it from the game. I generally eat healthy, too, at least during the season. But my one consistent vice is that of coffee. While I take my caffeine in many forms, hence Sean's push for me to be the face of a new energy drink on the market, coffee is my preferred vessel, and the stronger, the better.

The door chimes cheerily as I enter the coffeeshop. The cashier looks up and smiles for Bruno. I'm used to having women smile at me; I know I'm attractive, and I'm not saying that to be cocky. When you are told something enough, it becomes easy to believe it. However, whenever I'm with Bruno, that hairy beast steals all the attention, from males and females alike. If he weren't so damn adorable, I might resent him for it.

I order my double shot red eye and a pup cup for Bruno and make my way outside. If I even attempt to give Bruno his whipped cream inside the store, it will look like a Jackson Pollock of slobber and melted dairy all over the cafe. I pull Bruno to the side of the walking path and set down the cup. I barely get it on the ground before he's going to town, little droplets of drool and whipped cream splashing everywhere.

I'm in the middle of checking my texts when I feel Bruno's leash slide smoothly from out of my hands as he runs alongside a woman jogging by. He's keeping pace with her while I run behind him, yelling for him like a moron. Thank fuck the runner stopped, causing Bruno to stop and jump on her.

"He's friendly, I swear! I am *so* sorry! He's never done that before! Bruno! Get over here!" Of course, my dog has no plans to abandon the runner, and when I look up, leash firmly returned to my grasp, I can hardly blame him. Standing there, pink tinge to her cheeks, is a beautiful woman struggling under the weight of a massive canine. Lucky for all of us, she's laughing and petting Bruno behind his ears. I forcibly remove my dog and put him back on all four legs, continuing to apologize profusely.

"Ah, that's okay, this is my buddy, Bruno, right?" The woman laughs.

I eye her suspiciously. Bruno looks damn proud of himself; he should be, since I'm the only one unaware of their apparently deep, long-lasting relationship.

"I met him at Caffeine Kingdom a few weeks ago," she explains and a memory clicks into place. A beautiful blonde in a fuzzy pink sweater behind me in line, all giant chocolate eyes and wavy hair. Even then, she struck me as attractive; I would have stayed to chat with her that day, but she made no indication of her interest in me, only in Bruno. Go figure: my face gets recognized wherever I go in this city and this woman recognizes my *dog* instead. I mean, he's a handsome boy, if you're into slobber and shedding hair. I didn't wake up today and think my own dog would serve me an ego check so early in the morning, but here we are.

"That's right. I'm Jackson," I say, grimacing. "Again, I'm so sorry he jumped on you. I hope he didn't scare you." The woman gives me a quizzical look.

"Scare me? Nah, this big baby is just a lover." She continues scratching Bruno behind his ears, and I swear the smug bastard grins at me. He's so proud of himself, for once beating me to the attention of a pretty girl. I, on the other hand, am mortified. First, for being an irresponsible dog owner, and also for forgetting I'd met this woman before.

"I'm Amy. Bruno is always welcome to say hi and get some pets!" She replies cheerfully. "Well, I should keep going on my run. Nice to meet you. Be a good boy, Bruno!" Before I have a chance to say anything else, Amy is on her way, leaving both Bruno and me to watch her go.

CHAPTER FIVE

Amy

I could not be more embarrassed. There's a reason I started my run so early in the morning today, hoping to avoid running into others. Next thing I know, I've literally run into a dog and the most gorgeous man I've ever seen while I'm fighting for my life on this damn run. Bruno's owner initially seemed skeptical of me, narrowing his glacier-blue eyes my way. In hindsight, I probably sounded like a lunatic, knowing his dog's name instead of his own. I was momentarily stunned by the man's good looks—and not just those piercing eyes. His floppy brown hair, towering height, and five o'clock shadow combined in one person was enough to put my hottest book boyfriend to shame. Hopefully my new acquaintance attributed my blush to my workout, rather than my obvious attraction to him.

I work out, okay, but cardio is not my friend. Yoga is more my style. Yoga in the cocoon of my own home, without falling into the ego trap of comparing myself—good or bad—to the other practitioners in the room, is most especially my style. But my routine was getting stagnant and I really am trying to lose some of this weight. And what do I get for my efforts? Death by mortification. If my

44

heart didn't kill me on this run, my embarrassment would. Jackson is clearly in great shape; I could see the outline of his biceps through his henley. As if I weren't self-conscious enough about my figure, I run into the mortal equivalent of a Greek god on the sidewalk in Lincoln Park.

The good news is that my embarrassment fuels my run a little bit more, so I'm not huffing and puffing quite as much as I was when I ran into Jackson and Bruno by the time I get home. The run allows me some time to collect my thoughts and talk myself off the ledge. I try telling myself I'll probably never see them again, but seeing as I've already run into them twice, and they were right outside of Caffeine Kingdom, my favorite haunt, I resign myself to my fate of possibly seeing them again. Hopefully next time it will be under much more flattering circumstances.

I shake my head, trying to knock the self-conscious thoughts out of my brain. I have too much on my plate today to spend time dwelling on my own hangups. The pile of emails in my inbox necessitates working from home on a Sunday. There's a risk of funding getting slashed if the Illinois state congress doesn't approve additional funding proposals, and they seem to be dragging their feet on voting even more than they usually do. Which means I get to spend my weekend applying to and writing grants to allow for my work and the work of my colleagues to continue uninterrupted for the next few years. It's hard not to feel a lot of weight on my shoulders right now, even though I know it's not just me feeling the pressure. I even canceled brunch with the gang in order to get more work done. I was feeling motivated and ambitious this morning, wanting to start the day on the right foot (pun intended) by going for a jog. Now that I'm home, despite physically feeling better, I'm regretting that decision. I really could have used that extra time to begin working.

While what I really want to help me jump start my work is my standard dirty chai from Caffeine Kingdom, I know I need to make my morning caffeine in my apartment so I can get started sooner. I rush through a shower; luckily, my hair wash day isn't until later tonight, so I can get by with a quick body wash before booting up my laptop.

By noon, my head is spinning. Marianne, the administrative assistant to all the educators at the Chicago Museum Association, must have worked yesterday. My inbox is filled with information from potential grants that could benefit us. Unfortunately, a lot of them don't apply to us; we don't meet the eligibility criteria or the window to apply has already closed. I decide my best course of action is to start the research portion over myself. Marianne is wonderful, but grant writing is not her specialty, and it's hard for her to know what to look for.

I blink my eyes several times. The days I work in front of my computer are somehow more exhausting than shepherding large bands of small children through interactive museum exhibits. If we don't secure additional funding, positions are going to get cut, and while my position is less at risk than some of the newer employees at CMA, I am not willing to entertain that possibility becoming a reality for anyone. I am fiercely protective of my people, but the added layers of stress and anxiety breathing down my neck are not exactly conducive to work productivity. I've always struggled with internalizing my stress, resulting in a diagnosis of Generalized Anxiety Disorder in college. I work through it with my therapist every other week and supplement with a regular diet of yoga, but sometimes, work gets the better of me. It's hard for me to take breaks in these situations, even though Connie, my therapist, advocates for them. My breaks end up with me spiraling even more, fixating on all of the things I *could* be getting done if I wasn't taking a break. Sure, logically, I know I can't pour from an empty cup, but *emotionally* I ascribe to the "just power through" mentality. I know it's not healthy; I'm working on it. Sometimes.

After a few more hours sifting through application criteria and firing off endless rounds of emails, all of which are going to go unanswered today because no one other than me is insane enough to work on a gorgeous spring day, I decide to hit up Alicia to see if she wants to grab an early dinner. It's unseasonably warm today and we might luck out at some of the restaurants on Fullerton Avenue with outdoor seating.

Two hours later, Alicia and I are sitting in the sun, enjoying a slight breeze at Bowl Me Over, a new grain and pasta bowl cafe. I opt for a tofu and quinoa bowl with a basil tahini dressing, while Alicia orders a Southwestern sweet potato bowl with chicken on the side. As usual, we split our entrees in half and swap half of them, Alicia keeping all the chicken in her bowl. I tell her about the last grant I found during my research. It seems the most promising of all the options I found today, and the requirements are something we can easily fulfill if we get approved. Most of the requirements we already fulfill: host educational field trips relating to natural science, work with diverse groups of students, track data on field trip numbers and participants. This grant requires us to fill out a bit more paperwork following each group visit as well as administer pre- and post-activity surveys for the kids to answer. As long as we can use the additional supply of tablets a previous grant awarded us, this should be something easily accomplished with hopefully minimal effort.

I'm talking so much that Alicia is almost finished with her food by the time I make a dent in my bowl. Alicia smiles and lets me continue rambling; we've been friends long enough that she knows I just need to spew the information first, and we can dissect it all later. I'm about to put the most perfect forkful of sweet and spicy grains in my mouth when a large Rottweiler comes bounding up to me. Immediately recognizing the playful pooch as my friend from earlier this morning, I squeal out, "Bruno! Are you following me today?"

The dog gives me a grin, his stump of a tail becoming a blur. I laugh as Jackson, my newly introduced neighbor, shakes his head in embarrassment.

"Amy, right? I am so sorry; I swear I'm not following you. Bruno must have some magnetic draw to you or something." Jackson continues apologizing profusely, only stopping when he notices I'm still laughing.

"This handsome fellow is Bruno," I explain to Alicia. "And his owner, Jackson. Apparently they live in this neighborhood, too, and apparently, they love Caffeine Kingdom and taking walks wherever I am."

"I promise, I'm not stalking you," Jackson sputters, his ears turning red. His embarrassment is endearing, and the thought of stalking didn't cross my mind until Jackson voiced it. I often see the same people walking the same dogs at similar times in my neighborhood. In Lincoln Park and Lakeview, knowing your neighborhood dogs better than their human counterparts is pretty par for the course. I'm just grateful I actually remembered Jackson's name and didn't have to introduce him as "Bruno's owner" (or worse, "Bruno's *dad*") to Alicia.

Jackson apologizes again, tugging Bruno away. The dog reluctantly follows and I can't help but laugh at Jackson's rebuke to the oblivious puppy. "Dude, you can't just slobber on anyone and declare yourself as their best friend. I love you, but that's not how you make friends!"

I chuckle, returning to my food. When I glance up at Alicia, she is wide eyed and gawking at me.

"What?" I ask.

"Do you know who that was?" she asks, her voice a whispered hiss.

"Know who who was? My neighbor?" I don't know why Alicia is looking borderline offended right now. Alicia is never one to hold back her feelings, but her reaction seems a little extreme, given the innocuous situation.

"That's JJ Jeffers!" Alicia continues to hiss like a snake. At my blank look, she rolls her eyes. "All-star shortstop for the Foxes? Has his own shoe deal? His face is on half the bus stops in the city!"

"Oh. Well. Now I feel stupid for recognizing his dog more than him." I squint, trying to recall just how ubiquitous Jackson's–JJ's–face is. Alicia is right, as she often is. His face is everywhere. I don't know how I didn't make the connection. "I guess I never paid that much attention. Besides, he called himself Jackson. And it's not like I actually pay attention to what baseball players look like! I can't even tell you the last time I've seen a Foxes game!"

Alicia continues shaking her head at me the more I talk. It's not my fault I didn't recognize the guy. I recognized how annoyingly good looking he was, but I might have pegged him as a model before coming up with "athlete." Maybe I would have recognized JJ if he was walking around in his Foxes uniform? Honestly, half the team could be eating dinner at the table next to us and I wouldn't know it. I can appreciate sports and enjoy myself at games, but I don't follow any teams enough to know what any players, on any of Chicago's teams, look like on sight alone. Except for Michael Jordan; is he still around? I'd recognize him.

CHAPTER SIX

Jackson

W e're about to kick off a ten-day road trip and while I always like to go into road trips fresh off a win, hoping that momentum will carry us through our away games, that's not the case today. Luckily, we avoided being swept by Los Angeles, but they won two out of our three games. I'm in a shitty mood. Despite playing okay myself, our offense didn't put up nearly the run support needed to pull off a final win this afternoon. There is little time for me, or anyone else for that matter, to dwell on the loss. Getaway days are hectic. The team bus leaves the field an hour after the game ends, giving me barely enough time to do my post-game cool down, shower, grab my bag, and climb aboard.

The bus is relatively quiet today; everyone else knows we should have pulled out a win in today's game, too. Our manager, Benny, isn't one to harp on the losses or drill our mistakes into our skulls, but it doesn't stop the disappointment from pressing into us like an oppressive cloud. I'm hoping by the time we get on the plane, the gloom that has settled over the team will dissipate so we can go into our next series with clear heads. Sometimes our road stretches are only three or five games, but a ten game series is brutal. We play four games in Philadelphia, three in Boston, and three in New York before I finally make it back to Chicago for a well-deserved day off. I've made plans to meet up with a couple of the guys in Philly that I used to play with and who are still on the team. In New York, I'll meet up with my brother, Sean. While those activities are all things I'm looking forward to, I know I'll be exhausted by the time I make it home. I shouldn't complain though–the life of a baseball player is pretty luxurious. Case in point: the police cars escorting our buses to the airport so we don't even have to stop at lights or follow regular traffic patterns. The buses will pull straight onto the tarmac once we make it to O'Hare airport. The most taxing part of the trip is climbing up the stairs onto the plane. We really do have it good.

By the time I do make that climb up the twenty or so steps onto our chartered flight, my prediction about the mood of the team has proven correct. The boys' spirit has lightened. Tyler, our catcher, has started pumping tunes through his mini speaker, and a few of the guys–Warner James, Carter Perez, and Matteo Cota– have continued their tradition of a high-stakes poker game in the back few rows of the plane. I purposely chose my usual seat at the beginning of the season to be far away from them. I don't need anything remotely like that in my life anymore.

Caleb saunters back to the row across from me, handing me a full solo cup of red wine. "You seeing Thompson and Syzmanski tonight?" he asks, referring to my old teammates.

"Yeah, we're gonna hit up McNally's. Wanna join?" McNally's is a hole in the wall Irish pub near enough to the ballpark in Philadelphia to walk to, yet far enough away that we won't be bombarded by fans. It was my go-to spot after games when I played in Philly and I'm looking forward to reconnecting with my first baseman and outfielder.

"Nah, I'm gonna stay in. Jenny is pretty tired from treatment today so we are going to watch a movie together over FaceTime. We just want to do something low-key." I nod in understanding. Jenny and Caleb are a great couple and perfect for each other. While Jenny's prognosis has gradually improved with chemotherapy and radiation, it still kills me she has to suffer the way she has, and seeing the impact of her sickness on Caleb guts me as well. I'm glad they have each other. Jenny brings out the best in Caleb; he's a little more even-tempered with her around, which has translated to better focus on the field, especially when she's feeling okay. Jenny has relied on Caleb through her diagnosis and treatment. Even though they're not married yet, they are already living the "in sickness and in health" part of their relationship. A twinge of jealousy hits me and I'm immediately ashamed of myself. I have my supportive brothers and a found family in my teammates. Just because I've been a little unlucky in the romance department doesn't make it a bad life. And maybe if I'd made different choices in my own relationships, I wouldn't be sitting here on an airplane, pining over not having a relationship like my best friend's.

I used to have one like that. Not just a relationship, but a fiancee, too. I thought I had what Caleb and Jenny have. I thought so right up until I came home early from a road trip and found someone else balls deep in my future wife, Carolyn. I flash back to that moment, walking through the door of our shared townhouse in my mind.

I was hoping to surprise Carolyn so I hadn't let her know that our plane already landed. We just finished a quick game and were able to leave Cincinnati earlier than anticipated, so I knew she wasn't expecting me home so soon. But with the earlier schedule, I had been hoping to take her out for dinner that night.

"Okay."

It was all I could think of to say once my brain finally clicked back online. I stood there for what felt like an eternity, watching a man who was not me fuck my fiancee. It's true what they say about the feeling of time standing still; I have no idea how long I stood there frozen. It could have been minutes, it could have been hours, the soundtrack of their pants and moans playing in the background while my world slowly fell apart around me. I was powerless to stop the pieces from falling. I probably only stood there for a minute or two before I finally found words. Or one word. 'Okay' was all I said; what else could I say?

I turned and walked out the door. I could hear Carolyn squawking behind me but I didn't bother to turn around. For years, I built a life around her. My momentary brain lapse all but forgotten, now

I couldn't slow my thoughts down. All our plans: ruined. Our shared friendships: effectively over. My heart: shattered, along with my trust in the one person I had come to rely on more than anyone.

I sat on the steps to our townhouse, unsure of what to do or where to go. My mind was screaming at me to get out of there, but I couldn't make my feet move. I needed a plan. I needed to not feel this way. I didn't even know how I felt, I just knew I needed to not feel this.

Carolyn came outside a few minutes later, tying her silk robe around her waist, tears streaming down her face. How dare she cry when she did this to us? My emotions vacillated between anger and sorrow, then back to anger again. Then grief, and heartbreak, embarrassment, confusion, betrayal. How could one person feel all of this at once? I needed to think, not feel, but I couldn't think with all of these emotions swirling inside my already exhausted brain.

"I'm sorry," Carolyn whispered, as she sat next to me and grasped my hands. I slowly extricated myself from her grasp. I didn't know what I wanted in this situation, but I knew I didn't want her hands on me. Not when only moments ago, her hands were on someone else. I just looked at her, unsure whether I wanted to explode in anger or retreat into myself.

"It didn't mean anything, I swear. I love you, JJ." I still said nothing. "I didn't think you would be home so soo-" she cut herself off at the look on my face. "It doesn't matter. I'm so sorry. Please forgive me, JJ. Baby, please."

"Who is he?" My voice came out in a strangled whisper and I immediately cringed at how weak it sounded.

"Does it matter?" I didn't respond. Carolyn sighed. "His name is Corey. I met him at the gym. But I swear to you, it's just physical. It's not love!"

Disgust. That was the name of this overarching emotion I was feeling. I couldn't place it earlier, but I knew it then.

"How long?" Apparently disgust shut down my ability to say more than two or three words at a time.

Carolyn winced and I took a shallow breath, trying to prepare myself for the blow I know she's about to deliver.

"Three months," she whispered.

"THREE MONTHS?" There it is, the explosion of anger. "THREE MONTHS?" I repeated, not bothering to keep my voice down. In three months, I had met Carolyn and fallen in love three years ago. Three months' time was enough to alter your life's plans for another person. I would know. Three months was all it took for me to believe Carolyn was the one.

I stood abruptly, pulling my keys from my pocket. I needed to leave, to get my head on straight, to be anywhere but here. I guess the silver lining to finding out your fiancee is cheating on you right when you get home from a road trip is that my clothes—some of them, at least—were packed. I grabbed my bag and backpack and tossed them back in the car. Carolyn followed after me, crying.

"JJ, please! Don't leave! It's just...you're gone all the time! And I'm lonely! And sometimes even when you are here, I'm still lonely! And Corey was around, and attentive...I'm so sorry! Don't go, JJ. Let's just talk."

I reared back like she slapped me. I couldn't believe I was getting blamed for this. I needed to leave before I said or did something I would later regret. I got in the car while Carolyn was still talking and pulled out of our driveway. I didn't look in the rearview mirror as I pulled away.

"Where'd you go there?" Caleb has his concerned dad look on his face. I roll my eyes. The last thing I need is him thinking I'm reminiscing about my ex-fiancee. After I caught her cheating, I stayed at Caleb's for a few days before moving my things out of our townhouse and finding my own place for the rest of the season. Caleb was insufferable at that time. I know his attention came from a place of caring, but his level of concern was stifling. I'm glad I had his support, and I'm still so grateful for a friend like him, but I wanted to grieve the loss of my relationship alone so I could move on as fast as possible. I don't need Caleb thinking I've backslid on my "healing journey" as he called it (insert another eye roll here) because I actually haven't. But I know when I go out tonight, my old teammates will ask if I've moved on, and while I have moved on *from* Carolyn, I haven't moved on *to* someone else.

"Just thinking." I shake Caleb off and pull out my Nintendo Switch, joining in on the next game of Mario Kart my teammates are about to play. Julia, the lead flight attendant, comes around periodically offering ice cream, candy, dinner, and drinks. She always stops to chat with Caleb and me. She reminds me of my Aunt Mary. Julia really takes care of us. She's one of the kindest souls I've ever met and she always checks in with Caleb on Jenny's health.

By the time I make it to McNally's, Jayden Thompson and Grayson Syzmanski are already two beers deep but have ordered me my standard light beer. They're sitting at a high top in the back corner. I chuckle to myself. Some things never change; that exact table has seen many a drunken night from the three of us.

"Thomps! Man!" I greet my former teammates with a hug. We text periodically, but there's something about being able to get together with the guys you used to grind with, day in and day out, in your early career. Baseball schedules can be brutal with one hundred sixty two games in a season, so you better like the guys on your team. Lucky for me, Jayden and Grayson are as likeable as you can get.

"JJ! Glad to have you back here!" Jayden says, clapping me on the back.

"Now I just need to get you guys to Chicago!" I joke. "I'm thinking like, October?" The guys laugh, knowing while it's still early in the season, if Philly keeps playing the way they are, no one on that team will be playing postseason baseball in October.

After a few hours of catching up, I notice a warm feeling settling in my chest. There's something comforting being around people who just get you. The warm feeling, however, is quickly dispersed when Grayson turns the topic to the inevitable: my dating life (or lack thereof).

"So have you gotten back out there?" he not so subtly asks.

"I've thought about it. I just haven't done anything about it. I'm not willing to do online dating. I've heard too many horror stories. But I guess I'm ready to go out and meet someone, one of these days," I finish lamely.

Jayden slow claps. "Wow, what a show of enthusiasm," he deadpans.

"I'll get there." I reply honestly. "I'm ready," I say with a little more conviction.

"Good. It's been more than two years since the whole Carolyn debacle," Grayson states. As if I didn't know. For the first few months, Carolyn contacted me regularly, seeing if I'd changed my mind about ending us. I obviously never did, and never came close to it, but that didn't stop her from trying. After my trust was broken like that, I don't think I could have ever recovered even if we did get back together. I would constantly worry about what–or who–she would do while I was on road trips, when I went to work for the day, and who she was thinking about when she actually was with me.

I let go of my anger toward Carolyn a long time ago, too. I eventually got to a point where I could understand her feelings of loneliness. It's hard to be with a ballplayer. Our schedule is nuts, even when we are home. Off days are rare and never more than one day at a time, with the exception of the mid-season break, which is usually only four or five days long. For the last five years in a row, I've played in the All Star game during that time, so I didn't even get that break like most other players did. It was no excuse for Carolyn to cheat on me; I'm just saying I could understand her loneliness. I sold the townhouse we lived in, since it was in my name anyway, and started fresh. At least Carolyn let me keep Bruno after the breakup; he was the only thing I really wanted anyway. I found out a few months ago that Carolyn's still with Corey. So much for him meaning nothing. I'm mostly convinced she wanted to stay with me to mooch off my lifestyle. She of all people should know how deep that cuts me. It's almost as bad as her cheating. Thank fuck for therapy.

"It feels weird to get back on that horse though," I admit. "Picking up a girl at a bar is hard if she's a baseball fan."

Grayson and Jayden nod knowingly. It's hard to know if people are interested in you as a person or if they're after something else: the lifestyle, the paycheck, the fame. And in a city like Chicago, if you're with a ballplayer, the fans generally know about it. If a woman isn't interested in me initially for the fame, it's hard to knowingly subject her to that in the future. While I like to think I don't have major leftover trust issues from the "Carolyn debacle," as Grayson calls it, it's hard not to have a little hesitation about someone's motives when you first meet them.

"Maybe just rip off the bandage," Jayden suggests before looking around the room as if to find me someone to go home with tonight. I glance around the room, too, feeling relief when the only woman is a seventy-something grandmother with a bad wig flirting with the much younger bartender.

"Wanna be my wingman?" I joke.

"Don't tempt me. You know I'll have Grandma Sally taking you home in a heartbeat."

I finally make it home after what feels like the longest road trip of my life. My position as shortstop is always physical during games, so I'm feeling every minute of play on my body. I took a grounder to my inner thigh on a weird hop during the second game of the Boston series, and between that and my full social calendar in Philadelphia and New York, by the time we finish our crawl up the east coast, I'm ready to throw in the towel and crawl into bed. I make sure to stop at my downstairs neighbor's unit first.

"How was my tiny boy?" I ask Lisa as Bruno practically plows her over to get to me. Lisa is a force to be reckoned with, and is a runner and weightlifter, so while she's short, she can withstand some of Bruno's bull-in-a-china-shop tendencies. She swipes her dark hair away from her face as she bends to squish Bruno's face, planting a kiss on his nose. Lisa looks a little scary, with her partially shaved head, tattoos, and general no bullshit aura, but around Bruno, she turns into a simp.

"A perfect angel, as usual! I haven't taken him out since dinner, though." I thank Lisa. She never lets me pay her for her dog sitting services, which is ridiculous, but we've worked out a system. I put her on my restaurant delivery account so she can eat for free whenever she wants. I suspect she doesn't take advantage of it as much as I think she should, but at least I feel a little better about Bruno being with her so much during the season.

Bruno follows me to the elevator and we make the ride up to the fourth floor. My building only has four floors, so sometimes the elevator feels excessive. At other times, like tonight, when I'm pulling my luggage and walking with a ninety pound dog and feeling sore and exhausted, I'm grateful. I drop my bags in my place, and as tempted as I am to lay on the couch, I know Bruno needs his walk. He's lucky he's so cute.

I'm hoping I can get away with a quick walk with Bruno tonight, but he has other plans. Apparently feeling like he has to make up for lost time while I was gone, Bruno seems intent on sniffing every tree trunk and every blade of grass we encounter on this walk. I know for a fact Lisa lets him do this on her walks, too, so he isn't fooling me, but I just don't have the heart to pull him away. His bark of joy when he scared an unsuspecting squirrel filled me with so much contentment, I couldn't justify going back inside so quickly, so I let Bruno lead the way.

And lead the way he does, straight to the same target as he did the last time he fooled me into letting him lead the way: my gorgeous neighbor, Amy. She's walking towards us, about half a block away when I recognize her. Bruno does too, and his stump of a tail starts waggling, the motion traveling up his body, culminating in excited tippy taps of his front paws. Amy, though, doesn't seem to be paying attention, her eyes on her phone, one hand wrapped around a disposable coffee cup, the other's thumb scrolling across the screen. She looks incredible in yoga pants and an olive green hooded sweatshirt which somehow brings more attention to her chocolate eyes.

As we get closer, Bruno lets out another joyous bark. Amy grins as she looks up from her screen and recognizes my dog. Amy's smile is a thing of beauty, showing off a row of perfectly straight white teeth, crinkling her eyes, and pinkening her cheeks.

"Hi, Bruno!" Amy gushes. "Hi, Jackson," she says—with equal enthusiasm, I tell myself.

"Hey, Amy. You're gonna give this guy a complex, thinking he's the most important dog in Chicago with all the attention he's getting from a pretty girl." I cringe inwardly at my lame attempt at flirting. I guess I'm more out of practice than I realized. Amy beams at me from a crouched position where Bruno is licking her face.

"Ah, well that's because he *is* the most important dog in all of Chicago!" I don't know whether to be grateful Amy doesn't comment on my lack of game or whether I should be disappointed it didn't work. I don't have much time to think before Bruno shoves his butt into her leg, knocking her over onto the sidewalk. I gasp and yank my dog by his leash away from Amy, mortification seeping over every inch of my being.

"I'm so sorry! Bruno, no!" I start, but then I realize Amy is, as usual in these bizarre meetings, laughing.

"Bruno, I don't think you realize how big you are," she says, allowing me to help her to her feet. Amy appears unhurt, but I can't say the same for her coffee; her cup lays crumpled in the grass, brown liquid splattered across the sidewalk, the aftermath of Bruno's body turning Amy's coffee into a caffeine-laced grenade.

"We have to stop meeting like this," I joke. "Let me buy you a new coffee. Caffeine Kingdom is around the corner; they've gotta be open this time of night. It's not too late," I cross my fingers. I swear, I'm a responsible dog owner. Bruno has never jumped on strangers or knocked anyone else over–twice!—and now I'm sure Amy is thinking Bruno has never had a day of training in his life.

"It definitely is open. I just came from there." Amy gestures at her empty cup and between the lumps in the mangled cup, I can make out the familiar crown logo.

CHAPTER SEVEN
Amy

Well, this night took an unexpected turn. I had left my apartment dressed like a scrub in leggings, a sweatshirt, and a beanie, planning to grab a dirty chai and take it back to my apartment while I continued my work at home. I was planning on working late, possibly pulling an all-nighter, while I finish applying for the next grant on my list. The deadline is Friday, but I want to make sure I get it in early enough that I can stop worrying about it. The CMA could really use the additional funding, and I already have so many ideas on how we can expand our science summer camp if we get it.

Instead, I'm sitting on the back patio of the cafe, drinking a chai latte with no espresso. I made a last minute change to a decaffeinated drink when I decided to abandon my plans in favor of hanging out with a cute dog and an even cuter dog owner. Bruno might just be Jackson's wingman the way he keeps bringing us together.

Jackson leans forward on the table, his focus solely on me as I tell him about my job. His blue eyes are piercing, perfectly complimenting his shaggy brown hair that curls perfectly around his black baseball hat. He looks like he hasn't shaved in a few days.

Maybe that's how he always looks, but the scruffy look absolutely works for him. I want to run my fingers through his beard and hair. The whole time we sit on the patio, Jackson is an attentive listener, and even though we are just talking about surface level things like our hobbies, I have never felt so heard.

"I've done a little yoga for work here and there," Jackson says after I tell him about the remote and in-person yoga classes I take. "But I don't think I know enough about it to take an actual class in a studio. I'd need one of those yoga-for-babies classes."

"I bet you're great. I'm sure your balance is off the charts as an athlete. You'd kill in a yoga-for-babies class. Now a toddler yoga class? You may have met your match." Wait–am I flirting with Jackson Jeffers? I may have secretly looked him up after Alicia told me who he was, and the man has a *lot* of hype surrounding him. I felt a little creepy doing too much digging, so I limited my searching to Google images. Let me just say that I was not disappointed: a few years ago, Jackson was the face (or, more realistically, the body) of a designer underwear brand. It wasn't until I saw the ad campaign again in my search that I recognized Jackson from the billboards lining the interstate. So the fact that I am allowing myself to mildly flirt with this man who is so clearly outside of my league is a little startling; where did I get the audacity?

"I guess you'll have to give me some lessons," Jackson says.

Holy shit, is he flirting back?

Bruno gives a small snort as he snuffles around his long since empty pup cup, breaking the intensity of our little moment. "Maybe Bruno needs some lessons in grace, too." Jackson shakes his head. "I really am sorry he's been such a maniac around you. I swear he's not usually like this!"

"He's lucky he's so cute," I respond.

"I tell him that everyday." Jackson and I continue chatting. He tells me about his brothers and meeting up with his friends in Philadelphia. He mentions his fans and the media call him JJ, but his close family members and friends still use his full first name. Conversation is so easy with Jackson. We end up staying on the patio of Caffeine Kingdom longer than I expected. Bruno has been laying on the ground, fighting sleep, for the last forty minutes. Eventually, when one of the baristas comes outside to unplug the bistro lights and inform us the cafe is closing, we decide to finally call it a night.

Now that I'm home, I realize I wasn't in my head at all while talking with Jackson. Usually my anxiety rears its ugly head when talking to someone new for the first time: wanting to make a good impression, ensuring we don't run out of things to talk about or encounter too many awkward pauses, overthinking *what* to talk about, and then later overanalyzing every little thing that was said, every facial expression from my conversational partner, wondering if they really were enjoying the conversation or if they were just faking it to be polite. Sometimes, having an anxiety disorder is exhausting. Other times, like tonight, I don't notice it. But it is rare that I didn't notice it around new people.

I was mindful that I didn't tell Jackson exactly where I live–I've seen enough murder shows to know just because someone seems charming, doesn't mean they're not a serial killer, even if they are also a famous baseball player–when we parted ways on the walk back home.

I replay our conversation at the end of the night, just before we parted ways, and my giddy feeling intensifies.

"Look, I know we just met, but would you feel comfortable sharing your phone number with me? Or can I give you mine? Just so I can make sure you get home okay, obviously." Jackson had said.

"Obviously. Definitely no other ulterior motive than that," I had joked back.

"I take the safety of my neighborhood very seriously. I'll need you to text me when you get home." Jackson looked so serious. I couldn't resist. I gave him my number and he texted me immediately so I could save his contact information in my phone. I gave Bruno a kiss on his giant head, said goodnight to Jackson, and walked away, careful not to show either of them how giddy Jackson and this night made me.

Behind the closed door of my apartment, I try not to go down a path of overthinking all of our interactions and accept the night for what it was: great conversation, good coffee, and a little flirting.

My mind rests on our more flirtatious comments. Who am I that I'm not only flirting with Jackson Jeffers but being ultra confident, too? I feel like a new woman.

CHAPTER EIGHT

Jackson

The first thing I noticed about my neighbor, all those weeks ago, was how beautiful she was. Her brown eyes sparkled with joy when Bruno first knocked her over, and each time I saw her after that, they continued to shine. Each time I saw Amy, including the first, she wore more form-fitting pants, so of course I was immediately drawn to her killer ass. The woman has curves for days and I've always been into curvier women. But the second thing I noticed about my new neighbor, beyond her physical attractiveness, was her goodness. She has a light about her that I'm drawn to. I can't explain it, but I feel compelled to be around her more, which is kind of ridiculous, since we've really only had one, albeit lengthy, conversation. I haven't felt this kind of pull toward another person since Carolyn, and even then, it took several dates with her to feel that kind of an impact. I want to see Amy again, but I'm not sure if it's too forward of me to ask her on a date right away.

I feel so out of practice in the dating scene that I'm second guessing myself. I'm normally confident and don't waste my time overthinking. The mental skills coach for the Foxes, De'Andre, constantly reminds us not to think, to just act, when we're at the plate. *Overthinking leads to mistakes more than anything else,* he always says. I swear it's his favorite phrase. He probably has it needlepoint stitched to a pillow somewhere in his house. Normally, I consider myself a man of action. No need to break that habit tonight.

The dreaded double text. *Way to come on way too strong, Jeffers.* But I don't want to leave the last part unsaid, in case Amy is waiting for me to make the first move. I feel like I picked up on a little nervousness or self-consciousness in Amy in some of the things she said tonight. She has no reason to be self-conscious; I was hanging on her every word. I give it two minutes, and when Amy still hasn't responded, I toss my phone aside so I don't embarrass myself again and roll over in my bed. Tomorrow is an off day, so I can sleep in, but as exhausted as I was when I first got home from the trip, I feel wired now.

Bruno, snoring at the foot of my bed, has no such issues with sleep. I watch his feet twitch and smile. Sometimes I think Bruno knows exactly what he's doing when he gets into trouble and sometimes I think he really is that dopey and derpy. Either way, I love the block-headed troublemaker. I end up listening to a guided meditation De'Andre recommended to some of us and find myself drifting off to sleep sooner than anticipated.

When I wake in the morning, I feel refreshed. It's still morning according to my alarm clock, but I feel so well-rested that I double check the time on my phone to make sure my clock isn't wrong. It's then that I see Amy responded to my texts about twenty minutes after I sent the last one.

Amy

> I accept puppy snuggles in all forms, even derpy, uncoordinated ones that knock me over…I also accept coffee in all forms, even from new-to-me neighbors

I can't help the grin that spreads over my face. Maybe I'm not so rusty at this dating thing after all.

CHAPTER NINE

Amy

Jackson didn't respond to my text last night and I'm trying not to overthink it. He did tell me how exhausting his road trip was and how he had the day off today. I almost wish I had a full day of field trips and activities with students planned so I could keep my mind off of him. But then I think about how I didn't actually finish applying for the grant last night like I was supposed to, and I'm grateful to have a day free from scheduled activities so I can work on that. I decide to go in and work from my office in the planetarium so I'm less distracted.

Alicia is also working from her office as well and offers to help me finish the grant proposal, even though it benefits my projects more than hers. Alicia's specialty is working with students in high school and college. Last year, she also worked with a graduate student at the University of Chicago on her thesis. Young children are not Alicia's thing, and this grant focuses its funding on third through fifth grade science students. Still, two heads are better than one, and with her working simultaneously on the application from her laptop while I work on other sections on mine, we finish the work in half the time. I know I'm lucky to work with such a generous friend.

Alicia looks over my shoulder as I finish drafting the cover letter to the grant application. When we're both satisfied, I upload the application and supporting documents to the website, crossing my fingers I'll hear back soon. I close out of the grant application tab, causing the next tab on my browser to fill the screen. I'm not quick enough to close out of the tab or to shut my laptop before Alicia sees.

"Uh, why are you looking at Google images of JJ Jeffers? You can look out your bedroom window and see him, right? I thought he was your neighbor?" She wiggles her eyebrows at me, clearly trying to stifle a laugh.

"I cannot see him from my bedroom!"

"Interesting that that's the part you choose to respond to. Have you been thinking about dear old JJ in your bedroom, my little Amy?"

"No!" I answer quickly. Too quickly. Ugh! I came home from talking with Jackson last night and decided productivity would be hopeless, so I hopped in the shower, only to come back to my bedroom with a text from him possibly asking me out on a date? I decided the bold, confident Amy would respond flirtatiously, but when Jackson didn't respond, I chastised myself for reading too much into the texts. Maybe he really did feel bad about Bruno and just wanted to apologize. I wallowed in a bit of self-pity by searching for Jackson again online, limiting myself to pictures of his beautiful face. And body. I still can't bring myself to read articles about him; now that I know him personally, reading about him feels a little too stalker-y, like a boundary I shouldn't cross.

I spill to Alicia everything that happened last night, from Bruno knocking me on my ass, again, to talking with Jackson outside the coffee shop, to the late night texts. Alicia, like the good friend she is, tries to talk me off the ledge.

"No way, you did not read too much into it. A man doesn't spend over an hour talking at a coffee shop when he's exhausted if he's not interested," Alicia reasons.

"Yeah but maybe he was just being polite since his dog basically mowed me over?"

"He would have left after the coffee. He wouldn't have stuck around, not for an *hour*, if he didn't have some interest. Besides, he asked for your number! You told me he mentioned how tired he was after the trip, maybe he just fell asleep and that's why he didn't respond?"

She has a point. But at the same time, it was now three o'clock in the afternoon. I doubt he is still asleep now and he still hasn't responded. I can't help but feel a little foolish for putting myself out there and not having it be reciprocated. I try to push those and all thoughts of Jackson out of my head. I rationalize to myself by saying I never have to see Jackson again; he won't even remember my cringey text if we do happen to run into each other in the future. And as good as my rational brain is at logicing my way through things, my emotional brain throws a tantrum so loud my rational brain can't be heard over the screaming.

"Just try to relax, Ames. I think he'll respond, but maybe he won't, and if so, he sucks. Try not to waste any more energy on it until you know more information."

Alicia knows me all too well. She can see a thought spiral coming a mile away and usually does a pretty good job of heading it off. She pulls up aMUSEme, our favorite museum educator blog, and it serves as a good distraction from my nerves as we start to gather ideas for our upcoming summer sessions.

CHAPTER TEN

Jackson

I slam my palm against the tile wall in my shower. Bruno glowered at me when I got back from my long run; he was salty I didn't bring him along, but I couldn't be worried about how far or how fast I was making him run. I needed the burn in my lungs and the pounding of my feet on the asphalt. I'm sure my strength and conditioning coaches won't be pleased that I spent my off day–what was supposed to be a recovery day for me–doing a hard, strenuous run, but it was either run or commit a homicide, and I feel like my agent and publicist would appreciate my choices today.

This morning, I had made myself coffee at home and was just climbing back into bed to turn on the news, sip my java, and respond to Amy's text when instead I got a phone call. It has been awhile since I've seen the name on my caller ID, but my body reacted the same: cold dread, churning stomach, instant sweat sprouting on my forehead. Like always, I immediately declined the call. I declined it again when my phone started ringing again. And again, until I just turned my phone off.

Even thinking about this morning now, I can feel my heart rate pick up. I practice my deep breathing techniques, willing the blood whooshing through my veins to slow down. The relief is temporary, so I give up on a long, relaxing shower and choose one for functionality, spending just enough time to get clean before I turn off the water. Wrapping a towel around my waist but not bothering to actually dry myself off, I root around in my bed for my phone. Never one to make my bed in the mornings, it takes me a moment to find it within the sheets. I power it on and click on my brother's name before I even check to see if I have voicemails. I don't want to know.

Sean picks up on the second ring. "Hey, asshole. I've been waiting for you to call me about that energy drink deal. They wanted to add a couple pages to the contract they sent over last wee–"

"She called me this morning. Three times before I turned my phone off," I interrupt my brother. I don't know if I need to speak to my agent or my brother right now, but lucky for me, Sean is both, so I don't have to decide.

"Fuck. Did she leave a voicemail?" Sean's tone matches mine in its seriousness.

"I don't know. I just turned my phone back on. I panicked and turned it off when I saw her name on the caller ID a couple hours ago. I haven't checked my voicemail yet. Did she call you?" It's a pretty safe bet that when she doesn't reach me, Sean is next on her call list.

"Not directly. I'll check with Kevin." I hear my brother yell for his administrative assistant, then their conversation is muffled. "No, she didn't call here. Yet," Sean adds darkly.

"I'll check with Nate," I say. "Sean, I'll call you back later."

"I'll put some feelers out to see what she's up to now. I'll call Mariah, too, and give her the head's up." Mariah is my publicist, and I appreciate Sean taking the reins on this one. Mariah is wonderful, but I don't want to talk about this more than I have to. "Just breathe, Jacks. We don't know why she's calling right now; it could be nothing."

It's never nothing with her. I hang up on Sean and dial Nate, my other brother. He doesn't answer, so I'm forced to leave a voicemail. I keep it short and to the point.

"Nate, it's Jackson. Mom is back."

CHAPTER ELEVEN

Amy

The April weather lived up to the saying of "in like a lion, out like a lamb." At least I hope the month will end on an upswing, because the first two weeks of April were brutal. The weather oscillated from freezing rain to snow to hail to periods of bitter cold without any precipitation, with the exception of the one sunny day Alicia and I had dinner outside. I don't know what weather pattern was worse, but luckily, we seem to have passed the worst of it and the last few days have been warm, pleasant, and sunny.

"Amy!" I hear my name called in the transition between songs and pause the music on my headphones. I'm on my hot girl walk on my lunch break; I worked from home today so my schedule has a lot of flexibility.

Jackson jogs up to me; instinctively, I look around for Bruno but don't see him. "Amy! Hey! I was calling for you for a while like a lunatic. You should have seen the looks people were giving me."

"Hi, Jackson! Sorry! I didn't realize my music was so loud," I say, taking my headphones down and looping them around my neck.

"How are you?" I hate how breathless my voice comes out. I can't even blame it on my walk; I wasn't even going that fast.

"Look, I'm really sorry I've been MIA and didn't text you back. I didn't mean to ghost you; work got crazy and I was dealing with some family stuff. I'm on my way to work right now, actually. I'm double parked at Caffeine Kingdom but saw you walking and I needed to say hi."

"Oh, it's okay. You don't owe me any texts," I say, trying to convey a picture of nonchalance.

"Well, I wanted to text you. I *want* to text you," he corrects. "These last two weeks have been insane. Let me make it up to you by taking you for coffee when I'm not trying to run off to work. Please." Jackson looks so earnest that I can't help the small smile that crosses my lips.

"Okay. Just let me know what works for you. Your schedule is a little crazier than mine," I concede.

"I have a night game tonight and a day game tomorrow. Can we grab dinner or something tomorrow after the game? Or a drink if you don't want to do a whole dinner?"

I almost tell Jackson that we can just have drinks, that he doesn't have to take me out to a whole dinner, when I stop myself. I would love to have dinner with Jackson, so that's what I tell him. "Dinner would be great," I say shyly.

"It's a date," Jackson says with a wink. I try not to melt into a puddle in the middle of the sidewalk. "I'll text you later."

If Jackson could see me now, my "picture of nonchalance" is so far outside the realm of possibilities, it's not even in this solar system. I've changed my outfit six times and redone my hair three times. I finally settle on jeans, black wedge booties, and a slouchy sweater for tonight's date. I sweep my hair to the side in a thick braid and opt for minimal makeup. I don't know where we're going, and Jackson didn't give me a dress code, so this will just have to work. He had texted me an hour and a half ago, telling me to be ready in two hours and he would pick me up. I had texted him the address to my building, but not my apartment unit, rationalizing that even in the very miniscule chance I misread Jackson completely and he was a total creep, at least he didn't know *exactly* where I sleep each night.

I survey my room before leaving. It looks like a hurricane tore through my closet and deposited everything onto my bed. More to ease my nerves and pass the time than anything else, I hang my clothes back up, one by one. I pace my room for a little bit, trying to burn off the excess nervous energy. My phone starts ringing. "Jackson Neighbor" lights up the screen.

"Hello?" I answer tentatively. Who calls when texts work just fine?

"Hey, beautiful. I'm outside your building in the black Range Rover whenever you're ready," Jackson's voice comes across clear through the line. I peek down from my bedroom window, and sure enough, there's a black SUV that looks like it costs more than I make in two years double parked and idling outside.

"Okay, I'm on my way down now." I say. Very nonchalant.

I exit my apartment building, ready to hop into Jackson's car when he gets out first. Dark jeans and a black cashmere sweater drape over his body like they were made just for him.

"Wow, you look beautiful," he says, no hint of hesitation in his voice. And with equally little hesitation, he wraps me in a Jackson Jeffers hug, his slightly spicy, piney cologne enveloping me as much as his arms are. I could stay here forever, drinking him in, like the creep I am, but I let go when Jackson breaks the hug and walks around the front of the car to open my door.

"Oh, you don't have to get my door for me. That's really nice though," I say.

"I like doing nice things for beautiful women," Jackson replies. I can feel my cheeks flame. I know I'm not unattractive, but I also am well aware of my physical limitations as far as typical standards of beauty go. I'm certainly heavier than I'd like to be, as much as I'm trying to love and accept my body for what it is. But to be called beautiful by Jackson fucking Jeffers three times in a span of only minutes? My mind is malfunctioning just trying to process it.

Jackson drives us to a Turkish restaurant in Roscoe Village; we walk inside and I immediately fall in love with the dark wood interiors and tiny tea lights on every table.

"Is this okay?" Jackson asks. "I wasn't sure if you had dietary restrictions, but I feel like everyone likes Mediterranean food?"

"This is perfect, Jackson," I say, touching his forearm. "This is so thoughtful. I am a vegetarian, so this will be great."

Just like our first substantial encounter at the coffee shop, conversation with Jackson is easy again. He orders us a bottle of Turkish white wine and I'm thrilled to discover we like our whites similar: as dry as they come. The wine pairs perfectly with our mezze appetizer, and I couldn't be happier with Jackson's taste in restaurants. And wine.

Jackson tells me about the win the Foxes pulled off today and how Caleb, his best friend and teammate, is organizing a dog adoption event prior to one of the games next week. He mentioned that Caleb's love of rescue dogs is what caused him to visit a shelter and fall in love with a baby Bruno two years ago. I learn that Bruno's mother was brought to the shelter as a pregnant stray, and he and his littermates were born shortly after. I tell him how I would love to have a dog myself, but my long work hours and small apartment aren't conducive to a pet's needs. Jackson tells me about his love for pop punk and emo music. I share about the book I'm currently reading–a hockey romance with a detective/criminal twist–and growing up as an only child in the Chicago suburbs.

Jackson tells me about a bookstore down the street his publicist told him about that features all romance books. Jackson also let slip that his brother once tried to get him to model for a romance book cover series a few years ago.

"No!" I gasp in disbelief. "Did you do it?"

"Not even a little bit," Jackson chuckles. "If my teammates found out about that, they'd never let me live it down. Caleb already calls me 'pretty boy' enough. I don't even want to know what they'd say and do if they found me on a book cover." Jackson's eyes twinkle with mirth.

"You should be very flattered. Some of these men on my book covers...." I trail off.

"Oh yeah?" Jackson posits. "Tell me more about these books you like."

My cheeks flame further. I'm all for women owning their sexuality. I embrace my own. But there's a difference between reading my books, embracing my sexuality, and openly talking about the smut I read in the middle of a restaurant on a first date with my neighbor.

"I'll tell you when you're older," I deflect. Jackson just laughs, his good natured spirit spilling out of him and filling me up.

Our bottle of wine is empty and our waiter offers us the check. I glance around the room, startled to notice we are the only patrons left here. I wince at the thought of keeping the staff here longer than necessary while Jackson and I got lost in each other. Jackson apparently has the same thought because after he pays, the waiter comes back to verify if the tip he wrote on the tab was actually correct. Jackson shrugs, telling the staff he appreciates their service and staying late for us.

His hand on my low back, Jackson guides me to the car, opening the door for me yet again. As he starts the car, I'm struck yet again by the feeling that I don't want my time with Jackson to be over for the night. We're back in Lincoln Park before I know it and Jackson parks on the street outside my building. I go to open my door and he raises his eyebrow at me in warning. I laugh, rolling my eyes at him as he hops out of the car and opens my door for me.

"You really don't have to do that for me, you know. I can open a car door." I insist.

"I already told you I like doing nice things for beautiful women."

"You can't keep saying things like that," I murmur. I don't even want to know how red my cheeks are right now.

"If you hear something enough, you'll start to believe it. And you should believe it, beautiful. Now, is it okay if I walk you to the door?" I nod and we walk slowly to the door to my building.

"Thank you for dinn–" I begin.

"Thank you for doing thi–" Jackson says at the same time. We both laugh. The laughter dies down quickly when Jackson takes a step closer to me. I swear, I feel the electricity in the air, the crackling of energy on my skin as he slowly brings his hand to my cheek, tilting my face towards his. "Is this okay?" he whispers.

All I can manage is a small nod. Then Jackson's lips are on mine, soft and tender, as I lean into his touch. He tentatively licks the seam of my lips and I open for him. The kiss is gentle and sweet and perfect and I know if I'm not careful, this man could pull me easily into his orbit. Pushing those thoughts out of my head, I meet Jackson's tongue stroke for stroke. He lets out a quiet groan.

"Amy, you're going to be the death of me."

"Let's hope you don't die before the second date," I joke.

"I guess I can hang on a little longer," he retorts. "When can I see you again?"

Impulsive Amy answers before rational Amy enters the conversation. "Are you done seeing me tonight? Or do you want to come up for some coffee?"

Woah, when did I get so bold? Jackson is really bringing out a whole new side to me and I'm not mad about it.

His response is immediate. "I love coffee."

chapter twelve
Jackson

I knew the date was going well. I was having a great time, Amy seemed happy, the food was incredible. There's not a thing I would have changed. Then Amy invited me up to her apartment. I thought getting back into dating after Carolyn would be difficult, emotionally and practically. I did not account for it to be this easy, but I suspect that's because I'm doing it with Amy rather than with anyone else.

I try not to seem too eager as I climb the stairs behind Amy, our hands linked between us. I try not to get too distracted by the perfect way she fills out her jeans. I don't know if she really is offering coffee or something else, but I know I'll be happy with either option.

As soon as we enter her apartment and she locks the door behind us, I know she may end up offering me coffee eventually, but her plan really is for "something else." I hear the deadbolt click into place and Amy is leaning into me, up on her tiptoes. Even on her toes, she's not quite tall enough for our mouths to meet, so I dip my head and bend my knees, bringing our mouths level as she slides her arms around the back of my neck. Amy's tongue skims the seam of my mouth; this time I'm the one opening to her. Her teeth graze my bottom lip and it's like a switch has been flipped in me.

It has been so long since I felt this good in a woman's arms. Sure, I had my fair share of random hookups, especially in the months immediately following Carolyn's and my breakup, and while they all scratched a certain itch, this feels different. Despite our frenzied actions, our arms, hands, and lips exploring, I felt a sense of comfort, of peace, in our movements.

I run my hand down Amy's hip, slow enough that she can stop me if she wants, lifting her leg to wrap around my waist, my other hand tangled in her hair, tilting her head back as I pepper her jaw and neck with slow kisses. She lets out a soft moan and rocks her hips against me, but only once. I don't know if she is embarrassed or self-conscious, but if she is, I don't give her a second longer to question herself.

"Yes, sweetheart, that feels so good," I encourage. I rock my hips against her, allowing her to feel the effects of what she does to me. I drag my hand from Amy's hair down her body, skimming her breast, letting my thumb ghost over her nipple, until it comes to rest on her plentiful ass. I give it a squeeze and Amy moans against my lips, so I do it again, and again I am rewarded with Amy's sharp intake of breath and another rock of her hips against my erection. My cock is so hard, I wouldn't be surprised if I have indentations from my zipper carved into my flesh.

"Let me make you feel good, Amy. Can I please do that?" She whimpers and nods. "Where is your bedroom?" Amy slides her leg down to the ground in what I can only assume is an attempt to walk to wherever her room is, but I am not having any of that. I lift it again, securing it around my waist, lifting her other leg to join it so I'm fully supporting her. I hear her gasp as I knead the flesh of her ass. "Amy, baby, bedroom. Where is it?"

She points over my shoulder and I walk us down the hallway to her room, laying her gently on the bed, hovering over her while kissing her lips and exploring every inch of her with my hands. I squeeze her perfect breast and pinch her nipple, but it's not enough. Whoever invented sweaters should be put on trial as the biggest cockblock this century. Her sweater is so thick I'm surprised she can even feel what I'm doing. Unacceptable. I snake my hand underneath the fabric and pull down the cup of her bra, accessing her nipple and rubbing it with the pad of my thumb. Amy moans.

"Is this okay? You can tell me to stop if it's not what you want."

"Jackson, please keep going," Amy whimpers. I grind my cock into her center, eager for release. She doesn't need to tell me twice. I gently pull her to sit, pulling off her sweater. She doesn't think I see how her arms protectively curl over her lush stomach, but I do.

"Amy. You're beautiful," I reiterate, but she doesn't respond. I decide not to push it tonight. She has no reason to be self-conscious; I love everything I've seen about her body so far and I know I'll love what I haven't seen even more. But I also know women carry the weight of societal expectations on them all the time. "Is this still okay?" I check, and Amy nods, pulling me back in for a kiss. We float back down to the mattress after I unhook her bra.

I look down at the most perfect pair of tits I've ever seen, not too large, but still a good handful. A good mouthful. I decide to test my theory, kissing my way down Amy's chest. I'm not wrong. I swirl my tongue around her nipple before allowing my teeth to lightly graze it, while my hand gently squeezes her other breast. I switch my mouth to her other breast, her nipples peaked and pink and so fucking delicious. She arches into me, moaning quietly and running her hands up and down my back.

I kiss my way down Amy's chest and belly, hovering slightly over her as my hands work the button on her jeans. I run my tongue along the waistline of her pants, glancing up at her as I do so. Amy's eyes are closed in ecstasy, her hands curled around the blanket covering the bed.

"Is this okay?" I check. She nods. Slowly, painstakingly, I lower the zipper at the same time I slide myself to kneeling on the floor in front of her perfect body. Slowly enough for Amy to stop me, I pull her jeans down and off her, pausing briefly to remove her boots. Only a scrap of lacy purple fabric separates me from heaven.

Running my hands up the insides of her thighs, I bring my mouth to the apex, over her underwear, planting an open mouthed kiss right in the center. The noise Amy makes is exquisite; I love how responsive she is. Her arousal has seeped through her panties and the scent is intoxicating. I'm worried my cock will rip a hole right through my jeans if I don't get some relief, but I am nothing if not a gentleman.

"Lift up, baby," I instruct Amy and she lifts her hips enough for me to slide her thong down her thick thighs. I toss it in the pile with her jeans and the last rational thought in my lust-addled brain. Sliding my body slightly up her legs, I pause to stare at her glistening pussy, shiny with her arousal.

I take a moment to savor the sight, building the anticipation for both of us. Amy must mistake it for hesitation because she sits up and says, "Jackson, you don't have to if you don't want to."

"Amy. Are you serious? Do you want me to stop?" She hesitates. "I will stop if you want me to, just say the word." I run my thumb along her bottom lip. "I enjoyed kissing you here. I have a feeling I will enjoy kissing you everywhere."

"O-okay," she mumbles quietly and lets me gently guide her back down to the bed.

Not hearing further protest from her, I extend my tongue and swipe it through her folds. Amy lets out a loud moan in response, which spurs me on further. I, myself, moan in response to her taste. I knew she would taste good but I didn't anticipate just *how* good. I continue licking, sucking, and nibbling her dripping cunt, feasting like a man starved. Flattening my tongue, I work it in circles over her clit.

"Yes, yes, yes," Amy chants softly and I chuckle against her when I notice how hard she's gripping the sheets. I take both of her hands and place them on my head, never slowing the movements of my mouth against her core. Amy tangles her fingers into my hair and lightly pulls, and it's official: I've entered heaven. I spear my tongue through her pussy, fucking her with my mouth and tongue when she starts to move her hips.

"Yes, baby, ride my face. Let me make you feel so good," I praise. As if waiting for my permission, Amy complies, taking what she needs from me, turning me on even further. I buck my own hips against the side of the mattress, desperate for a little relief. I suckle Amy's clit, sliding one finger inside her slick pussy and curling it slightly. I take my other hand and press it along her low belly, adding just enough pressure where I can start to feel my finger on the inside from the hand that's on the outside of Amy's incredible body. I add another finger and her hips move faster. She's full on riding my face right now and I cannot get enough. Some of the guys I've played on teams with aren't into oral sex that much, but I was made for eating pussy. And Amy's pussy is the most delicious of all.

"Oh, please don't stop," Amy whimpers. I want to laugh. Asking me not to stop is like asking the sun not to shine; I'll do whatever she needs me to. The only way I'm stopping is if she tells me to, and since she's telling me the exact opposite, I apply a little more pressure on the top of her belly with my hand and make faster tongue flicks on her clit. When I latch my mouth onto Amy's clit and suck hard, I feel her fully come undone under me, screaming my name. Her pussy walls are fluttering around my fingers as I keep a gentle curling motion going. I continue gently sucking her clit until her legs stop trembling and her aftershocks subside. I place one last kiss on her perfect pussy before detaching myself and sliding up next to her on the bed.

I wipe my mouth before planting gentle kisses on her neck and jaw. I don't know how Amy feels about kissing after I eat her out, and right now, she seems so blissed out I'm not sure she's even registering my kisses along her neck. Her eyes are closed as she tries to regulate her breathing. She's silent for so long I'm starting to get worried she's hurt or scared.

Finally, she speaks. "That...was...incredible," she whispers. "Thank you." She sounds in awe.

"You're welcome," I whisper back, chuckling and pulling her body close to me.

"I've never–" She cuts herself off. I don't say anything, waiting for her to continue if she wants. "I've never been able to come from that before," she admits. "That was so, so good." My ego instantly skyrockets.

"I'm glad," I say, kissing her temple. I slide off the bed and pull back Amy's sheets. "Come here." I help her under the covers so she's laying underneath, naked and sated. She reaches for my belt, eyes sleepy but lust-filled.

"No, pretty girl. Not tonight. Just rest." She looks startled, which then morphs into self-doubt. I can see the exact moment when Amy's anxiety kicks in because it plays across her face like a scene from a movie. I take one of her hands in both of mine. "Nuh-uh, pretty girl. You don't get to overthink this tonight. I just want tonight to be about you. You relax. There will be plenty more opportunities for more with us, but tonight, you rest." I kiss her knuckles gently.

As soon as Amy told me she had never been able to come from oral before, I knew I wasn't going to do anything more tonight. As much as my dick is currently protesting, I want to leave Amy relaxed, unthinking, and boneless, and I know she isn't going to be able to do that if she starts thinking about ways to please me. I can already see how quickly Amy's exhaustion starts settling in after I gave her what I hope was an orgasm of a lifetime–and given the arousal coating my face and fingers by the time she was done, I'd say I did a pretty good job of that. I don't need to put more on her tonight.

Besides, I mean what I said about us having plenty more time to do everything else together. There is no way in hell I am done with this girl.

CHAPTER THIRTEEN

Amy

I stretch my arms overhead, luxuriating in the full body release I experienced last night. I've never slept so well in my life. My mind replays the events of last night: our date. Jackson's refusal to let me open my own door. The incredible wine, food, and conversation at the restaurant. Jackson's kiss, morphing from sweet and tender to hurried and passionate. His hands all over me. His tongue...his tongue! That man is talented on and off the ball field, I learned.

I have always been in touch with my sexuality, even more so since discovering romance novels. That being said, I also don't make a habit of hooking up on a first date, but last night's activities were a testament to my insane levels of attraction to Jackson. I know a lot of guys deliver oral sex as a polite, perfunctory act, something to get through so they can arrive at the main act. Not so with Jackson; he acted like going down on me *was* the main event. Last night, I wasn't sure if Jackson and I were heading straight to sex or if we were just hooking up, but I didn't want anything we did last night to have been done out of a sense of obligation. Jackson's enthusiasm in eating me out erased any doubts about him not being into it.

Rolling over, I grab my phone. I don't remember plugging it in to the charger last night and I briefly wonder if Jackson did it for me. I was half asleep by the time he pulled the covers back and helped me slide into bed. My eyes grow wide as I realize Jackson didn't allow me to reciprocate last night. My face heats with embarrassment; our first date and he walked away with an erection–I felt how hard he was when we got back to my apartment–because I was too tired to return the favor. He probably thinks I'm selfish, that I'm –

My thoughts are interrupted as I unlock my phone to a text from him. He must have sent it last night after he left.

Jackson Neighbor

Goodnight sleepyhead. I had a great time tonight with you.

Clutching my phone to my chest, I smile. How is this man real? He seems to always know what to say to quell my anxious thoughts. I'm tempted to call out sick today and spend the day at home, reminiscing about our date. As much fun as that sounds, I've got back to back meetings with our directors this morning that I can't miss. I begrudgingly get out of bed, cursing my steady employment. I send a quick text to Jackson first, then vow to push him out of my mind for the rest of the work day.

I succeed somewhat in focusing on my work. It helped that we got approval for one of the smaller grants I had applied to. It gave us an additional $18,000 in transportation and nutrition funding to assist children from low income areas in accessing our summer camp programs, which means we need to get the ball rolling on outreach and marketing in those areas. The grant requires twenty-five children to be enrolled from lower socioeconomic status areas in order to maintain the funding. While eighteen grand sounds like a lot of money on the front end, it gets spent quickly, especially when trying to make it stretch all summer to feed and transport children. I couldn't be more thrilled, though. It's always been important to me to build museum education programs for all students, not just those who are fortunate enough to be able to afford it.

It's one o'clock before I realize I haven't eaten yet today. Alicia's knock on my door startles me. I'm sure I look all kinds of crazy with piles of paperwork on my desk and spreadsheet printouts surrounding me. I'm pretty sure I have a pencil stuck in my ponytail.

If Alicia thinks I look as insane as I feel after crunching numbers all day, she doesn't let on.

"You haven't eaten yet, have you?" She asks hopefully, holding up a plastic salad container.

"You are a lifesaver. I didn't even realize how late in the day it is. I feel like I haven't gotten a second to breathe since I walked out my door this morning!"

"Then let's eat and not deal with work for the next half hour." I knew Alicia was my friend for a reason. "I've been dying to hear about your date! How'd it go? Oh my god, you're blushing! Was it that good?"

"Leesh, it was so good. We went to this adorable Turkish place in Roscoe Village. We'll have to go back because the food was so good. We ordered this mezze plate–"

"Girl, I'm glad you ate, but those are *not* the details I came in here for," she interrupts. "What was JJ like? Did you hit it off? Is there going to be a second date? And why are you blushing? Did you jump his bones?" Alicia douses her salad in a sickening amount of dressing.

"No one says 'jump his bones,' anymore, Alicia. This isn't 1998. But no, I didn't jump his bones...but we did hook up," I pause, briefly reliving my memories of last night. She twirls her hand in a *go on* motion. "The kiss was unreal. It started all soft and gentle, but when I invited him in for coffee...

"Yeah, coffee," Alicia snorts sarcastically.

"I mean, I would have been okay with coffee if that's what he really wanted!" I protest. Alicia gives me a *yeah right* look, raising her eyebrows. "But he definitely didn't want coffee," I add quietly. I fill Alicia in on all the details from last night in between bites. She is a good audience, gasping and sighing in all the right places.

"So you're obviously going to have a second date, right?" she asks.

"I mean, we didn't plan anything, but I'm guessing so? I haven't heard from him yet today," I say, checking my phone for the first time in a few hours. Just a check-in text from my mom. I try not to feel too disappointed, even though I know that's an irrational response.

"So what are you going to do now? Are you still wanting something casual?"

I give Alicia a look. "Yes. That's all my heart can handle. And men will say they want serious when they really want casual. I can't do another Patrick."

"Patrick was an asshat. I don't know what his deal was, but he was obviously not the guy for you. I can't blame you for being hurt by him; I would have been, too. He *told* you he wanted to be serious. Hell, the guy sent you listings of houses in good school districts. You don't do that if you're not serious." She rolls her eyes and shoves a huge forkful of salad into her mouth. "You still don't know what happened to spook him?"

"No, and I don't care," I tell her honestly. "I've moved on, but I've learned my lesson. Even if men say they want a serious relationship, they don't. So I can play that game, too. If I keep things light and unserious, then I don't have to get hurt either."

"But how long can you play that game? Don't you want to get married or live together or something?"

"Honey, I can play that game forever." I'm hoping my heart believes me more than Alicia does, given the skeptical look on her face. I'm saved from further scrutiny by the pinging of my text message alert. She raises her eyebrows at how quickly I jump to look at my phone but says nothing. The text is just a confirmation of my dentist appointment next week. I try not to look disappointed as I set my phone down. Alicia doesn't have to say anything to me; she knows I was hoping the text was Jackson and the look she gives me says more than words.

"Shut up," I grumble. "I'm getting there."

Alicia holds her hands up in surrender. "I said nothing!"

The thing is, she didn't have to.

CHAPTER FOURTEEN

Jackson

We've been down by two runs since the sixth inning. Now, it's the bottom of the eighth and the top of our order is due up to bat, which means I'm batting third this inning and am currently in the hole. I'm standing on the top step of the dugout, next to Samuel "Benny" Benjamin, our manager.

"I think it's gonna be a slider, low and inside," Benny murmurs. Sure enough, about two seconds later, the pitcher delivers a slider for a ball, low and inside. Caleb, the batter at the plate for the Foxes, doesn't swing. He steps back on his back foot, resetting his stance and preparing for the next pitch. I squint at the pitcher as the opposing team's catcher lobs the ball back to him, trying to pick up on whatever Benny is seeing. Benny speaks again, using his hand to cover his mouth to avoid the chance of lip reading. "Look at the flick of his wrist going into his setup. When he flicks it like that? Fastball. Last pitch, that slider? You can see him take an extra half second to spin the ball in his glove before his setup."

It's so subtle, I missed it, but now that Benjamin has pointed it out, it's as obvious as a flashing neon sign announcing his pitch.

"Holy shit, you're right," Kennedy, our hitting coach says. He leaves my other side to walk slowly down the dugout, quietly informing the guys the opposing pitcher is inadvertently tipping his pitches. I'm chomping at the bit for my turn at the plate. Benny waves Hayden Oliver, our first baseman, over. Oliver bats before me in the lineup and is standing in the on deck circle, ready for his at-bat. Hand over his mouth, Benny shares the information with Oliver, who nods once and resumes his practice swings in the on deck circle, keeping both eyes narrowed on the pitcher. Caleb draws a walk and after two more pitches, Oliver hits a perfectly placed hit between left and center field, just shallow enough for the outfielders to have to play it on a bounce.

I dig my feet in next to home plate, readying my stance. *Slider,* I think to myself about half a second before a slider makes its way across the plate. It's called a strike, but I don't mind. It wasn't my pitch. I'm waiting for a fastball, preferably a little high and slightly outside, my preferred pitch. I don't have to wait long, as my opponent delivers it the very next pitch. I don't think; muscle memory takes over as I swing the bat, connecting perfectly at the fattest part of the barrel of my bat. As soon as I feel it connect, I know it's what our broadcasters call a no doubter. The pitcher knows it too, judging by his body language as he turns to watch the ball fly out of the ballpark and onto the street outside left field.

I round the bases, pumping my fist, as we take the lead with no outs and potentially only half an inning left to play. This feeling right here? This is what every little boy dreams of in baseball and this is why I have the best job in the world.

"JJ, let's talk about your homer in the eighth," Robin, our on-field reporter, asks me after the game. I am slotted for the post-game interview on the field given my hit was the one that drove in the winning run.

"Yeah, a fastball high and outside. It was what I was looking for," I reply. I don't tell Robin or anyone outside the Foxes organization that the pitcher was accidentally showing what pitch he was going to throw immediately before delivery. We still have two more series against this team this season and if their pitching coach doesn't figure it out before we play Minneapolis again, our offense will absolutely use that information to our advantage. No need to ruin the fun.

"You, Andrews, and Oliver make a great team the way you guys turned three double plays in today's game. You've been hitting offense and defense hard lately. What is your secret?"

"No secret, Robin. Just working hard and being surrounded by some great guys. I'm lucky to have talents like Caleb and Ollie behind me. Baseball season is a grind, but it's a lot easier when you have teammates who work as hard as these guys do. It makes my job a lot easier," I say, flashing the camera my signature JJ smile.

I'm a big believer in giving credit where credit is due. You couldn't find two more opposite personalities between Caleb, constantly joking and rarely serious, and Hayden Oliver, the most serious person I've ever met. The uniting feature between the two of them, though, is their work ethic. Oliver eats, sleeps, and breathes baseball when he isn't wining and dining supermodels, which seems to be his only hobby outside of baseball. Caleb has a little more balance in his life, but when he's at the ballpark, he is locked in on the work.

The interview wraps up, but not before Soji and James throw an entire cooler of orange sports drink all over me. I knew it was coming because Robin took one giant step back from me in the middle of the interview, stretching her arm holding her microphone towards me while moving her body backwards to avoid the incoming assault. I laugh, dripping orange all the way through the dugout and back to the clubhouse. I make sure to stop at Soji's locker and shake my sopping hair at him, flicking orange droplets onto his face and torso, as he shoves me away laughing. I peel off my uniform and head for the showers. It's not until I'm in the shower, facing the hot spray that I can pause my baseball brain and bring my other thoughts online.

My mind immediately zeroes in on Amy and the noises she made last night when I made her come. *Nope, shut that down real quick,* I tell myself. I can't be walking around naked in the clubhouse with an erection. But damn, do I want to see her again soon. I debate the merits of asking if she's free tonight for another date. It's a quick turnaround from last night and I could be coming on too strong. But at the same time, I *want* to come on strong to Amy: I'm into her and I'm not interested in playing games. It's better she knows right off the bat that I want to see her again and I'm willing to make that happen as soon as possible.

My mind made up, I turn off my shower head, wrap a towel around my waist, and head back to my locker, my shower shoes squeaking on the tile floor. I don't bother getting dressed before my phone is in hand, fingers flying across the screen.

Me

Do you have any plans tonight?

I don't have to wait long before I'm rewarded with a response. When it comes through, I can't stop the grin on my face.

Amy

Wow, you had a great game today! Congratulations! I don't have any plans yet. Why?

Me

Did you watch my game?

Amy

Maybe. Just wanted to see if you were as good as they say you are.

I don't miss Amy's wording inadvertently revealing she's been googling me.

Me

And what's the verdict?

Amy

You're okay, I guess.

Me

Ouch. So I guess that means you don't want to go out with a mediocre ball player tonight?

Amy

Hmm, I'll have to think about it. Depends if any amazing ball players ask me out instead.

Me

They better not.

<winky face emoji>

Amy

Haha, lucky for you, you seem to be the only ballplayer I know.

Me

Does that mean I get to pick you up in an hour and take you out?

Amy

I suppose I can make that work. <winky face emoji>

"Who are *you* texting with that look on your face?" Caleb tries to read my texts over my shoulder. I hide my grin while powering off my screen, but I don't respond. "Jackson Jeremiah Jeffers, are you texting a woman?"

"You know my middle name is Alan." I frown.

Caleb ignores me, pretending to wipe a tear from his eye with a loud sniff. "Don't frown, you'll get wrinkles and your new lady love won't want an old man. My little Jacky boy, growing up so fast!" He spins, plopping down on the folding chair in front of his locker, crossing his legs and propping his chin on his hand and staring at me intently. "Tell me everything."

I laugh at the teenage girl masquerading as a grown man next to me. "There's not a lot to tell. Amy is a neighbor. We went on a date last night and I am going to take her out again tonight."

"Two nights in a row? Tell me more. Don't hold back, Jackie boy!"

I roll my eyes. "There's not too much more to tell. Bruno might be in love with her already. He has this weird magnetism to her. He keeps finding her in the neighborhood and running up to–and into–her." I smile at the memory of Bruno's goofy doggy grin whenever Amy pets him.

"Bruno: wingman of the year," Caleb remarks.

"You're not wrong. I swear, he noticed her first. He might be jealous when he finds out I spent time with her yesterday without him."

"What'd you do yesterday? And what are you doing tonight? When are you going out?"

"Slow down, Barbara Walters. I don't know what we're doing tonight yet; I only asked her out about seven minutes ago. Last night we went to this Turkish place," I pause, wondering if I should tell him about Amy inviting me up to her place after.

Like a shark sensing blood in the water, Caleb homes in on that pause. "And after?" he asks expectantly.

"She invited me up to her apartment, but a gentleman doesn't kiss and tell."

Caleb scoffs. "Jackson Jeffers!" This time, he left off the made up middle name. "If I know one thing about you and the ladies, it's that you are a gentleman in public and only up until the second she realizes she doesn't want you to be one in private."

He's not wrong.

I just laugh in response. The noises Amy made? The way she dug her fingers into my scalp as my tongue swirled across her clit? Her arousal coating my fingers as I sunk them into her perfect pussy? Those memories are for me and me alone.

I have enough time to take Bruno for a long walk before heading out to pick up Amy. Caleb, for all of his juvenile messing around after the game, came up with the perfect spot for Amy and me to grab a drink or two before figuring out dinner plans together. I couldn't get us tickets to the show this late in the evening, and while I could have asked our team secretary to pull some strings to get us in, I'm not sure about Amy's opinion on the activity as it is, so we'll just hit the bar instead.

Amy looks radiant as she comes to the car. She's wearing tight black pants, ankle boots, a low cut top, and a denim jacket. I hop out of the driver's seat, pulling open her door as she reaches me. I bend down to hug her, inhaling her jasmine and orange blossom scent.

"Hi, Jackson," she says shyly. "Thanks for picking me up."

"Thanks for agreeing to come out with someone of my mediocre status," I joke with a wink. Amy's cheeks flush an adorable pink. She climbs in just as fat raindrops begin to fall. By the time I pull up to the venue, the sidewalk is wet, but there's a brief reprieve in the rain, allowing us to safely get inside without getting soaked.

"You brought me to a laundromat?" Amy asks skeptically.

"Well, a good ballplayer would bring you on a good date. But a mediocre one brings you to get your laundry done," I continue the joke. "Pull on that handle there." I point where Caleb told me to earlier.

Amy grasps the handle and the entire front panel of the washing machine pulls back, leading to a secret entrance of a bar filled with moody lighting and curved velvet couches. The walls are lined with massive posters featuring magicians from a long-forgotten era.

"Welcome to Chicago Magic House," the receptionist greets us. Amy's grin stretches across her entire face as she looks at me, in awe of her surroundings. "Are you here for the show or just a drink?"

"Just some drinks," I answer.

"Just drinks" hardly covers our experience over the next hour. While Amy and I wedge ourselves into the last few remaining seats on the couch and place our drink order, a magician walks up to the bar and introduces himself as The Great Zamizi. With his bushy mustache and slicked back hair, The Great Zamizi is every part old school magician mixed with cheesy dad jokes. I can practically feel Amy vibrating with excitement.

The Great Zamizi entertains us with small but impressive magic tricks while sprinkling in both terrible and great puns. He periodically asks for audience participation and while I see Amy rapt with attention, I also notice she refrains from raising her hand or looking too eager to participate when Zamizi asks for volunteers. I am more than okay sitting on the sidelines as well; I don't need to call more attention to myself in this city. I'm enjoying every second of being a normal person on a normal date.

I cringe when I notice a man across from me nudge and whisper to the woman next to him, who quietly gasps and not-so-subtly takes her phone out to take a photo of me. I'm used to it, but I can only hope that's the extent of her fangirling. As much as I love the fans, they aren't always aware of boundaries and their situational awareness typically goes out the window when they see an athlete in public. It's hard sometimes not to feel like a zoo animal, but having my photo snapped is far better than having a date interrupted by uninvited conversation, and given Amy's clear inclination tonight to remain firmly away from the spotlight, I'm hoping the woman opts for the more polite, albeit slightly creepier, route. Luckily, Amy appears oblivious to the woman's actions. The bar patrons who have tickets to tonight's show are soon ushered into the theater, leaving Amy, myself, and some other stragglers to close out our tabs.

"Do you want to grab some dinner?" I propose as I close out at the bar.

"I'd love to. What did you have in mind?"

"Wanna check out the neighborhood? See what's around?" We parked about a block away and street parking in this area was limited.

"That sounds great! I'm up for anything."

I love exploring new neighborhoods and don't mind walking, but when we exit the bar, we're confronted with a massive thunderstorm. Sheets of rain pour down from the sky making it impossible to not be completely soaked by the time we make it anywhere. I spot a pizza restaurant across the street. It looks like nothing special, with a couple metal tables and chairs inside in front of an ordering counter, but it's well lit and dry.

"Pizza?" I ask, pointing across the street. Amy's responding smile is radiant.

"That's perfect! I don't need anything fancy and that seems to be our driest option!" she says cheerfully. I can't help but match Amy's grin. Carolyn only ever wanted to eat at high-end restaurants with a dress code and reservations made weeks in advance. While I enjoy a nice meal here and there, sometimes a rainy night hanging out with a saucy pie is just what the night calls for.

After we order, we take a seat at the rickety metal table. There's a small, plastic, fake plant on our table, butting up against the window. Amy touches the leaves as we laugh about some of Zamizi's finest dad jokes.

"That was such a fun place!" Amy gushes.

"We'll have to go back sometime for the actual magic show. Sometime when I know my schedule a little bit better; maybe on an off day or something?"

"Your schedule is kind of crazy. When do you get days off?" she asks. It's hard for people outside of baseball to understand the schedule and the demands of a one hundred and sixty two game season. I pull out my phone and bring up the schedule from the Chicago Foxes app I keep on my home screen.

"We are required to get an off day every one to two weeks, but sometimes we get them more frequently than that. It just kind of depends on how the schedule shakes out throughout the season." I show Amy my screen. "Our next day off isn't for another week and a half, but it'll occur when we're on the road. We're actually in Seattle for the next one."

"Ooh, I love Seattle! My parents and I went there when I was a kid before we took an Alaskan cruise." Amy tells me about her vacation and her time in Pike's Place Market the day before embarking on the cruise.

"I've always wanted to go to Alaska," I tell her. "I guess it'll have to wait until retirement since the best time to visit is the summer," I say with a shrug.

"That must be hard, not getting to take vacations whenever you want."

"It's not so bad. I get to travel to some really cool places with the team, and my schedule is really flexible between November and early February. I didn't grow up taking a lot of vacations as a kid, so I haven't planned a ton of travel during my time off, but it's something I want to start doing more."

Our pizza arrives and between bites, Amy and I talk about dream vacations (Greece for her, New Zealand for me), the best food we've ever eaten (Kung Pao tofu for her, Morimoto sushi for me), and our favorite spots in the city (the library for Amy, the dog beach for me).

Two hours and a mostly finished cheese pizza later, Amy's and my conversation winds down. Caleb's Magic House suggestion could not have been a bigger success. Amy won't stop gushing about the experience and her excitement is so cute, I know I'm going to be buying us tickets for the full show at some point in the very near future. I had a great time too, but I have a feeling I could be happy shoveling shit as long as Amy is happy. I tell myself we're just lingering in the pizza parlor to wait out the rain, but the truth is, the rain stopped about an hour ago and we're still here. I enjoy talking to and laughing with Amy more than I have with another woman in as long as I can remember. She is funny and sweet and has a heart of gold. She just finished telling me about her busy day of meetings and how she had resurfaced from her office after a long day of paperwork only to narrowly miss getting puked on by a child in the lobby of the planetarium. Her reaction in this story is to laugh, while all I can feel is disgust.

"The poor mother's face when her first child puked, followed by the sibling sympathy throwing up right after! I felt so bad for her, but all I could think of was how relieved I was to stay out of the splash zone," Amy chuckles. I'm not sure my reaction to the situation would be so good-spirited, but throughout my conversations with her, I've realized Amy is the type to find the good in every situation. Her laughter dies down and we experience our first lull in the conversation of the night.

"Should we head out?" I suggest.

"Sure." I'm not ready to end my night with Amy but I think my ass has fallen asleep on this hard metal chair and I'm starting to lose feeling in my legs. Previously, Carolyn suggested I wasn't attentive enough, causing her to cheat, so I decide now with Amy, I'm going to be more upfront with my affections and attention so there's no question where I stand with her.

"No pressure whatsoever, but would you want to come back to my place? I know a hairy, four legged guy who would love to see you."

"You know I can never say no to Bruno," Amy teases. Even if she is just coming for Bruno, which I don't think she is given the heat I saw flash in her eyes at the invitation, I couldn't be happier. We stand to leave, and I grasp Amy's hand as we walk out the door and to my car together.

CHAPTER FIFTEEN

Amy

This date could end right now and I would be thrilled. But then Jackson invited me back to his place and confirmed I did not misread the lust I saw spark in his eyes when I first saw him tonight. As self-conscious as I can be about my body, I know these pants compliment my figure and, for once, I'm not constantly worried about how my clothes are laying on my body. Jackson has a strange ability to put my mind at ease, whether it's with what he says or the way he looks at me, I'm not sure, but I feel a sense of calm around him I don't typically get around new friends.

Not that Jackson is just a friend. We haven't defined what we are and I'm not going to push that. I'm happy just getting to know him and seeing where this takes us. And right now, it's taking us back to his place after what I can only describe as a perfect date. I'm practically giddy with anticipation after last night's adventures.

A small thought in the back of my mind reminds me that Jackson Jeffers is a famous athlete, and a man, and that I shouldn't allow myself permission to fantasize about notions of romance, getting swept off my feet, and finding my happily ever after with Jackson. Sure, I like him, but I know he's likely only looking for fun, and I shouldn't get my hopes up. The only way I'll survive any relationship with my heart intact is if I keep reminding myself of reality. Casual is the way to go. Besides, that's what I want anyway, I tell myself.

Jackson squeezes my hand, bringing me back to the present moment. He held my hand all the way to the car and, after buckling himself in and pulling the car back onto the road, promptly picked it back up, where our hands remained clasped together on the center console of his car. "You okay there? You got quiet on me."

Of course Jackson would pick up on me lost in my thoughts. I've never met someone so observant. "Yeah, of course," I respond honestly.

"Are you worried about coming over? I don't have any expectations."

"Jackson, I am in no way feeling pressured by you. I want to come over, if the invite still stands." The man is such a cinnamon roll but I appreciate him checking in on me so much.

"Of course it still stands. Amy, I cannot wait to have you over. I know Bruno will be stoked, but if we're being honest here, I invited you over for my own selfish reasons. I might get jealous if Bruno hogs all your attention," he tells me with a wink. It's the second time he's winked at me tonight and that little action does something to me. Desire pools low in my belly at the sight, or maybe it's the anticipation of what's to come, given what already transpired last night.

"We can't have that. I promise I'll give you plenty of your own attention, too," I say with a wink of my own. Jackson's responding grin is filled with heat and I swear he drives just a little bit faster back to his place.

When we arrive at his building, he clicks a button on his rearview mirror. A gate across the drive slides open, allowing us entrance to the underground garage. Jackson's building isn't huge, just a few floors, but the parking structure is a huge perk. Chicago parking, especially in this part of the city, is such a pain, but Jackson lives too far from the ballpark for him to walk to work. It makes sense that he'd need a place with guaranteed parking nearby.

He presses the button in the elevator in the parking garage to go to the fourth floor. When the doors open, Jackson guides me to the far door. It looks like there are only two units on each floor, but the hallway is so quiet, I feel like I'm in a library.

I'm not sure what to expect when we get inside, but Jackson's place is nicely decorated, even if it is a little sparse. The modern loft feel is supported by an open floor plan, high ceilings, and exposed ductwork. It almost seems at odds with the fluffy blankets draped across his large gray sectional, but somehow, the juxtaposition works. I have only a moment to admire the surroundings before Bruno comes bounding out of one of the back rooms. He looks almost like a cartoon dog the way his legs scramble, trying to come to a stop on the hardwood floors once he realizes he'd rather be running towards me than to Jackson.

"Wow. Okay, I see where I stand," Jackson looks affronted but Bruno doesn't even notice. He leans his heavy back end against me, silently demanding butt scratches, but this time I'm ready for him and have already braced myself.

"Hello, handsome! I missed you so much!" Bruno beams in response, tongue lolling out the side of his mouth, as if the only possible reason for me to be standing in this living room is to see him and only him. I can't help but laugh. I take off my shoes and stumble only a little–Bruno still leaning most of his weight against my legs–and Jackson reaches out a hand to steady me.

"Do you want me to take your jacket?" he offers. I slide it down my shoulders and Jackson hangs it in his front hall closet. There's something so domestic about the action that I can't even name the emotion it elicits. Bruno trots off to find one of his toys and comes prancing back into the room, where he jumps onto the couch and begins loudly chomping on the stuffed moose he brought in.

"Can I get you something to drink?" Jackson asks.

"Water would be great, thanks." I had a drink at the bar and two beers over the course of our long dinner so I'm definitely not even tipsy, but I want to make that point clear to Jackson, too. That whatever happens tonight, I'm going into it with a clear head. Jackson pulls out a bottle of water for each of us. Just as I'm wondering how this is going to transition to hooking up or sex, Jackson's words interrupt my thoughts.

"Amy. I'll kick myself if I don't tell you just how beautiful you look tonight."

I'm working on accepting compliments without downplaying them, my newest homework from my therapist, so I tuck my hair behind my ears and quietly whisper, "Thank you."

Jackson takes a step closer to me, angling his body in front of me as he grasps my chin between his thumb and index finger, lifting it slowly so we make eye contact. His gaze drops to my lips as his tongue darts out to wet his own. I barely have a moment to take a breath before his lips are on mine, the hand holding my chin shifting to gently grasp the side of my jaw and neck while his other hand grips my hip. We both groan together as his tongue slides inside my mouth and I'm reminded what a talented muscle that is.

I swear fireworks go off inside my brain. All thoughts cease as I'm consumed with the sensations around me. Jackson's spicy pine scent, his squeezing grasp on my hip at odds with the gentle way he holds my face. I bring my hand to Jackson's chest and am met with a solid wall of muscle. Slowly sliding my arms up around his neck, Jackson's kissing becomes more passionate, frenzied, while his hand on my face slides slowly–painfully slowly–down my neck and finally to my breast, giving it a gentle squeeze. I pull Jackson's lower lip into my mouth, dragging my teeth across it and biting gently. And right in front me, that small action causes Jackson to become unhinged. He groans, deepening the kiss and squeezing tighter both my hip and my breast. My moan mixes with his as he breaks away from me.

"Off, now," he instructs, tugging at my shirt. I grin in response and lift my arms as Jackson tears my shirt from my body and immediately ducks his head to run his tongue along the top curve of my breast. My nipples pebble underneath my bra and a rush of arousal fills my panties. Closing his mouth around my nipple, he sucks over the lace of my bra and I throw my head back in ecstasy. Not wanting to neglect my other breast, Jackson repeats the motion on my other nipple. My hips involuntarily buck toward him and he backs me toward the back of the couch. Not even lifting his head from my breasts, he first unclasps my bra with expert precision and then begins on the buttons of my pants.

My brain is scrambled and can hardly keep up with what is happening as Jackson slides his hand down my pants. He lets out a low groan when he discovers how wet my panties are, cupping me over them.

"You're so wet, Ames. Is this all for me?" I nod shyly. "Gorgeous, nothing makes me happier than to turn you on. You need to own that shit," he murmurs against my neck, gently suckling where my neck and shoulder connect. "Are you going to let me make you feel good again?" Again, I nod. "God, you tasted so good last night. I can't wait to do it all again. I've been dreaming of ways to make you scream all day."

"Please," is all I can think to say.

"Baby, you never have to beg me. Not tonight, at least," he adds darkly. He slides his hands down my panties and drags a thick finger through my wet folds; I gasp in response. "All you have to worry about tonight is telling me to stop if you want me to."

Stop? I never want him to stop. After last night and what Jackson's expert fingers are doing to me now, I can't fathom a world in which I'd ever want him to do anything but keep going. My heart is pounding so fast I'm surprised it's not filling the room with its beats like surround sound. Jackson withdraws his hand and I gasp at the sudden emptiness. He slides both hands to my waistband, pushing my pants down to right below my ass, giving him just enough room to replace his fingers in my wetness and move them with a little more range of motion. The heel of his palm is pressed firmly against my clit and my body is reeling from the sensation. It feels passionate, sexy and raunchy at the same time, panties to the side, getting fingered by Jackson with my pants half on in the middle of his living room.

"Come for me, Ames. Give me one on my hand and then I'll bend you over the bed and fuck you like you deserve. I'll make you come so many times, baby. That's it, just like that. Ride my fingers." Jackson is almost breathless as he speaks.

Last night, Jackson employed a little bit of dirty talk, but I am wholly unprepared for the flood of dirty talk coming my way tonight. I love it. It heightens the entire experience in a way I've never felt before. I've never been with a man who talks dirty before and I've never felt comfortable enough to ask for it, despite enjoying it in the books I read.

I don't tell Jackson I'm not that kind of girl. My head is too foggy, too lust-addled to explain I've never been a multiple-orgasms-a-night girl. That I've tried it, with other guys, by myself...all to no avail. It's the truth, but something between my brain and my mouth has short-circuited and I can barely form the thoughts, let alone articulate the words. Jackson doesn't seem to notice I've gone silent, my involuntary moans and heavy breathing mixing with the lewd sounds his fingers are making against my wetness.

"That's it. Give it to me. Scream for me."

And I do.

My tightening muscles give way to a screaming orgasm ripping through my body. I couldn't control my moaning and babbling if I wanted to. Jackson continues working his fingers until I come down, floating back to earth. I try to regain control of my breathing as Jackson slowly removes his fingers. I open my eyes to see him grinning down at me. I close my eyes again. What just happened?

Before I can overthink this, Jackson whispers, "Beautiful. Baby, I wish you could see how incredible you look when you come. How amazing you felt squeezing my fingers."

Well. That stops the overthinking. I've always felt a little vulnerable after an orgasm...I can't describe the feeling other than to say I feel slightly embarrassed by how I look and sound in the O moment. It's silly, I know. The whole point of this was to come, but there's something about the actual act of coming that makes me self-conscious in the immediate aftermath. It's almost as if Jackson knew that and chose the exact right words to let me know there was nothing embarrassing and everything sexy about my reactions. I open my eyes again to see him looking at me with adoration.

"Are you okay? Can you walk?" He smoothes my hair and begins kissing me again, softly, sweetly. "Come on. I've got you," he whispers, pulling my pants the rest of the way down and helping me to step out of them. He then takes my hand and pulls me to the bedroom.

Jackson is still fully clothed when I perch on the edge of the bed wearing only my underwear. The adoration in Jackson's eyes has morphed into lust again as he slowly begins unbuttoning his shirt. He reaches the last button, leaving his dress shirt hanging open while he works the buttons on the sides of his sleeves. Why is that so hot?

My awe of Jackson's body doesn't stop after my initial perusal. How is this man real? His chiseled pecs lead to a six pack and an annoyingly sexy Adonis V, all covered with a light smattering of brown hair. While my Google image stalking–ahem *searching*–let me know Jackson's body is incredible, I was wholly unprepared to experience it up close, naked, and personal. I've never seen someone so cut in real life. I bite my bottom lip and glance back to Jackson's face. He knows he's caught me blatantly ogling him and smirks.

Whatever.

I'm shameless in checking out his powerful chest, ripped abs, and strong, muscular forearms. The man has no idea the panty-melting power in his forearms. Jackson, finished with unbuttoning his cuffs, pulls his shirt off, letting it pool at his feet. Slowly, drawing out the show, he unbuckles his belt and unzips his pants. They fall to the ground, belt jangling. He steps out of his shoes and socks and I'm left breathless, staring at him in only his boxer briefs, the thick outline of his cock straining against the thin material. I'm aching to pull him out. While I know I can't orgasm again, I'm not ready for the fun to be over.

I slide to my knees in front of him, placing my hands on the front of his thick thighs. Jackson pulls a sharp intake of breath and I revel in how powerful it makes me feel. I may be on my knees, but that little gasp lets me know I am the one in control at this moment. Jackson's thighs flex slightly under my touch.

"Take it out, baby. I'm dying here. You look so pretty on your knees, staring up at me."

I've never minded blowjobs. I can get into them—like them, even—if my partner is appreciative, but they've never turned me on the way they can for some of the women in my books. But the hungry way Jackson is looking at me right now? And his words—holy shit, this man's words! I get it now, book ladies! I absolutely understand how a blow job can be a turn on for the giver. And my drive to please this man, to give him the same pleasure he gave me only minutes ago, spurs me to lick my lips in preparation to return the favor. Jackson's face darkens with lust.

Gripping the waistband of his boxer briefs, I slide them down his thighs. His cock springs forward and I'm momentarily stunned. I knew he was going to be big based on the hard outline I saw before I pulled him out, but I don't think anything could have prepared me for this. Thick, hard, with an angry vein running along the underside and a drop of precum on the tip.

"Jesus, Amy. You better do something about this or I'm not going to be able to control myself with you looking at my cock like that." Now I'm the one who smirks. Jackson looks to the ceiling as if praying for resolve. I take the opportunity to run my tongue along the underside of his length, right along that glorious vein. He lets out a low, rumbling groan which only serves to encourage me further. I pull the tip of his engorged cock into my mouth, swirling my tongue around the crown, tasting his saltiness.

"Fuck yes, Amy," Jackson breathes. I pull him deeper, bobbing my head down his length, stretching my lips across his girth. It's a tight fit, given how thick he is, and there's no way I can take his whole length in my mouth. It won't stop me from trying to get as much in as I can, though. I hollow my cheeks and pull him to the back of my throat. The noises this man is making are so sexy;

I'm turned on more than I ever have been before from engaging in foreplay.

"God, you look so gorgeous with my cock in your mouth. Take me deep again. Suck it hard." Never one to admit defeat, I do as I'm told. The tip of Jackson's cock hits the back of my throat, gagging me, and I breathe through my nose. Beside me, Jackson clenches his hands into fists, attempting some modicum of control over himself.

"Shit. You feel so good." I grab the base of Jackson's cock, the part that doesn't come close to fitting in my mouth, and squeeze gently. He follows with another groan as I twist my hand, mimicking a pepper grinder motion. Jackson's breathing picks up and his hips involuntarily rock, the tip of his cock hitting the back of my throat repeatedly. He fists my hair roughly and I'm pleased to discover that turns me on too. I've never had a man pull my hair before and watching my sweet Jackson lose control like this, take what he wants like this, is a turn on in and of itself. He pumps a few more times, then pulls his hips back, keeping a tight hold on my hair. He pulls himself all the way out of my mouth and I pout. I was enjoying myself, enjoying him getting lost in the sensations, and I wasn't ready to give that up yet.

"Don't look at me like that, pretty girl. If you keep sucking my cock like that I'm going to come down your pretty throat."

"So do it," I challenge. Jackson's eyes glint with lust and some unnamed emotion. Excitement? Promise?

"Oh I will. Just not tonight. I told you I would bend you over this bed and fuck you like you deserve, and I intend to keep every promise I make to you. Now get up, and turn around."

CHAPTER SIXTEEN

Jackson

Amy does exactly as she's told and, fuck, if that doesn't make my dick swell even more. I couldn't be happier with the direction the night has gone. When Amy came undone under my fingers, when her breathy moans turned into outright screaming—and screaming *my* name—I knew there were few things that could top this night. Then she gave me the best head I've ever had and it took all my willpower to rip my cock out of her mouth. There's no way I am going to end the night coming down her beautiful throat when I could draw more orgasms out of her. I am going to come with my cock buried in her soft, warm pussy tonight. But seeing Amy follow my instructions without question, turning her beautiful body toward the bed, almost brings me to my knees.

"Good girl," I murmur as Amy looks over her shoulder at me. "You're doing so well, baby," I continue, bending and pulling a condom from my discarded pants pocket. I rip open the foil, rolling the condom down my length and stepping closer to her. I wrap my arms around Amy's shoulders from behind, pressing a soft kiss to her ear. She leans back into me, pressing her ass against my hard cock.

"Are you ready to get fucked the way you deserve?" I whisper against her ear. I feel her shudder against me. "I know you're turned on, baby. I know if I bend you over and touch this gorgeous pussy, I'll find you dripping for me again, won't I? But I still need your words, Amy. Are you ready for me?"

Amy's voice is barely a whisper as she breathes, "Yes."

"Good." I release my hold around her, kiss her neck one last time, and slowly drag her panties down her legs. Placing my palm between her shoulder blades, I gently press her chest onto the mattress.

"Baby, you're soaked," I murmur, dragging a finger through her folds. "Did you like sucking my cock?" She nods, and while I'd rather hear her words, I also know tonight I've pushed her probably as far outside her comfort zone as I'm willing to make her go. There will be plenty more times for us to push boundaries further. Later.

"Good." I run my cock along the length of her pussy, coating myself in her wetness. "God, you feel so good. We can stop if there's anything you don't like. Just tell me. But you've been such a good girl, so good to me, and I'm going to reward you." I notch myself at her entrance and push in, just the tip.

She stops breathing. "Breathe, Amy. I need you to relax and breathe. I'll take care of you." Amy again does as she's told and it allows her to relax enough for me to thrust in another inch. "You're taking me so well. You're doing so good, baby." She whimpers. I felt how much she enjoyed dirty talk when my fingers were buried in her, the extra gushes of wetness coming hot on the heels of my words, so I know talking her through it is going to loosen her up enough to take all of me for the first time. I love being vocal in bed; it's one more reason I'm convinced Amy is the right girl for me.

I push in a little more, gritting my teeth. It's almost painful for me to go this slow, but I'll do whatever she needs in this moment. This woman is intoxicating and all consuming, and I'll go whatever pace is necessary to allow her to warm up and get what she needs.

"Jackson," Amy whimpers. "Please."

I don't know what she's begging for, more or faster, but hearing her beg causes me to lose a little more of my control. "I've got you, baby," I say, thrusting hard the last few inches until I'm fully seated inside her. I give her a few moments to adjust to me while also taking a few moments myself to regain my composure. Amy feels so good, so warm, so wet, so *perfect*. I need to get a hold of myself if I want to make this last—for both our sakes.

"God, you feel so good. You're so tight. I'm gonna start moving now; are you ready?"

And fuck if it doesn't do something to me when Amy says "please" again. The last tether of my control snaps and I go feral for this woman. Gripping her hips to hold her in place, I kick her feet out wider and push in deeper. Amy's tiptoes are on the ground, barely touching it, and her hands scramble for purchase against the raised bed as I begin a relentless pounding into her from behind. She fists the sheets as her breathing turns ragged and I continue slamming into her. She begins moaning, and that noise, paired with the obscene sound of skin slapping together, makes me come a little more undone. I'm not ready to finish yet–far from it. I need to coax another orgasm from my girl first before I can even think of coming myself.

"Fuck, Amy, you're so good. Just like that, keep squeezing me. Your pussy is so perfect," I praise. Amy moans again and I can't help but smile. My girl loves dirty talk and might have a bit of a praise kink. I love it. "Come for me again. Scream my name," I instruct.

"I can't," Amy breathes. Her words come out stuttered due to the onslaught I'm putting her body through behind her. "I've...never...been...able to..."

I halt my movements, not understanding. "Baby, you came earlier?" I question, thoroughly confused now. There's no way this girl faked her orgasm earlier, not with the way her pussy was strangling my fingers, squeezing the life out of them. I know women can fake an orgasm, but I'm confident enough in my own skills, in my own experience, that the thought didn't even occur to me that Amy might do that.

Amy squeezes her eyes shut further. "I mean, I can't...not more than once...I've never been able to." And damn, if my sweet little Amy doesn't seem embarrassed by that.

I can't help but laugh. "Oh baby, don't you worry about that. Let me worry about that. I'll get you there." I resume rocking my hips, slow at first, then rapidly, resuming my earlier pace.

"It's okay if you don't, Jackson. It's not a you thing. I just can't," she says definitively, almost sadly.

Part of me feels sad for Amy, that she may have had a man make her feel badly about not orgasming multiple times. That's more of a them issue than a problem with Amy's ability to perform in the bedroom or receive pleasure. I have no such concerns, but that doesn't stop me from feeling anger towards anyone at any time making Amy feel like she isn't good enough.

"It still feels good, though, even if I can't finish," Amy goes on, as if she needs to reassure me. I don't need to be placated in this situation; I have no doubt how this is going to end for Amy. She just doesn't know it yet.

CHAPTER SEVENTEEN
Amy

Crack. I hear the sound of Jackson's palm against my ass a second before I felt the sting. He immediately soothes the pain, squeezing and rubbing his palm against my ass cheek, never ceasing his relentless pounding into me.

"I told you to let me worry about that, baby. You just hold on." Jackson grunts out behind me.

Holy shit. I've never been spanked before. My mind is reeling. My inner feminist is appalled, while my inner sex goddess is shrieking, kicking her legs in the air and giggling. Jackson Jeffers just spanked me. And I liked it.

"You like that, Amy? I felt your pussy strangle my cock when I smacked your ass."

I can't breathe. I don't even know what to say. Of course I liked that. Why did I like that? It's so degrading...isn't it? I've read about spanking in my books, but never thought I'd be into it. In fact, I distinctly remember rolling my eyes at scenes that included it.

"Come back to me, Amy. Where'd you go? I love your beautiful brain, but let's turn that off for right now, yeah? Let me make you feel good."

Of course, Jackson noticed me getting lost in my own thoughts. *Shut up, brain,* my vulva is practically screaming, *it's my turn now!*

I close my eyes, gripping the comforter, as Jackson slams into me again. My toes barely reach the floor and I know I'll have bruises against my hips, either from being slammed into the mattress or from Jackson's controlling grip. Either way, I love it. I've never been fucked like this before and I can't believe I never knew what I was missing. Jackson must notice I'm barely hanging on-literally. In one swift movement, he's bending his knees, sweeping my legs up and folding them under me, so they are now on top of the surface of the mattress, all while remaining inside of me. I'm in the kinkiest version of a child's pose in yoga, which allows me to become a little more stable on the bed. It also changes the angle of Jackson's cock hitting inside me, and a string of unintelligible words fly out of my mouth as a result.

"Oh holy shit. Fuck…just like that. Yes…right there. Oh please, don't stop. That feels so good," I can't stop babbling. This feels different from the build of my orgasm before, and a part of me almost feels crazy enough to think I might be building toward another one? The thought has me hopeful, excited…is this what multiple orgasms feel like? Or does this just feel good because it's sex, and sex with Jackson? I wonder if I really can lose control again? Is it truly possible for me to come more than once a night? Is this actually happening? Can I…aaaaand it's gone. Whatever that amazing feeling was, orgasm or not, I killed it by overthinking.

"Baby, I will spank your ass so hard you'll be wearing my palm print the rest of the night if you don't turn your thoughts off. I see you overthinking." Jackson punctuates his next words with thrusts. "Let. Me. Do. My. Job."

It's so hard to turn the thoughts off, and it's even harder to see them coming in order to prevent them. I swallow and breathe through Jackson's continued thrusts, vowing to turn my brain off. I take another deep breath and will the thoughts out of my mind.

"There she is," Jackson murmurs. "I told you I was going to fuck you like you deserve, now let me do it." He snakes his hand up my spine, grasping the back of my neck. He squeezes gently, just once, but leaves his hand there. I can't explain the feeling that washes over me. Is it weird to say I feel safe with Jackson's hand around my throat? Because for some reason, I do. Jackson's other hand comes out of nowhere from underneath me, rubbing my clit roughly. I can't help the deep moan it elicits. There are so many sensations occurring at the same time. Jackson's hand around my throat. His cock pounding into me. The slap of his hips against my ass. And now his skilled strumming of my clit by his talented fingers. Before I know what's happening, I shatter around him. I think I scream his name, but maybe I just scream.

"Yes; scream my name. Fuck!" Jackson exclaims as he chases his own release. As I'm feeling the aftershocks of my own—second!—orgasm, I feel Jackson stutter his hips, coming with a final shout, before collapsing on top of me.

Our breathing slows and after a few minutes, he rolls to the side and pulls out of me. He kisses my shoulder and gets up to dispose of the condom. I slide my hips to the side to stretch my legs while keeping my eyes closed. Jackson returns with a warm washcloth and cleans me up. He lays next to me, tracing slow patterns on my back as I work to regulate my breathing.

I open my eyes to see Jackson looking at me with concern. "Was that all okay? It wasn't too rough, was it?" He looks almost panicked as he smoothes my hair away from my face. My heart melts a little bit at the worry in his tone.

"Jackson," I whisper, trying to collect my thoughts. "I've never had sex like that. It was...incredible. Everything was incredible."

The look of relief on his face makes emotion well in my throat. The transition from sweet, cinnamon roll Jackson to bossy sex god Jackson back to a cinnamon roll would give me whiplash if it wasn't so absolutely perfect. I sigh contentedly as Jackson nuzzles into my neck. It's then that I realize my brain has been mercifully quiet the last several minutes.

CHAPTER EIGHTEEN
Amy

I replay my night with Jackson over and over again throughout the course of the next several days. I slept like the dead in Jackson's bed after we had sex. I had tried to get up after several minutes of post-coital cuddling, intent on going home and maintaining what I had hoped would be a casual attitude toward Jackson and our relationship in general. Instead, he pulled me closer and told me while I could leave if I really wanted to, he wanted me to stay the night. So I did.

In the morning, I had woken to my clothes folded neatly on the nightstand, Jackson's heavy arm draped around my waist. He must have collected my clothes from his living room floor when he took Bruno out at some point in the night. Bruno must have heard me stir because before Jackson could fully wake, I heard the click of Bruno's nails on the floors. I had about four seconds to prepare myself before ninety pounds of fur and love effectively cannon-balled his way into the bed, wedging himself between Jackson and me. It was such a bizarre way to wake up that I couldn't help but laugh.

That morning, Jackson and I had walked together to Caffeine Kingdom with Bruno. Jackson bought us our usual coffees: a dirty chai for me, a cold brew with two shots of espresso for Jackson, and a pup cup for Bruno. The boys then walked me to my apartment. Jackson gave me one hell of a goodbye kiss before he left to get ready for his game.

Now, Jackson is on a four game road trip in St. Louis, but he's been keeping a steady stream of texts and phone calls going without being overbearing that it keeps me reassured I didn't say or do anything embarrassing to scare him off. Brains are weird that way, and mine happens to work overtime when it comes to worry. One of my favorite yoga instructors often says that worry and anxiety are a form of meditation–it's a singular focus on one thing, even though it's an unproductive use of meditative energy. By that logic, I should be great at meditation. I'm working on it, at least. My therapist, Connie, is great, and she's teaching me to give myself a lot of grace while I'm still learning to manage my anxiety the best I can. Some days are better than others, but Jackson seems to almost instinctively know what to say or do to not only make me feel better, but to prevent some of the impending anxiety from rearing its ugly head. It's enough to make a girl fall for him if I didn't know better.

I'm still keeping my heart guarded at a comfortable distance from Jackson, but it's getting harder and harder the more I interact with him. Old habits die hard and I've always been one to wear my heart on my sleeve. That alone has caused my heart to be broken countless times, but this last time, with Patrick, was the worst, because it was the blow I never saw coming. Patrick lulled me into a false sense of security with his pretty words and empty promises, and I swore to my battered and bruised heart that never again would I let someone in like that. If you don't let them into the most vulnerable crevices of your heart, they can't destroy it. So I'll keep my wits about me and a relatively tight grip on my emotions and Jackson won't be able to pull a Patrick, even if he wanted to.

My mom is driving into the city tonight from the suburbs. There is a retro movie theater not far from the ballpark that is hosting a film noir festival this weekend with old movies playing nonstop. Once patrons buy tickets, they can come in and out as they please all weekend to catch one or more movies. My mom and I have always loved old movies. I grew up watching Sunset Boulevard and Casablanca with her, longing for the golden age of film. We have lunch plans at a nearby cafe before we plan on spending the rest of the day inside the movie theater.

Over soup and salad, I fill my mother in on work and all of the new grants I'm hoping to get. Realistically, I know I'll be lucky to get even one more than I've already gotten, but given that some of the budget we were hoping to get from the state was severely slashed during legislative negotiations, I'm hoping to squeeze every drop out of these grants that I possibly can. My mother has always been my biggest fan. My stepfather is supportive as well, but, never having had children of his own, I think he is more than happy to give my mom the time she needs to spend with her only daughter while he remains at home, installing their new landscaping. My mom and stepdad didn't meet until a few years ago, when I was already in college, so I didn't grow up having a relationship with him. Gary is kind and supportive, even if he is a little awkward about showing his affection. Still, I consider him as close to a father figure as I'll get.

My mom tells me about the new landscaping they're putting in the backyard. She's a few years away from retiring as an elementary school principal, and they're preparing to transform their back-yard into an oasis for when that time actually comes.

"Elizabeth's wedding planning is almost done. I was talking to your Aunt Nicole yesterday and they've got pretty much every-thing set." I'm not surprised. My cousin Elizabeth is an event planner; she's marrying her high school sweetheart in October. Of course she would have everything complete by now. We chat about her upcoming bridal shower and bits of family gossip. My phone dings with a text from Jackson. I glance at it briefly, planning to respond to it later when I'm not in the middle of lunch.

Jackson Neighbor

Hi beautiful. We're about to start our pregame stretch here but just wanted to let you know I'm thinking of you. I hope you have a great time with your mom today!

I roll my lips together, attempting and failing to suppress the goofy grin spreading across my face. My mother picks up on it immediately.

"What's going on?"

"Nothing, just a nice text from someone." My mother knows me better than that and doesn't let me off the hook so easily.

"Does this someone have a name?" She wiggles her eyebrows at me.

"Yes, his name is Jackson. He's just a neighbor." I stop trying to hide my grin; resistance is futile at this point.

"Interesting. Diane and I text every week and I never have that look on my face when I text her."

"That's because Diane is the neighborhood gossip," I say, not sure what point I'm trying to make.

"If you don't want to tell me about this Jackson, that's fine. But it's nice to see you get excited about a boy again. And another J name!" she teases.

For a little while in high school, I dated a string of guys who happened to have names that started with the letter J: James, Justin, Jason. It became a running joke in my family that I only dated guys with J names.

"Just make sure you don't forget to tell me when it becomes serious." She throws a wink my way. Never one to push or pry, my mother gives me enough of her opinion to let me know her thoughts without trying to sway my own opinions.

"It won't get serious. I'm not looking for anything serious right now." Or ever, I silently add. She gives me a knowing look. What she knows, I'm not sure, but she certainly seems to think she's on to something. She says nothing more about the subject.

After we finish lunch, we head to the theater. We make our way down the dimly lit aisle and shuffle in to the middle of the row. The old-school, red velvet upholstered seats don't compete with the cushy recliners of newer movie theaters, but there's something about the vintage vibe of this place that makes me fall a little in love with it, even if it has fallen into a bit of disrepair.

My mom and I watch 'The Killers' first, a 1964 film starring Ronald Reagan before he was president. The "special effects" and gunfight scenes are laughably bad compared to today's acting and technology, but we love it. It's the perfect way to pass the afternoon and keep thoughts of a certain blue eyed Adonis at bay.

CHAPTER NINETEEN

Amy

"So what's the deal then?" Danny asks over brunch the day after my movie marathon with my mother. Tim, Danny, Alicia and I are at Over Easy, a new brunch spot that opened in Lakeview East.

"Yeah, this one hasn't filled me in on too much dirt," Tim remarks, jerking a thumb at his boyfriend. Danny rolls his eyes in response as he sips his espresso martini, but I catch a hint of a smirk. Tim loves gossip as much as Danny does; there's no way they haven't already discussed my love life.

"What do you want to know?"

"Um, everything?" Tim pulls out his phone and a minute later is apparently reading Jackson's stats from an official baseball website. "Ooh, he's six foot two! Good for you. One hundred ninety pounds, solid. Bats left-handed, throws righty. Ames, if this is all I have to go on, you know I'm going to die from a lack of information. Please give me more to go off of or I'm going to Google Image search him and make up my own details."

I snort. "Go ahead, I might like what you come up with," I challenge.

"Fine. JJ Jeffers: Chicago Foxes shortstop by day, international spy by night. With these custom suits I'm seeing him in, there's no way he just hits a ball with a stick and people pay him millions of dollars. And a face like that? World leaders would spill secrets for him. Amy, he's gorgeous, but is baseball all these women he's pictured with are into? There's definitely more to him. I'm going with spy; my mind is made up."

"He's not a spy."

"That you know of!"

"Fair point. But I'm pretty sure he's not a spy. He spends pretty much all of his time at the ballpark." I decide to throw Tim a bone and give him a little more information. "He has two brothers, one of whom is his agent. He's got a rottweiler named Bruno who might just be the love of my life. And he lives in Lincoln Park, a few blocks from my place."

"That boilerplate information is exactly the type of stuff a spy would share. Generic enough to be believable without specifics that would cause him to get him caught in a lie." When Tim gets on a roll like this, it's best to let him run with it. "I need the *deets* on your boyfriend."

"Woah. *Not* my boyfriend. Absolutely not." I don't miss the way all three of my friends simultaneously share a look.

"Amy, sweetheart, you talk to the man every day–and *he's* the one initiating the communication with you," Alicia begins. "Which, I'd like to point out, you are not unhappy about. Your face lights up like a Christmas tree whenever he so much as texts you. You've been on two dates on back to back nights and are already planning to see him again for a third. I know you've already slept together–" Tim whips his head in my direction so fast I'm surprised he doesn't strain a muscle "--and the sex was mind blowing. So don't try to tell us that you're not into him or he's not boyfriend material."

"We haven't discussed what we are or what we want out of this arrangement. Besides, I have no expectation of exclusivity–we've been on *two dates.* You guys are as bad as twelve year old girls at a slumber party."

"What *do* you want out of this?" Danny cuts to the chase.

"I don't know. I'm just here to have fun. I don't want to be pressured to figure out what we are or are not at this stage. For all I know, Jackson has a girl in every city and I just happen to be his Chicago girl."

"Okay," Alicia says gently, "and if that's true, how do you feel about that?"

"I don't have a right to feel one way or another about it," I respond evasively. "You always hear stories about athletes and their little black books."

Alicia tuts. "You always have a right to feel however you're feeling. But he's been calling you and texting on this road trip. That doesn't sound like just a hookup situation to me," she counters.

"Well, add it to the mystery surrounding Jackson Jeffers then. Maybe he really is a spy. Because I didn't think someone telling me they loved me, that they wanted to marry me, that they wanted to have *children* someday with me was just a hookup situation either, but that's apparently what my relationship with Patrick turned out to be. Lesson fucking learned." I say with a lot more bite than I intended. Alicia flinches. "Sorry," I add in a whisper.

"At the risk of sounding like a white man seeped in toxic masculinity, not every man is like Patrick," Danny adds softly.

I know Danny is right; he and Tim are proof of that. But Tim is gay and while Danny is attracted to all genders, he's so head over heels for Tim that his sexuality is a moot point in this conversation. My history with the pool of available men leads me to believe most men who are attracted to women are not willing to settle down and are just looking for a fun time. A small, secret part of me hopes I'm wrong, but I quash that thought almost immediately. My heart can't afford to hope after Patrick left it shredded.

"We just want you to be happy, Ames. Whether that's with JJ or someone else or no one at all. Whatever you decide, we're happy for you." Tim tells me, his voice full of genuine empathy instead of sympathy. I'm struck by just how grateful I am for this group of friends and their endless support.

"Thanks," I whisper. "In lighter news, Jackson invited me to watch one of his games. He thought I might get nervous being by myself with all the other baseball wives and girlfriends so he suggested I bring you guys along. What do you think?”

“*Other* baseball wives and girlfriends? As in, you’re lumping yourself in with the WAGs?” Danny wiggles his eyebrows suggestively. I open my mouth to respond; he holds up a hand to stop me. “I know, I know. I’m just playing.”

“Ooh, what about tomorrow? We could extend the weekend and play hooky from work?” Alicia suggests. I check the game schedule published on the Foxes’ website.

“Looks like there’s a one o’clock game tomorrow. I probably have to work from home for a couple hours, but we could take the afternoon off? What do you guys think?”

“We’re in,” Danny and Tim say simultaneously.

chapter twenty

Jackson

I've played eight rounds of Mario Kart on our flight back from St. Louis. The flight itself isn't that long, but I'm restless and unfocused. My mother called twice on our road trip. Both times I let the calls go to voicemail; she didn't leave a message, but that didn't prevent my blood pressure from spiking each time I saw her name light up the screen. My brother, Sean, says he's handling it but I need him to handle it faster. Or better.

I haven't always had such a fraught relationship with the woman who birthed me. My mom was a great caregiver when my brothers and I were younger. Once my dad died, however, so much of my mother died with him that it made it possible for the darkness to reach through the cracks in her heartbreak. I don't remember the day we were told my dad died of a massive heart attack (I'm told not remembering is a fairly common trauma response), but I do remember the weeks after. We grieved together as a little, broken family surrounded by my dad's larger, extended family. My mom was an only child whose own parents passed away before my parents married, so when my dad died, his family swooped in to support us in the immediate aftermath.

What I do remember of my dad is that he was kind with a boisterous laugh that filled the room. He's the one who instilled the love of all things athletic in my brothers and me. He was larger than life and my favorite person in the world. When you love as hard as my dad did, it's not surprising to see the world crumble around your loved ones when that love is suddenly ripped away. We did okay at first. My dad worked hard enough and had a good enough life insurance policy that we weren't at a huge financial risk initially. My mom had to go back to work eventually, but we were never financially destitute.

Surviving financially, unfortunately, did not equate to really surviving, and we definitely were not thriving. My mom was irrevocably broken by my dad's passing, and when my dad's extended family eventually trickled back to their own homes and returned to their own lives, moving forward in the grieving process, my mom stood still. She wasn't able to move forward in her grief, shoving it inward until it ate her alive. In hindsight, it seems so much of her own identity was wrapped up in my dad, and once he was gone, she no longer knew who she was. She might have been able to work through it if she didn't have such terrible coping mechanisms.

Instead of seeking help, my mom sought company in the form of boyfriends. Now that I'm well into adulthood, with several years of therapy under my belt, I can see that my mom not only didn't want to be alone, she didn't know *how* to be alone. It doesn't excuse her for hopping from one man to another, but it certainly explains things. Laurie Jeffers was always physically beautiful, with dark hair and bright eyes, but she didn't hesitate to remind my brothers and me that a single woman with three young children was viewed as a woman with baggage, and we should minimize our impact on her life, and by extension, the lives of her boyfriends. Some of her boyfriends were fine, nice even, but most men didn't stick around long enough to meet us. The ones who did were hardly men we wanted to know anyway. Most men whisked my mom away from the house for hours and sometimes days at a time.

It forced my brothers and me to rely on each other. Nothing like trauma bonding to bring a family together, right? Sean, being the oldest, always made sure we had food to eat as my mom's escapades didn't always allow her the flexibility to remember to go grocery shopping. Money wasn't the issue most of the time; my mom just needed to remember she had three other mouths to feed at home and most times, it seemed she just couldn't be bothered to do that. It would have been lonely if it didn't draw Sean, Nate and myself closer together. It's probably the reason we're so close today, despite being separated by geography.

Sean and Nate excelled in school, giving them a sense of importance they didn't get from home. While I did okay academically, I excelled in sports, especially baseball. Baseball gave me an identity and a purpose outside of scraping and clawing for some semblance of importance alongside my brothers at home. As my skills on the ball field increased, I started to get scouted, first by colleges, and then by professional baseball teams.

My brothers were by my side the whole time, keeping me grounded and helping me hone my skills long after practice ended each night. Nate picked up the housework while Sean cooked, giving me time to sharpen my fundamental skills. Sean parlayed his protective instincts and experience essentially parenting me as a student athlete into a successful career as a sports agent. To this day, I am one hundred percent certain I wouldn't have gotten baseball scholarships or been signed by a major league team if not for my brothers. They've never asked for anything in return, but I take care of them nonetheless. I bought Nate his house in Milwaukee and I've made Sean incredibly rich in his own right as my (and many of my teammates') agent.

Growing up, if my mom was just physically and emotionally neglectful, I think my brothers and I could have gotten by and adjusted well enough with a little therapy or time and hindsight to process everything. Instead, my mom met Ron, who was and still is not only emotionally abusive toward my mother, but a gambling addict. He preyed upon my mother's insecurities, sinking his claws into her vulnerabilities and solidifying himself as an unyielding presence in her life. He also introduced her to the world of poker, blackjack, and, worst of all, sports betting.

My mother is a fully fledged gambling addict. Not that she would ever admit to it, but she is the literal textbook definition of an addict. Repeated and ongoing betting? Check. Continued betting even though it's negatively impacting her life? Check. An inability to stop or control her gambling? Absolutely. Gambling when she's stressed? Yep. Hiding the aftereffects of her disastrous gambling? Every time.

She lost her job several years ago and relies on her bets to "break even" or make her some semblance of an income. The last I heard, she and Ron were living out of a seedy, extended stay motel outside of Austin, but that was years ago. She could be anywhere, I suppose, and I would have a better idea of where she was staying if I ever picked up the phone to find out.

But I can't, because not only am I dealing with the emotional fallout of an addict as a parent, the trauma of childhood neglect, and the anger about what my mother put us through growing up, but because my mother's drug of choice is gambling, my livelihood is at risk if I interact with her in any way.

Like many professional sports, baseball has extremely strict anti-gambling rules. Players and staff are not allowed to bet on baseball. Period. Some people think you can bet as long as you're not gambling on games involving your own team, but that's not true. Any betting within the sport at all is cause for sanctions, fines, or suspensions. I could get permanently thrown out of the league if I bet on baseball, regardless of whether or not I bet on the Foxes. So my mother finding her favorite vice in sports betting is one of the most dangerous things she could have chosen to do with herself. Logically, I understand an addiction isn't a choice, but emotionally, it's hard not to feel rage toward her actions when it comes to *sports* gambling.

It wasn't too hard (physically, at least) to cut my mother out. Due to her neglectful nature, she probably didn't even realize my brothers and I had collectively decided to cut her out when I was in college. At that time, Sean had already graduated and was almost finished with law school, so I imagine it was harder for my mother to notice his lack of communication with her. Nate, being only two years younger than me, was almost in college at the time. Perhaps my mother just thought we were getting busier and busier, but she never bothered to pick the phone up to actually find out.

Emotionally, cutting my mother out wasn't that difficult for me, either. I suspect Sean struggled more, given that he is older than Nate and me. He remembered a lot more of the good times and the old mom we had back when Dad was still alive. Sean claims he has no issues cutting Laurie Jeffers out of his life and that he hasn't looked back once, but he had such a different experience with her during his formative years that I can only hope he's being honest. My brothers, especially Sean, sacrificed so much for me to have the life I do now. The guilt over what they gave up gnaws at me daily, despite their reassurances that they'd do it all over again if they had to.

Now that my mother is a gambler, I cannot have any sort of contact with her. I don't know how she tracked down my phone number; it's risky enough that she's found me and called me, regardless of whether or not I picked up. Sean's been working overtime to notify regulators in the league that while my mother is reaching out to me, I am in no way communicating with her.

I pull out my phone and block my mom's most recent phone number. I should have done it the first time she called me a few weeks ago, but when I didn't hear from her again, it was honestly easier to shove all thoughts of her and her many betrayals from my mind as soon as I informed my brothers of the situation. I wouldn't be surprised if my mom finds another way to contact me in a few months' time. She periodically goes through cycles of remembering she actually has children; sometimes she even wants to talk to us when she remembers we exist. I'm protective of my privacy but it's important to me—and my brothers—that I be able to live my life semi-normally. I don't give out my phone number to others unless I absolutely have to; Amy was the first person I voluntarily gave my number to in years.

Amy. That woman is a bright spot in my storm cloud of a day. All I want to do is call her, ask her if she wants to grab coffee or go on a walk with Bruno and me when I land, but I'm trying not to overwhelm her with my interest. Carolyn drilled into me that I wasn't attentive enough in our relationship and while I don't believe that caused her to cheat—we'll chalk that one up to her terrible personality—it's made me hyper aware of my actions toward women I'm interested in. I won't make that mistake again;

if I'm into a woman, I'm all in, and she will know it. And right now, I'm finding myself all in on Amy.

The sex with Amy has been nothing short of phenomenal; our chemistry is off the charts. But more than that, I want to be around Amy for who she is as a person. Her mere presence has a soothing effect on me. I'm in awe of how her mind works and seeing her passion for working with children is inspirational. Her laugh is infectious and her ability to really analyze a situation makes me want to bounce all of my ideas off of her.

Our flight is landing in Chicago in a few minutes. The flight time between St. Louis and Chicago is minimal and when the plane gets low enough where my cell reception kicks back in, I can't help my grin when I see Amy's text from earlier.

Amy

> Great win! I talked to everyone at brunch today, and as long as you're totally okay with it, we'd love to go to the game tomorrow. Alicia and I are planning on taking the afternoon off. Danny and Tim are in too. Are you sure you don't mind getting us four tickets? I know that's a lot.

I shake my head, smiling to myself. My beautiful girl never wants to give her equally beautiful mind a rest, but I'm okay with it.

My girl. We haven't had a conversation about what our time together means, so Amy doesn't know she's mine yet, but if I have my way, she'll know soon enough.

Chapter Twenty-One

Amy

"Can I see your tickets, please?" The usher–Dale, if his nametag is to be trusted–asks us. He scrutinizes my phone where I swipe through the app housing our tickets. Dale shows us to our seats which are one section back from the field, behind home plate. Even as someone who doesn't religiously follow baseball, I can tell these seats are in a perfect location.

Danny, Tim, and Alicia follow me into the row. I'm carrying a salad we picked up at a concession stand on the way to our seats. Danny and Tim are laden with two beers apiece, but I am not ready to start drinking. For some reason, I'm on edge with nerves. I know Jackson can't see us from the dugout and we only made vague plans to meet up after the game, but I can't help but feel like I need to be "on" for some sort of performance. Alicia rubs my arm soothingly, picking up on my stress.

"These are great seats, babe. You'll have to tell Jackson thank you from us."

"You're coming out with us after the game though, right?" I ask, alarm in my voice. My anxiety is at an all-time high, and I am not ready to be abandoned by my friends in a few hours.

"Of course. We're all going to be there and we'll also thank Jackson ourselves," Danny interrupts. He's seen the evolution of my anxiety over the last decade I've known him. He's a little more abrupt about dealing with it than Alicia, who tends to take a softer approach, but both strategies are effective.

A booming voice comes on the announcement system, asking us to rise and remove our hats for the national anthem. The game begins shortly after, and my breath catches in my lungs when I see number nineteen run out onto the field. Jackson is wearing bright blue, high socks up to his knees, and this, paired with the white uniform and blue pinstripes, make him look like an old fashioned ball player from eras long ago. The scruff of a new beard, or maybe just not shaving for two days, covers Jackson's lower face and accents his high cheekbones. The brim of his orange hat is tilted up as he tosses warm up throws with the other infielders. Even from our seats, I can see how attractive he is and it steals my breath away.

"Shortstop, right?" Danny confirms. "Wow."

"Yeah," I say breathily. The row in front of us is unoccupied, but a man in the seat in front of that turns around to look at us. He's got a strange look on his face, but I ignore him. There are weirdos everywhere, baseball games appear to be no exception.

The game moves forward at a relatively quick pace. I know enough about the general gist of baseball to get by. Three strikes and you're out, four balls is a walk, the game is scored in runs, not points. Beyond that, my understanding of baseball strategy is meager at best. Alicia and Danny know more, but they also know I'm not here for a lesson in Baseball 101, so they don't pester me with details. I'm here to watch Jackson and enjoy the afternoon sunshine. Jackson's first at bat ended in a strikeout and his second was a grounder which was quickly thrown to first to get him out. But he made a great defensive play, if the cheers of the crowd were any indication, so I felt like so far, it is a decent game for him.

Jackson's third at bat comes in the eighth inning. The Foxes are up by one run. When his name is announced on the PA system, Danny, Tim, Alicia and I cheer a little louder than we did earlier in the game. I think we all feel Jackson could use a little extra encouragement offensively. At our louder cheers, the man two rows ahead of us peeks over his shoulder at us again. The man next to him is still talking on his phone, which he has been doing for the last two innings. How anyone could even hear enough to have a phone conversation in the middle of a baseball game is a mystery to me. I felt a little bad for his friend; it's rude for that guy to ignore him to talk on the phone the whole game. No wonder he keeps dividing his attention between the game and us; he's probably bored.

Jackson's third at bat is a hit; a double to deep left field. For a second, I think it might hook foul, but it stays in fair territory and allows him to make it to second base easily, standing up and not needing a slide into the base. I've never seen someone run so quickly in real life. The more I watch Jackson Jeffers play the sport he loves, the more impressed I become.

Everything he does on the field seems natural, which I know isn't true, but I think even with a lifetime of practice, I could never do the things Jackson does. He moves with a natural grace I know I'll never be able to achieve. When he reaches second, the crowd goes crazy, as he drives in an additional run to put the Foxes up by two. My friends and I join in the cheering for Jackson.

"Amy! This is so fun!" Tim exclaims. The man two rows ahead of us turns around again. *What is this guy's deal?* It's not like we're being any louder or more obnoxious than any other fans in the stadium. I'm about to roll my eyes when he climbs over the seat behind him and stands in the row in front of me, flashing me a handsome grin. Not as handsome as Jackson's, but it's still nice.

"Oh my god, are you *the* Amy?" he asks evasively. His friend turns around and hangs up his phone. It seems like he just noticed his friend is no longer sitting next to him. The men look like they could be brothers except that they're dressed as differently as possible. The original guy who climbed over the seat is wearing a Jeffers jersey over navy shorts and flip flops. Phone Call is wearing navy slacks, a polo, and brown dress shoes to match his brown belt. He almost looks out of place being so dressed up at an outdoor sporting event, but the look somehow works for him.

"Um, who are you?" I ask softly but not rudely.

"Are you the Amy my brother won't shut up about?" I give him a blank look, clearly lost in this conversation. He sticks out his hand. "I'm Nate Jeffers. Tell me you're Jackson's Amy." Out of the corner of my eye, Tim's eyes practically bulge out of his skull.

"Oh um, yeah, we're … friends," I finish lamely. Nate gives me a knowing look.

"We've heard all about you." By now, Phone Call has stretched his long legs over his seat and joined Nate in the row in front of us. They simultaneously sit down, angling their bodies towards me.

"I'm Sean," Phone Call reaches his hand out to shake mine. "Our brother is Jackson," he adds unnecessarily. I introduce my friends to the Jeffers brothers and we all begin chatting immediately.

"Jacks doesn't know we're in town yet. I hope we're not crashing the party," Nate begins. "I live in Milwaukee and Sean is Jackson's agent so we try to catch a few games together during the season. We thought we'd surprise him today. Do you guys have plans for tonight?"

"Not really. We said we would meet up but we never really talked about the details. But it's more important for you guys to go out with him. I can see Jackson anytime."

"Nah, we can all go out together," Sean insists. "I have some clients I want to meet up with later tonight, but maybe we can all grab drinks after the game for a bit."

The game finishes up with a win for the Foxes. Nate suggests we wait at a bar, rather than sitting around at the stadium for Jackson. He tells us the players usually take about an hour to leave after the games, finishing up interviews, press conferences, stretching, and showers. There's no shortage of bars in the area surrounding the ballpark, so we have no problem finding two tables at a nearby tavern. Alicia and I pull them together while Nate and Sean offer to buy the first round.

They bring back the drinks, Danny and Tim helping carry, and Nate slaps a round tin on the table. We look at the tin as he opens it and explains the rules of the game on the cards inside. We have to find a picture on our card that matches one of the drawings on the card face up in the middle of the table. When we do, we have to name the picture and put our card on top of it as fast as possible. The game repeats until someone runs out of cards and is declared the winner. Sean opts out of the game, people watching and texting with an intense look, almost a scowl, on his face while Nate orchestrates the game.

I'm learning that the way Jackson's brothers dress is not the only way in which they are polar opposites. Sean couldn't be more serious, while Nate is all fun and games, from what I can tell. The game is fun, and the Jeffers brothers are introduced to just how competitive and cutthroat my friends and I can be. After forty-five minutes, Nate has clearly regretted his decision to bring this game over.

"So, Amy, you're neighbors with our brother," Nate begins vaguely.

"Yeah, Bruno took the liberty of introducing us several times before we started hanging out," I laugh. "Speaking of your brother, I should probably tell him where we're at if we want to meet up."

"I already did," Sean reports. I can't quite get a read on him. Nate seems like an open book, jovial and smiling. Sean's face is impassive and he seems unimpressed with just about everything. I can't tell if he's just not that expressive, or if he's actually pissed off about something. I try not to let it bother me. I want to make a good impression on Jackson's brothers, which I realize is ridiculous, since Jackson and I haven't even defined what we are with each other yet. I may never see Nate or Sean again.

"Jacks is five minutes out from leaving."

That only gives me about five minutes to worry about what I look like and how I'm going to greet him when he arrives, seeing as the bar we're at is across the street from the clubhouse entrance. The salad from earlier and the two beers I've had since arriving at this bar start to churn in my stomach. It's one thing for me to greet Jackson when we're meeting for an agreed upon date. It's another to see him for the first time in days, in public, with his brothers and my friends watching. The conversation shifts to something else, but I couldn't say what, as I'm consumed with whether I should hug or kiss Jackson hello. Lost to my thoughts, Danny and Tim seem to be picking up the conversational slack. Alicia gives me an encouraging smile.

"There he is!" Nate announces, looking over my head with a grin. Sean and Nate stand at the same time, each giving their brother a tight hug.

"I see you've met Amy," Jackson says, bringing his arms around me from behind and pressing a chaste kiss to my temple. So much for worrying how I'd greet him. I melt into him, pressing my back into the solid warmth of his chest. "Hey, Ames," he whispers in my ear. Goosebumps immediately speckle my arms in response.

"Hey," I whisper back. "Great job today." Turning around, I drink him in. Wearing designer jeans, a light blue linen button down that perfectly matches his eyes, and a backwards baseball hat, Jackson is a vision straight from my daydreams. Shaking my lustful thoughts from my head, I quickly introduce him to my friends.

"This is Alicia, I think you met her a few weeks ago at that patio restaurant where you saw us. And these two are Danny and Tim." My friends all shake Jackson's hand and give him words of congratulations about the game today. My pulse pounds in my ears when Jackson sits next to me and places his palm on my knee, drawing little circles on the outside with his thumb. The movement is so small but so subtly possessive that it's such a turn on.

Nate disappears and reappears a few minutes later with another round, including an extra beer for his brother. I'm happy to take a back seat to the conversation blooming around me. Nate talks about his and Sean's last minute decision to head to Chicago this morning and catch the game. Sean was able to get tickets through his own professional connections, rather than through Jackson, and thus, was able to keep their presence a surprise.

Looking from Jackson to his brothers, there's no doubt about their familial connection. They all have the same straight nose and dark hair and they look at each other with such pride and love, there's no doubt they're all brothers.

Nate shares the last time he saw Jackson was during spring training, when he and some friends flew out to visit him in Arizona. Sean apparently has more frequent contact with Jackson, which makes sense, given their professional ties as well.

After catching up for a little bit, we return to playing the card game. Nate sighs, picking up his small stack of cards.

"I hope you're ready for this, Jacks. These four have been kicking my ass every round. Your Amy is a little cutthroat!"

I try not to blush at Nate's term of "your" Amy, but Jackson either doesn't seem to notice or be bothered by it.

"Bring it on, Ames," he tells me, eyes twinkling. "I'm pretty sure I can handle whatever you throw at me."

Chapter Twenty-Two

Jackson

I can't stop grinning like an idiot in the back of this bar. All of my favorite people are here. I can't believe Sean and Nate pulled off a surprise visit–Nate is an open book and he can't keep a secret to save his life. Nate tells me what he has for breakfast in the morning every time I talk to him, so the fact that he kept me in the dark about his impromptu visit is actually a pretty impressive feat for him.

Sean, on the other hand, is a vault. He can, and probably does, keep secrets like it's his job. It's probably what makes him a good lawyer and an even better sports agent. The way he can negotiate killer deals and argue revisions in contracts is intense; I've been in the room before while it's happening and it stresses me out, and I pride myself on being normally unflappably laid back.

I couldn't be happier that my brothers are here and that they've gotten to meet Amy. I probably should have prepared her a little more, had I known they were going to meet her, knowing that she gets a little nervous about being thrown into new social situations. She's amazing in social situations and you'd never know her inner turmoil before, during, and after these scenarios, but if I can avoid stressing Amy out in any way, I'd like to do so. Having my favorite people squeezed into one table is such a balm to my earlier stress of my mother's calls that I almost forget that that's the likely reason for my brothers' surprise visit.

"How long are you guys staying?" I ask, eyeing Nate's beer. Milwaukee isn't too far from Chicago and an easy drive, but even if Nate stops drinking now, after a day of beers in the sun, I'm nervous for him to get behind the wheel.

"I got us a suite at the Westin," Sean answers, correctly guessing where my thoughts were heading. Of course he did. Sean doesn't do anything half-assed. Even if he's in town for one day, he gets a suite or a penthouse at a nearby hotel. It's a little over the top, but the man can afford it, so I don't give him too much shit about it.

"I've got a few contacts I've got to meet up with while I'm in town. I'll head back to New York in a couple days, assuming everything goes according to plan," Sean continues. He's always wheeling and dealing with players, teams, and business partnerships. I know better than to ask for details, because Sean won't divulge them anyway.

"I'll head home tomorrow morning," Nate tells me.

"So, JJ," Amy's friend, Tim, interjects when there's a lull in the conversation. "Would you say you're a well-connected guy? Know a lot of people in a lot of different circles?"

"I guess?" I'm not sure where he's going with this, but Amy rolls her eyes and fills me in.

"Tim is convinced you're an international spy."

My brothers burst out laughing. It's not often that Sean is surprised, or, to be honest, humored, but it's good to see both emotions flit across his face.

"What?" Tim asks innocently. "I've seen pictures of you in custom suits, surrounded by rich people. You've got this air of mystery around you."

"I could see it," Sean says, suppressing a grin. "If this whole baseball thing doesn't work out for you, Jacks, you could give espionage and assassination a try. Might want to start with being a little less warm and outgoing first, though."

"I stand by it," Tim says, metaphorically digging his heels in.

"I'll keep that in mind for when I retire," I say as Amy giggles and I can't help but bask in the sound. I want to hear it every day.

Later, Alicia and I find ourselves alone at the table. Amy is in the bathroom, Tim and Danny called it a night about twenty minutes ago, and Sean stepped outside to take yet another phone call. The man might actually have an aneurism if his phone is not connected to him at all times. Nate went up to the bar to grab another round, only minimally protesting when I insisted he put the whole tab on my credit card.

"So I hear your boy Bruno has a thing for my girl, Amy," she begins.

I laugh. "Yeah, I think he's got a bit of a crush," I say, pulling out my phone to show Alicia pictures of Bruno. There's no shortage of photos and videos; like any good pet parent, my dog takes up most of my camera roll.

"He's adorable," Alicia exclaims, oohing and aahing at all the right spots as I scroll through my photo library for her.

"Yeah, I think I'll keep him around," I deadpan. "Amy seems to love him almost as much as I do, so I'd say he's got a pretty good gig going on."

"Ha, I bet. She's excited about you, too, you know," Alicia adds quietly. "She's trying not to wear her heart on her sleeve so much these days, but you guys seem good together. I know it's early days, but I'm glad she's met you."

"I'm glad I met her, too," I respond with a smile. It's true. I wasn't exactly seeking out a new relationship, but I'm certainly glad I've found one.

"Just be upfront with her though, okay? I wouldn't be doing my best friend duty if I didn't say this. And that's all I'm gonna say about it. She's been through a lot so if you're not feeling it anymore, at any point, just tell her."

Not feeling it? I can't imagine a scenario where that would be the case. Yeah, Alicia is right: it is early days. But the connection I feel with Amy is stronger than what I felt with Carolyn, and I almost married her. I'm not saying I'm going to marry Amy, but as we continue getting to know each other, I've not only liked everything I've learned, I've been enthusiastic about learning more.

"I'm in on this one, Alicia. I really like Amy. But thank you for being such a good friend to her."

Alicia just nods, but I see the smile peeking out behind her glass as she takes a sip of her beer. While I'm curious about whatever Alicia is alluding to, I'm not going to pry about Amy's past. If there's information she wants me to know, she'll tell me eventually. Right now, I'm just happily along for the ride, and when Amy returns to the table with a smile on her face, I'm happy to bask in her glow.

Chapter Twenty-Three

Amy

Jackson left for his road trip a few days ago. He went to Denver first, and today is his day off in Seattle before playing three games there. After that, he'll come back to Chicago. We've communicated every day he's been out of town, mostly via text, but with some phone calls and video calls interspersed. He hasn't had too much down time on the road, but he's told me about some of the coffee shops he's explored in the mornings near his hotel in Denver. The other night, he explored breweries with his friend and second baseman, Caleb Andrews. That night, Jackson sent me progressively blurrier photos of the craft beers he was sampling. It was really adorable to know he was thinking about me when he didn't have to.

Yesterday morning, an extra large dirty chai from Caffeine Kingdom was delivered to my apartment. Jackson claimed he had no idea who could have sent it, but the smile he tried to hide behind his hand on our video chat told me he was behind the thoughtful gesture.

I signed up for a new weeklong stress relieving yoga series at my studio. Classes in this series are held every other day and at the end of every class, the instructor leads us through physical exercises designed to release tension in the psoas muscle through tremoring movements. It's a different type of yoga than what I'm used to practicing, but I really like it so far. It makes the walk home after the class pass by in a blur as I'm still feeling the zen-like aftereffects long after the classes end.

I love yoga. There's something mentally freeing about working my body in a way that pushes me without making me feel like I want to give up the way I do during some forms of cardio, like running. I feel such a connection to the practice that last year, I went through the training to become a yoga instructor.

For a while when I was going through the training program, I was dead set on teaching classes to the public at a studio or park district. My passion, personal experience, and even my teaching background through museum education led me to believe I'd be a good yoga instructor. I still believe that. However, the reality of finding the time to teach at a studio that actually had class openings at a time that worked with my schedule was daunting. If I'm being honest with myself, I'm not quite ready to take the leap and teach classes to anyone other than my friends right now. I'm still glad I took the classes and got certified. It's helped me progress my own practice immensely. My passion for teaching yoga is still here, even if I'm not ready to bite the bullet and actually do it right this second.

I've taken a handful of continuing education credits for yoga for special populations, like cancer patients and pregnant people. One day, maybe, I'll add teaching yoga to my resume, if I feel like I'm in a situation where I can work less at the museums to accommodate teaching. But a very real part of me feels like pulling back from museum education would be too hard, or too scary, for me to really consider that right now. So I'll keep on using yoga for myself and maybe eventually branch out to teaching others.

Tonight, my legs are jelly on my walk home. Tonight's class was a nice distraction from work stressors. With the recent budget cuts, our program directors have started throwing around terms like "workforce reduction" and "program revisions." The words themselves all hint at major changes coming soon, but we won't know what the changes will look like or who, specifically, they will affect, until right before they happen. My stress levels are off the charts, but as there is little I can do to control the situation, I've been trying really hard to preserve my mental energy for things I can control. It's not going great.

I pride myself on my job. There's probably a slightly unhealthy amount of my job tied into my identity, but I love what I do. I'm very good at what I do. Lately, however, work has been consuming me mentally and emotionally, which impacts my ability to disconnect from it outside of work hours. And the decision fatigue is real: I'm exhausted by the idea of even having to figure out what I'm going to eat for dinner when I get home tonight. Last night, I ate olives, cheese, and a couple crackers for dinner. Of course, I washed it all down with a giant glass of my favorite sauvignon blanc, so at least I was balanced?

If I'm being honest, I'm a little worried that I haven't heard from Jackson much today either. I find myself falling into the pathetic trap of wanting to hear from him. I look forward to his texts every day, and beyond the initial good morning text I got this morning, I haven't heard from him. I guess I had expected him to be a little more communicative on his day off, since he wouldn't be going into the ballpark. As soon as that thought pops into my head, I chastise myself for it. Jackson is not my boyfriend. Sure, we're casually seeing each other, but he has no obligation to communicate with me all day. I am not acting like a casual, nonchalant woman right now.

I cringe inwardly at my internal monologue as I reach my apartment and unlock the main door. I trudge slowly up the stairs, my legs heavy after class. Once I shower and settle on the couch, I open my Kindle app on my phone, hoping to get further in my hockey romance.

I'm in the middle of reading a scene that should have contained off-the-charts levels of spice and I find my mind wandering. I'm supposed to be reading the pivotal scene in the book where the female main character realizes what she's been missing out on by resisting the male main character's advances and I cannot stay focused. I sigh, exiting out of my e-reader app, resigned to doing nothing productive with my brain the rest of the night. I'm going to call it an early night and watch a true crime documentary in bed until I fall asleep. On my way to bed, my phone vibrates with an incoming FaceTime call. 'Jackson Neighbor' lights up my screen and I release a breath I didn't know I was holding and I pick up the call.

"Hey, baby," Jackson says softly as his grinning face fills my phone screen. "How are you? I feel like I haven't talked to you in forever."

I can't help the small smile from creeping onto my face. "I know, even though we just talked last night," I commiserate. All worries about Jackson's feelings vanish. I had convinced myself, in the back of my mind, that he was no longer interested, or that he found something better. I know, logically, that's unrealistic, especially because he sent me a good morning text twelve hours ago. But my brain was back to playing its old tricks on me again when I hadn't heard from him because I thought he would have had some flexibility in his day to be able to communicate more.

"I'm sorry I didn't get a chance to talk to you more today. After I texted you, I fell back asleep and woke to Caleb and a couple other guys pounding down my door, wanting to do a food tour of Pikes Place Market. We kind of did one thing after another and I haven't had a second to myself since then. I didn't even know they had all that stuff planned. I kind of just wanted to chill and talk to you." Jackson's eyes are contrite.

"Tell me about the food tour. What was the best thing you ate?" I ask, trying to tamp down on some of the relief I feel that Jackson didn't decide to start hating me in the hours since we last talked. *This is so not casual. Get it together, Amy.*

Jackson tells me everything that he ate. I'm impressed he can actually remember everything, because the man has an appetite like no one else I've ever met. He shares funny stories about the guys he hung out with and all of their activities. The grin on my face keeps getting bigger; Jackson's enthusiasm is contagious and I'm genuinely happy for him to be able to do something fun on his day off, rather than sit around in a boring hotel room.

"Enough about me. Tell me about your day," Jackson instructs.

"There's not a lot to tell about my day. Work is getting super stressful and they're talking about possibly eliminating some programs, or at the very least slashing the budgets for them, so we'll have to make a lot of changes in a really short amount of time. Nothing is finalized yet, but Alicia and I are a little worried about job security." I take a deep breath. "Okay, a lot worried," I amend.

"I'm so sorry, Ames," Jackson coos. "That sounds so stressful. What can I do to help?"

"Nothing, just listening is helpful. There's not a lot that can be done until we know more, so I'm trying not to stress."

"How's that going for you?" he asks softly.

"Not great," I admit. "I have Generalized Anxiety Disorder, so the whole not-knowing-what's-going-on is really not great." I wince. I know that being upfront about mental illness is beneficial and I trust Jackson that the information about my anxiety isn't going to make him completely run for the hills, but a part of me is nervous to disclose just how significant my anxiety actually is. There's something about anxiety being clinical, being *diagnosed*, rather than just an emotion everyone feels, that is really daunting for me. I had no problem sharing the diagnosis with my friends and my parents, but I think that was because it came as the least surprising bit of news to my loved ones. Jackson is still so new that I'm not sure how telling him is going to go over, but it's probably best to rip the bandaid off and let him see what he's dealing with sooner rather than later.

"Thank you for sharing that with me, Amy," Jackson responds softly. That wasn't exactly the response I was expecting. I don't know what I was expecting, but his gentle acceptance wasn't quite what I had received from past boyfriends. Not that Jackson is my boyfriend.

"What helps you most when you're anxious?" He follows up with a question I have never been asked before. When I'm silent, he elaborates, "Like, is it best if you're distracted when you're anxious? Or does it help to talk things out?"

"I guess it depends on what I'm anxious about. Sometimes talking it through is helpful, but sometimes it makes things worse." Jackson nods in understanding. "I've never really had someone ask that before. Most people just give me sympathy when I disclose my anxiety."

"Is that helpful?" Jackson asks without judgment.

"Not even a little. I can't help that I have an anxiety disorder. There are things I can do to manage it, and a lot of the time, I don't feel like it impacts me too much, but I guess it's been a part of me for so long, even though I didn't get diagnosed till a few years ago, that sympathy kind of makes me feel bad. Like my life isn't as good as it could be, which is not how I feel. I'm really happy with my life, even though I get stressed about things easily and think about things more than most people. I know people mean well and they probably just don't know what to say in response, but it still kind of sucks to hear."

Jackson nods, listening intently. I knew I hated when people's responses to my anxiety disclosure is "I'm sorry," but never really thought about why until Jackson asked me. It feels nice to be able to speak honestly about some of my challenges without feeling judged, and I tell Jackson so.

"Baby, my job is not to judge you. My job is to care about you, and listen to you, and make you feel good. There's no room in all of that for judgment."

Excuse me while I melt into the floor.

"How do you always know what to say?" I whisper. Jackson laughs.

"I don't, sweetheart. But I did have a college teammate who had pretty significant anxiety and depression. He preferred to be distracted when he got really in his head, and once his teammates knew that, we were better able to support him. I'm under no delusions that what we did cured his mental illness, but it did seem to help. So if you think of something I could do to make things better for you, I would like to hear it. But it's also okay if you don't know."

Wow. I've never felt so seen before.

"Thank you, Jackson." I don't know what else to say.

"You're welcome," he smiles. "Now, tell me about your yoga class tonight. Second one in your new program, right?"

When I wake up the next morning, it's not to another dirty chai on my doorstep, but instead, to what looks like a custom gift basket filled with bath salts, gourmet herbal tea, soothing face masks, a lavender candle, and a fluffy blanket. Tucked into the note is a gift card to the romance bookstore in Roscoe Village Jackson told me about on our first date.

Amy, since I can't be there in person to help you with this stressful time at work, I hope these items can fill the void until I get back.

-Jackson

Chapter Twenty-Four

Amy

The last week of May is a whirlwind. We are able to stave off some layoffs at work by increasing the cost of field trips for the next school year. It isn't a great solution, and I feel terrible that the increase in pricing is likely going to impact some schools' ability to participate in our programs, but I suppose it's better than eliminating programs altogether. We're still not out of the woods, especially since we've been told that the field trip price increase is not a permanent or effective enough solution to make any lasting assurances, but Alicia and I still have jobs, as do the myriad employees funded under the museum education umbrella of the CMA. The next round of budget decisions won't happen for another few months, so we're safe for now.

Jackson and I have gone out on a handful of dates in the last few weeks. We see each other basically whenever he is not on the road and his schedule allows. When he has day games, he arrives at the ballpark early enough that I feel bad keeping him out late the night before. The Foxes' stadium is in the middle of a neighborhood, which lends itself to a unique game day experience, but caus-es most games to be scheduled during the day, to accommodate neighborhood noise ordinances. Between my job, Jackson's schedule, and my yoga classes, I haven't seen him as much as I would have liked to, but that doesn't stop him from being so attentive and communicative. Every morning, I'm greeted with a good morning phone call or text if Jackson is on the road, and usually a good morning kiss if he's not.

I have to admit, I don't hate waking up in Jackson's bed most mornings when he's in town. Bruno's less than gentle wake up calls took some getting used to, but Bruno shows his love in very physical, very ungraceful ways. I wouldn't change it for the world.

Jackson and I still have not had a conversation about our relationship. Part of me is relieved, because that means expectations haven't solidly been placed on it. Without expectations, I can't be let down. As much as I tell myself otherwise, though, I know that's not realistic. I'm finding myself craving Jackson in all ways when I'm not around him: his touch, his words, his smiles...if I'm not careful, I'm going to get hurt. I keep telling myself I need to pull back, to put up a little more fortification around my heart, but then I see Jackson, or hear from him, and I immediately forget I'm supposed to be on the defensive.

Jackson doesn't seem concerned about defining our relationship, and I suppose, on the surface, I probably seem the same way. So when he called me this morning and asked if he could take me out for a romantic date after today's game, I started feeling a little apprehensive. Last night, the Foxes arrived back in town from a road series. Their flight didn't arrive until midnight, and they have a day game today, so I haven't actually seen Jackson in person in several days. But the fact that Jackson used the term "romantic date" makes me feel like he wants to have that conversation tonight.

If work wasn't so crazy today, I wouldn't be able to stop thinking about the date and what Jackson could possibly want to talk about, but because everyone is worried about their jobs and the longevity of our programs, everyone seems to be working double time to increase productivity, myself included.

I feel like I've been staring at my computer screen for hours. The numbers on the spreadsheet I'm poring over are starting to blur together and when I see Jackson leaning against the doorframe of my office, I swear I'm hallucinating. He smirks as I blink confusedly at him.

"Hey, pretty girl. You didn't answer any of my texts or calls, so I figured I'd drive down to see you. Alicia spotted me in the lobby and brought me down here. You doing okay?" Jackson asks as he walks toward me. His look of concern morphs into amusement as he takes in my disheveled state. He pulls a pen out from my messy bun, where I had put it–and promptly forgotten about it–hours ago.

"I am so sorry!" I gasp, grabbing for my phone and seeing that it's completely dead. "I guess I got sort of caught up in all this work.

I didn't even realize it was…" I pause, looking at the time on my computer, "6:30! Jackson, I am so sorry!"

"Shh, it's okay, baby," he coos. "Are you still up for our date?"

Luckily I chose to wear a dress to work today, so if I ditch my blazer, I can still look presentable at a restaurant without needing to go home and change first. My hair is likely a whole other story, but some things can't be helped. I stand, frantically gathering my things, feeling guilty that I kept Jackson waiting.

"Wait." Jackson holds my face in his hands and kisses me slowly and thoroughly. "That's better. I'm not in a rush, Ames. Take your time; the restaurant will still be there."

"I know, but I feel terrible!"

"Amy," Jackson admonishes. "It's forgotten. Are you at least making headway with some of the programs?" I had told him yesterday how stressed I was about rearranging some of our summer camp programming to accommodate hiring fewer instructors.

"Getting there," I promise. We climb the stairs near the back offices of the planetarium and emerge at the staff parking lot. Jackson encourages me to leave my car overnight so we can take one car to dinner and back to his place. He promises to drop me at work tomorrow morning with a smile and a kiss to my forehead, so I agree. It's not even funny the things this man could get me to do just by sending me a smoldering look or giving me a damn forehead kiss. I'm putty in his hands.

At dinner, a swanky, trendy, Italian restaurant on the Chicago River, Jackson and I are seated at an intimate table near the back of the dining room. As the hostess walks us back to our table, I don't miss the whispers and pointed glances that follow Jackson. A few people make small comments to him as he walks by, congratulating him on today's game or some play that he made last week. He takes it all in stride, politely thanking them but not further engaging in conversation. I can't help but swell with pride at how well-loved Jackson is.

He orders us a bottle of Chianti because I had said weeks ago that I had never tried it when we were discussing the movie 'Hannibal.' How he even remembered that tiny morsel of information is lost on me, but it makes me smile nonetheless. Still, I feel bad that he's spending $120 on a bottle of wine that I may not even like.

"Jackson, what if we don't like it? You've never had a Chianti either!"

"One, who cares if we don't like it? Then we'll get something else. But more importantly, I don't think we'll know if it goes well with fava beans if we don't try it!" I giggle.

The waitress brings out the bottle Jackson ordered and he lets me do the honors of trying it first.

"It's delicious, but I'm not exactly convinced it will enhance the taste of human liver," I remark. Jackson's responding laughter is infectious, while our server, who has clearly never watched 'Silence of the Lambs,' looks at me like I'm a giant weirdo and leaves the bottle at the table.

By the time our meal is finished, I feel like I'm bursting at the seams with the amount of food I've eaten. Everything was incredible and lived up to the online reviews I checked out on the way over. I feel like I've eaten my weight in cacio e pepe, so when the waitress returns to offer dessert, Jackson and I both decline.

When Jackson offers for us to walk for a little bit along the river instead of picking up the car from the valet right away, I'm relieved. I don't think I can sit with my full stomach much longer, and walking might help my nerves, which have been steadily increasing all meal long because we still haven't discussed whatever it is Jackson wanted to talk about when he suggested a romantic date.

"So what did you want to talk about?" I ask when I can't take the suspense any longer.

"Talk about?"

"You said you wanted to go on a romantic date. We've never done that before, and all through dinner we didn't really talk about anything of major importance and so I was just wondering why you wanted to do a romantic date?"

Jackson chuckles at my confusion. "Can't I just want to take you out? You deserve a romantic date. I wasn't aware I needed an ulterior motive to take you on one."

Oh. I feel like an idiot now. I had built this up to be something more than it was in my head, and I'm not sure how to feel knowing I was wrong. I blow out a breath.

"I thought you were going to make this like super serious or something," I say with relief.

"Make what super serious? The date?" I nod. "We can be serious if you want." Jackson adopts a monotone voice. "Taxes. Heart attacks. Other serious stuff."

I give him a gentle push as I laugh along with him. He snakes his arm around my waist and pulls me close to him as we walk along the sidewalk above the river.

"You know what I mean. I thought you were going to make this a serious conversation about *us*." I don't know why I'm pressing the issue, since I don't want to have this conversation.

"We can talk about us. What do you want to talk about?"

My shoulders stiffen. "I don't know. I don't really want to talk about us or what we are. I just thought you were going to."

"Amy, I'll always be happy to talk about us. But you brought it up, which means you've been thinking about it. And it's you, so I'm guessing you've been overthinking about it, too." I hate that he's right. And maybe in some way I do want to talk about it because if we don't, and he's dating other people, which he's entitled to do, *since we haven't talked about us yet,* I don't think I'll feel great, either. But there's not a way I can bring that up without a ton of awkwardness because beyond a casual dating relationship, I don't know what I want.

"Ames. I can *feel* you overthinking about it. What do you want? I never brought it up before because I didn't want to pressure you. Did I interpret that wrong?" Jackson stops walking, turning me to face him.

"Ugh, I don't know. I don't know how I feel."

"Okay, that's okay. Can I tell you how I feel?" I nod. "I like you, Amy. It's been a long time since I've liked someone the way I like you. I have no interest in dating other women and I haven't since I met you. If you want to be exclusive, I'm all in. I already am. If you need something less serious, then let's talk about that, too."

I don't know why, but my emotions start to rise. I'm so frustrated with myself for not knowing how I feel when I'm the one who brought this up. Of course I like Jackson; who wouldn't? He's kind, attentive, thoughtful, funny, and absolutely gorgeous. I want to throw my arms around him and tell him exclusivity with him, not having to share him with any other women, is all I've ever wanted, but the fact that I feel that way is practically a guarantee that my heart won't survive once this is over. I handed Patrick my still-beating heart straight from my chest when he said pretty words to me too, and he strangled the life out of it. I'm not sure I can go through that again. So while Jackson is telling me pretty words and that he wants to be exclusive, it's hard to trust that he won't change his mind in a few days or a few weeks. I believe *he* believes he wants exclusivity, but does he really?

"I don't know what I want, Jackson." His face falls and I quickly add, "I'm not seeing anyone else either though. I just don't know how serious I'm ready to make this."

Jackson pulls me close, resting his chin on the top of my head. "Ames, I'm not asking you to marry me. But I'm crazy about you and if we're being honest, I *really* don't love the idea of seeing you with another man while we're figuring this out. I'm not going to tell you what to do if you're still figuring out how you feel, but if you're not ready to be serious, then let's slow it down. I'm not in a rush either. But I would prefer we slow it down together, while you're not seeing anyone else."

"Yeah, of course," I say, and a tidal wave of relief sweeps over me. Exclusive I can be. Serious? Not likely. But exclusive I can happily do. As we stand there embracing, a feeling of embarrassment creeps over me. I brought this up without any idea of how I wanted it resolved, only to create an awkward, uncomfortable conversation when we didn't even need one. "Are we okay?" I ask timidly.

"What? Of course, baby." Jackson shifts to hold me at arms' length so he can look into my eyes. "I hope you're not feeling bad about this conversation. You can talk to me about anything, okay?" I nod. "Now, can I take my girlfriend home and into bed so I can show her just how okay we are?"

CHAPTER TWENTY-FIVE

Jackson

I wake the next morning with Amy in my arms, her blonde hair spilling over my chest. For a brief moment last night, I thought I had spooked her. She stood by the river looking like a deer in headlights when I told her I wanted to be exclusive. It turned out she was freaked out by getting serious, rather than being exclusive, but for a moment, my heart stuttered. After all Carolyn put me through, I don't think I could have handled it if the end result of our conversation last night was that Amy wanted to keep seeing other people in addition to me.

After Alicia's comments several weeks ago at the bar and Amy's general skittishness when it comes to discussing more serious topics between us, I had a feeling she wasn't ready for the "what are we?" conversation, so I hadn't brought it up. I was shocked when she did, but I guess that just shows how much it was weighing on her mind.

I had wrapped Amy in my arms by the river and promised to bring her home and show her the girlfriend treatment. The girlfriend treatment really wasn't any different from how I'd already been treating Amy, but when I called Amy "my girlfriend," interspersing the new title several times during dirty talk, I could tell she liked it.

I had laid her down on my bed, telling her I was going to eat my girlfriend's pussy, and the whimper that left her mouth after those words is something I've replayed in my head over and over in the hours since. Then, when I praised "my girlfriend" for her cock sucking skills, Amy glowed and redoubled her efforts to suck my soul out through my dick. And later, after two more rounds of sex, Amy draped herself across my chest as she came down from her fourth orgasm of the night, she whispered, "Thank you, boyfriend." It was never about exclusivity.

Tonight, I have a night game, which means I don't have to head in to work until later afternoon. Amy already agreed she would take the morning off work, seeing as she worked late last night anyway, and I would drop her off at the planetarium on my way into the ballpark. Even though the museum complex is in the opposite direction of the ballpark from my house, I'd happily sit through Chicago traffic with Amy just to spend more time with my girl.

My girl. It feels so good to say and think those two words. I'm irrationally happy about the new term, about officially making Amy mine. She was mine from the first moment I tasted her, but now she knows it, too. Thinking back to the first time Amy let me taste her has me hardening beneath my sleeping girlfriend. I slide out from underneath her, knowing if I'm going to do something about my growing arousal, I need to take care of Bruno's needs first.

I slip out of bed, throw on some sweats and a tee shirt, and walk over to where Bruno is snoring on the couch. He's laying sprawled across the cushions, belly up, legs spread, the picture of doggy contentedness. What a freeloader. When I rouse him to take him outside, I swear he rolls his eyes at me for waking him so early.

"I regret to inform you that 7:30 isn't that early, sir," I tell him. Somehow, Bruno must have gotten the memo that I didn't need to go in to work as early today and had planned on sleeping in. I guess he'll just have to pencil in a nap to his already packed schedule, I think, rolling my eyes as Bruno huffs to his feet.

By the time we make it back inside, it's already 8:00. As much as Bruno grumbled about being woken up, as soon as we were outside, he made a point to sniff every leaf and blade of grass outside our condo. I was hoping I could get away with just taking him out to the bathroom without doing a walk so I could get back to the sleeping angel in my bed, and while we only paced the area in front of my building, Bruno sure took his sweet time about it. It gave me plenty of time to figure out how I wanted to spend my morning with said angel.

Amy is still asleep when I finally do return to bed. She is sprawled on her back across half of the mattress, one leg hanging over the edge of the bed and peeking out from underneath the sheet. I can't resist touching her perfect body, sliding my palm up her draped leg as I gently skim the sheet over her other leg and out of my way. Amy never redressed after our activities last night, and a naked girlfriend is how I prefer my girlfriend.

She slowly starts to stir, not quite awake as I drag my tongue along her inner thigh, leaving a trail of goosebumps in its wake. I love how responsive Amy is to me, even when she's only half awake. She moans and flutters her eyes open enough to see me hovering over her core.

"Hey, baby," she mumbles sleepily. Other than calling me her boyfriend once last night, Amy has been careful not to use any terms of endearment toward me before now. I cherish this moment of vulnerability.

"Hey, girlfriend," I respond. Amy's eyes close and she smiles sleepily, only for her eyes to fly back open when I drag my tongue across her perfect pussy.

"Oh, shit," she breathes. I continue my ministrations, sucking each of her pussy lips, in turn, into my mouth, planting an open mouth kiss right at her entrance. The sounds she makes are exquisite. I'll gladly wake her up this way every morning just to be able to hear and taste her like this. Amy drags her hands through my hair, gently scraping her nails across my scalp and the move is so comforting, so intimate, that I can't help but let loose a moan of my own. It vibrates across Amy's pussy, and I know the added reverberations edge her just a little bit closer to her own release.

Meanwhile, my cock hardens to steel in my sweats. I rock against the mattress just once to ease the swelling tightness in my pants.

"Baby, you taste so good. I can't wait until you're dripping down my chin." Amy begins rocking her hips against my face and I grin, loving how much my girl loves my dirty words. "That's it, angel, ride my face." Amy groans and picks up her pace. I add in one finger, then two, curling them just like she likes. When I latch my mouth onto her clit and suck hard, she comes with a scream. She does, indeed, drip down my face, and I make a mental note to start as many of my mornings like this as possible.

CHAPTER TWENTY-SIX

Amy

The breeze on the planetarium terrace picks up, scattering petals from the planter boxes strategically placed along the patio. Elementary students are gathered in small groups across the terrace, practicing using various meteorological tools and recording data. This is one of my favorite lessons when the weather cooperates. The terrace is two stories and sits on the side of the planetarium. The view is incomparable and one of my favorites in the city. Whenever I can, and whenever the weather allows, I try to take my lunch break here because if I position myself in one direction, I get a view of the city skyline. If I shift in the other direction, I get a view of Lake Michigan.

Today, the sun is shining and while the breeze is a little more intense than I would like, it's perfect for the clusters of students to measure things like barometric pressure, temperature, and wind speed. I smile, watching the kids hunched over clipboards, recording their data to compare against other groups.

STEM summer camp through CMA has been going strong for about a week and a half. It's given me enough time to get to know the kids and learn their personalities and interests. I've already figured out that Shaela, a fifth grader from the south side of Chicago, is a natural with anything math-related. And Bashir, a third grader from Portage Park, is a science whiz. Twins Milo and Maximus are mischievous but sponges for everything they've learned so far.

The brightest spot of my day is when King, a second grader with Down syndrome and autism, joins us for hands-on experiments each day. King comes with his aide, Rich, who is equally as wonderful. My mom and I spent a weekend last month modifying some of the activities to King's level and I think we did a pretty good job. At times, Rich has to make some on-the-fly changes based on how cooperative King is able to be that day, but for the most part, everything goes according to plan. Even though King only joins us at camp for about an hour each day, it's important to me that he's included in as many of the activities as he wants to be involved with. Science and museums are for everyone, and camp is meant to be for everyone as well.

We have thirty-three students enrolled in my STEM summer camp session; other museum educators have similar numbers enrolled in theirs. The groups rotate which museum campus they visit each day so each campus isn't overwhelmed with groups. Today, my camp is at the planetarium, but tomorrow we'll be at the Humanities Museum discovering anatomy.

Typically, the first few weeks of STEM summer camp is spent rotating through the various Chicago museum campuses with different hands-on activities scheduled at each one. It allows the kids to find their passion within the field while exposing them to careers and opportunities they may not learn enough about during the school year. So far, the kids have learned about entomology at the Field Museum, zoology at the aquarium (we'll be heading to the zoo later this summer, too), chemistry at the science museum, math and geometry within artwork at the Art Institute, and sociology in the Field Museum, in addition to today's lesson in meteorology at the planetarium. They'll eventually be adding to their repertoire with archaeology, anatomy, psychology, astronomy, computer science, engineering, natural resources and conservation, and the scientific method.

As the daughter of an elementary school principal, to say I'm geeking out about the program I developed for my campers is the understatement of the year. It doesn't hurt that the group of kids I have this year (and every year, if I'm being honest) are smart, kind, and enthusiastic learners. It makes the six hours we spend together every weekday fly by.

I tap my yoga chimes, which make a surprisingly loud sound given the small, handheld device and the buzz of chatter amongst my campers. The children know the chime is signaling the end of the camp for the day, and it's time to transition to cleaning up, sharing data and what they loved about today's lesson, and heading home. I've specifically designed this time of day as a great way for me to get feedback about the day's lesson to shape future camp planning. The campers are thoughtful and insightful in their reflections on what worked well for them and what they didn't like as much. I not-so-secretly love hearing their passion for each day's activities as well.

After the kids have loaded the buses and cars, one student is still left lingering on the front steps of the building with me. KJ is normally a relatively relaxed, subdued camper who has a particular passion for computer coding, but I can feel the tension radiating off him as the minutes tick by and his mother still has not pulled up to pick him up. I reassure him that I'm sure his mother got caught in traffic and is probably on her way; KJ doesn't say anything but gives me a nervous smile in response.

After fifteen minutes waiting outside, however, I suggest we go inside and wait for KJ's mother there.

"I'm sure everything is okay. We can call your mom together from my office and make sure," I do my best to reassure him. Each parent from my group this year so far has been very reliable and on time to pick up their children. We provide the option of bussing to more central locations near the children's homes, but KJ's mom elected to transport him every day. KJ's sister, Amaya, previously participated in my summer camp program, so I know their mother a little bit, and she's always been responsible and on time, so I try not to give KJ reason to panic even though I'm starting to become concerned myself.

She doesn't pick up when I call her, but I leave a cheery voicemail reassuring Ms. Harris that KJ is safe with me, and that we'll be inside the planetarium waiting for her when she arrives. However, when I haven't heard from her an additional twenty minutes after I left the voicemail, I text Ms. Harris from my personal cell phone. I try to make a point not to give my personal contact information to parents, but I also understand texting is sometimes more effective than calling from a landline. Ms. Harris doesn't answer her texts either.

I set KJ up on a coding-for-kids website on my laptop while I shoot a text to Alicia and ask her to check through KJ's application for an emergency contact phone number. I also send a message to Jackson to inform him I'm likely going to be late for our date tonight. Jackson had a day game earlier today and we made vague plans to get dinner together on one of the neighborhood patio restaurants so we could bring Bruno along.

My phone buzzes with a reassuring text from Jackson letting me know he's not in a rush and that he just left the ballpark about fifteen minutes ago. I tap out a quick message, telling him I'll let him know when my camper's parent arrives and when I end up leaving work for the night. Alicia pokes her head into my office.

"Hey KJ!" She says, and her attempt to imbue cheeriness into her tone makes me smile. "We have an emergency contact in your file for a Daisy Wade, but when I called, it said the number was disconnected. Is Daisy a neighbor?"

"No, that's my grandma," KJ replies. "What do you mean the number was disconnected?"

"I'll try again, maybe I dialed the wrong one," Alicia promises with a smile. When she locks eyes with me, though, I know Alicia has already verified the number and called it more than once. The minutes crawl by and I give KJ the granola bar leftover from my lunch when his stomach begins to audibly growl. I keep up a steady stream of chatter so KJ doesn't worry more than I can tell he already is. Not that I would admit it to KJ, but I'm worried too; it's almost 6:30, a full ninety minutes after camp ended, and we haven't heard anything from Ms. Harris. I hope she's okay. Twenty minutes ago, I waved Alicia home when she offered to wait with us, telling her we were fine, and I didn't mind hanging out with my buddy KJ.

I can tell by the amount of times KJ asks me what time it is that his nerves are mounting. I try calling Ms. Harris again, but it goes straight to voicemail now. At least earlier, it rang a few times before I got her voicemail. Again, I send out a silent plea to the universe to allow Ms. Harris to be safe.

KJ and I are both startled by a knock on my open office door. I look up to see Jackson standing there, looking as handsome as ever with two day old stubble and an olive green baseball cap–on backwards, as usual. He is carrying several bags that he sets on my desk when he walks in the room.

"Hello, Ms. Stone," he says formally, clearly unsure how to address me in front of my camper.

"Ms. Stone? That's your real name?" KJ asks curiously. I let the kids call me by my first name. Several years ago, I worked with a camper who had speech challenges and struggled to make the "st" sound. Ever since then, I've allowed the kids to call me Amy and no one has had any difficulty pronouncing it.

"The kids call me Amy," I explain with a laugh. "What are you doing here, Jackson?"

I see KJ watching Jackson out of the corner of my eye. He's got a strange look on his face, like he's trying to place how he knows him.

"I thought I'd bring dinner to you both tonight," he tells me with a wink. "I figured there's no reason for you both to sit here hungry when I can fix that."

"You're JJ Jeffers!" KJ finally pieces it together. He apparently is a Chicago Foxes fan, based on the hushed awe in his voice.

"I am." Jackson nods. "What's your name?"

"KJ. Harris," he adds quickly.

"Alright, KJ. Looks like KJ and JJ will be dining together. I hope you like cheeseburgers? I wasn't sure what you might like to eat, so I hope I guessed right with burgers, but if not, I also picked up chicken tenders and grilled cheese, too." Jackson begins unpacking the bags and opening styrofoam containers. Jackson's attention to detail and thoughtfulness render me speechless. He gives my shoulder a nudge when he notices I haven't said anything for a moment. He hands me a box containing a falafel burger,

Greek fries, and tabbouli from my favorite Greek diner in our neighborhood.

KJ's eyes widen at the amount of food spread out across my desk. Jackson gestures at the boxes. "Dig in," he instructs. KJ hesitates only a second before sliding the cheeseburger box closer to himself and picking up a french fry.

"I knew it," Jackson says with a grin. "Burgers are the best. This restaurant makes the best ones in town."

"Thanks," KJ says quietly. I can't tell if he's still momentarily stunned at the prospect of eating dinner with a famous athlete, still worried about his mom, or some combination of the two. I, myself, am momentarily stunned by the generosity of my man.

We begin to eat in relative silence until Jackson breaks the silence by asking KJ about his day at STEM camp and his favorite experience this summer so far. I'm happy to sit back and watch KJ gush about coding and how he wants to design his own video game and maybe eventually build robots. I hadn't known about the robot thing. Jackson tells KJ his favorite subject in school was science but nothing was better than PE. KJ laughs and tells Jackson about playing kickball in PE at school.

It turns out KJ is a huge Foxes fan, so when Jackson offers to play catch with him in the hallway outside my office once we finish eating, I wonder if I'm going to have to help KJ pick his jaw up off the floor.

"You want to play catch with *me*?" KJ asks incredulously.

"Of course I do!" Jackson replies enthusiastically. "It's not everyday I get the opportunity to throw a ball around with a future scientist and robot builder!"

My heart swells. Jackson indulges KJ in a way that builds his self-esteem without coming across as phony. Kids can always tell when the adults around them are disingenuous, and Jackson seems like a natural in his interactions with KJ.

When the boys leave my office to play catch with a rubber band ball (the closest thing to a baseball I could find in my office), I busy myself by cleaning up my office. I package up the extra food for KJ to take home later. When I'm done, I lean against my door frame and watch KJ and Jackson.

Jackson lobs the ball softly to KJ, who bends his knees slightly to catch the rubber band ball between both hands. He returns it to Jackson with a little more heat than I was expecting. Jackson has to jog a few steps to the side to catch it, but he does so easily. KJ is putting his all into each of his throws, clearly trying to impress Jackson. Jackson ensures he keeps up a steady stream of specific, positive praise for him. I don't think KJ's grin could get any bigger. It's overtaking the lower half of his face and it is nothing short of adorable. Jackson looks over his shoulder and catches me watching the show and throws a wink my way. Something shifts in my chest, watching the way this man interacts with a young fan, taking away his anxiety over his mother, and knowing he's mine? I'm in trouble.

I need to walk away into my office before I start to examine my own feelings and why my heart physically aches. I make another attempt at reaching Ms. Harris. Luckily, she picks up this time and the panic in her voice is evident in her greeting.

"Ms. Stone, oh my gosh, I am so sorry! I'm on my way! Is KJ okay?" She's speaking so quickly I almost have trouble understanding her. "My neighbor collapsed outside and I thought he was having a heart attack so I took him to the hospital but he was unconscious so I had to stay with him and my phone died and I just got in the car to charge it now and I didn't even realize how late it was because it was just chaotic and they were using the paddles on his chest right in front of me and oh, my poor baby KJ has been waiting this whole time! He must be so upset with me!"

"Ms. Harris, it's okay! KJ is safe. I've got him at the planetarium with me. Everything is okay. Please don't rush. Please don't worry. KJ has already had dinner, so just get here when you can." I cannot imagine how stressed Ms. Harris feels, but if her tone and jumbled words are any indication, I'm sure her head is spinning. She attempts to tell me she'll get to the planetarium as soon as possible, but I placate her with reassurances that there is no rush and to drive safely.

After we hang up, I pop my head outside of my office to let KJ know his mother is okay and is on her way to get him. He smiles with relief but almost seems a little sad to have to stop playing with

Jackson. I laugh to myself when I notice Jackson seems a little sad to stop playing catch as well.

When Ms. Harris arrives, she calls me and we meet her outside, since the main area of the planetarium is already closed and locked up for the night. I walk KJ to his mother's idling car and my heart breaks for her when I see the guilt written all over her face over how late she is. At this point, it's nearly 8:00 and the sun has already mostly set. As mildly disappointed as I was to have to shift around my date with Jackson, it was a minor inconvenience to make sure everyone was safe and well-cared for.

Ms. Harris gives her son a hug and the tears threatening to spill from her eyes start to trickle down her cheeks. I help KJ into the car, laden with bags of the extra meals Jackson ordered.

"I'm so sorry, baby! Mr. Rivera needed help and I was the only one home! I promise this will never happen again!"

"It's okay, Mom." KJ truly looks unbothered. "I got to have dinner and play catch with JJ Jeffers!"

Ms. Harris is clearly not the same level of Foxes fan as her son, given the confused look she levels at him. "Who?"

Jackson steps forward and shakes Ms. Harris's hand through her open window. "Hi, I'm JJ. Your son is wonderful."

"Mom, he plays shortstop for the Foxes!"

"Oh. Oh, wow. What are you doing here?" Ms. Harris's eyes dart between Jackson and me, and when she sees the warm smile he directs at me, a knowing one of her own makes an appearance on her face. "It's so nice to meet you. Thank you–thank you *both* for taking care of my baby. I don't know what I'd do if you didn't stay late to make sure he was okay."

"Really, it was nothing. Please don't spend another second worrying about this," I assure her. As Ms. Harris drives away, Jackson stands behind me, snaking his arm around my waist and pulling my back to his chest.

"You're a good one, Ms. Stone."

I shrug. "I love KJ. I love all the kids in my program. I'm just glad everything is okay. Ms. Harris doesn't have a lot of support. She's a single mom just trying to do her best, but there's no question she's doing her best for her kids."

Jackson is quiet so long I wonder if he hears me. The only indication he hasn't walked away is his arms still banded across my stomach and the warmth of his chest on my back.

"You're a good one too, JJ Jeffers. You were a natural with KJ. He completely forgot about his worry about his mom when he was playing catch with you. I could see it on his face." Jackson is still quiet. "You okay back there?"

"Yeah, I'm good. I just lost myself a bit in my head. My mom…" He fades into silence, then tries again. "KJ's mom has so much love for him. It's so obvious from the way she looks at her son. My mom never looked at my brothers and me that way. Or maybe she did before my dad died, but after he was gone, she was…very neglectful."

I slowly turn in Jackson's arms and bring my palm to his cheek. He closes his eyes and leans into my hand and my heart breaks for a younger Jackson, trying to win the affections of an absent parent. My heart breaks for an older Jackson, too, who carries the pain from his neglectful mother.

"It's why my brothers and I are so close. We learned from a young age to rely on each other instead of our mom. Sean bore the brunt of the responsibility since he's oldest, but it sucked for all of us."

"I'm so sorry, Jackson." He slowly opens his eyes. "Do you want to talk about it?"

"I think I've said all I want to say about it tonight. Very few people know about my childhood."

There's that feeling in my chest again, the warm ache that I don't want to explore. "Thank you for trusting me," I whisper instead. While I'm curious to know more about Jackson's upbringing, I'm confident he'll share more when he's ready. I'm honored he trusted me enough to share that side of him and it makes his brothers' surprise visit a few weeks ago that much sweeter.

"Let's get you home," Jackson changes the subject. "Will you stay at my place tonight?"

"Of course," I say without hesitation. We walk toward Jackson's car, again electing to leave mine in the staff lot for tomorrow. I'm grateful my bosses are so accepting of flex time; because I stayed three hours late tonight, they won't think twice about me coming in three hours late tomorrow. Tomorrow is Friday, which means no campers, and mostly just preparing for the following week of STEM camp. I was able to do some preparations while KJ was coding in my office and again while KJ and Jackson were playing catch. Jackson has a night game tomorrow, which means we'll have plenty of time to sleep in tomorrow morning.

"Thanks for being so cool with me crashing your KJ party," Jackson says as we zip along Lake Shore Drive toward Lincoln Park. There's nothing in the world like a Chicago summer, and there are still plenty of people enjoying the beaches. Beachfront bars have their bistro lights on and with the car's windows down, I can hear live music and bar chatter wafting toward us when traffic forces Jackson to slow down.

"I meant it when I said you really helped! Thank you for bringing us dinner. You're always welcome to crash my work events. Especially if you bring Moonshadow Diner."

"Seeing you with KJ helped me better understand your passion for your work. It was cool to see you in action." I smile and we fall into a companionable silence until we reach Jackson's apartment.

When Jackson parks and turns off his car, he gently grasps my chin and tilts my head toward him, planting a soft kiss against my lips. "That's better," he whispers. "I wasn't sure if I was allowed to kiss you in front of KJ."

"As a general rule, I think you're always allowed to kiss me," I reply honestly.

"Is that right?" A wicked gleam sparks in Jackson's eyes. "In that case..." He presses his lips against mine and traces the seam of my lips with his tongue. I open, allowing him entry into my mouth and he deepens the kiss. I let out an involuntary moan as his hand slides down my neck to cup my breast while his other hand slides up my leg toward the apex of my thighs. I don't know how Jackson does it, turning an innocent kiss into one that leaves me panting, ready to beg for more, but it takes almost nothing for my body to respond to him, always ready for more with Jackson. He cups my sex over my jeans and we both share a groan. The next second, Jackson pulls away.

"Don't move," he warns as he exits the car. Before I have a chance to ask him what he's up to, he's opening my door, unbuckling my seatbelt, and swinging my legs out the car door. When Jackson kneels in front of me, I gasp. He unbuttons my pants but says nothing other than "lift" to slide my jeans down my legs and off my body. He tosses them unceremoniously on the floor in front of the passenger seat.

"Jackson!" My mind has finally caught up with my mouth. "Someone could walk in on us!" The parking garage is empty of people right now, and Jackson's big body admittedly shields much of me from anyone who might be walking by, but my self-consciousness about the possibility of someone seeing us like this doesn't allow me to fully relax. Some people might find the prospect exciting, arousing even, but I'm not in a place where anyone other than my partner seeing my half-naked body is something I'm happy to risk.

"No one's down here, baby," Jackson reassures. "I can't go a minute longer without tasting you. I need you." His words, or maybe the feral look in his eyes as he says them, settle something in me and I slowly spread my legs a little wider. "Good girl," Jackson praises. And before I can register what is happening, Jackson's mouth is on me, eating me out in his parking garage while I writhe on the passenger seat.

chapter twenty-seven

Jackson

This is my dream. I've had a fantasy about eating Amy out in the car since we started dating. I don't know what it is, but something about getting to hear her scream my name with my head between her legs in my car is as sexy as it gets for me. As it is right now, my cock is ready to punch a hole through my pants.

Amy's vocalizations start as a small whimper; she's clearly still a little self-conscious about someone walking by. The thrill of getting caught is all the more arousing for me, but Amy doesn't share that feeling. She doesn't know this yet, or at least not fully, but I would never let anyone but me see her in all her glory like this. I can tell by the way she still sometimes covers her stomach when I take off her clothes that she's not totally comfortable with her body. I can only tell her that her body is perfect so many times; she has to feel it herself. In the meantime, I'll keep reminding her and worshiping her all the same.

Amy's moans get slightly louder after I flatten my tongue and swirl it around her clit. She's starting to lose some of her self-consciousness in the heat of the moment and I am here for it. I look up to find her leaning back, resting her mid-back against the center console as her hips gently start to rock. I love when Amy gets to this point, when she starts to lose her inhibitions and get lost in pleasure. It's so damn sexy to see her let go a little bit that I have a feeling I could get addicted to this moment when her anxiety is stripped away and I'm left with the real Amy. I'm crazy about all of Amy, but when she can finally let go? That's my favorite version of her.

She opens her eyes and catches me watching her. The moment of eye contact is so intense, so fucking hot, that I make sure to force my tongue to slow down, drawing out her pleasure. She reaches her hands toward me, then seems to think better of it before hesitating again. At this point, I know Amy well enough to see some of her self-consciousness flit back in. We're not having any of that right now. I want Amy to stop thinking and just *feel*.

"Baby, keep your hands in my hair or holding onto the seat until I tell you otherwise. That's my rule and if you break it, I get to punish you. Deal?" Amy hesitates. "You'll always have a choice with me, Ames, but sometimes, I'm going to whittle your choices down to a couple options to give your brain a break. But I will always, always take care of you, no matter what choice you make. Now, can I please eat this dripping cunt?"

Amy twines her fingers in my hair in response and I redouble my efforts, rewarding her for following my directions. I don't particularly care where Amy keeps her hands while I'm licking her perfect pussy, but if I don't interrupt her thought patterns, she is either going to overthink it now, in the moment, or revisit her actions a hundred times later. Neither sound like great options to me, so I'm going to try something new and see if I can get Amy to turn that brain off again.

I pump one finger, then two, into her swollen cunt, never stopping my tongue's pressure on her clit, and it's only a minute more before Amy explodes around me. Her pussy walls flutter against my fingers and I can't help the moan that escapes my lips when I anticipate what they will do around my cock later. Amy's screams echo in the garage and I'm filled with a sense of male pride knowing I did that to her. I continue licking her as she comes down from her orgasm and sighs.

I pull away from my version of heaven, wiping my mouth. Amy looks disheveled and sated. Her hair is a mess, just the way I like it.

"Thank you," she whispers and I laugh.

"Amy, that was as much for me as it was for you. I could spend all day down there and it'd be one of the best days of my life." She blushes but I know she loves it. Still crouching in front of her, I help her back into her jeans and sandals. She threads her fingers through my hair and my eyes flutter closed at the intimate gesture. Amy playing with my hair is my favorite non-sexual way she touches me. My scalp prickles in delight as I stand in front of her. She drops her hands and immediately gives my hard cock a squeeze.

I chuckle. "Oh, little girl, what did you just do?" I groan. "Did I give you permission to do anything with those hands other than hold the seat or pull my hair?" Amy's eyes widen when she realizes her mistake.

"What? You were serious?" she exclaims. I don't miss her thighs squeezing together at the look I send her way, silently reminding her she's about to be punished. "I'm sorry," she whispers. "I forgot."

"It's okay to forget," I tell her, kissing her temple. "But now you can choose Option A or Option B to help you remember next time."

"What's Option A? And what's B?" she asks with a small amount of trepidation in her voice.

"I can't spoil the surprise. But I meant it when I said I would always take care of you, so don't be afraid. You'll like it."

"Option B then," she says with a grin. I wasn't sure how Amy would react to the idea of being punished. I've never tried it with a girl before, but her answering grin tells me that at least so far, she's into it. My excitement is mounting with hers as we step into the elevator and ascend to the fourth floor.

When we get inside my condo, we're of course greeted by Bruno's shenanigans, slobbering and whining for Amy to pet him. When Amy's around, I play second fiddle to her for my own damn dog, but I can't even pretend to be mad about it. Bruno knows what I know: any second spent basking in Amy's attention is time well spent. After a few minutes of Bruno butt scratches and Amy's words of affirmation reminding Bruno he is the best boy in the world, I take a seat on the couch, spreading my legs to accommodate my growing erection at thoughts of what's to come. I motion Amy over to me with two fingers.

"Come here." She stands between my knees and places her hands on my shoulders. Her hand shakes a little. "Are you afraid?"

"No. I'm...turned on." She says, wincing with embarrassment at her admission.

"Good. You're about to be even more turned on. Remember we can stop at any time, but I think you'll enjoy this. Now take off your pants."

Amy whimpers and does as she's told. I shift a little in my seat, trying to ease the physical tension on my swollen cock. I love how much she trusts me. I'll never do anything to betray that trust and I am confident she's going to enjoy her punishment as much as I am. Amy is now bare from the waist down, having removed her lacy thong as well. I try and fail to hold back a groan.

"You are so beautiful, Ames. Now come lay down."

Amy lifts her leg to straddle my waist. I place my hand on her hip to stop her.

"Uh uh, pretty girl. You're going to lay across my lap." I chuckle at the confused look she sends me. "If you can't keep your hands to yourself when I tell you to, I'm going to keep mine on your ass. Repeatedly. Until my handprint on this ass helps you remember when I give you a rule, it's to make sure you're enjoying yourself and thinking of nothing else. Are you ready to get your gorgeous ass spanked, baby?"

Amy's pupils are blown so wide I can barely see the browns of her irises. I'm turned on by how turned on she is; I can smell her arousal as she positions her body across my lap, turning her head to rest her cheek against the couch cushion. I grab one of her ass cheeks and squeeze it roughly as Amy groans. The noise runs straight to my cock. I take a deep breath, willing my dick to be patient; he'll get his turn later.

"We can stop at any time, just tell me," I remind Amy. Before giving her a chance to respond, I bring my hand down on her ass with a satisfying crack. I immediately rub the point of contact, soothing the area, as Amy moans.

"Do it again," she pants. "Please."

I didn't think I'd have my girlfriend begging me so soon tonight, but I'm not complaining. I do as she asks because I, too, can follow directions. I spank her four more times, each time resulting in louder moans from Amy. She's wiggling on my lap and rubbing against me so much it's hard to focus. I've never spanked a girl like this before, with her laying across me, but I suspected Amy might like it, given her earlier reactions to the occasional ass smack in bed. I love that my girl is kinky and into this. I'll gladly give her whatever she needs and then some. Gently rubbing the globes of her ass, I coax her up. She straddles me, panting and planting open-mouthed kisses on my neck.

"Amy, you've made a mess of my pants." It's true. Her wetness leaked out of her pussy and soaked through my joggers, causing them to stick to my skin on my thigh. Knowing Amy is so wet because of me makes my cock twitch against her exposed, dripping pussy. It's not going to take much to make me come tonight.

I swipe a finger through Amy's wetness before bringing my finger to my mouth and licking it off with a groan.

"You like having your ass spanked, Amy?"

"Yes," she murmurs breathlessly against my neck, grinding shamelessly on my lap.

"You did so well. I told you I'd take care of you and that you'd like it." I pause briefly, and Amy nods against my neck. "But I'm not done with you tonight. You've been through a lot right now so I'm going to give you another choice. You want to get fucked hard on this couch right now, or should I take you to my bed and fuck you sweetly and slowly?"

CHAPTER TWENTY-EIGHT

Amy

I'm so turned on I can barely think. My ass tingles from where Jackson spanked me and thinking of that alone causes another gush of wetness to my core. I'd be embarrassed about the wet spot on Jackson's pants if my mind wasn't so lust addled. Between going down on me in the parking garage to my spanking on his couch, my lower body is on sensory overload and I don't want it to end.

"Fuck me here, Jackson," I pant. "Do it hard. Please, I need you."

Apparently Jackson doesn't need telling twice before he grabs my hips and tosses me onto the couch beside him. I bounce lightly and giggle at how feral he's become. I guess I'm not the only one who enjoyed the spanking.

"Shirt off," Jackson commands. His eyes are dark and gone is the sweet Jackson who brought me dinner and played catch with a little boy so he wouldn't panic about his mom. In his place, a wild, commanding, domineering Jackson remains and I scramble to do what he tells me. I like making others happy, but pleasing *this* Jackson is like a primal urge, an instinct I can't ignore–not that I even want to. I can't rip my shirt off fast enough, moving swiftly to remove my bra while Jackson undresses just as quickly and rolls on a condom.

Before I can say another word, Jackson is slamming into me, thrusting inside me to the hilt. The stretch is so good and I shudder to think what it would feel like if I weren't so wet from the foreplay in the garage and on Jackson's lap earlier.

Jackson's thrusts are relentless, inching me further up the couch with each thrust. He's so deep inside me, hitting a spot I didn't even know existed. I wrap my legs around his waist and hold on. There's little else I can do; his movements are all-consuming. Between the spanking and his assault on my pussy now, I know it will hurt to sit down tomorrow and I love every second of it.

"Oh god, Jackson...yes, god, please!" I don't know what I'm praying for, what I'm begging for, but Jackson gets the message and continues pounding into the same spot. He wraps one hand around my throat, holding me in place and preventing his thrusts from moving me further on the couch. His other hand roughly cups my breast and then pinches my nipple hard. I scream, shattering around him.

Jackson keeps up his pace as he works me through one of the most intense orgasms I've ever experienced. Nonsensical words fly out of my mouth; I swear I start speaking in tongues. My body is lit up in pleasure and Jackson continues playing me like a violin as I come down.

"Good girl. You take my cock so well," Jackson praises. My body is limp in his hands, wrung out from pleasure. "Remember when you thought you couldn't come multiple times in one night?"

"Mmm" is all I can respond. Jackson presses my left knee toward my chest, deepening his access and making me gasp.

"Fucking love how flexible you are. My cock is so deep inside your perfect cunt. I love making you scream." His gentle bite on my collarbone is at odds with the unyielding snap of his hips. I make a mental note to thank whoever is in charge of Jackson's workouts for developing the power behind his hips. Jackson's abs contract against me as his grunts grow louder, chasing his own orgasm. He comes with a shout, burying his head in my neck as he finishes.

His movements slow and Jackson rests his head on my chest while I play with his hair.

"Mmm, Ames, I love when you play with my hair," he murmurs.

After a few minutes, he peels himself off of me, our sticky bodies slick with sweat. "C'mere baby," he says sleepily. "Let me take care of you."

"I think you've been doing that all night," I laugh.

"Not stopping anytime soon, either." Jackson lifts me with ease and carries me to his shower. He positions me outside the stream of the spray while the water heats up. Soon, steam is billowing out of the shower, hot jets of water shooting out of both shower heads in his giant shower. There's a built-in bench in the corner that I'm tempted to sit on, but Jackson pulls me to his chest, running his hands up and down my water slicked body. It's not sexual per se, but comforting and reassuring in a way I haven't experienced yet.

We take turns washing each other, the clean, soapy scent of Jackson's body wash infusing my pores. When Jackson washes my hair, my throat constricts. The action is so gentle, so intimate, and I don't know why I want to cry. I'm just glad Jackson is standing behind me and can't see me try to reign in the emotions I'm sure are playing across my face. We stand together in the stream while Jackson peppers my neck and jaw with kisses while whispering how perfect I am. This, too, makes me want to cry, and I don't know why. Jackson's tenderness is so endearing and I think I'm just not used to it.

When we're done showering, he wraps me in the fluffiest, most luxurious towel I've ever felt. He wraps his own around his waist without drying himself off, and I find myself subconsciously licking my lips as I watch the droplets of water on Jackson's chest slide down his perfect abs and underneath his towel.

"You're trouble," Jackson says, catching me staring at him and slowly shaking his head.

"The good kind of trouble, though, right?"

"Always." Jackson again lifts me and carries me to his bed. What is with this guy carrying me everywhere? I mean, my legs are jelly from the incredible sex, and I do feel precious when he carries me around like I'm this petite little thing, but there's no way this is actually as easy for him as he's making it seem. Right?

Jackson lays me gently in his bed, rounding to the other side and laying himself to face me. He strokes my cheek and I can feel my eyes becoming heavier with exhaustion.

"What was Option A?" I ask, unable to contain my curiosity.

"Option A? For your punishment?" I nod. "I would have edged the hell out of you all night." I shudder. I'm glad I chose Option B. As if he could read my mind, Jackson laughs. "You would have liked that option too, eventually. Once you finally came, it would have felt explosive. And I would have made you come again and again."

I can't help the moan that escapes my lips at that. I'm not exactly inexperienced in bed, but I'm discovering so many new things with Jackson that I had no idea turned me on so much. He shoots me a roguish grin.

"Maybe we'll try that one of these days too." He says it like it's a suggestion, but part of me hopes it's a promise. I begin tracing lazy designs on his chest with my finger.

"How are you feeling? Now that we're not in the heat of the moment, talk to me, Ames. Did I hurt you?"

"Hurt me?"

"How's your ass?" he asks, pulling me closer to his chest as my cheeks flame.

"Ugh, it's so good. I've never...done...that before."

"Me neither," Jackson admits. For some reason, that gives me such a strong sense of satisfaction that I'm momentarily distracted from the conversation. "I don't want you to go along with anything because you think I want it, though, Ames," he continues. "Even if I tell you you're going to be punished, if you don't want it, we stop."

"No, I don't want to stop. It was fun. It was...god, I loved that. So much." I groan just remembering it. Jackson pulls my face away from his chest and kisses me tenderly.

"I thought you would."

No more words are spoken from either of us as Jackson rolls me underneath him, still kissing me, opens my towel, and makes sweet, slow love to me.

When I wake up the next morning, I reach toward Jackson but find his side of the bed empty. The sheets are cool to the touch, indicating he left the bed awhile ago. I strain my ears to listen for him in the rest of the condo, but it's silent. Not even the click of Bruno's nails against the floor can be heard.

I sit up, holding the sheet to my naked chest. I know no one is here, but for some reason, I can't break all of my patterns of modesty, even though Jackson constantly praises my body. I spot a notepad on Jackson's pillow that I missed earlier. In a tidy scrawl, the note reads:

ANGEL, I WENT TO GET US COFFEE AND TAKE BRUNO FOR A WALK. I'LL BE BACK WITH A DIRTY CHAI SOON. RELAX AND HELP YOURSELF TO ANYTHING IN THE HOUSE.

LOVE, JACKS

Why is Jackson signing his name with the nickname his brothers use so endearing? I need to remember to not get so caught up in my feelings for him, lest we encounter another Patrick situation, but it's getting harder and harder. Jackson seems to wear his heart on his sleeve, which is helpful at times, knowing where he stands. But I still can't quite bring myself to trust what might be the depth of his feelings for me.

Whew, Patrick really did a number on me.

The longer I stay in bed, the more I replay the events of last night in my head. There's a dull ache between my legs and I smile at the reminder of Jackson's talents in the bedroom...and the garage...and the living room. I decide to get out of bed and actually do something productive with my morning before I make myself so horny replaying last night's escapades that I pounce on Jackson as soon as he walks in the door. I've always liked sex, but sex with Jackson is on a whole other level. It's like I can never get enough, even though the ache in my nether regions might indicate I need to take a little hiatus.

I get out of bed, stretch, and throw on one of Jackson's shirts I find draped across the back of the chair in his bedroom. It comes down almost to my knees and I decide to forgo wearing anything else for the time being.

I'm rummaging around Jackson's refrigerator when I hear a key slide into the lock at the front door. I don't bother lifting my head from inside the fridge as I greet Jackson.

"Hey, baby, do you mind if I eat this banana yogurt? It's my favorite flavor."

"You must be Amy," a feminine voice says.

I whip around so fast I'm surprised I don't strain something. A woman is standing in Jackson's front hallway with a direct line of sight to me standing half naked in his kitchen. I pull at his shirt, sliding it further down my legs, even though it's already long enough to cover almost all of my thighs.

"Um, yeah, hi. I'm Amy."

Really smooth, Stone.

Why is there a beautiful woman standing in Jackson's condo? And why does she have a key to his place? And why is she so beautiful? She's got long, chestnut hair pulled over one shoulder, the other side of her head shaved close. A septum ring glints on her nose, catching the light streaming in from the window. She's wearing tight black jeans and a tiny tank top that shows off her generous...assets. Tattoos scatter her arms and torso.

"I'm Lisa," she says, as if that explains anything. She's grinning at me, and it seems like the kind of smile that is truly genuine, not one simply offered with a polite greeting, though I can't figure out why she would be giving me such a warm smile. I'm still waiting for further explanation that doesn't seem to be coming. Instead, Lisa says, "I've heard so much about you."

"Oh, um, hopefully good things?" I say meekly. I'm trying not to let my confusion show. Does Jackson make a habit of giving a key to beautiful women who are not his girlfriend? Is this a crazy ex who kept her key after Jackson broke up with her and she's here to exact revenge on his new girlfriend by murdering her? I might need to tone down how much true crime I watch.

"Girl, only good things!" Lisa replies enthusiastically, oblivious to my continued confusion over who, exactly, she is. Thankfully, at that moment, Jackson walks through his still open front door, Bruno's unattached leash looped casually around his shoulders and a drink carrier with two cups in hand.

"Lisa! What are you doing here?" Jackson seems confused, but not angry. Maybe Lisa isn't a murderous ex. Bruno, the ultimate traitor, saunters up to Lisa for pets, which she readily supplies.

"What are *you* doing here? I thought you had a day game?" she responds, matching the confusion on Jackson's face with a look of her own. I'm sure we're quite the sight, should anyone stumble into Jackson's place: three people looking varying levels of confused, staring at each other.

"It got changed to a night game a few weeks ago. They wanted to make it the nationally broadcast game of the week. I guess I forgot to tell you." Jackson smiles. No one has explained what this woman is doing here, but Jackson's relaxed posture is helping me to not immediately fear for my life.

"Guess I should have just looked up the schedule instead of relying on the old printout you gave me in January."

"That, or you could actually become a baseball fan and pay attention to these things," Jackson teases.

"Never gonna happen, big guy."

Big guy? Is she flirting with Jackson right in front of me?

Jackson must sense my shift in emotion. He sets the coffees on the counter in front of me.

"Amy, this is Lisa, my neighbor. She takes care of Bruno while I'm out of town and when I have long days at the ballpark. Lisa, this is my girlfriend, Amy." It suddenly makes sense why Lisa would have a key to Jackson's place. The relief I feel is palpable, but I can't help immediately suspecting Jackson might be attracted to Lisa more than me. Hell, *I'm* attracted to Lisa and I'm as straight as an arrow! My earlier relief must have been plastered on my face, because Lisa immediately pieces my thoughts together.

"Oh my gosh, I'm such a space cadet! I didn't even tell you who I was or why I had a key to your boyfriend's place! My fiancee, Desiree, and I rent the unit below JJ. We love our Bruno time. She'll be bummed when I tell her we won't have him for another few hours. I'll get out of your guys' hair so you can enjoy your morning! I'll come grab Bruno around five." Lisa blurts out all of the information so quickly I barely have time to digest what she's said before she's rushing out the front door.

"So that's Lisa," Jackson drawls. I laugh as I take the drink Jackson holds out to me.

"She's stunning," I admit, unable to hold back on my comments.

"Yeah, she's pretty." I'm weirdly relieved Jackson doesn't try to deny her beauty. "But I prefer this girl right here." He presses a kiss to my temple. "Lisa is a great neighbor, though. It would be really hard to keep Bruno with my schedule. I don't know what I'd do without her or Des stepping up."

"What made you get a dog? I can't imagine it was an easy decision to adopt this guy knowing how often you're on the road."

Jackson sighs. "I used to be engaged. My fiancee and I adopted Bruno together when we were still engaged." He pauses. I don't know what to say. Was Jackson's fiancee one of the gorgeous women I'd seen him photographed with during my early Google searches of him?

"What happened?" I ask, then immediately follow it up. "You don't have to tell me if you don't want to. I don't want to pry."

"Amy, you're allowed to ask questions about my life. You're my girlfriend. You're entitled to know about my past, especially since it brought me to you." Jackson takes my hand and brings me to the couch in the living room. "Carolyn and I met years ago when I was playing in Philly. We got engaged and she obviously came with me when I signed with the Foxes. We bought a place together in Lakeview and adopted Bruno shortly after. He was such a troublemaker when we first got him. Caleb and his fiancee, Jenny, do a lot with the local rescues around here, so when they showed me his picture, I knew I had to have him. Carolyn and I went to the shelter that day and adopted him when he was nine weeks old. We adopted him together, but he really bonded with me." Jackson's eyes crinkle at the corners as he remembers. "I was so happy. Until I wasn't." Jackson takes a long sip of his coffee before continuing. "I came home early from a road trip and found her in bed with someone else. She'd been sleeping with him for three months." He rushes through the last part of his story, as if slowing down to relay the information would be too painful.

"I'm so sorry," I whisper. I don't know what else to say. I reach out and squeeze his hand, hoping to convey my sympathy, my care, my *something* that would be enough to take away what I can only imagine is the pain from his life crumbling around him when he found out.

"Anyway, I obviously broke it off right then and there. I moved out immediately and sold the house, since it was in my name. I haven't really looked back since then. She's still dating that guy, and we broke up years ago."

A bevy of emotions wells up inside me. Anger–no, rage–at Carolyn for hurting the world's kindest, most genuine person. Sorrow for the pain Jackson had to have gone through. Worry for where Jackson's head is at now.

"What is going through your head?" Jackson says with a small laugh. "So many emotions are playing out on your face."

"I'm so angry that someone could hurt you that way!" I blurt out.

"I'm over it now, but yeah, it really sucked for a long time after. In the years since it happened, I've learned more about myself and realized even without the cheating, Carolyn and I probably weren't the greatest match. She was really consumed with the status of being an athlete's girlfriend, which I didn't totally pick up on until after the breakup. She tried to blame the breakup on me and the baseball schedule–" I gasp at the audacity. Jackson shakes his head, smiling at my reaction.

"What a bitch," I mumble.

"Yeah," he huffs. "I don't use that term often, but if the shoe fits...anyway, she didn't fight me on taking Bruno, which was really the only thing I cared about anyway." At the sound of his name, Bruno comes trotting over, stuffed giraffe in his mouth. He stares soulfully at Jackson, slowly squeaking the toy in his jaw. Jackson scratches behind Bruno's ears. When he stops, Bruno takes it as an invitation to climb onto the couch with us, resting his head on

Jackson's lap. "Thanks, bud," Jackson murmurs, stroking Bruno's head.

"How could she not want this face?" I say, reaching across to give Bruno some pets of my own.

"Right? If that's not a direct reflection of her character, I don't know what is!" The mood is slightly lightened. "Anyway, if nothing else, I learned to be a more attentive partner, since Carolyn claimed I didn't pay enough attention to her during baseball season. Or, at least, I hope I am?" The hopeful look Jackson gives me makes my chest ache.

"Jackson, you are the best boyfriend I have ever had. You're attentive and thoughtful and I've never questioned your commitment to me." He sighs in relief and my chest cracks a little further. "Come here."

I press Jackson's head to my chest, holding him close as he wraps his arms around my waist. My fingers immediately begin to absentmindedly play with his hair.

"Mmm, I love that," Jackson hums. I close my eyes and relish the quiet calm.

CHAPTER TWENTY-NINE
Jackson

The gravel crunches under our feet as Amy and I walk from the parking lot to her yoga studio. She convinced me to join her for today's class before we swing by her apartment and I drive her to work. I don't have to be at the ballpark until 2:00 today, so I have plenty of time. I'm sure my strength and conditioning coaches would rather I get my workout in at the field today before the game, but I can't deny Amy anything. The excitement telegraphed across her face when she suggested I join her in class was so adorable, there was no way I was going to tell her no. We park in the back lot and are making our way to the front door of her studio when Amy verifies with me, yet again, that I actually want to do this with her.

"Baby, I love spending time with you. Besides, you never have to convince me to work out. I don't know that I can make this a regular thing during the season, but during the offseason, I'm here whenever you want me."

I don't miss the look of unease on Amy's face. I don't know all the details, but I know the last guy she dated treated her poorly and Amy can be a little skittish whenever we talk about plans further into the future or anything remotely resembling getting serious. It's getting harder and harder to match Amy's slow pace when all I want to do is spend time with her and get serious, but I'm trying to respect her unspoken wishes. It doesn't help that I don't know the full story between her and her ex, but I'll wait until she's ready to tell me.

"Come on," I urge her inside with my hand on the small of her back.

After I get registered, sign a waiver and take off my shoes, I enter the room we'll be practicing in and lay my mat next to Amy's. She's already starting some gentle stretching warmups on her mat, so I begin to do the same.

The instructor comes in and walks us through a series of sun salutations. My rusty yoga skills are slowly coming back to me. It helps that this class is relatively repetitive, but I often sneak glances at Amy. Not just because she looks incredible in yoga pants and a tight top, but because she really knows what she's doing. It's fascinating to see her in this light, excelling at something she's passionate about. I got to see glimpses of it yesterday when I visited her at work, too.

This yoga instructor seems really focused on anatomical alignment, which I appreciate, since I need all the tips and verbal cues in the poses I can get. Amy told me George, our instructor, was her favorite because of his cuing and his overall themes for his classes.

He happens to be one of the studio owners, and I can tell he's been doing this for a long time.

Today's theme seems to be all about choices. I catch Amy's eye when George first introduces the topic and see she's fighting a smile as well. I throw her a wink. Somehow, I don't think George was thinking about the kinds of choices I gave Amy last night when he designed the structure of today's class, but it makes the rest of the hour that much more enjoyable. George talks about how we always have choices: whether we do a pose in yoga or sit it out, whether we speak our mind or remain silent, whether we enter into a meeting we're dreading with a good attitude or one of disdain. I can see why Amy enjoys his classes; George expertly weaves storytelling and theme into the poses he's selected for today's class. We reach our final resting pose quicker than I realize. I spend a lot of my time in savasana replaying the choices Amy made last night.

When the class ends and Amy and I emerge, blinking, into the bright late morning sunlight, I know she's still thinking about last night, too.

"So a class all about choices, huh?" I say, poking Amy's side.

"Right?" Amy's excited, scrunching her nose at the coincidence. She gently hip checks me on the way to the car. "It's like a sign from the universe."

"What does the sign say?"

"That I'm right where I'm supposed to be." After a thoughtful pause, Amy adds, "That maybe we're right where we're supposed to be."

For all of Amy's hesitation, all of her communication that she doesn't want something serious, that she's hesitant to get into a deep, serious relationship, her one simple statement calms my heart and lets me know we actually are on the same page.

I grasp her hand as we walk to the car. She no longer fights me on opening the door for her.

"I was thinking of having people over on Monday. We have an off day and we can barbecue on the roof. Would you want to do that with me?" I ask.

"That sounds great!" I love her enthusiasm. "I'll have to work but can come as soon as the kids leave!"

"Perfect," I say, kissing her on the tip of her nose before she ducks into my car. I shut the door, rounding the front and getting in myself. I continue the conversation while I start the engine. "Feel free to invite Alicia, Danny, and Tim. And whoever else you want. I'll ask some guys on the team and I'm sure they'll bring their wives and girlfriends, too."

"That would be great!"

After I drop Alicia off at work, I have about an hour to kill before I need to be at the ballpark myself. I take Bruno for a walk and fire off a couple texts to my brothers, just checking in. Bruno happily saunters along on our walk and I get lost in thoughts of Amy again.

I'm fine with taking control for Amy if it means she can rest her overworked brain. I can't imagine what it's like to always be thinking, to always be "on." I don't mind being domineering in the bedroom as long as Amy still likes it. And as long as I get to spoil her everywhere else. In fact, I'm beginning to suspect I prefer it that way.

CHAPTER THIRTY

Jackson

I fall back against the outdoor lounge chair on my roof. The barbeque is in full swing, and I just finished wiping the floor with Warner, our right fielder, in darts. When I first bought my condo two years ago, I made the rooftop of the building, half of which I own, my outdoor oasis. Between the cushy seating area in front of the outdoor television under the pergola and the game areas where I have ping pong, darts, and bags set up, there is an oversized island in the center, currently laden with food. One side of the island also houses the grill, while the other includes a mini fridge and kegerator. I wanted a place where I could hang out with teammates and loved ones without being bothered like I might be in public.

Amy worked all weekend to help me prepare for the gathering. I would have put out a cheese board and an assortment of chips and fruit, but with Amy's help, we went all out. In addition to the items I planned for, she created table nachos. Spread across half of the island, Amy laid out layers of chips, homemade nacho cheese sauce, shredded cheese, cilantro, onions, homemade salsa, black beans, and jalapenos. She also put out little platters of cut fruit at various seating stations around the roof. The charcuterie board she put together was immaculate. She made four different kinds of salad too, now sitting in large bowls sprinkled around the island; Amy wasn't kidding when she told me she loves to cook. Her happy hums while preparing everything filled my kitchen this weekend. I suspect she channeled some of her nervous energy about meeting my teammates and their significant others into the overabundance of food. She had nothing to worry about; everyone has been so welcoming and they were so excited to meet her, but I know her anxiety gets the best of her sometimes.

I'll start grilling burgers, hot dogs, and brats in about an hour when people start to tire of the snacks and are looking for a more substantial meal. The music is playing, drinks are flowing, and under the twinkle of the bistro lights strung across the rooftop patio, everyone is mingling and seems to be getting along well.

Alicia collapses on the couch next to me, sweaty and out of breath from playing a particularly rousing game of ping pong with Caleb, Hayden Oliver, and Tim. From the looks of it, she and Caleb won, but Ollie and Tim gave her a run for her money.

"Thanks for having us over. It was really nice of you to include us," Alicia says, speaking apparently on behalf of Danny and Tim as well.

"You're always welcome over here. I love hosting and putting the space to use."

"You've done a great job with the place. Your teammates seem pretty cool too. Everyone is really easy to get along with."

"We've got a good group," I admit. While I get along with all of my teammates, I'm not close with everyone. "Your ping pong partner and I went to college together. We were teammates and roommates, actually."

"Really?"

I tell Alicia about some of the shenanigans of a much younger Andrews and Jeffers. She laughs, spilling her drink a little as she readjusts herself on the couch. We're reaching the point in the night where I might have to start grilling early if everyone else is as tipsy as Alicia.

"I love seeing you and Amy together," Alicia loudly whispers, as if she's sharing some big secret.

"I love being with her. She's great. The more I learn about her, the more time I want to spend with her. I know I'm lucky." Alicia gapes at me. "What?"

"I don't know, I guess I expected you to play it cool a little bit more. Not be so vocal about how much you care for her."

I give her a quizzical look. "Why wouldn't I want to brag about my girlfriend? She's really cool and I'm happy being with her."

"A lot of guys tend to downplay their affections, I guess."

"Nah, I've never been one for that. If you care about someone, you need to let them know it. Not just with your words." I would know firsthand about the importance of actions over words. If words were enough, my mom would have been parent of the year and I'd probably be married to Carolyn by now.

"Can I ask you something?" Alicia blurts out of nowhere.

"Sure thing," I respond.

"What do you want from your relationship with Amy?"

I raise an eyebrow. "Are you asking my intentions for your best friend?"

"Well, sort of. I'm just trying to look out for her. The last guy she dated seemed to have her best interests in mind and then broke up with her out of the blue. She was really confused and honestly, pretty devastated. They seemed to be totally on the same page about everything and he completely blindsided her."

"Is that why she's hesitant to talk about a serious relationship?" I ask. Finally, I'm getting some insight into where Amy's head is at when it comes to us.

"Yeah. He really hurt her," Alicia says quietly.

"His loss. To answer your earlier question, I'm completely crazy about Amy. I'll have her in whatever way she'll allow. Right now, she keeps saying she doesn't want anything serious, so I'm not going to pressure her. But the second she's ready, I'm there. I'm all in on this one, Alicia." Alicia just smiles. I hope that bodes well for me.

I know Amy says she doesn't want anything serious, but I suspect she's just as in this as I am. And just like I can read her anxiety, I can read every other emotion she feels and I know she isn't faking this. I know I'm not misreading Amy's feelings and how much she cares about me, even if she doesn't like the term "serious."

But that's okay, I'll meet her where she's at and we can both pretend she wants to keep this casual.

CHAPTER THIRTY-ONE

Amy

"I had to ask him to untangle my sweater from my nose ring the first time we hooked up," Hailey laughs, covering her mouth. Elijah McClintock's wife continues, "I thought I would be all sexy and put in this new spiral nose ring, which totally caught on my sweater when Eli took it off over my head. It ripped the shit out of my piercing. Blood was pouring everywhere and poor Elijah had no idea what happened."

Jenny and I howl with laughter. Hailey has been married to Elijah, the starting third baseman for the Foxes, for two years now. She's animated and high energy and in the middle of telling us her most embarrassing moment when she and Elijah first started dating.

"Seriously, I had to throw the sweater out between the giant snag from my nose ring and all the blood...that baby was a lost cause." Hailey snorts a little when she laughs, which just makes Jenny and me laugh even harder.

"What about you, Amy? Any embarrassing stories with JJ?" Jenny turns to me. I was nervous about meeting Jackson's teammates and their wives and girlfriends, but I should have known

I had nothing to worry about. Jenny especially has been warm and welcoming; I fell into easy conversation with each of them so quickly. Even now, Jackson occasionally catches my eye from across the roof, checking on me, but I'm happy to give him a smile and nod each time, confirming that I really am doing well.

"The first time I encountered Jackson, Bruno knocked me flat on my ass in the middle of a coffee shop. Then, when I met him again, Bruno did it again, only this time, he spilled my entire drink all over the sidewalk." The girls laugh alongside me.

"I don't think I have any embarrassing stories from when Caleb and I first got together. I can't even tell you how many times I've thrown up on him from the chemo, though." Jenny's words sober us a little. Jenny waves off our looks of sympathy. "It feels like we've been together for so long that the early stages of our relationship seem like a blur."

Tyler Edwards' girlfriend, Carly, joins us as she tops off a new beer. We're standing around the island, munching on nachos and fruit, and conversation is easy. These women are delightful; they're warm and welcoming and really funny. Their significant others are crazy about them, and it's really sweet to see so many examples of healthy relationships. Each woman is stunningly beautiful in her own right; it's hard not to feel a little bit of pressure to perform and live up to the standards they've set, even though I know that's just an arbitrary rule I've placed on myself.

"Now that you know a few of us a little better, Amy, will we be seeing more of you at the games?" Hailey asks.

"I don't know," I answer honestly. "This whole thing with Jackson is so new. I don't want to overstep."

The women all share a look. "Girl, JJ would want you there! You're not overstepping. They get a certain number of tickets for free each season, so it's not like you're even costing JJ anything," Jenny says, incorrectly guessing the reason for my hesitation.

"Oh, I wouldn't want to take the tickets from his family or someone else who could use them," I answer hurriedly.

Carly answers gently, "Amy, you're not taking someone else's spot. JJ wants you there. Besides, if someone else needs tickets from JJ, he can always ask for more or ask another one of the guys for their unused tickets. We've gotta talk to Deb and get you a badge."

The women explain that Deb, the woman in charge of the Foxes' family program, can make me an ID badge which would allow me into more restricted areas before, during, and after games, like on the field and in the family room. The wives and girlfriends (they affectionately call themselves WAGs, too) all wait for their men in the family lobby after the game, they explain to me.

"We call them a WAG badge," Jenny says.

"Hey JJ!" Carly shouts across the roof. "Should we hook Amy up with a WAG badge?"

"Hell yeah!" Jackson shouts back, standing from where he's been sitting on the couch with Alicia, watching Warner, Caleb,

Tim, and Danny play ping pong. Jackson makes his way over and I mumble that it's not necessary to have anyone make me a badge. He shakes his head at me and kisses the top of my head.

"You can do whatever you want, Ames, but the second you want a WAG badge, you let me know and I'll have Deb make one for you. She's great; she really won't mind doing it."

"I'll think about it," I lie. While I love being Jackson's girlfriend, everything about our relationship is shiny and new. Given how casual things are between us, I'd hate to have someone go out of their way at their job to make me a badge if Jackson and I don't have any long term plans. And let's face it, I'm not about to make any long term plans with him anytime soon. Or anytime. Old Amy might have done that, but New Amy keeps things easy, less serious, more fun. Jackson and I may have agreed to exclusivity, but we never agreed to anything long-term. And I'm not about to rock the boat to ask.

CHAPTER THIRTY-TWO

Jackson

The Foxes are on another lengthy road trip, hitting all of our rivals in the Midwest. It's not a bad trip because the flights are short, but it does suck a little to be away from home that long. Between Amy and Bruno, I'm missing home and missing my own bed. The hotels we stay at are nice. They're all expensive and luxurious, and I'm sure if I actually spent more time in the rooms, I'd appreciate them more. It's mid-June, so we're not quite at the halfway point in the season, but I'm feeling the drag of the season sooner than I usually do.

"Hey pretty girl," I say as Amy's face fills my phone screen.

"Hi, Jacks!" She responds enthusiastically, and the use of my nickname fills me with an unexpected warmth.

"God, I miss you already," I tell her honestly. It's been five days since I last saw her in person, and if I have anything to say about it, that's five days too long.

"You do?" Amy's surprise seems genuine. I just shake my head slowly; one of these days, I won't have her questioning my commitment. I feel a flash of uncharacteristic anger that the fucknugget Amy used to date didn't make her feel appreciated enough.

"Sure do. A few of the guys were talking about plans over the break and I realized I never asked you if you'd join me. We have a midseason break for four days next month. Wanna go somewhere? My treat."

"That sounds like so much fun! What were you thinking?"

"It depends on what you feel like doing. I'll send you the dates so you can put them on your calendar. Some of the guys who are staying in Chicago are renting a boat and going out on the lake for the day. We were invited to join them, but if you'd rather go somewhere else, I wouldn't say no to getting out of town either."

"Is there anywhere you've always wanted to go but haven't been able to?" she asks me thoughtfully.

"I travel a lot for work but don't always get to explore places or do a lot of things when I'm in town for games. I wouldn't mind revisiting some places either, especially if you've never been to them. We should probably stick to something domestic though, since we've only got a few days. What kind of things do you like to do on vacation? Are you a beach person? Or a sightseer? We can be as relaxed or scheduled as you want. I'm just happy to get away."

"That leaves a lot of options! I haven't been able to travel as much as I would like. I'm not too much of a beach person, but I would love to hike! We could relax and hike and take it easy. Maybe a place where we can get a good mix of activities and downtime?"

"I know the perfect place. Have you ever been to Telluride? Caleb and Jenny went there a few years ago and haven't stopped talking about it since. I'll book us a place with spa access." Amy's face is so lit up in excitement I don't need to hear her verbal response to know she's into this idea. "Let me take care of this for us. You won't have to worry about anything."

On our flight to Cincinnati, I read one of the in-flight magazines when I couldn't sleep. It talked about a concept called "decision fatigue." When someone has to make a lot of decisions on a regular basis, they can get burnt out on it and the idea of making more decisions in their personal life is exhausting. I haven't asked, but I suspect Amy might experience that from time to time. She seems indecisive more often after work and during the week than she is on weekends. If I can lessen her load by making a few choices for her and just verifying if they fit her needs, I can happily take that on.

Amy and I talk about what we could do on our trip. I'm planning on chartering a jet to get us there; otherwise, the journey can be long and I'd like to maximize our time in our destination, rather than waste time getting there.

Amy thinks she can get one of the directors to cover her kids at camp for the days she'll be gone as long as she gives them enough notice. She says a month should be plenty of notice but I send her the dates while we're still talking so there's no delay.

Talking to Amy from my hotel room is easily the bright spot of my mornings on the road. It's slowly becoming more and more apparent to me that my interactions with Amy significantly impact my mood. If I get to talk to my girl on her lunch breaks, I'm a happy man. If the schedule doesn't allow for us to connect, I'm disappointed and quiet on the bus ride from the hotel to the ballpark. I'm not sure when I became such a sap. What I do know is that Amy makes me happy and I want to make that feeling last as long as possible, even if she's a bit of a commitment phobe.

Only four more days until I'm back home and back to my girl.

CHAPTER THIRTY-THREE

Jackson

Our flight home from our road series was later than anticipated. We first were delayed due to an unexpected downpour, then went into extra innings after coming back from a two run deficit in the seventh inning. We ended up losing when Cincinnati hit a walkoff homer in the tenth. To say I'm ready to be home is the understatement of the year.

Because we got home later than scheduled, I told Amy to stay at her place for the night rather than waiting up to meet me at my condo when she has work the next day. Selfishly, I would have rather had her come over, but I know that would just make work today more difficult for her. Today is another off-day for us, so at least I got to sleep in.

Hayden and I meet up for coffee and he comes back to my condo to play video games for a bit. Once he leaves, I book the trip for Amy and me to go to Telluride next month. I reserve us a room in a luxury hotel in Mountain Village, just a gondola ride over the mountain from the more touristy side of Telluride. I suspect Amy will like Mountain Village a little more than Telluride. From what I can tell from my online research, Mountain Village seems more spa- and hotel-oriented. I will be booking a few appointments at various spas to ensure my girl leaves our trip feeling pampered.

I take Bruno on his second long walk of the day, because apparently I don't know what to do with myself on off days anymore. I take care of some paperwork Sean wanted me to work on, sign a stack of photographs for my publicist to use for charity events, and talk to Nate on the phone for a few minutes to catch up. Amy gets off work in an hour. I can wait for her here, but I'd rather surprise her at work again.

I was able to book a reservation at a Michelin starred restaurant in River North, which is closer to the museum campuses. It makes more sense to leave from Amy's work rather than crisscross the city all night.

By the time I park outside the planetarium, it's almost time for Amy to go home for the night. Chicago traffic is becoming more and more impossible to predict these days, and the normally quick drive took me longer than I planned for. Luckily, I can see Amy's car across the lot near employee parking, so I know she's still here.

By now, museum staff and even security know me as Amy's boyfriend and greet me when I walk in. I return their warm greetings and see myself to Amy's office in the basement. It's generally off-limits to the public, but I've visited her here enough that no one thinks twice.

When I make it to the threshold of Amy's office, she doesn't notice me at first. She's scrolling, staring at something on her computer screen that is making her scrunch her nose in the most adorable way. She's got a pen tucked into her ponytail. She's also got another pen absentmindedly dangling from the corner of her mouth; she's clearly forgotten about the original in her hair. She looks so fucking cute I can't stand it.

I lean against the door frame, admiring Amy at work. When she looks up and notices me, she jumps a little.

"Jesus, Jacks! Way to creep up on a girl!" she says, clutching her chest. There's that nickname again. *Jacks.* I'll never get tired of her saying it.

"I thought I'd swing by and see if you're interested in hitting up L'Âme. I made a reservation for 8:00." Amy takes a sharp inhale.

"L'Âme? That new French restaurant?"

I smirk. "Wanna go?"

"I would love to! How did you manage to get us a reservation? It's impossible to get in there!" I shrug. The real reason is that I had Sean call in a favor, but that doesn't sound as romantic or cool. I walk toward her desk, leaning over it to cup her cheek and give her a slow, lazy kiss.

"I missed you, pretty girl."

Amy kisses me back, pulling my lower lip into her mouth and sucking gently. "I missed you too. Oh my gosh, I'm so excited to go to L'Âme! Can I finish sending a few emails first? Then I'm all yours."

"Babe, take all the time you need. We still have a couple hours but since L'Âme is closer here than our places, I figured I'd intercept you before you made it home."

Amy gets to work finishing her tasks for the day. I take a seat in front of her desk. Amy's office isn't big. It's barely big enough to fit two chairs in front of her desk. When we had dinner here with KJ a few weeks ago, we were forced to get cozy, but luckily KJ is little so it wasn't too terrible. It's a little more spacious without a third person in here, but "cramped" seems to be the overall theme of the room.

I pull out my phone and chip away at some of my emails and texts myself. Phones aren't allowed in the dugout during games, so I consistently have a backlog of communication from friends and family members in my texts that I respond to usually several days late. After about half an hour, during which several people have poked their heads into Amy's tiny office to say goodnight, Amy announces she's done for the day. I'm pretty sure we're the last employees left here, except for security. Amy is nothing if not dedicated to her job.

She starts to gather her things, preparing to leave.

"We've got some time before eight. What do you want to do to kill time before dinner?" She's distracted, rummaging through her purse for something so she doesn't notice me round her desk to stand right behind her. She straightens up and turns, almost bumping into my chest.

"Hi," she says sheepishly as I remove the pen from her hair. "Oh, I forgot I put that there."

"I think it's adorable," I say before kissing her upper lip, gently sucking on it as Amy melts in my arms. "I have an idea of something we can do to pass the time."

I lift Amy's hips onto her desk and stand between her legs. She's wearing the sexiest sundress I've ever seen, with little lemons all over it. I slide her green cardigan off her shoulders. The lack of a sweater makes the swell of her breasts that much more noticeable and I can't help myself. I need a taste. I pull gently on the fabric, freeing her gorgeous nipples and take one into my mouth. Amy immediately moans and brings her hands to my hair. I let go of her breast with a pop before taking the other into my mouth and sucking hard. Amy squirms on top of her desk and I know if I were to check, my girl would be dripping for me. I love how responsive her body is.

"What are my rules tonight?" Amy asks innocently, and the look she gives me as she licks her lips goes straight to my hardening cock.

"No rules, baby. Just let me have my way with you."

"I suppose I can do that."

I slide my hands up Amy's luscious thighs, hitching the skirt of her dress higher. Amy is practically writhing on the desk, fidgeting in anticipation of what's to come.

"Jacks..." She moans. I squeeze her thighs under my hands, sucking and pulling on her nipple. Amy's hands slide down my chest and fumble with my belt. She palms my hard cock outside of my pants, almost giving up on the belt buckle when it doesn't immediately come undone. I groan right along with her.

My hands reach the apex of her thighs and I hook my thumb under her panties.

"Baby, you're soaked."

"Mmmhmm."

I slide my thumb over her clit and Amy jolts. I huff a laugh, hooking my fingers around the waistband of her panties. She lifts her hips and I pull them off, at the same time kneeling in front of her. She looks like a goddess, all heat and desire. She looks powerful and sexy and *mine,* I think as I lower my mouth to her drenched pussy.

Amy sucks in a breath and I groan at the taste of her. I'll never get tired of this; I can never get enough of Amy. I've always liked eating pussy, but Amy's is a fantasy come to life.

"God, baby, you taste so good. Lay back and relax. I'm going to be here awhile." I throw her ankles over my shoulders and feast.

Thank goodness everyone seems to have left for the night because Amy is not holding back. Her sweet little gasps interspersed with low moans are the soundtrack of our evening and I'm planning on playing it on repeat until we have to leave for dinner. When I slide one finger in Amy's cunt and curl it slightly, she comes immediately.

I don't slow down.

"Jacks, Jacks, Jacks," Amy chants, and I can feel the build of another orgasm in the shaking of her legs. I add a second finger, then a third. When I apply pressure to the outside of Amy's abdomen, I'm rewarded with a gush of wetness to the lower half of my face.

"Hell yes," I mutter, continuing to stroke my fingers. Amy is silent and I think she may have stopped breathing. I pause, glancing up at her. "You okay, love? Talk to me."

"Oh my god," Amy moans. "That was....I've never..."

I laugh. "Buckle up. I'm just getting started with you. I've got two hours to kill and plan on making you come at least two more times." Amy whimpers.

I know we both hear footsteps in the hallway at the same time because we both freeze. They're still far enough away that I know–or hope–their owner hasn't heard anything, but the sound is getting closer. Amy's office door is wide open.

She scrambles to pull her dress up at the chest and down at her waist to cover herself. Her discarded panties on the floor are behind the desk and out of the line of sight. I quickly and quietly rise and make it to the door in four strides. I guess it's good that Amy's office is tiny; the door isn't that far away. I snick it shut and turn the lock quietly.

Amy is standing behind me breathing heavily.

"Oh my god," she mouths, covering her face in embarrassment.

"It's okay. No one saw or heard anything. I've got you, Ames." We listen quietly, barely breathing, as who I assume is security walks past Amy's office door and continues on. Amy closes her eyes and presses her forehead against the door, sighing in relief.

"I guess we won't be adding exhibitionism to your list of kinks," I joke, trying to lighten the mood.

"I can't believe that almost happened," Amy groans. I love to make her moan, but I'd rather she be making those noises in pleasure, rather than embarrassment. I pull her back into my arms.

"I'm not done with you," I whisper against her neck, my voice full of promise. Amy's breath catches as I walk my fingers down her chest, pinching her nipple through the fabric of her dress. She grinds her ass back into my erection. I'm still hard from earlier; almost getting caught did nothing to soften me and all I want to do is fuck Amy against this door.

"Do it," she taunts. I guess I voiced my desires aloud.

"Put your hands on the door," I instruct, my voice instantly gravelly with desire. My dick is so hard it's almost painful. I pull it out of my unbuttoned pants while throwing the bottom of Amy's skirt up around her tilted hips. I can't get the condom on fast enough, but once I do, I drag my cock through her wetness.

"I love how wet you are for me. You're ready for my cock." I say it as a statement, rather than a question. The answer was already revealed when I saw Amy's arousal sliding down her thighs.

"Jackson, I need you," Amy pants, pressing her ass back toward me. I bring my hand down on her right ass cheek and am rewarded with another gush of wetness on my cock. I'm not even inside her yet, just notched at her entrance. She's so drenched that I slide in on one thrust easily.

"You feel as good as you taste, Amy. Your pussy was made for my cock. I've been thinking about fucking you all day." I tell Amy how I missed her between thrusts, keeping up a steady stream of praise. "You're such a good fucking girl, taking my cock so well after being without it for a week."

I reach around and fondle Amy's perfect tits as they're pressed against her door. The door rattles within the hinges each time I power into Amy. I spank her again and she screams, shattering around me. The sensation of her pussy walls fluttering around me sends me into sensory overload. I grip her hips tighter before spilling my load inside the condom.

Pressing my forehead into Amy's shoulder, I pause to catch my breath. Amy is breathing just as hard as I am, a slight sheen of sweat across her brow.

"Baby, you are so beautiful. So perfect. You did so well." The words spill out of me, reminding Amy how exceptional she is and how much I missed her. As we stand together, pressed against each other, catching our breaths and collecting ourselves, I'm struck with a not-entirely-unexpected thought.

I love Amy.

That thought should scare me, given how skittish Amy is about commitment, but I find the feeling of loving Amy comforting, like wrapping myself in a warm blanket in front of a bonfire on a chilly

Midwestern evening. I can love Amy quietly from the sidelines, subtly from beside her, and loudly when she's ready.

One thing is for sure, though: I will keep steadily loving Amy, whether she's ready for it or not. Right now, she's not ready to hear me say it, so I'll keep it to myself. She'll absorb my love through her skin by osmosis. I'll let it seep through her pores until it becomes a part of her. Because she just as equally has become a part of me.

Just because I can't tell her I love her yet, it doesn't mean I don't feel it and I won't continue to show it, even if I keep those three little words to myself.

CHAPTER THIRTY-FOUR

Amy

"Okay, but this is my favorite room," I say, pulling Jackson toward a closed door. In all of his years of living in Chicago, he told me he never actually visited any of the museums we have here, including the planetarium. I can't imagine having all of these museums at my fingertips and not taking complete advantage. As it is, I spend a good deal of the time I work here in awe of my surroundings.

I push Jackson into the darkened room. I can just barely make out where to walk by little illuminated lights on the floor. He takes a few tentative steps inside, but when he sees I've stopped by the control panel on the wall by the door, he slows. I wave him toward the middle of the room.

"Go in the center. That's the best spot." I direct him further into the room. There's nothing in the middle of the floor he can trip on, but I guess my ability to see in the dark is a little better than Jackson's because he walks hesitantly forward. "Look up."

"Okay, what am I suppos–"

Jackson's words are cut off when the star show begins. The domed screen ahead of and above him swirls with gray and purple storm clouds as fans in the walls circulate a cool breeze. The "winds" pick up, tousling Jackson's perfect dark hair. He grins. The sky above him opens up to a dazzling thunderstorm, imaginary raindrops falling from the screen as flashes of lightning temporarily light up the room before plunging us back into near darkness. Thunder rumbles in the background, steadily growing louder, sending vibrations through the floor under our feet.

The show itself is spectacular, morphing from treacherous thunderstorms to serene stargazing conditions, but I'm caught up in the awe on Jackson's face. I suspected he would like this exhibit–who wouldn't? I didn't expect the childlike wonder and joy on his face to be so transparent. Seeing Jackson in awe makes me fall a little more for him, and I caution myself yet again about getting too close. In a tiny recess of my mind, however, I already know I'm in trouble. Because once Jackson inevitably lets me go, I'll be left hollow. I tried to shield myself from him, fortifying the defenses around my heart, but I did exactly what I was afraid of. I still gave Jackson a piece of my heart. I should have known it would be impossible to resist his charms. The way he swooped in and provided me with steady, unwavering and attentive care? How would anyone be able to resist?

Now I'm terrified for the moment when he decides to stomp on that precious piece of my heart he doesn't even know belongs to him.

CHAPTER THIRTY-FIVE

Amy

"L'Âme means soul in French," our waitress explains to us. "Please enjoy the heart and soul we've put into your meal." With a flourish, she sets down an amuse bouche and begins explaining the ingredients and what sounds like an incredibly complex preparation method.

I'm practically bouncing in my seat with giddiness. I love to cook, although what I do is more playing around than the science experiments they conduct here at L'Âme. Danny would lose his mind if he knew we were here. He loves everything cooking and molecular gastronomy; the amount of time we've spent in his apartment kitchen probably qualifies us to work in a kitchen somewhere professionally, but it's just a hobby for us.

Our server is explaining the adjustments they made to their typical recipe to allow for the meal tonight to be plant-based. My heart swells at the thoughtfulness, realizing Jackson must have made arrangements for my dietary restrictions.

"Jacks," I hiss after the server leaves. "You didn't have to make them change the menu for me!"

"Amy, it is their job to accommodate dietary restrictions. They didn't seem to have an issue with it when I mentioned it earlier."

We haven't even ordered yet. The amuse bouche came shortly after we sat down, so I haven't even had a chance to look at the menu and parse out what I can and cannot eat. I wasn't going to make a fuss; I'm used to having more limited options at certain restaurants and French cuisine generally doesn't scream vegetarian-friendly. I'm just happy to be here, soaking up the experience that is L'Âme. But there Jackson goes, making the moment even more special, more memorable, just by being his normal, thoughtful self.

We order cocktails, and Jackson's comes out in a small, wooden chest. Upon delivery, the chest is opened and sweet-smelling smoke wafts out. The man who delivers it explains that the smoke not only flavors Jackson's drink, but the scent prepares our palates for the whiskey-based cocktail. My drink falls on the opposite end of the spectrum: pink and girly in a martini glass with a liquid-filled orb floating on top. The server explains that as the sphere's ice casing melts, the liquid inside infuses the drink, changing the color to lilac and modifying the flavor profile to be more floral and tempered. The pink part of the drink is fantastic, tiny bubbles of effervescence popping on my tongue; I can't wait for the evolution as time wears on.

The meal progresses, with each dish more fantastic than the last. We start with kombucha-infused plant "caviar," followed by cream of pumpkin soup with coconut foam, before transitioning to celeriac root "scallops" with balsamic toffee beets.

Throughout the meal, Jackson and I chat. He asks me what my happiest childhood memory is, and I pause, chewing a "scallop" contemplatively.

"Probably when my dad chaperoned my field trip in first grade to the science museum. I don't even remember too much about the actual event. I was just so excited to have my dad there, instead of my mom. Not that my mom isn't amazing!" I add quickly. "It's just that all the other kids had their moms with them, but *I* got to bring my dad."

"Are you close with your dad? You don't mention him much."

"We're more of the touch-base-every-so-often kind of father/daughter duo," I explain. "We're really different people. He and my mom were never married, and they split when I was in fifth grade. He lives in the Bay area now, out in California. He's a sculptor."

"How often do you get to see him?"

"Not very. The last time I saw him in person was a few years ago when he came to Chicago for an exhibition one of his pieces was in. He's really talented. But he also is a bit of a loner, so he's happier holed up in his studio in San Francisco. We video chat every few months but we kind of are always searching for conversational topics when we talk, so we tend to keep our chats on the shorter end. It's okay though. I know my dad loves me, and I obviously love him. We just have a less traditional relationship that works for both of us."

Jackson nods his head.

"What about you? What's your happiest childhood memory?"

Jackson takes a long time to answer. So long, in fact, that I start to worry he's not going to answer me.

"I don't really have a lot of happy childhood memories," he reluctantly admits. "My childhood was not really traditional either. My dad died when I was young, and my mom's life kind of went off the rails at that point. Once it was no longer socially acceptable for us to be stuck in the grieving process for my dad, and the rest of our family went back to their lives, my mom kind of...lost herself. It was really hard in the beginning, but when my brothers and I stopped expecting her to be a parent, it got easier." I cover my mouth. Whatever I expected Jackson to say, it was not that. My mom is one of my best friends. I can't imagine giving up on her parenting me as a child.

"What do you mean, you had to stop expecting her to be a parent?"

"As I've gotten older, I've tried to give my mom some grace, but I don't think I'll ever forgive her for essentially abandoning us. My mom still *technically* lived at our house," Jackson says with a sigh.

"Technically?"

"She slept at home, sometimes. But after the family left following Dad's funeral, she kind of went from man to man, I guess trying to find herself in them. I lost count of the number of men she dated; she didn't bring all of them home, so I guess I'll never actually know. We were kind of left to our own devices, Sean, Nate, and I. Sean took on the brunt of the responsibilities. He was essentially thrown into parenting in high school."

He takes a sip of his drink, as if he's fortifying himself to continue his story. I don't know what to say, so I don't say anything.

"Sean basically raised me. Raised Nate, too. My dad left us enough money that we could scrape by financially, but Sean filled every other hole there was in the loss of not only my dad, but my mom, too." Jackson swallows. "I guess my happiest childhood memory was spending time with him and Nate, playing catch. It didn't happen often when all three of us could just be kids together, but when it did, even then, I knew it was special."

My eyes fill with tears as I watch Jackson share his trauma. I cover his hand with mine and give him a gentle squeeze.

"I'm so sorry that happened to you," I whisper. Jackson clears his throat. "Where is your mom now? Do you have a relationship with her now?"

Jackson laughs grimly. "I wish my mother forgetting she had three children was as bad as it got. When I was in college, she started dating Ron." He says Ron's name with a sneer, as if the name itself was poison. "Ron ruined the last little scraps of decency left in my mother. If I envision my mother's dependence on men as something of an addiction, her relationship with Ron makes a lot more sense. He somehow sunk his claws so deep into my mother, she lost all sense of herself. I don't know the details of their relationship. I don't want to know. I don't know if he was abusive toward her or just a dick. But he also introduced my mother to a few new vices. Drinking is one, but that was never as bad as showing her the seedy underbelly of the gambling world. When sports betting became more ubiquitous a few years ago, my mother latched onto that like it was her last, dying hope. I don't even know if she and Ron are still together, but he seems to have made a lasting impression regardless."

I let that information wash over me, sink into my skin. Jackson has had to deal with so much. So much that I didn't know about, that probably very few people know about. He's remarkably well adjusted given all that he's been through, and I tell him so.

"That's what years of therapy do for you. I finally started therapy in college, and it helped me sort through everything. But when your mother abandons you at a young age, you kind of realize there's nothing life can throw at you that will be worse than that. So there's that, I guess," he finishes with a shrug.

The tears I've been holding at bay finally slip loose, tracking down my cheeks and splashing onto my lap.

"Don't cry, baby," Jackson soothes, cupping my face and gently swiping my tears with the pads of his thumb. "I'm okay, really. I made it through. I'm on to bigger and better things."

"I know, but I wish you didn't have to experience any of that," I say, my voice trembling. Trying to stave off a fresh wave of tears as I think of the child Jackson was, struggling through the loss of both parents in two very different ways, I lean into Jackson's hand. "Your mom doesn't know what she's missing," I whisper.

"You're right. She doesn't," he adds sadly. "But I mean it, I'm okay. I just don't share that with a lot of people. I hate that it's part of my history, even though I know it's made me a stronger, more resilient person."

"Thank you for trusting me with your story," I say quietly. Jackson nods.

"Now that I've ruined dinner with my sob story–"

"You didn't, Jacks. I'm glad you told me. I'm proud to know all parts of you."

We finish the meal with coffee (of course) and black sesame pudding spheres which are as gorgeous as they are delicious. My mind is still reeling with all Jackson shared with me tonight. I try to reconcile the Jackson I know–the strong, handsome, thoughtful man–with the child Jackson must have been. I send a silent prayer of thanks for Sean and Nate and their help in molding Jackson to be the man he is today.

CHAPTER THIRTY-SIX

Jackson

Walking into the ballpark the next day, I feel somehow lighter. There are a few fans waiting outside the player parking lot–nothing like the amount that was there on opening day, but now that the Foxes have been doing so well this season, more and more trickle by the entrance to the gated lot each day. I make a point to stop and sign autographs and chat with each of the fans briefly.

The jokes and smiles come easily today. To be honest, they come easily most days and especially most times I interact with the fans, but today, there's an added feeling of lightness to my interactions. The lightness continues as I stroll into the lobby of the building that houses our clubhouse, greeting the security guards on my way.

"You seem to be in a good mood, pretty boy," Caleb remarks as I reach my locker and begin changing into my athletic shorts and moisture-wicking tee.

"Andrews, you should be in a good mood, too. We get to play baseball today," I remind him.

"We do that everyday," he quips.

"Yeah. We're a couple of lucky bastards." I flash him a grin which he returns slowly.

Tonight's game ended up being a loss for the Foxes, but I played well. It's hard when you have almost the best game of your career but your team still loses. Conflicting emotions are warring inside me, even as I do my postgame interview.

"JJ, you had a night careers are made out of," Robin, our field reporter, starts. "What do you think contributed to your success both on the field and at the plate?"

"Robin, it's all about the hard work, putting it in with my teammates. We've got a great group of guys, and between the coaching staff, our dieticians, and my strength coach, I'm feeling stronger and more confident than ever. I wish we could have pulled off that win tonight, but we'll be back stronger and better than ever tomorrow afternoon."

I finish the on-field interview with Robin before I'm shuffled off to the post-game press conference in one of the media rooms inside. I'm seated between Caleb and Benny, our manager.

"Caleb, you seemed distracted tonight. Care to comment on your night?" Caleb *is* distracted tonight. Jenny learned of the results of another scan this afternoon and called Caleb during batting practice to relay the news that while the cancer hasn't spread, it hasn't shrunk as quickly as her doctors were expecting. He spent half an hour after that call alone in a locked training room trying to collect himself before finally allowing me in to talk to him. He practically had to beg Benny to let him play tonight, telling him that having him sit on the bench would only allow him to stew in his emotions further.

Jenny and Caleb have been through so much already. Instead of being able to enjoy their engagement and plan their wedding, all of their free time is spent shuttling to and from doctor's appointments and working on Jenny's battle with breast cancer. It's not fair. I hold a level of anger with the universe for what it's done to my best friend and the love of his life, and I hate that this is outside of my control. Instead, I try to focus on what I can control, which is the direction of this interview right now.

Caleb takes a deep breath, ready to take responsibility for his less-than-stellar play tonight. Under the table and outside the view of the media, I press my thumb into his knee, forcing him to pause.

"I think I can speak for everyone when I say we wish the Foxes could have pulled off a win tonight," I start. The question wasn't directed at me, but there's no way in hell I'm allowing Caleb to answer or for him to in any way feel like what happened on the field tonight was his responsibility. I catch Benny's eye out of my peripheral vision and realize he was half a second behind me, about to take the question himself, too. I'm momentarily reassured to confirm that everyone loves Caleb and Jenny and has their backs.

"It'd be great if we had a crystal ball and could anticipate every play, but that also wouldn't make for very exciting baseball. I think the best we can do is review the tape from today and learn from our mistakes and be better tomorrow," I say.

"Easy for you to say, JJ," Tom Stafford, a reporter for one of Chicago's biggest newspapers jokes. "You made no mistakes tonight. Talk about a career maker."

"Sure I did. I could have flipped the ball to Andrews faster in the third, and that could have been a double play that ended the inning. Instead, we only got the out at second. That's on me," I respond honestly. "And I struck out in the fourth. Who knows, if I had gotten a better jump on that ball, I might have been able to hit for the cycle."

It's doubtful, but still a possibility. I ended the night with a single, double, and two-run homer–just a triple shy of the cycle. While I would have loved to have done that, as it would have been the first time in my career and something many players don't ever accomplish, my goal right now is to take the heat off of poor Caleb. After a few more mundane questions, we're dismissed so the press can talk strategy and tactics with Benny.

Benny is a natural with the press. I'm not terrible at interacting with the media, but I'm never one hundred percent comfortable with them like he is. Benny can laugh and joke around with the press and there's no doubt he's having a great time doing it. My jokes feel a little more practiced, a little less loose. There's a reason Samuel Benjamin is running this team.

Caleb and I hit the showers.

"You okay, man?" I ask him tentatively. I know he's not, but I need to say something to break the tension billowing off of the man.

"I'll be fine," he says through gritted teeth.

"Really? Because I'm worried you're going to crack a molar with how much you're grinding your jaw there."

"I'll be fine. I have to be. Jenny is counting on me to be the strong one right now. And playing like shit isn't helping. The last thing I need is the entire city on my back, too."

"Let's take a step back. The questions at the press conference were out of line, which is why Benny and I took that off your plate. Just because you have one off game doesn't mean the city will abandon you. We lost as a team. Not because of you." Caleb just shakes his head and begins aggressively shampooing his hair. "You and Jenny are in this together. You're allowed to be angry at the cards she was dealt. You're allowed to be fucking enraged that she has to go through more treatment than what the doctors originally predicted," I continue, echoing the sentiments I told him earlier in the training room.

"I wish it were me, instead of her," Caleb grits out.

"I know. Me, too, man." I sigh. It's the truth. Jenny doesn't deserve this; Caleb doesn't deserve this as her partner. "Go home, Caleb. Be with her. Let me send over food tonight. It'll be one less thing for you guys to worry about." Most of our meals are provided for us at the ballpark, since we spend so much time here anyway.

The postgame meal has been set up since the ninth inning, but Jenny's treatment makes her nauseous. These days, all she seems to be tolerating is fruit and smoothies.

When we get back to our lockers and are drying off, I place an order at Green Jungle, Jenny's favorite place for acai bowls. At least in smoothie form, Jenny can get more protein and nutrients blended in. I wish there was more I could do, but for now, I'm as stuck as Caleb feels.

Amy is waiting for me when I get home. I gave her the code to my building a few weeks ago and she knows where I keep my spare key. I walk in the door, exhausted from my day, and fall into her arms. As I stand there, holding Amy as much as she holds me, her fingers running through my hair the way she knows I love, I know that I've truly arrived home.

Because home is wherever Amy is.

CHAPTER THIRTY-SEVEN
Jackson

I breathe deeply, soaking in Amy's jasmine and orange blossom scent. I find myself craving the fragrance. Kim, one of our trainers, walked by the other day with a mug of jasmine tea, and the smell was both oddly comforting and arousing at the same time. Amy buries her head deeper in my chest.

"I'm sorry about the game, but Jacks, you looked *fantastic!*" The way she spoke the last word, tinged with a sense of awe and pride, makes my chest hurt.

In my years of therapy, I did a lot of intensive introspection and really developed my self-awareness. I learned that sometimes I doubt whether I'm enough for people, since I clearly wasn't enough for my mom. I worked through most of that, but when Carolyn more than clearly communicated I wasn't enough for her, I revisited therapy again for a few months. Now, I'm pretty solidly self-aware and self-assured, but that doesn't mean I don't benefit from reminders here and there that I really am enough. And given Amy's reluctance to get more serious, her praise soothes me in a way I didn't realize I needed.

It makes me wonder what sort of reassurances Amy needs. She says she doesn't want something serious, but her actions in our relationship indicate otherwise. We're together all the time when I'm in town, she had no problem committing to exclusivity, and she's met my brothers. Yes, she still balked at the WAG badge, but I'm beginning to realize that maybe Amy is uncomfortable with the *idea* of a serious relationship more so than the reality of it. After my conversation the other week with Alicia, I know that Amy has been burned in the past and she's trying to protect herself from it happening again. But seeing as I have no intention of letting Amy go unless she tells me to, she doesn't have to worry about that with me. She just doesn't know that yet. I recognize that it will take some time for her to believe me, but she at least should know the true depth of my feelings.

"Amy," I start before kissing her deeply. "I want to tell you something. Let's go lay down."

I see Amy's nerves yet again play out on her face. It was probably not a great idea for me to start a conversation that way, but I suppose it was better than saying, "We need to talk."

"It's nothing bad!" I reassure her. "I just want to lay with you and catch up."

She follows me to the bedroom. I strip down to my boxer briefs, ready to climb into bed when I catch Amy undressing. There's something so domestic about getting ready for bed together in a completely nonsexual way that makes what I'm about to tell Amy that much easier. My blood heats as I watch her change into one of my old t-shirts. She's swimming in it, and the way it drapes over her body results in a boxy shape, but there's something so sexy about her wearing something of mine that awakens the possessive side of me.

"What?" She asks when she catches me staring.

"Nothing, I just love seeing you in my shirt."

"Would you like to see me out of it?" She flirts back, and as much as I want to take her up on that offer, I want her to know that what I'm saying are truly my thoughts and feelings, rather than something spoken in the throes of passion.

"Yes. Absolutely. But first," I put my hand gently on her wrist, preventing her from taking off the shirt she just put on, and kissing her nose, "let's talk."

"Okay." Amy reluctantly lowers the bottom hem of my tee and I almost regret temporarily turning her down. We climb into bed facing each other and I brush Amy's hair behind her ear. Every time I look at this woman I'm momentarily stunned by her beauty.

"I'm going to say this because you need to know. You deserve to hear it. And I'm saying it with no expectation of hearing you say it back." Amy sucks in a sharp breath; she knows where I'm going and the surprise flitting across her face surprises *me*. I can't believe Amy didn't see this coming. I'm not sure how she could be so oblivious to something so obvious to me. "You deserve to know that you are loved and cherished. And that I'm the one doing the loving and cherishing. I love you, Amy. I'm proud to know you and I love you."

CHAPTER THIRTY-EIGHT

Amy

My breath wooshes out of me.

My mind is reeling and both my mouth and my brain forget how to work. I blink stupidly at Jackson. How is it possible that the world just keeps spinning, people keep walking by on the sidewalk beneath Jackson's apartment, everyone keeps on living, while my brain and lungs and heart stop—while my organs forget how to organ?

Jackson chuckles and kisses my forehead. "Stop overthinking, Ames. It's okay. I really don't need to hear it back but I did need to say it. It changes nothing about us because I've felt it for a while but needed you to know it finally."

This changes nothing? That can't possibly be true. It's already changed things. I had no idea that was what Jackson was going to say. For a moment, when Jackson said he wanted to talk, I experienced a brief period of blinding panic when I thought he was going to give me the "it's not you, it's me" breakup speech.

"Ames, let's watch a movie."

I know Jackson is changing the subject to stop me from freaking out, and maybe it slows the thoughts in my head a little, but I know even as I smile up at him and let him pick a movie from his multiple streaming services, I'll be thinking of this the whole movie.

I was right. The movie Jackson chose for us last night was a comedy, but my head was swimming and all of the jokes fell flat. My laughter came a second or two too late each time and I think Jackson could tell my mind was elsewhere. I'm not sure what he expected.

I believe Jackson loves me. And under normal circumstances, Old Amy would be thrilled with the news. A small part of me *is* thrilled. But I keep trying to stuff that part back into the box I keep my hopes for my relationship with Jackson in. Because Patrick loved me too, or so he said.

At lunch today with Alicia, she can tell my mind is elsewhere. While we stand in line at the bagel shop and deli a few blocks from the museum campus, she eyes me, concern etched on her face.

Our number is called and after grabbing our sandwiches, we make our way to a corner table in the back of the cafe. We had plans to eat outside at the picnic tables on the small sidewalk the deli turned into a patio, but the humidity on the walk over was too much. The chill from the air conditioner has already frozen our sweat, but if we were to eat outside, we would be more miserable, so inside it is. The deli is buzzing with activity at prime lunch time. Normally, Alicia and I don't get enough time to make it off campus for lunch during summer camp, but it's Friday, meaning we have more flexibility in our schedules since the campers are home.

"Spill it. You've been quiet and more in your head than usual. What's going on?"

"Jackson told me he loved me last night." Alicia starts to squeal in excitement but cuts herself off at the lack of enthusiasm on my face.

"And this is a bad thing because...?"

"I don't know. I'm trying so hard not to get sucked into a place where I can get hurt again. This was supposed to be a fun, casual thing...a fling, even!"

Alicia's face is almost pitying and I know immediately that I'm not going to like what she's about to say.

"Girl, that ship has sailed. Tell me what is so wrong with JJ Jeffers loving you?"

"Shh!" I hiss and immediately look around. Chicago media can be ruthless, and I don't need the whole city knowing my boyfriend is in love with me. Okay, even I know how ridiculous that thought is. I shake my head at myself. "Okay, there's nothing wrong with it. I'm happy about it. I mean, I felt a little blindsided when he told me." Alicia's eyes bug out of her head when I say this, but she remains silent, letting me process out loud.

"Jackson is amazing. He's perfect, really. There's nothing I would change about him. I feel lucky to be loved by him. But it wasn't what I expected when I got involved with him and I guess I'm just...scared," I finish lamely.

"You don't want another Patrick situation," she observes astutely.

"Exactly," I sigh in relief that at least my best friend understands. "I guess...I don't know, if I'm being honest with myself, I'm so relieved he loves me. I know, deep down, that it's a good thing. And when he told me last night he had something to tell me, I had a moment of panic when I thought he was going to end things." I pause, and Alicia gives me a *go on* gesture, twirling her hand in front of her.

"The fact that I panicked about that tells you what, exactly?" I swear, Alicia could have been a therapist in another life; she has mastered the contemplative silence strategy. I chew my veggie sandwich, thinking.

"That I don't want Jackson and me to end. That I want to see where this relationship goes."

"Do you think you can do that with one foot out of the door?" Damn. She's good. I shoot her a scowl and she smiles because she knows she's right.

"Fine. I can't. But Leesh, when this ends, it's going to destroy me. Utterly gut me. Far worse than the damage Patrick did."

"Why is that?" Alicia asks, but based on the look on her face, she already knows the answer, even if I'm not ready to admit it to myself. When I don't answer, she continues. "Besides, who says it has to end? He loves you, which, might I add, is the least surprising news ever. Have you seen the way that man looks at you? He thinks you hung the moon and all the stars around it. You don't fall in love and then end things–and I know what you're going to say about Patrick but can we please forget about that twatwaffle for five minutes? We're never going to know why he changed overnight, but that's no longer your problem. He sucks–you know it, I know it. And anyone who would pull the stunt he did on you never really loved you to begin with. I'm sorry, I know that's harsh, but it needed to be said."

I don't say anything for a long time. I pick at the seeds on my everything bagel, no longer interested in eating my sandwich. A part of me knows Alicia is right. A part of me has known that far longer than this conversation would indicate. I'm still so afraid of Jackson shattering my newly repaired heart. Patrick left it in such a fragile state that I'm afraid any more damage will be permanent.

"I'm not ready to get hurt again," I whisper.

"I know, babe. But that's part of life, whether you're in a relationship or not. It's killing me to see you hold yourself back just because of one asshole. Are you really going to let Patrick have that much control over your life?"

I know she's right. Cognitively, logically, she's absolutely right and I know it deep in my bones. It doesn't stop the emotional side of me from wanting to run and hide when I think of not the power that Patrick holds over me, but the power Jackson unknowingly holds over me when he holds my battered, bruised heart in his hands.

CHAPTER THIRTY-NINE

Amy

The next few weeks pass by in a blur. Jackson had two road trips with a home series interspersed between them, so I haven't seen him as much as I would have liked, but that doesn't stop us from calling, texting, and video chatting regularly. When Jackson is home, we spend our nights together. When he's on the road, I fill my nights with yoga, reading, and spending time with my friends.

I feel a little guilty for neglecting Danny and Tim a bit now that I'm spending more time with Jackson, but they waved me off when I expressed it to them. "When you date an international spy, you have to make sacrifices to see him when he's in town," Tim had joked.

Jackson has a day game today and then four days off for the mid-season break. I'm meeting him after the game and we're driving to O'Hare airport together. Jackson booked us a chartered flight to Telluride and I can't wait. I feel a little guilty that he's spending all this money on me, but he insists he can afford it (which I believe) and that I'm worth it (still working on believing that one). I'm finishing packing with the Foxes game on the television in the background. I stop folding the shirt in my hand to watch Jackson's at-bat.

"Now up, number nineteen, JJ Jeffers," the television announcer says calmly. "Jeffers has been struggling at the plate a bit these last few games, batting .197 in his last twenty-five plate appearances." I wince. The announcer isn't wrong, but Jackson is just in a little slump. There's not a reason for him struggling; that's just the way baseball is sometimes, Alicia and Danny reassure me. Jackson hasn't said anything to me about his struggles at the plate other than that he's frustrated and wishes he could do better. He's still doing great in the field, but of course, the announcers don't talk about that.

"He takes a pitch outside for a ball," the television continues. I realize I'm clutching my shirt so tightly it's going to wrinkle it and I won't be able to pack it. We leave in a few hours, which won't be enough time for me to do a load of laundry or iron it because I have barely started packing. I place the shirt neatly inside my suitcase when I hear the unmistakable crack of a wooden bat against a ball, followed immediately by the roar of the crowd. It's not a home run, but Jackson hit the ball deep into the pocket of right field, allowing the runner on second base to easily score.

I send up a silent cheer as Jackson reaches second base on a slide and the hit puts the Foxes up by a run. Jackson needed that. If the Foxes can pull off a win today, it will be much easier to go into the midseason break. Everyone, Jackson included, is much happier when the Foxes win.

That'll shut you up, I think to the announcer. I'm fiercely protective of my man.

The Foxes end up maintaining the lead and winning the game. Jackson texts me after and lets me know he should be at my place to pick me up in an hour, which gives me plenty of time to finish packing, even if it is sooner than expected. Usually, Jackson doesn't leave the ballpark until at least an hour after the game ends. He lets me know that there are no scheduled workouts after the game for anyone. Jackson's strength and conditioning coaches must be as eager as their players to get their vacations started. Apparently there's a mandatory team workout the first day back from the break to make up for the early release today.

At four thirty exactly, Jackson calls me to tell me he is double parked on my street, ready to take me to the airport. When I open the front door to my building, lugging my overpacked suitcase behind me, I see him standing outside the passenger side of his car, leaning against the door with his arms crossed. When he sees me with my suitcase, he jumps into action, taking it from my hand and giving me a quick peck on the lips.

"Not a light packer, I see," he jokes, lifting my heavy suitcase with ease and placing it in his trunk.

"Seeing as you wouldn't tell me the details of all of our plans, I had to come extra prepared."

"If all goes according to plan, you'll be naked most of the trip, so I'm not sure why you felt the need to pack so much." He winks. My core throbs in anticipation. "I meant because you'll be at the spa so much, dirty girl." I scowl at him as he opens my door and helps me climb in. Jackson just laughs.

"Look what came in," he says as he climbs in the car after closing my door. A lanyard hangs from his finger. On the end is an ID badge with my name and picture on it. He puts the car in drive as we head towards the airport.

"What is that? And where did you get it?"

"This, pretty girl, is your official WAG badge!" Jackson is more excited about this than I am. I didn't realize he was going to have one made; I thought he was going to wait for me to tell him when I was ready.

My lack of enthusiasm must show on my face, because Jackson rolls his eyes and mumbles, "It's just a badge, Amy, not a marriage proposal. Just take it."

He's silent for the rest of the ride and I can tell it's because of my reaction to the badge.

"I'm sorry. Thank you for having that made for me. That was really thoughtful," I tell him, leaning across the center console of Jackson's Range Rover and giving him a kiss on the cheek when we stop at the next red light. The tension in Jackson's shoulders and around his eyes lessens visibly. He sighs.

"Look, I'm not trying to pressure you with this. But you *are* my girlfriend. It just would be nice if you weren't always dragging your feet about it."

He has a point. I've been a terrible girlfriend in that regard. I think back to my conversation with Alicia a few weeks ago and internally vow to do better. Jackson is everything I've wanted and if I don't start getting my shit together, he's not going to want to stick around. My self-preservation is going to be the death of me.

The plane is incredible. As soon as I finish climbing the stairs of the tiny jet bridge onto the chartered jet, a flight attendant greets me and offers me a drink.

"Oh, um, I would love one."

"How about champagne?" Jackson suggests from my side.

"Is that really an option? Do you have champagne?" Jackson laughs at my naivete, but the flight attendant gives me an indulgent smile.

"Of course, I'll bring you each a glass. Make yourselves comfortable. I'm Carissa; let me know if there's anything I can do to make the flight more enjoyable for you."

I look around the cabin in awe. It's small, but the flight to Colorado isn't that long. The seats are basically oversized armchairs facing a small table. There's a small loveseat along the side as well.

With his hand on the small of my back, Jackson guides me to the chairs. I place my purse on the empty seat next to me as Jackson sits in the seat across the table.

"This is so nice!" I've never been surrounded by such luxury and five star service when it's just the two of us. The only thing comparable was our experience at L'Âme and even then, we were surrounded by tables and other diners. Jackson seems to be enjoying my astonishment and giddy reaction when the flight attendant brings us our champagne, leaving the bottle in a chiller bucket on the table. Jackson's earlier annoyance with me seems to be forgotten, but I'll make a point to make it up to him this weekend. Jackson is so selfless, and Alicia is right; I need to get over the effects of Patrick and stop holding myself back.

"So do you want to hear about our plans or do you want to keep the air of mystery?"

"No, I'm too excited! Tell me everything."

"It's going to be kind of late by the time we get in, so I thought we could just hit up the hotel bar tonight and settle in. But tomorrow we could do a hike if you wanted, then spa reservations during the day, and dinner at a place where it's supposed to be the best spot to view the sunset. We have more spa reservations the following day too, and I thought we could spend our downtime relaxing or shopping. They have yoga in the morning in the little main area of Mountain Village too."

"Jacks, that all sounds amazing. Thank you so much for planning everything. I've been looking forward to this so much!"

We spend the rest of the plane ride curled up on the loveseat together, having migrated over there to be closer to one another. Jackson is playing video games on his Switch and I am snuggled up with my Kindle.

"What are you reading now?" Jackson asks conversationally while still manipulating his controller.

"Can you talk and play at the same time?" I'm surprised. I guess I expected him to be one of those guys that zones out.

"I'm a man of many talents." He throws me a wink. I roll my eyes. "Don't worry baby, I'll be making your eyes roll back in a different way soon after we get to the hotel." His eyes darken with promise and I squeeze my thighs together. "Don't look at me like that, Amy. This plane is too small and too open to join the mile high club. Unless you want to give Carissa a show?"

I lightly shove his arm, causing his finger to slip off the joystick. He laughs.

"Now I just lost in Mario Kart!" He fakes disappointment, then turns his game off. Jackson angles his upper body toward me and pulls my hand into his, resting it on his lap. "Whatcha reading, Ames?"

"Well, I started a new romance this morning when I was laying in bed, procrastinating on packing. It's about this hockey player who falls for his best friend's younger sister."

Jackson gasps, looking wounded. "You're reading *hockey* romance? Where's the baseball romance?"

"There's not as many baseball romances as there are hockey. Besides, there's something different about hockey. I don't really watch it or follow a team, but I can eat up a good hockey romance."

"Is it the missing teeth? Or the sliding around wearing knives on their feet that does it for you?"

I huff. "Don't make fun, Jacks. I get a lot of good ideas from these books."

"Ideas?"

When my cheeks pink and I don't respond, Jackson plucks my Kindle out of my hands and begins reading, holding the device in his far arm, just outside of my reach. After about thirty seconds of trying to get my Kindle back, I give up. Jackson's likely read too far already. After about a minute of reading, Jackson turns back to me with a look of stunned silence.

"Holy shit, Amy. *These* are the books you read?"

"Don't make fun, Jackson. They're easy reads and they make me happy." I immediately go on the defensive.

"Baby, I'm not making fun. I'm just surprised! Had I known you were reading these kinds of books, I would have asked for recommendations. This is awesome. I'm *way* in support of this. When Sean mentioned the book cover thing, I just thought it'd be like a chick flick." He hands me back my Kindle and gives me a look of rapt attention. "Now tell me. What sort of good ideas do you get from these books?"

I fidget in my seat. Carissa is far too close not to overhear anything I might say to Jackson. It's bad enough he made those mile high comments earlier. He nudges me, glancing over at Carissa and correctly interpreting my hesitation. She's busy reorganizing the compartments in the galley, so I doubt she's listening, but I don't want to embarrass myself anyway.

"You don't have to tell me, honey. You can show me later." He smirks. This man will be the death of me.

If I thought the chartered plane to Telluride was luxurious, I was not prepared for the hotel in Mountain Village. As we pull up to the porte-cochère, I take in the stacked stonework and flickering real flames inside the lanterns. Upon registration, we are offered a choice of a glass of champagne or their homemade spiced whiskey. A little sugared out from the champagne on the plane, we both elect the glass of whiskey, Jackson taking his on ice.

The front desk host takes us on a tour of the property while our bags are being delivered to the room. I may have died a little bit and gone to heaven. The area we're staying in, Mountain Village, is very appropriately named. The hotels in this area are situated in a semicircle around a large, grassy area, which, we're told, hosts yoga in the mornings. Mountains surround us on all sides. Little fire pits dot the perimeter of the grassy area, surrounded by a mix of wooden adirondack and lounge chairs draped with cozy blankets. The mountain air is noticeably thinner up here, and our tour guide recommends some remedies to combat the feeling of dizziness.

We continue walking, whiskeys in hand, around Mountain Village. The host points out breakfast cafes, various spa locations, and where to pick up the gondolas to take a trip into Telluride proper. Large gondolas float above us, tethered to thick cables pulling some over the mountain toward the larger town and some in the opposite direction. Unattached gondolas are sprinkled throughout Mountain Village, serving as places to eat or take a private phone call. Tall ceramic pots spill purple-leafed vines while narrow green stalks stretch skyward from the middle.

"I may have fallen in love with this place already," I admit. The host smiles; she must get that reaction a lot.

By the time we are brought to our suite, I should be used to being impressed, but the more I see of this place, the more amazed I am. Jackson really went all-out for us by booking this suite.

The fireplaces in both the living room and our bedroom are roaring upon our entrance, casting a cozy and welcoming glow to the place. The kitchen is open and airy, containing a large wooden dining table under an artistically hung chandelier and massive, stainless steel appliances. If I was planning on doing any cooking this trip, I'd be enthralled, but Jackson already listed all of the restaurants and breweries he wants us to try. The kitchen leads to the living room, which, in addition to the large stone fireplace, houses an overstuffed couch, two armchairs, and a coffee table, artfully decorated with knick knacks on the surface that match those on the fireplace mantle. The living room opens to a large balcony with outdoor seating where Jackson and I will likely spend our mornings and evenings. Almost every seat in the place has a blanket neatly folded across it; whoever designed this place perfectly married luxury and cozy all in one and I am a big fan.

"Jackson, this is stunning," I say as I wander into the bedroom, where I am, yet again, awed by the luxury and attention to detail. The bed is massive, much larger than a standard king size mattress. The vaulted ceiling with its exposed beam down the center gives the room an even bigger feel. I gasp when I reach the bathroom, which houses the largest bathtub I've ever seen. I've always wanted to take a bath when both my knees and my boobs are covered by the water and it seems I'll get my wish.

"I'm glad you're happy." Jackson stands behind me, wrapping his arms around me and pressing a kiss to the top of my head. I shiver as he slowly drags his nose against my jaw, planting soft kisses against my neck and collarbones. My hand drifts up behind me to cradle the back of Jackson's head.

Jackson trails one hand lower toward the waistband of my leggings while the other cups my breast. I press back into Jackson, feeling the hard outline of his erection through his jeans.

"Mmmm," I hum as Jackson's hand slides beneath the band of my leggings and into my panties. I can feel his smile against my neck when he finds me soaked.

"Always so wet for me, Amy." I shamelessly grind back against his length. "So needy, tonight. You gonna show me something you've learned from your books?" Jackson pinches my nipple gently as he slides his other hand low enough to insert one finger into me. I pull away, turning my body toward Jackson. The initial surprise on his face morphs into heat and awe when I lower to my knees.

"Fuck my face, Jacks."

He sucks in a sharp breath. "You are perfect, Amy," he praises as I begin unbuttoning his pants. As I lower his zipper, he steps away for a moment and taps some buttons on a control panel on the wall.

"What are you doing?"

"Heated floors." He smirks at me. "So at least you can be more comfortable when I shove my cock down your throat." His dirty words turn me on further and I bite my lip and look up at him, letting him see the heat in my eyes mirrors that shown in his. I pull out his length and stroke it a few times, cupping his balls with my other hand. Jackson closes his eyes for a second, getting lost in the pleasure.

"Open up, baby," he says, tapping his tip against my lips. I happily oblige. Jackson cups my face in both hands. "You look so good on your knees for me, Amy. You're a fucking goddess." He takes a deep breath. "Are you ready for me?"

I nod, my mouth too full to make any sort of intelligible noise. He holds my head still and slowly snaps his hips forward. He pauses, letting me adjust to him and I take deep breaths through my nose, allowing my throat to relax further. Jackson must sense when I do, because he then sets a ruthless pace against me.

"Tap my thigh if it gets too much," he warns, but I know I'll never admit defeat. A few times, Jackson activates my gag reflex and I have to breathe deeply through my nose again. Tears stream down my face and the noises of pleasure Jackson makes motivate me to relax my throat even further. The warmth under my knees actually does feel nice, a thoughtful little touch to make the experience more comfortable for me. I moan around Jackson's length, continuing to massage his balls, drawing out the sexiest groan from him.

"I don't want to come down your pretty throat tonight. Not yet anyway." Jackson draws his hips back and I hollow my cheeks, causing him to pull out of me with an audible pop. "You were so good, but I'm not ready to come yet. I need you to come a few times first."

Jackson holds out his hand, helping me to stand. As soon as I'm upright, he steps out of his pants and underwear and bends at the waist, hoisting me over his shoulder and carrying me to the bedroom. I get an up close shot of Jackson's bare ass and I can't resist giving it a little smack.

"Careful, pretty girl," Jackson growls in response. In the giant mirror on the opposite side of the bedroom I can see Jackson's massive dick bounce with each step he takes. When we reach the bed, he tosses me on it and steps back to remove his shirt. He quickly slides my leggings and thong off, tossing them on the floor before pressing my thighs wide and absolutely devouring me.

There is no hesitation from Jackson, no moment to catch my breath and prepare for the assault of his tongue laving away at my soaked core. Jackson's earlier relentless pace while his cock was down my throat fully matches his enthusiasm for eating me out. He's always been talented at oral sex, but this is on a whole other level. My hands clutch the comforter, desperate to ground me in any capacity.

Jackson readjusts my legs, bending my knees further and placing the soles of my feet on the tops of his shoulders. This new angle exposes me in a less flattering light, but I have little time to feel self conscious as my arousal slides further toward the mattress and down the crevice between my ass cheeks. Jackson seizes the opportunity to lick a long stroke from my ass to the top of my clit. The moan I release is unearthly.

"Dirty girl," Jackson murmurs against me before swirling his tongue against the puckered hole. The feeling is different but equally as intense as the attention he had been giving my pussy.

When Jackson thrusts two fingers inside me and thumbs my clit, I come immediately. He continues tonguing my rear entrance like he can't get enough and I'm too far gone to do anything to stop him.

"Jacks," I gasp as I feel the crest of another orgasm coming on swiftly. He must feel it too because he redoubles his efforts and speeds the pace of his fingers thrusting in and out of me. I release a long, unflattering moan as a gush of arousal splashes Jackson's face.

"Fuck yes," he mutters, lapping up every drop.

Holy shit. We've been here less than an hour. If things keep going this way, I don't know how I'm going to survive this weekend, but if I don't, I know I'll die a very happy woman.

CHAPTER FORTY

Jackson

I press my hands into the pillowtop mattress, using my upper body to push myself to standing in front of Amy. I stare at her, admiring the rise and fall of her chest as she works to catch her breath. The swell of her breasts press against the flimsy neckline of her top. Her nipples are sharpened to points beneath it. She looks exquisite. If I didn't just make her come twice from eating her out, I'd devour her again.

I love seeing Amy like this: hair a mess with that freshly fucked look, and I haven't even properly fucked her yet.

"You good?" I smirk at Amy, who opens one eye to peer at me.

"You may have just killed me. I'm gonna need a minute."

She still hasn't caught her breath, so I walk to my suitcase and pull out one of the boxes of condoms I brought, preparing us for later. Amy props herself up on her elbows to watch me open the packaging.

"We haven't really discussed it," she says breathlessly. I mentally pat myself on the back for the lingering effects I've created on my girlfriend. "But I'm on the pill."

"That's good to know," I say, trying not to assume where this is going.

"So, um, if you wanted to skip the condom, I'd be okay with that. I got tested after my last boyfriend. I wondered if he had cheated on me since the breakup came out of nowhere," she hastily adds.

"Amy. You're in my bed and really talking about your ex?" I quirk an eyebrow at her.

"Sorry!" She winces.

"I'm kidding. I'm glad to know you're clean. I am too. We get tested during spring training and I have only been with you since that time. Are you sure you're okay with this?"

"I am if you are. I've just..." I see her self-consciousness creep in and wait patiently for her to finish her thought. "I've always used a condom. I've never gone without before."

"Me neither." Carolyn was adamant about not getting pregnant, which, in hindsight might have been because if she had gotten pregnant near the end of our relationship, she wouldn't have been able to easily determine who the father was. The thought threatens to sour my mood and I shove it out of my head.

Amy is glowing. I can't tell if it's the normal post-orgasm zen that washes over her or if it's due to my admission that we'll be sharing an experience new to the both of us, but she looks gorgeous. I tell her so, and she blushes easily.

I lean over the bed, caging Amy between my arms and kissing her deeply. She tastes like whiskey from her earlier drink. She gently sucks on my tongue and I let out a groan.

"How do you want me to fuck you, baby?"

She pulls me close and I delve in for another kiss. "Can we, um, maybe have you behind me, but I'm laying flat against the bed?"

I pull back to look at her, reestablishing eye contact. "Of course we can, baby. Anything you want. I don't ever want you to be shy about asking for what you want from me."

Amy nods and I pull back, allowing her to sit up so I can strip her out of her shirt and bra. I gently circle her nipples with my thumbs, feeling them tighten under my touch. I give Amy one last kiss before pushing her back on the bed and guiding her to turn over. I climb up between her spread legs and drag my bare cock through her wetness, parting her lips with my fingers. She moans in pleasure just before I slide inside, bringing my hands to her waist to anchor myself as I begin to thrust. Taking Amy bare was simultaneously the best and worst decision I made tonight. The initial glide into her warmth, with no condom on to dull the sensations, is enough to make me come. Through sheer force of will, I hold my orgasm back.

She feels so good, so tight in this position, but she surprises me not by sliding her legs wider, but bringing them closer together, making the fit feel even more snug. I bring my knees to the outside of her hips and she hooks her ankles, one over the other, tightening her grip on me even further. I take slow, deep breaths against the tightening sensation in my testicles.

"Holy shit, baby. Those books really do give you great ideas," I praise. "You feel so tight. I can feel your slick pussy squeezing my dick…You ready for me to go faster?"

"Please," Amy murmurs, her voice muffled by the pillow against her face. I pull my hips back until I'm almost fully removed from Amy before slamming back in. She screams and the sound is so absolutely primal that, yet again, I'm worried it's going to make me come immediately. I circle my hips and Amy's screams transform into moans as more arousal coats my cock. She's so wet I could slip out of her easily if I'm not paying attention.

I remove one hand from Amy's side, continuing the swiveling motion of my hips, replacing it on the bed by her head, allowing me to lower myself and get even deeper. The movement is rewarded with Amy's ensuing moans, letting me know it's just as good for her.

"You take me so well, Amy. I'm never going to get tired of fucking you. Your pussy was made for my cock." My mouth brushes the shell of her ear and with this most recent round of praise, Amy presses her ass back into me. She gasps and I assume the movement dragged her clit across the sheets. "Do it again baby, rub your clit across this bed. Use it to get off."

Amy repeats the motion and my cock twitches inside her at how well she follows my instruction. It means she trusts me enough to let go of her self-consciousness. She has nothing to be embarrassed about; I want Amy to get off in every way humanly possible.

I pick up my pace, slamming into Amy as she rocks back into me. The force causes me to reach the deepest parts of Amy and my eyes to roll back into my head. It takes every ounce of my composure not to come before I draw out one more orgasm from my girl. Luckily, I don't have to wait long; on the next thrust, Amy's pussy pulses around me and her muffled screams echo in the high-ceilinged room.

"That's my girl. Scream. Let everyone know who owns this pussy."

"Jackson!"

"That's right. Whose pussy is this?"

"Yours!" Amy gasps as I draw out her orgasm longer.

"Damn right it is," I manage to grit out before tipping over the edge and following Amy's orgasm down into an abyss of pleasure and relief.

I collapse on top of her, mindful to throw my forearm out to take most of my weight. It takes me several moments to gather myself before I'm able to push up off of her. When my softening cock pulls out of her, she whimpers. I place a kiss against her sweaty forehead.

"Are you okay, my love?" She nods as I roll to the side, keeping a hand against her back. I gently stroke her back as she looks at me with eyes full of such devotion, I swear she's about to tell me she loves me.

Except she doesn't.

Shaking my head, I try to hide my disappointment. I don't know why I expected Amy to fall in love with me when she's shown nothing but resistance to deepening the relationship. It's not her fault; she's told me every step of the way what she wants—and what she doesn't—but my stupid heart hoped otherwise.

I won't let this ruin the weekend. I walk out to the kitchen to bring back our whiskey glasses, taking the moment to collect myself. I've handled plenty of setbacks and disappointments in my lifetime; this one shouldn't be all that different.

Yet somehow it is.

I need to get over this, or at least put these uncomfortable feelings on pause before I walk back into the room. It's not Amy's fault that she doesn't love me. I had just hoped, for once, I'd be enough for the woman in my life.

CHAPTER FORTY-ONE

Amy

The rest of our time in Telluride passes in a blur of breathtaking hikes, gorgeous sunsets, good food, and even better sex. Jackson has induced so many orgasms this week that I'm worried I'll go through withdrawal when we get home.

It's our last day here. Jackson requested a late checkout so we could spend as much time here as possible. Our flight home isn't until eight tonight, so we're soaking up the last bits of vacation relaxation as possible.

Luckily, Jackson has a week of games at home before he goes out of town again. We haven't discussed our plans, but I assume we'll spend as much downtime together as possible during that week. Even then, I'm a little worried that the reduction in orgasms due to our schedules might be detrimental to my health. I should really discuss this predicament with my doctor.

Last night, we stopped at the bar in the hotel lobby and brought our drinks to the hot tub. It was a particularly chilly night, due to an increase in wind and a predicted thunderstorm overnight. We weren't surprised to find ourselves the only ones brave enough to weather the elements to enjoy the hot tub. As long as I slunk low enough in the water to keep my chest submerged, I felt warm enough. And when Jackson slid his hand beneath my bikini bottoms, I warmed even faster. Under the water, he hooked one of my legs over his thick thigh, spreading me open, thumb strumming my clit and fingers spearing inside of me. I came apart on his hand faster than I ever have before, burying my face in his neck as I moaned.

Now, I'm sitting on the balcony, wrapped up in a blanket to ward off the remaining chill from last night's storm. I've got my phone in hand, about to video conference my mom on her lunch break. Jackson is out for a run. I opted out of the additional physical activity; we already hiked this morning and the altitude is messing with my head a bit. Jackson was reluctant to leave me when I told him about my altitude sickness, but he's been running a lot lately and I didn't want to mess with his routine. Each time he's come back from his run, he seems a little more relaxed.

There was one point this weekend, shortly after we got here, that I felt like Jackson got a little moody, but he covered it well. Or I misread him. But I'm pretty sure something is off. Usually, Jackson is pretty open about whatever is on his mind, and since he didn't bring anything up, I'm trying to convince myself that it's just my anxiety making me overthink things.

My mom picks up on the second ring, her smiling face filling my screen. "There's my girl!" she exclaims. "How is your trip?"

"Mom, it is so gorgeous here. Look." I flip the camera screen so she can partake in my view of the mountains. "Everywhere is like this. We're in this little subset of Telluride called Mountain Village, and we can take these cute little gondolas over the mountains into the town of Telluride itself. It's adorable. It's artsy and there are so many cute clothing boutiques there. I had to stop Jackson from trying to spend his whole paycheck in this one store with the cutest sweaters and accessories."

My mom mirrors my excitement. "It is beautiful, Ames. I'm so glad you're having a good time."

"I am," I gush. "Every meal we've had has been so good. I've probably gained ten pounds. And the hikes are just insane. We have to go slow because I'm so affected by the altitude, but Jackson seems to be adjusting to it better than I am. He's actually out on a run now."

Several weeks ago, I filled my mother in on my relationship with Jackson. She's well aware of his success on the field and recognized him from his energy drink billboards that have recently gone up along I-55 (thank goodness she recognized him from those ads, rather than when he was briefly the body behind the underwear campaign). Even more so, though, she seems to be happy that Jackson makes me happy. She's supportive of the relationship without prying.

"So obviously things are going well between you two," she says, raising her eyebrows and giving me a look. I'm not sure where she's going with this, but I suspect she's about to grill me.

"Mom, don't give me that look." My mother feigns innocence. "You look like you're about to start planning a wedding. This is not something serious."

"Is that right?" Her tone suggests indifference, a non confrontational lilt to the rhythm. Her face, however, is nothing but a map of intrigue.

"What does that mean?"

"It means that he told you he loves you weeks ago and you're telling me that this isn't serious. Your face lights up when you talk about him." I say nothing. My mother interprets my silence as a green light to continue throwing my hypocrisy in my face. "You mentioned last week that maybe we should all get together for brunch the next time that Jackson is home." I wince, knowing she's right. "Organizing a brunch for your boyfriend to meet your mother isn't exactly casual now, is it?"

I hate that she's right. I didn't bring up the brunch idea to Jackson yet, mostly because it was an off the cuff comment I made to my mother without thinking. I sigh.

"Mom, I don't know what to do. I really like Jackson. Alicia and I talked a lot about this a few weeks ago when he first told me he loved me. And I'm really trying not to be scared about this getting serious." Tears prickle the backs of my eyes; I can feel myself getting more stressed by the second. My mother's face softens, reading the anxiety lining my own.

"Why are you upset about this?" she asks gently.

"Because I'm tired of my heart getting ripped apart by men!" I exclaim with more frustration than I intended. I rein it back in. "Jackson is a famous baseball player, for god's sake!"

"I'm not sure what his job has to do with anything," she says patiently. I breathe deeply, annoyed that my mom is not understanding this. "He treats you well, you're happy with him, you *really like him*. What's the problem?"

"I'm not doing this with another J name." I cringe at my lame excuse. I'm grasping at straws here; I know it and my mother knows it, too. She gives me an admonishing look.

"Look, Amy. I can tell you're getting upset by this and I'm not saying this to ruin your last day on your trip. But you seem to be putting a lot of arbitrary rules on yourself as far as relationships go." I open my mouth to argue, but she forges ahead. "Keeping it casual? Not another J name? Not allowing yourself to fall in love?" She ticks off each question on her fingers, then pauses, and my mouth hangs open, at a loss for what to say. I'm not in love with Jackson.

Right?

"Amy, I get why you're doing it. You've been hurt quite a bit in the past when you've worn your heart on your sleeve. As your mother, I can't tell you it hasn't concerned me in the past how hard you've loved, even at the risk of getting hurt. A mother never wants to see their child get hurt. But over the last several months, I've watched you guard your heart so fiercely that now I'm more concerned that you'll miss out on all that life has to offer. The pendulum of your attitude toward relationships has swung so far to the opposite side that I'm afraid you've lost sight of yourself."

My mom is sounding like an echo of my conversation with Alicia a few weeks ago. Apparently I haven't done as good of a job at opening up and braving my fears as I had thought I was. Certainly not well enough if someone else is forced to have the same conversation with me a few short weeks later.

"Amy," she finishes out her speech. "You can't keep punishing Jackson for Patrick's mistakes." Her final statement hangs in the air and hits me like a load of bricks. I hadn't realized I'd been doing that, but now that she puts it like that, there's no other way around it.

Of course my mother is right. The rules that are preventing my heart from breaking are the same rules preventing me from truly living. From finding not just happiness, but *joy*. *Love*.

It's at this moment that I realize I no longer want a guarded, safe, unlived life. I wanted a safe harbor at all times. A safe harbor, with no waves, made for sailboats that never left, never are used to their true potential, resulting in a lot of bored sailors. I can't control the wind, but I can adjust my sails and leave the safety of the harbor. I want to choose joy. I want to choose love, even if that means I risk heartache. But I can't keep living my life in self-imposed bubble wrap, holding myself back because I don't want to crack, to break. The cracks can let the light through, and I'm finally ready to let that happen.

After I hang up with my mother, I sit on the balcony reflecting for a long time. From my spot on the elevated veranda, I can see as Jackson rounds the corner, finishing out his run. He spots me and gives a little wave. As he stretches and cools down from his run, I think about our adventures together. I can't help but compare my relationship with him to those with my previous boyfriends.

I allow my mind to wander back, flipping through the memories of my exes like an old magazine. There were lots of good memories, plenty to make me cringe, and no shortage of heartache. Even looking back, with some notable exceptions, the good outweighed the bad. But none of those relationships come close to the good I experience in my relationship with Jackson.

Somehow, undetected by me, Jackson has snuck in and picked up the shattered pieces of my heart. Unbeknownst to me, he put them back together, somehow better, stronger, more solid than before I had broken. And the truth hits me like a freight train: I do love Jackson—because how could I not? Jackson is selfless, kind, thoughtful, and more loving than I sometimes deserve. He is patient and understanding and sexy as hell. Importantly, I like myself more when I'm with him, too.

In all the time I spent denying the depth of my feelings, Jackson Jeffers remained the steady constant in my life, as reliable as the tides. And like the tides under a midnight moon, his steadfast presence brought me a peace I never allowed myself to acknowledge until now. I am done running. I'm done convincing myself this will all blow up in my face. There is still a miniscule chance that it will, but I'm no longer willing to forgo this love. The risk is too great. And I'm powerless to stop it.

Every man in my life–past, present, and likely, future–pales in comparison to Jackson Jeffers. I should have known I've been in love with him based on the way my mind immediately eases around him, like sliding into a warm bath. Of course I can see a future with Jackson because I can't imagine a scenario in which I'd be happy being without him.

I feel so stupid for not realizing sooner how much I do love Jackson.

Now I just need to become brave enough to tell him.

CHAPTER FORTY-TWO

Amy

When Jackson got home from his run, the sight of him in front of me took my breath away. Sure, I watched him stretch from several hundred yards away, but to gaze upon him in all of his sweaty, muscled glory is something else entirely.

He quirks a brow at me when he catches me licking my lips and staring.

"You okay there, pretty girl?"

"Yeah," I respond, my mouth suddenly dry.

"You sure? Because you're looking at me like you're about to maul me."

I cross the room slowly, taking him in and not bothering to hide my blatant ogling of his body.

"Maybe I am," I admit.

"Let me take a shower first. I probably stink," Jackson laughs. *Pass, unless I can join him in that shower,* I think. Instead, I fist his tee shirt and bring him closer to me. Even on tiptoes, I'm not quite tall enough to reach his lips. I curl my hand around his neck and pull his mouth to mine. He groans and opens further, allowing my tongue to sweep inside.

Jackson's initial hesitation about his sweatiness or any potential odor forgotten, I feel the moment when his resistance to me crumbles. He grabs my hips and pulls them flush against him.

"I can never say no to you," he groans, lifting me and wrapping my legs around his waist. He kisses me like he can't get enough of me, and I kiss him back with equal fervor, trying to pour all the love I have into my actions, afraid to voice the words aloud just yet.

Jackson walks us in the bedroom and deposits me on the bed. I lift my sweatshirt over my head and he groans at the sight of my bare breasts.

"You haven't been wearing a bra all day? If I had known that, I would have fucked you much sooner."

I giggle. "No, I took it off after our hike."

I shimmy out of my leggings as Jackson rips the clothes off his body with so much enthusiasm I can't help but laugh. A strand of his dark hair falls in front of his eyes, and I'm momentarily stunned that this gorgeous man is all mine.

"I can't wait to watch your tits bounce when I fuck you. You sure you don't want me to shower first?"

"No, Jacks. Please. I need you." I'm practically whimpering with need. Jackson launches himself on the bed and roughly grabs my hips, guiding me to straddle him as he kneels on our unmade bed.

"Bounce on my cock baby. You're going to come at least three times for me before we leave tonight." I do as I'm told, Jackson holding my hips and helping to lift me up and down on his shaft.

"Jacks!" My breath catches in my throat.

"Fuck yes. Say my name when I impale you with my cock." He buries his face against my heaving breasts, never ceasing his lifting of my hips. I'm nearly boneless, teetering on the precipice of a mind-blowing orgasm.

As I shatter around him, I can't help but wonder how much my own heart might soon be shattering right along with it.

CHAPTER FORTY-THREE

Jackson

I climb the few stairs on the jet bridge to the plane behind Amy with a self-satisfied smirk on my face. I can't help but notice she's walking a little funny and I'm filled with a sense of pride. I lightly tap her ass as I follow her.

"You good there, Ames? You're walking a little funny." She looks over her shoulder with a gasp. I laugh.

"It's your fault," she grumbles, reaching the top of the landing and stepping onto the plane.

"You're damn right it is," I say, pulling her into a hug.

"You're pretty proud of yourself, aren't you?" Amy pushes against my chest, attempting to push out of my arms. I tighten my grip and give her a chaste peck on the lips.

"Of course I am."

"Smug bastard," she mumbles, taking a seat on the couch. We don't have the same exact plane or flight crew as when we arrived, but the layout is the same. The flight attendant introduces herself as Maggie and offers us a drink, but we both decline. It's late and we both have to work tomorrow. I only have the all-team practice, but Amy is back to working a full day. Luckily for her, tomorrow is a Friday, so it's lighter for her because the campers won't be in attendance.

"Did you decide if you're working from home tomorrow?" I ask as Amy snuggles against me, placing her legs across my lap. I pull her legs in tighter to me, absentmindedly rubbing circles on her shins with my thumbs.

"Yeah, probably," Amy says between yawns.

"Close your eyes, baby. Get some rest. I'll wake you up when we land."

As Amy quietly sleeps next to me, I can't help but think about our last afternoon on our trip. After fucking Amy on my lap and again against the shower wall, she told me when I take control in the bedroom, it allows her to fully switch off her brain. I consider it to be the highest compliment of my skills. Not wanting to seem ungrateful, I bent her over the bed one last time and took her from behind, after which we took a nap together. By the time we woke up, it was that awkward time between lunch and dinner, but having missed lunch, we were starving. We opted for ice cream at one of the cafes in Mountain Village, even though the air still held a crisp chill. After we ate, we came back to the room to reluctantly pack before I slipped Amy's pants down and ate her out from behind, pressing her chest against the wall. We ate a light dinner at the hotel bar before finally leaving paradise.

The way Amy looked at me over dinner was unlike any way she had looked at me before. My stupid heart stuttered, yet again mistaking her gaze for one of love. At this point, I'm frustrated with myself for continuously hoping for something my girl clearly can't give me.

I contemplate if spending time away from Amy, even just for a night or two, will allow me to reset my emotions and rid myself of that pesky hope that Amy and I could be anything more than what we are. I've always told myself I'll take Amy any way I can get her, but the dull ache in my chest right now might be telling me something different.

I don't want to be apart from her, but I also don't want to have to convince my own girlfriend to love me. I don't want this to be the end of the road for us, either, though. I'm so conflicted with what to do and how to feel and how to make the literal pain in my heart stop.

I sigh, closing my eyes and resting my head against the back of the couch. Sleep doesn't come. By the time we touch down in Chicago, I'm no less confused about what I want and where to go from here.

CHAPTER FORTY-FOUR
Amy

The gentle bumps and jostling of the plane touching down on the runway lures me from a deep sleep. The ride back to Chicago wasn't long, but I'm surprised I slept so soundly, especially after the nap Jackson and I took earlier today.

At dinner, I was so close to telling him I loved him, but I chickened out. *What is my deal?* I *know* Jackson loves me. Telling him I love him back changes nothing about the fact that I do love him. So why is telling him so difficult?

I blink the sleep from my eyes and focus on Jacks. He looks terrible. Okay, not terrible, because the man always looks steal-your-breath-from-your-lungs good, but he looks terrible for *him.*

"Are you feeling okay?" I ask, placing the back of my hand against his forehead.

"I'm fine," he mumbles. He gently pushes my legs off his lap and helps me to stand. He won't make eye contact with me, which is weird.

"Jacks, honey, what's going on?"

"I'm just tired," he says evasively, gathering his things, still not looking at me. I can feel the panic start to creep in. Something is wrong, but Jackson isn't telling me. "Seriously, don't worry," he adds, finally looking me in the eye. Some of my worry starts to melt away.

Jackson is quiet on the ride back from the airport. He no longer seems sick, but just lost in his thoughts. I reach over to play with the hair on the nape of his neck, but the movement makes him look more conflicted, almost anguished.

"Thank you for the perfect vacation, Jacks." He nods and I wish he would tell me what's on his mind. I hate seeing him like this and I wish I knew how to fix it. Maybe he is just tired. He scrubs a hand down his face, the scrape of his stubble lightly audible in the otherwise silent car.

I'm yet again struck by how beautiful Jackson Jeffers is. His straight nose, vibrant blue eyes, the scruff of a few days without shaving only adding to his attractiveness. Even more than my physical attraction to my boyfriend, I'm convinced he's the perfect man. Sure, he's not without his flaws, the biggest right now being his lack of communication about how he's feeling if he thinks I'm not going to like what he has to say. His devotion to me, the way he devotes himself to all the things he loves, is so admirable.

When he drops me at my apartment, he lingers outside my door, no doubt wanting to extend this vacation as much as I do. Exhaustion lines the corners of his eyes and I'm glad he has a light day tomorrow, with only a sports radio interview and a team workout planned. I'm not sure if he'll want to do dinner tomorrow night, after spending so many days together, but I'm already cataloguing the work I'll need to complete if he does. After one last lingering kiss, he retreats to his car while I actively suppress a sigh of contentment. It really was the perfect vacation.

After five straight hours of staring at my computer screen, I could use a break. My eyes are dry and itchy and there's only so many different ways I can stretch a budget when planning next week's lessons on human anatomy at the Humanities Museum. There are so many ideas and creative ways the kids can learn about their bodies, but with tightening purse strings, I have to be mindful of what I include. I can't blow my remaining summer budget on one week, just because summer camp happens to be held at my favorite museum campus.

At this point, it's time to blow my personal budget on caffeine. I haven't heard much from Jacks today, which isn't too unusual; I'm sure he's catching up on life now that we've re-entered the real world. Closing my laptop, I place it gently on the coffee table in front of me. I need to get away from these four walls and my computer screen. Caffeine Kingdom will do the trick.

CHAPTER FORTY-FIVE

Jackson

"**M**r. Jeffers, I'm so sorry to inform you that we're running a bit behind in today's show. We had to move your segment back an hour to accommodate some last-minute changes. Is this something that will work for you, or will we need to reschedule?"

I run my fingers through my hair. It's not ideal, but I also have more flexibility in my schedule today than usual, so I can't really complain. The poor assistant that is calling to deliver the news is clearly frazzled; she's speaking so quickly that it takes me an extra second or two to process everything. I'm worried if I tell her to reschedule she might spontaneously combust.

"That's okay," I tell her, actively reminding myself not to release the sigh I want to make. "Are they just going to call me when they're ready?"

"Yes, sir. I'll call you with a ten minute head's up and then again immediately before you go on air. I'm so sorry for the inconvenience."

I shake my head, even though the poor woman can't see me. "No problem." We hang up. Mariah, my PR agent, would be so proud of me for not rescheduling. She and Sean set up this interview as a way to generate more buzz around me and the Foxes in general, but also to prime the market for the release of my new energy drink partnership. I've never been an incredibly savvy businessman, instead sticking to what Sean and my financial advisor suggest, but they haven't led me astray so far and I don't anticipate them starting soon.

I play a couple rounds of Mario Kart to kill time, and before I know it, my phone is buzzing again. I glance at the caller ID; it's a Chicago number I don't recognize, so I assume it's the sports radio assistant calling me with a countdown until I go on the air. I answer and am met with a different female's voice.

"JJ? Hello, are you there?"

I swear, my blood turns to ice at the sound of her voice. I'm mildly relieved to discover that it's not my mother calling, but instead the second to last woman I ever want to talk to. My momentary surprise has rendered me speechless, but I jump into action after I quickly recover.

"Carolyn?" I wish I could say, all these years later, that I didn't recognize her voice, but the truth is, she was such a massive part of my life for so long that I'm afraid her cadence and vocal quality will forever be seared into my brain.

"JJ," she breathes, relief evident in her voice. I scowl immediately. Had I recognized her new number, I would have sent it to voicemail immediately before blocking her. I have nothing to say to the woman. "I was hoping to reach you. I've been thinking about you a lot lately. I was at your last game, right before the midseason break. You played really well."

I grunt noncommittally. I don't even care that I'm coming off rude. I need her to get to the point so I can free my phone line for the interview.

"It brought up a lot of memories, JJ." A beat of silence passes; I'm sure she's waiting for me to confess how much I miss her. That's never going to happen. She continues, "I've been working on myself a lot, JJ. Going to therapy, figuring some stuff out."

"That's good," I tell her, and I mean it. Therapy is great; everyone should do it. Especially Carolyn.

"Anyway, my therapist suggested it might be helpful if you and I talked some things through. Got a little closure on everything, you know?"

I feel my eyes widen in incredulity and I'm glad she can't see me. I want to provide a snarky response about not needing any closure, or this conversation coming several years too late, but I stop myself. Because if Carolyn really is putting in the work, then who am I to judge her timeline? I don't really have a desire to speak with her, but if this is standing in the way of her making self-improvement progress, then I should meet with her. To intentionally not do so would kind of be a dick move, even if I don't actually owe her anything.

"Please, JJ. Can we just meet for dinner or drinks or something? There's so much I need to say, so much you deserve to hear. Please?"

Her pleading is what gets to me. I have to admit we had some great times together. Sure, they were mostly all tainted by the way the breakup happened, but things were good in the beginning. Carolyn is a unique personality. Loud, unafraid of calling attention to herself, boisterous. Before she got too snobby, she was the kind of girl who would down a pizza and a six-pack with the guys. She could follow my stats better than some of my coaches. She was fun—when she wasn't actively cheating on me, that is.

"Fine. I'll meet you for coffee in two hours. No dinner." She needs to go into this understanding there is no way this can be misconstrued as a date.

I don't hate Carolyn. Maybe I should. She has certainly done enough to warrant it. When I think about her, I have a general feeling of apathy regarding her. Enough therapy has taught me that there was a small amount of good that came with dating her. Namely, Bruno and the fact that I know where my boundaries are.

However, meeting Carolyn at Caffeine Kingdom was a bad idea. I wanted to go to a public place, neutral ground, but as soon as I enter the coffee shop, I realize this is the opposite of neutral.

This is my safe space. I'm worried that Carolyn's presence will taint it. I don't want every subsequent visit here to remind me of the worst breakup of my life. Right now, Caffeine Kingdom is where I met my future wife for the first time (if she ever comes around to the idea of marrying me)—and I'm not talking about my cheating ex-fiancee.

I step outside, my red eye in hand, digging my phone out of my pocket to text Carolyn with a change of venue when the woman herself walks up. Fuck.

We end up sitting outside on the patio. It's an equally bad choice as inside because while I didn't meet Amy on this patio, this is the spot where we had our first real conversation. It's the spot where I realized how fascinating and intelligent and sweet Amy is. And now, I'm seated across from Carolyn, her nose wrinkling on her vapid face when the dog at the table next to us sniffs us when we sit down. I offer him a friendly scratch behind the ears when the owner grants me permission, sitting heavily across from the woman I once loved.

Looking at Carolyn, I can't fathom what I ever saw in her. She's nothing like Amy. She's materially obsessed. Her makeup is caked on, as if she's trying too hard to make herself appear younger. She always was self-conscious about being two years older than me.

"Aren't you going to offer to buy me a coffee at least?"

"No." My answer is simple. My tone isn't rude but my message is clear. Carolyn got the last dime out of me years ago. "What do you want, Carolyn?" I ask wearily.

She reaches across the table and tries to grasp my hand. I immediately yank mine back, placing it safely on my lap. She pouts. It looks ridiculous, a thirty year old woman pouting in public.

"JJ, I've been doing a lot of thinking."

I bet you have, I think snarkily. *Thinking about my bank account, I'm sure.*

"I miss you. We were so good together, baby." I stare at her, incredulous. I have to admit, a small part of me is curious. Why now, after all these years, is she crawling back to me?

"What, exactly, about us made us work so well?" She blinks and stares at me, as if it never occurred to her that I would question her. "I'm serious, Carolyn. What was so good about us?"

"The sex was hot," she replies boldly.

The sex was good, I'll admit that. Light years away from the quality of sex I'm having now, though. I roll my eyes at her. I change tactics.

"What did you want to talk about? You said you've been going to therapy." Carolyn's eyes dart right and left. Some people can be skittish about others learning they go to therapy. I make a note not to mention the T word. "What have you been working on?"

"About that...therapy wasn't really my *thing*." I wonder briefly if she actually ever went, or if this entire therapy thing was just a ruse to tug at my heartstrings.

"Not your thing," I repeat, my tone flat.

"Yeah, whining and crying about the past, woe is me..." She rolls her eyes theatrically. "I think, now that some time has passed, we can look at our relationship with fresh eyes. And when I went to your game last week, it really solidified some things for me."

I really try not to glare at her. I must succeed, because she plows on.

"I miss you, JJ. I think we should give us another shot."

I'm glad I didn't make the mistake of sipping my drink, because there's no way I wouldn't have spit it all out on her overly caked-on face. After a pause, I ask, "What about Corey?"

"Corey is...Corey," she offers by way of nonexplanation.

"What does that even mean?"

"It means he's not you. He doesn't give me what you and I had. We had so much history. *Have* so much history. It's the foundation we can build upon for an even better life." Looking at Carolyn sitting across from me, I wonder what I ever saw in her. She's beautiful, sure, despite all the crap caked on her face. Her personality is garbage, though. How I could have gone from rock bottom with Carolyn to shooting for the stars with Amy is frankly amazing. Carolyn can't hold a candle to Amy because the truth is, no one can. Even with all of Amy's hesitations, she's the one for me. I've never been so sure of anything.

"Are you fucking serious right now?" My words are clipped and I know I'm losing some of the carefully curated control I gathered for this meeting. "Are you still with Corey?" Carolyn's responding shrug tells me everything I need to know.

"JJ, you know I took care of you. It's time you took care of me, too."

Ah, there it is. I was wondering how long she'd wait until she hit me up for money.

This time, I can't hold back my scoff. "Care, you jumped into the first available bed each time I went on the road. If this is your way of convincing me that I'm missing out on some great love, you're doing a real shitty job of it." Her jaw drops in indignation. How dare I call her out on her shit?

"JJ, let's face it. You aren't exactly a cakewalk of a boyfriend either. You're not exactly *husband material*," she hisses the last two words, as if they scald her tongue. "You have so much damage from your deadbeat mother and your unhealthy codependency on your brothers..."

My blood boils. My grip on my coffee cup tightens; I hear the plastic crinkle and buckle. Carolyn, never having been close with her own family, could never understand why I love my brothers so much.

"All right. I think we're done here." I go to stand and again, she reaches across the table to grab my wrist. "Get your hands off of me." My voice is low, deadly, but somehow, Carolyn is too willfully ignorant to recognize the lethality of my tone. I'm not a violent man, but this will be the last time Carolyn Whittier touches me.

A sharp intake of breath sounds behind me. I recognize the gasp, the barely audible noise, before I even turn. Because of course I do. I'd recognize everything about Amy blindfolded and struck deaf. Because that's what happens when your soul calls to another's. You magnetize toward the other without conscious thought. But as I turn my shoulders toward my soul's counterpart, Carolyn's claws still clinging to my wrist, there's nothing but hurt and betrayal written on Amy's face before she turns and runs in the opposite direction.

CHAPTER FORTY-SIX

Amy

You don't know what you saw. Give him a chance to explain.

I repeat those thoughts over and over in my head as I sprint away from Caffeine Kingdom. I thought working from home today would give me greater productivity. I deserved to reward myself for getting through my inbox by getting an iced dirty chai. Instead, I saw Jackson...I'm not sure what I saw.

Well, I know I saw a woman holding onto my boyfriend. But my brain isn't sure how to interpret it. I refuse to be one of those women who makes a knee-jerk reaction without hearing everyone out. The miscommunication trope is my least favorite in all my romance books, but I realize it exists for a reason. Because it really happens. My brain—or my anxiety, or both—is screaming at me to run and hole up in my apartment. To crumble into my own hurt and betrayal without giving Jackson a chance to defend himself.

Feet pounding on the pavement sounds behind me. I slow to a walk, my chest heaving less from exertion and more from the adrenaline coursing through my system. There's no way I'll ever outrun Jackson Jeffers; few people can. It's not even worth trying.

My shoulders hunch forward as Jacks rounds in front of me. I refuse to look at him, afraid he'll see every emotion playing on my face like a movie screen.

"Amy, please. Please look at me."

I lift my chin, but my eyes stay glued to his chest. I can't bring myself to make eye contact. This is my worst fear played out. Thinking about my prior relationship, I have no idea if Patrick was cheating on me, but honestly, it's the only explanation that makes sense. Seeing that woman's hand wrapped around my current boyfriend's hand, seeing the intensity in the way he looked at her, and the wild desperation in which she returned his gaze...it's hard not to wonder if Jackson is cheating and what it is about me that screams "easy to cheat on."

Am I boring? Or just that much of a pushover?

"Please, Amy. It's not what it looks like. Please let me explain." I nod, still refusing to look at my boyfriend. "Can you look at me please?" Jackson's voice is quiet.

I shake my head, just once, but he sees it and doesn't force the issue.

"Do you want to talk right here? Or can we go back to my place? Or yours?"

I don't know what I want. I just want this ache in my chest to stop. I want the whirring of my brain to stop, my mind to stop magically conjuring up scenario after scenario, each one worse than the last: Jackson cheating on me. Jackson leaving me. Jackson never loving me, but using me as a pawn in some sick game that I can't understand.

He nods, as if he's making up his mind. "Come on, let's go to my place." He holds out his hand, but I don't take it. After a few seconds, he drops it sadly to his side. He takes a few tentative steps toward his building and when he sees me follow him, he breathes out a deep sigh of relief.

The normally short walk to Jackson's is excruciating. He doesn't say anything else, so my mind is left to its own devices. When we get inside, there's no Bruno to greet me. He must be with Lisa and Desiree.

"Do you want to sit down?" he asks, gesturing to the couch.

I shake my head again. He's being so nice, it's going to break my heart even more. He sits heavily.

"Amy, that was Carolyn, my ex-fiancee." At my stricken look, his words come rushing out, tumbling over one another to assure me nothing happened. "Amy, I swear to god, nothing happened. This is the first time I've seen her since we broke up. There's nothing going on between us. There will never *be* anything going on between us again."

As he speaks, his elbows resting on his knees, his head drops lower and lower between his shoulders. When he looks up at me though, anguish is written all over his face. I feel anger at myself for wanting to comfort him.

"I swear, Amy. She asked me to meet her. I was just going to get it over with, so I could say I did it and I could leave with a clear conscience."

"Why?"

"She said she was working on herself. That she'd been in therapy for a while and just wanted to talk. For closure." His face is so earnest that I know it's the truth. Jackson could never deny anyone who is trying to work on themselves. "She just wanted to get back together. She hadn't been working on herself. She just wanted another piece of me." His face is the picture of disgust.

"Why didn't you tell me?" My voice comes out as a shaky whisper.

"I didn't want to worry you. I figured if I told you ahead of time that I was meeting with her, it would have heightened your anxiety. You would have been so worried leading up to and during it. I never want to be the cause of your distress, Ames." His blue eyes are bright with unshed tears. "I'm sorry. I should have told you."

I nod curtly. I know I have an anxiety disorder, but it's no reason to keep me in the dark. Jackson has never once treated me differently because of my anxiety. Until now. I can't help but wonder what else he's kept hidden from me, convincing himself it was in my best interest not to know.

"I need some space," I tell him honestly. He swallows and nods, refusing to blink. The emotions swirling in my brain leave little room for me to think, and if Jackson keeps looking at me like I'm breaking his heart, I know I'll cave. I'll tell him it's not a big deal, but I'll always wonder. And even though it's breaking my heart a little bit not to throw myself into his arms, I steel my spine and walk out his door.

chapter forty-seven

Amy

The rest of the night is a blur of swirling emotions. I talk separately to Alicia, then Danny, who puts me on speakerphone so Tim can partake in my emotional meltdown.

I don't actually know if Patrick cheated. It was one of the many confusing things about our breakup, and never getting closure meant I never got answers either. But seeing Jackson with a woman who only has eyes for him (sort of) brought back an all-too-familiar feeling of nausea. He was acting weird in Colorado. Is this why? Did he pick up on me falling for him and start to feel some sort of guilt? Or was his withdrawal trying to find some way to balance the multiple women in his life?

The blood whooshes in my ears. I'm trying not to jump to any conclusions, but my nervous system is still in flight mode. No surprises there; I've never been a fighter.

"I believe him," Danny says, his voice slightly tinny from the speakerphone. After several minutes, he conferenced Alicia in so we could all pick apart my love life together. I don't have much to say in response.

"For what it's worth, I do too. The shitty thing is, you'll probably never know for sure. I hate that for you, but it's the truth." The thing is, Tim is right. But even if Jackson didn't cheat, he made a conscious choice not to tell me something, which makes his meeting with Carolyn even shadier. Alicia clears her throat.

"Tim is right. But I've got to ask, Ames...and don't shoot the messenger on this one, but are you sure this is what is bothering you?"

"What do you mean? Of course this bothers me." I throw my hands up in frustration.

"Yes, but is *this* the issue? Are you sure you're not....you know...self-sabotaging?" Alicia's words hang in the air and I feel them like a slap. Danny lets out a low whistle, but the call is otherwise eerily quiet. "Amy, you know I love you more than life itself. But you've kind of been dragging your feet on this relationship, even though you agree you're happy and it's what you want. Is this a convenient way to break it off with JJ while maintaining your dignity?"

My chest tightens. It's not because of her original statement, as jarring as that was to hear. Alicia has always been perceptive beyond all reason. It's her follow up response about ending things with Jackson that makes me feel like a piece of my chest was just carved out. Tears instantly spring to my eyes.

"Amy," Alicia whispers. "Talk to us. What's going on?"

"I don't..." My voice breaks but my friends patiently wait for me to compose myself. "I don't want things to end." It's not until I say the words out loud that I realize just how profoundly I mean them.

"Oh, honey, things don't have to end. I'm just saying that you seem to be at a critical crossroads. Sometimes it seems like you're fighting against yourself and your own self-interest, you know?"

I hiccup, my body's revolt against my waning attempts to hold back my tears. I fail spectacularly and give up the fight. I ugly cry in the middle of my kitchen, my friends listening quietly on speakerphone as my emotions pour out of me.

"I almost told Jackson I loved him last night." Somehow, my friends' silence grows.

"Almost?" Danny finally asked.

"I chickened out. He hasn't said it to me since the first time and I kept psyching myself out and convincing myself he doesn't feel that way anymore."

Tim—or maybe Danny—sighs. "Ames, the way he looks at you? It's obvious he loves you."

I nod uselessly, using the sleeve of my comfort hoodie to sop up my tears. I hiccup loudly again.

"So, what does this mean?" Alicia asks gently.

"That I love him. And I can't lose him over this."

Over the next several minutes, I slowly regain my composure. We wrap up the call with promises to get drinks later in the week. I assure my friends I'll keep them updated once I figure out how to tell Jackson that I love and forgive him.

My true crime television show is barely holding my attention. I'm restless tonight. I want to text Jackson and tell him to come over, but at the same time, I asked for space, and maybe I should use this time to figure out how to tell him I love him. A quick knock sounds on my door. I mute the television and peek out the peephole, but no one is there. The landing is empty. I open the door to find a large paper cup with a Caffeine Kingdom logo on it, the spicy scent of chai and espresso floating in the air. A creak on the stairs pulls my attention to the landing, where Jackson is frozen.

"I'm sorry," he whispers. "I know you asked for space and I'm going to give it to you. But I wanted to deliver that and then you opened the door faster than I thought you would. You caught my escape." He smiles softly. I stoop to pick up the drink and breathe it in deeply.

"Jacks," I sigh. "Please come in."

A flash of disbelief crosses his face before he bounds up the few remaining stairs and into my apartment.

"Amy, I'm sorry. I didn't mean to keep you in the dark. I know it makes my decision to meet up with Carolyn look even worse. I really was trying not to stress you out, but not telling you made it look like I was purposely trying to hide it. I'm so sorry. You know I'm an open book with you."

The thing is, I believe him. Prior to today, I never had any reason to doubt Jackson or his intentions. He's always been open and honest with me, but he's always made every effort to ensure my mental health was protected. So the guy messed up? I've been messing up practically every step of the way in this relationship because I've been resisting what is now clearly inevitable. Jackson deserves someone who wants him every second of every day. *I* want him every second of every day, but he doesn't know that. A while ago, Jackson told me I deserved to know how loved I am. It's literally the least I can do to return the favor. I need to get over my fear of rejection and tell him. Setting the coffee on the counter behind me, I take a deep breath and swallow my nerves.

"Hey Jacks," I start, hating the way my voice trembles. I pull his hand into both of mine. "I have something to tell you." I pause, taking a deep breath. "I...I love you, Jacks. And I just wanted you to know. That I love you, too."

Jackson blinks once, twice, three times. He attempts to say something but no sound comes out. He clears his throat and tries again.

"What?"

I experience a moment of sheer terror as I wonder if he no longer feels the same way I do. He hasn't told me he loved me since the first time, but did I mistakenly attribute that to him not wanting me to feel pressured?

Jackson must read the fear on my face because he reaches out and cups my face in his hand, preventing me from turning away.

"Say it again, baby."

I let out the breath I didn't know I was holding. "I love you, Jackson."

"Amy," Jackson sighs. The look on his face is nothing short of a miracle. He smiles softly, his eyes filling with tears. "You love me?"

My own eyes spill over. I hadn't realized they had been collecting tears in response to the look Jackson is giving me. I nod vigorously.

"I love you, too, Amy." He kisses me softly and I try to pour every ounce of love in my cells into this one kiss. He breaks away slightly, resting his forehead on mine and laughs softly.

"C'mere baby."

He tugs me over to the couch and pulls me down until I'm straddling him. It's not sexual; we just need our bodies as close as they can get. Jackson clutches me to his chest, planting frantic kisses on my ear, my forehead, my hair.

"I've been waiting, hoping to hear you say that for so long."

"I'm sorry it's taken me so long to get there," I say as he wipes away my tears. "I'm sorry if I made you feel like I didn't love you. I've loved you for a lot longer than I was willing to admit to myself. I was so afraid to say it."

Jackson's breath catches at my admission.

"I'll take care of you, baby. I know you're scared. I know you've been hurt and I promise I'll do everything I can to never let you hurt again," Jackson promises.

CHAPTER FORTY-EIGHT
Jackson

I *have something to tell you.*

I love you, Jacks.

I love you, Jacks.

I love you, Jacks.

I didn't realize how much I needed those words until Amy spoke them into existence. *I just wanted you to know. That I love you, too.* A unique feeling has washed over me since she told me. It's calming and energizing all at the same time. I possess a deep sense of peace. Simultaneously, my body hums with energy; I feel so alive since Amy told me she loved me. It's what I've wanted for so long. I feel so lucky to not only have this incredible woman by my side, but to be on the receiving end of her love? There is nothing better.

I finally fall asleep around four in the morning, Amy at my side. She fell asleep easily, tucked into my chest, my arm wrapped around her. I stayed up for hours after she drifted off, just marveling at the sleepy sighs she made, the way her fingers twitched upon initially falling asleep, the feel of her silky strands against my chest.

When my alarm sounds a few hours later but several hours too soon, I stretch carefully, mindful not to wake her, only to find her side of the bed empty. Rubbing the sleep from my eyes, I take in my surroundings. A steaming mug of coffee rests on a stone coaster on my nightstand. Bruno stretches lazily from his oversized bed by the door. Amy is seated on the chair in the corner of the room, her feet propped on the foot of the bed, knees bent so her laptop can rest on top of them. She quietly types away for a moment before realizing I'm awake.

"Good morning, my love," Amy chirps cheerfully. A goofy grin firmly affixes itself to my face.

"You've never called me that before."

"Yeah, well, I decided I'm going to try this thing where I tell you how I really feel. You know, because I love you and all."

My grin widens. I'll never tire of hearing Amy tell me she loves me. "I love you, too. Now get over here, woman."

Last night, we came back to my place after I made love to my girl-friend at hers. We spend most of our time at my place anyway due to Bruno, so I never realized how loud her downstairs neighbor plays his music. It was late by the time we left her apartment too; Amy just shrugged when I pointed out the thumping vibrations coming through the floor. Apparently this happens all the time. Now that I know that, I want Amy to spend even more time at my place, as if wanting her in my arms and in my bed weren't reasons enough.

Amy volunteered to keep an eye on Bruno and take him for a walk while I went to work today. Since it's a day game, I asked Amy to work here instead of going back to her place; I'm practically giddy at the idea of coming home to my girl. In my house.

Amy sets her computer aside, stands, and walks over to me. Scooting myself upright, I reach for her hand. She leans over me and plants a sweet kiss on my lips. I want to deepen it, to turn it into something more, but I want to check in with her first.

"I was thinking..." I say, unsure how to begin.

"Ooh, that's a dangerous thing," she quips. I roll my eyes, stupid grin still firmly in place.

"Would you be okay if I gave you a key here?"

"To your place?"

"Yeah. I mean, it makes sense, especially since you'll be spending the day here, to come in and out. I thought maybe if we got you your own–"

Amy silences me with a kiss, pressing me back with her palm against my chest. When she pulls away, she seats herself on the edge of my bed. "I would love that."

I narrow my eyes on her. "Who are you, and what have you done with my girlfriend?"

She giggles, and it's fucking adorable. "I told you. I'm trying a new thing. No longer hiding how I feel and all." She twirls her wrist in the air as she explains.

"I love this idea," I say, pulling her back in for another kiss. The lingering kiss turns into several more. All I want to do is drag Amy across my lap and show her how much I love her new perspective, but I have to get to the ballpark. I groan, pulling away from her at last.

After dressing and making several more assurances that I'll be home soon, and after Amy promises me she's fine taking Bruno for his morning walk, I grab my backpack, toss on my hat, and get ready to walk out the door. As I cross the threshold into the hallway outside my bedroom, Amy calls over her shoulder.

"Hey Jacks?" I turn. "Have a good day. I love you."

Any day will be a good day when Amy Stone tells you she loves you.

CHAPTER FORTY-NINE

Amy

"You're here!" Hailey squeals from two seats down from me after Dale, the usher at the Foxes game, shows me to my seat. She stands and throws her arms around my neck and I return the gesture.

This is only the second Foxes game I've been to since dating Jackson and I was a little nervous to show up alone, which is why I waited until the second inning to actually make it to my seat. Hailey plops down in the empty seat next to mine. Jenny leans over her to give my hand a squeeze.

"I'm glad you made it, Amy. How was your break?"

Hailey, Jenny, and I fill each other in on our respective breaks. Jenny and Caleb stayed in town due to her treatments, but they were able to take a day and spend it at a luxury spa. Hailey and Elijah visited his parents in Detroit. We fill the game with chatter, pausing briefly when each of our men come up to bat. Jackson has been playing well since we got back; yesterday's game was spectacular both offensively and defensively for him.

"I can't believe I didn't get your number at JJ's barbeque the other week," Jenny says. "I've been wanting to text you and invite you to our book club. I don't know if you're a reader, but you really don't have to be. It's more of a social time. We usually get together when the guys go out of town. It's hard being away from them, so leaning on each other is really important. Although I guess you're from here, like me, so you also have other support."

"I'd love to join. I do like to read, but it'd be nice to be with people who are missing their men as much as I miss mine when he's on the road." I pause, then decide if I'm being honest with Jackson about my feelings, I should open up to his friends' significant others too, especially if I'll be seeing a lot more of them. "I feel like Jackson and I turned a corner over the midseason break and we're more serious about our relationship now. It would be nice to get together with people who are down in the trenches of baseball life."

Jenny's eyes twinkle in delight. Hailey claps her hands excitedly.

"I'm so happy for you guys! Being a baseball wife can get lonely during the season. It's really important to surround yourself with good people. Let's get together for drinks–or mocktails," she hastily adds, glancing at Jenny. I guess she can't, or doesn't want to, drink while actively in treatment. "--and trashy television. Amy, what is your work schedule like? You work in a museum, right?"

I tell the girls about my job, which they had never heard of before. Since Jenny is from Chicago, though, she grew up attending field trips at the various area museums, and easily recalls her experiences. Hailey, on the other hand, grew up in a small town without access to museums until college.

"We should all visit some of the museums together! Amy, you can show us all the best exhibits. It'd be like insider information!" Hailey's excitement is contagious. "Unless that would suck for you, staying at work longer?"

"No one ever needs to convince me to enjoy a museum. It's one of my favorite things to do when I visit a new city. I don't really "get" art, but give me a good history or science museum anyday."

"Wait till you start joining JJ on road trips! We don't go on all of them, but when there's a new city I want to explore, or friends to visit there, Elijah will book me a flight out and I can stay with him on the road. Every once in a while, usually a few times a season, the Foxes sponsor a "family trip," where all the WAGs and kids are allowed on the team plane and in the hotel. They bus us from the hotel to the games each day too. Earlier this year, the family trip was in Miami, but Elijah said they'll probably do another one in August or September."

I feel a pang of sadness for missing out on the first family trip. I don't know when it was, but I'm guessing Jackson didn't feel comfortable inviting me on it since I was, admittedly, kind of dragging my feet in the relationship. The girls and I continue talking about anything and everything; they're easy to talk to and easy to listen to. I'm looking forward to spending more time with them.

When Jenny asks about local yoga studios offering gentle, beginner friendly classes, I have to actively remind myself to rein in my excitement so I don't look like an actually insane person. It took me a while to discover the perfect yoga studio for me based on what I was looking for, so I've visited a lot of them in the area. I tell Jenny about the programming at my favorite studio, and how they sometimes put on weeklong programs for people with cancer. I mention that I love my studio so much, I got my certification to teach through their yoga teacher training program and how I get a lot of my continuing education credits through them as well.

When Jenny's eyes widen, I realize I've been gushing about yoga, not really stopping for a breath, for several minutes.

"Sorry," I mumble. "Sometimes I get carried away and forget not everyone loves it as much as I do."

"Never apologize for your passions," Jenny tells me gently. "I love it. I would love for you to teach me."

I stare at Jenny, blinking. I haven't actively sought out yoga teaching positions because I'm concerned not enough people will join my classes each week. But working individually with Jenny? That not only sounds manageable, but fun.

"I'd love to," I tell her honestly. "Whenever you feel up for it, let me know. We'll have so much fun!"

The game winds down with the Foxes winning. Hailey and Jenny tell me that usually, they remain in the stands until the crowd dies down a bit before making it onto the field. They pull out their

WAG badges, which allows them on the field to either wait for their guys to say a quick hello, or to walk straight to the waiting area where we'll hang out for another hour before the guys finish up. I tentatively pull my badge out of my purse, still not quite feeling like I should own something so special.

"Ooh, Deb got you one already! I was going to see if you wanted me to text her and ask her to make you one!"

"Jackson got it for me right before the break. I still don't know if I deserve one, since I'm just a girlfriend and not a wife or a fiancee…" I trail off.

"Psh, girl, please. First of all, JJ is crazy about you, so who cares what anyone else says? Besides, you have to be a girlfriend before you can be a wife," Hailey reminds me.

I never allowed myself to dream of the possibility of being Jackson's wife. I've only recently adjusted to the idea of being in love with him. But his wife? I'm stunned to discover that not only does that idea *not* terrify me, but it's exciting. The possibility of someday being Jackson's wife, of knowing he is coming home to me every day, of calling him mine in a way no one ever has before…it's a comforting thought. I remind myself to not get too far ahead of myself, but now that I've admitted I'm in love with the man, I'm experiencing a greater depth to all of my feelings when it comes to him.

I spent so long denying my feelings to myself, that it seems finally admitting them has opened a sort of floodgate to all my emotions regarding Jackson. Yes, I'm still a little scared I will end up hurt, but that was a possibility before I told him I loved him, too. Jackson has never given me a reason to doubt him, leading me to the conclusion maybe Patrick was just an exception to how most people in relationships act.

The girls and I make our way toward the field, flashing our IDs at the security guard manning the gate access to the field. Friends and family cluster in small groups along the third base line, waiting for the players and staff members to pop out to say hello or to run the bases with their small children. I didn't know going on the field was an option, so I didn't prearrange to meet Jackson here; all he knows is that I'm at the game and that we'll meet up in the family room when he's ready to leave. So when a warm pair of hands grip my hips from behind, I jump. Jackson's laugh fills my ears.

"Easy there, pretty girl," he chuckles, turning me around. "Jumpy?"

"Jacks! I wasn't expecting you!" He looks incredible. I've never seen Jackson look unattractive, but in his uniform, eye black on his cheeks, hair messy without his hat? He's on a whole other level. Once again, I can't believe he's all mine.

He quirks a brow. "Really? At my baseball game, you weren't expecting to run into me?"

I give him a playful shove. "You know what I mean. How did you know to meet me out here?"

"Andrews. He was on his way out to meet Jenny and saw you were with her and told me."

"Oh. That was nice." Jackson shrugs.

"So do I get to kiss my girlfriend, or what?"

"I suppose," I flirt, batting my eyelashes at him. Jackson doesn't waste a second, pulling me closer and cupping my neck. I tilt my head back and he gives me a surprisingly long, sexy kiss, given that we're in public and there are still plenty of fans in the stands. When we break away, Caleb is openly gawking at us while Jenny fans herself dramatically. I feel my cheeks heat in pleased embarrassment.

"Hey, Jen," Jackson greets, reaching around me to give Jenny a side hug. She cautiously returns the greeting. It's one thing for Jackson's friends to see him be affectionate towards me in private, like on the roof of his building, but apparently a whole different thing to see him so public with his affections. I don't hate it. Normally, I'm not the biggest fan of PDA, because I'm so worried it might make others uncomfortable, but I'm finding I crave the attention and love Jackson so openly gives me by staking his claim on me. Plus, I'll never say no to how this man touches me.

Jackson remains on the field only a few minutes longer before he has to return to the clubhouse. He tells me it might be a little longer than an hour before we can leave, as he has a longer postgame workout scheduled; I don't mind. I'd wait forever for this man. Before he turns to head back into the dugout hallway leading to the lockers and weight room, he gives me a brief kiss, then pulls me close under the guise of a hug, whispering in my ear all of the things he's going to do to me when we get home.

CHAPTER FIFTY

Amy

I scoop the fluffy, sticky rice onto the soy paper in front of me, trying not to rip the delicate fiber and failing miserably. I'm in Danny and Tim's kitchen for sushi night. Danny is next to me, cutting sushi grade fatty tuna that he picked up earlier today. Alicia and Tim are sitting on the couch; she is sitting cross-legged, turned to face him, as she tells him an animated story about her latest dating disaster. The Foxes game is on in the background with the volume up so we can listen while we work.

"JJ Jeffers is on a thirteen game hitting streak since returning from the midseason break. Let's see if he can continue his monumental progress. This man is pure talent at the plate." I roll my eyes at this announcer, who, a few short weeks ago, was complaining about Jackson's lack of prowess in the same location. Jackson is the hardest worker I know and he's never wavered in his commitment to the team. Now that he's doing well, everyone is singing his praises. I'm angry that the announcer's commitment to Jackson is dependent on his performance.

I tune the broadcast out and focus on not shredding my poor attempt at a sushi roll, layering cucumber, avocado, and carrot across the bed of rice. I wet my fingers and gently pull the soy paper casing over the filling. The roll is lumpier than it would be if I had used nori, but I just can't get on board with the taste. Danny's rolls, complete with tuna, avocado, and cream cheese, look professionally made, the nori holding it together neatly. As he drags his knife through the roll, making six equal pieces, I marvel at his skills. My culinary prowess is not best demonstrated on sushi night, but Danny's is. He even created a new cocktail for us tonight using Japanese whiskey and sparkling plum wine. When he initially described it, I wasn't sure how it would taste, but the flavors work well together.

The drinks are flowing and we're slowing down on how quickly we consume the sushi rolls. As I dunk my last roll into my dish of soy sauce, my phone vibrates with an alert. I ignore it, knowing Jackson is on deck and I don't want to miss his at bat. He's already gone two for three tonight, with two singles and a run batted in. My phone vibrates again, and again, signaling multiple texts. Jackson steps up to the plate, looking relaxed yet focused. The first pitch is a ball, which Jackson watches cross the plate below his knees. The second pitch, however, is right where he told me likes to hit it, a fat pitch slightly high and outside. As soon as we hear the crack of the bat, everyone knows that ball is not staying in the park. The pitcher's shoulders hunch and he crouches at the mound in frustration; I'd almost feel bad for him if it didn't signal Jackson's success.

Jackson grins as he rounds the bases, his arms rising above his head, making a motorcycle revving motion with his hands, the team's universal signal of success. Danny, Tim, Alicia and I all cheer together from the couch. Alicia almost spills her drink during the excitement.

When things die down, I finally remember to check my phone. I have four texts from Jared. Jared? It takes me an embarrassing amount of time to recall who Jared is and why the guy I went on two dates with months ago is texting me.

Jared

> this u?

> i guess this is why u ghosted me all those months ago.

> [link to blog post]

> i mean good for u i guess.

I click on the link. It takes me to what looks like a fan website for the Foxes entitled Foxy Fanatixxx. I scroll through the post and am stunned to see my picture on the page. The photo shows Jackson kissing me on the field after a Foxes game. It must have been taken last week. I skim through the article, where "JJ JEFFERS HAS A NEW MYSTERY WOMAN" screams in bold lettering across the top. The writing that follows is largely unnecessary; the entire two paragraphs continuously say the same thing, a reiteration of the headline. I don't know how I feel about the article, other than shock.

I don't say anything for several moments. Wordlessly, I hand my phone to Alicia, who reads the article faster than I did and passes the phone to the guys. No one says anything for another minute. Alicia looks at me with concern.

"How are you feeling about this?"

"Weird. I don't know," I tell them honestly. "I mean, everyone always watches Jackson and sneaks photos of him when we're out together, but no one has ever cared about *me*. No one *should* care about me."

"Apparently, given the amount of retweets and likes this post got, a lot of people do care about you. Or at least who they think you are?" Danny is still scrolling, presumably shuffling through the comments at the end of the post.

I know better than to read through the comments. I've seen enough of the internet to know people can be cruel, and I'm choosing to protect my mental health.

"How did you find this?" Tim asks.

"Do you guys remember Jared?"

"That guy who wanted to date his sister?" Alicia screeches.

"He didn't want to date his sister," I begin. "Well, okay, maybe he did. He had a weird relationship with her to say the least. But yeah, that guy. He just texted it to me and said 'no wonder you ghosted me.' Which, I might add, I did not! I let him down easy after our second date and haven't heard from him since."

"Probably for the best, seeing as he's a grown ass man who can't capitalize or spell the word 'you.'" Danny has clearly switched back to my texts. I snatch my phone back, but he has a point. "Are you going to respond?"

"Not worth my time." I can't deny that I'm a little curious, and maybe a little scared, about my presence on a blog dedicated to the love lives of the Chicago Foxes.

When I get home later that night, I do some more digging on the Foxy Fanatixxx blog, mindful not to scroll too far down, lest I accidentally peek at the comments. The blog is filled with articles and posts from women (and the occasional man) claiming to have hooked up with various Chicago athletes, most notably the Chicago Foxes. Warner James seems to be the topic of the most posts. The right fielder is attractive, but given that the blog also has writers claiming to have slept with Caleb Andrews, the world's most devoted fiance, I doubt the veracity of anything posted there. Still, I can understand the appeal of a website like this to the public in general. I just don't know how I feel about myself starring front and center.

The good news is that half of my profile is obscured by Jackson's hand and the photo is taken from several rows back in the stands, so unless someone were to look at a side-by-side comparison of me and the photo, they likely couldn't tell it was me.

When Jackson calls me from his hotel room later, I tell him about the post. He's apologetic for dragging me into the less pleasant side of his fame, but as of right now, I'm not as bothered by it as I thought I would be. It probably helps that my name is not attached to the story and my face isn't readily identifiable.

"Are you feeling unsafe? Do you want to stay at my place? There's a little more security there," Jackson suggests.

"No, I'm fine. I guess I'm just surprised that anyone cares about me, but I know they just really care about who you're dating, rather than about me personally."

"They should care about you. They don't know what they're missing," Jackson says with a flirtatious lilt to his voice. "Can we switch to a video call? I want to see you and make sure you're really feeling okay."

We started the call on the phone because Jackson was on the bus back to the hotel and he wanted more privacy. Now that he's in his room, no one can overhear him or peek over his shoulder at his phone screen. I tap my screen and the call changes to video format. Jackson looks worried.

"Are you sure you're okay? I can't control the fans or the media, but I wish you didn't have to deal with this."

"Babe, I'm fine. It's just weird. But maybe now the women of Chicago will back off my man," I joke. Jackson's eyes soften at the realization that I'm not freaking out about this. "Let's talk about something else. Thirteen game hitting streak, huh?"

"Yeah," Jackson shrugs. "You know that's your doing, right?"

"What is?" I'm not following Jackson's logic.

"What happened thirteen games ago? Two weeks ago exactly, if we're getting technical?"

"I don't know?" I pull up my calendar on my phone. Two weeks ago was July 20th. There is nothing on my calendar. If I didn't know Jackson's birthday is in December, I might have started panicking that I missed his day.

"We technically got back to Chicago from the midseason break, then we were driving after midnight..." Jackson waits for me to fill in the blanks, but I'm coming up short. "I pulled the car over and you told me you loved me," he finishes slowly.

My brows raise. "That's not the reason you're on a hitting streak," I tell him skeptically.

"It's the reason I've felt like I'm floating for the last two weeks. And when I feel good, I play good. Simple as that." That's a gross oversimplification of things, but I'm happy to hear that Jackson is so excited about the way our relationship has progressed. Jackson continues, "Amy, you make everything better by being you, and your impact on me is no exception. I must have done something good in a former life to be able to know you, to have you in my orbit. The truth is, though, my world revolves around you. I am so grateful to call you mine."

I still don't know how to respond when Jackson gets romantic with me. I'm not used to being doted on to this level. I enjoy it, of course, but it's still an adjustment.

CHAPTER FIFTY-ONE

Amy

The next several weeks pass in happy bliss. Things with Jackson have never been better, and his road games are easier (on me, at least) because I've joined the WAGs' book club. Hailey and Jenny were accurate in their description of the book club; it really is just an excuse to socialize and drink, but the women were kind enough to move their regular start time to a little later in the day to accommodate my work schedule. Mei, Kaito Soji's wife, and I are the only women who work regular hours, but she works from home and generally makes her own hours as a consultant, so the women all insisted the adjustment was easy. I insisted they didn't have to make a change just for me, but Jenny reassured me they were happy to do it and it allowed us to still be together at the start of night games, so we mostly watch the games together as well. It's hard not to be optimistic about the state of my relationships–not just my relationship with Jackson, but with the other women at the games, too.

Now that I have a key to Jackson's place, I've been spending more time there than usual. He initially pushed for me to spend my days and nights there when he was out of town because Pete

Peterson below me was a menace. Jacks had finally had enough one night, taking matters into his own hands and banging on his door. When Pete came to the door, all he said was, "Holy shit, you're JJ Jeffers," like an idiot. Jackson snarled something about keeping his music down, and it hasn't been as much of an issue since.

Spending more time at Jackson's place wasn't much of a hardship, once I got over my initial worry that I was imposing too much of myself on Jackson's physical space. Bruno still spends his days with Lisa and her fiancee, Desiree, when Jackson is out of town, because my work schedule can be unpredictable. But when I work from Jackson's condo on Fridays, Bruno and I are inseparable.

I ring the doorbell to Caleb and Jenny's penthouse, hitching my yoga bag filled with extra props higher on my shoulder as I wait for Jenny to answer the door. When it opens, she greets me with a wide smile. She tells me she's been feeling good for the last several days, as she has had a short break between rounds of chemotherapy. We've been getting together on a weekly basis for some gentle stretching yoga, which Jenny attributes to a decrease in her general joint fatigue and soreness.

I start setting up the mats, blocks, and blankets, preparing to take Jenny through some supported yin poses to allow for nervous system and fascial relaxation. Jenny is the perfect yoga client: she's vocal about what she needs and where her body is at each session, but is open to new poses and experiences. After each session, we catch up, drinking tea and chatting in her sunny kitchen.

"I appreciate you spending your Saturday morning with me," she says, giving me a look of genuine kindness.

"This is fun for me, too," I assure her. "This allows me to flex my creative yoga muscles, practicing my cueing for getting you in and out of poses. Plus, it's nice to spend time with someone who understands how much I miss Jackson when he's out of town."

"I get it. I promise, it does get a bit easier once you get into the routine of baseball season. But sometimes, especially at night or during really long road stretches, the loneliness can be crushing," Jenny admits sadly. I release a sigh of relief; I feel terrible that Jenny feels the same way when Caleb is out of town, but the solidarity is comforting. "That's why it's so important we support each other. Caleb has been with the Foxes his whole career, which is really unusual. But some of the other wives have told me the families aren't as supportive on other teams. It can be really isolating for the wives and girlfriends whose partners are on different teams."

I quietly reflect on how grateful I am that Jackson is with the Foxes, before a new worry starts poking at me. "What do you think the chances are that Jackson will get traded to a different team?" I ask her, grimacing at the possibility.

"I guess anything is possible, really. The guys don't have a lot of control over where they end up; those decisions are made by the higher ups in the organization and we basically go where we're told. But if JJ continues playing well and the Foxes stay in contention for the postseason, I'd say it's probably not likely anytime this season. More than anything, it depends on what his contract looks like and how much time is left on it." I make a mental note to ask Jackson his opinion. I have no idea what stipulations are in his contract, and I don't feel like it's my place to ask about all the details, but it'd be nice to know if there is suddenly going to be an expiration date on our relationship if Jackson is abruptly no longer playing for the Foxes.

When Jackson and I have our regular video call later that night, I ask him just that.

"Do you think you'll get traded?" I blurt out after he greets me, barely giving him enough time to get into his hotel room and set his backpack down after his win against Detroit.

"Um, why do you ask? Is there a rumor going around or something?" Jackson looks worried, and I try not to read into it, but apparently my face did not get the message to portray calm instead of panicked. "Baby, what's going on? Where is this coming from, Ames?"

"I was talking with Jenny today, and she mentioned the possibility of anyone being traded at any time, and while I guess it's always been a possibility, I've never really thought of it as it relates to you before and I'm not sure how I feel about that or what it would mean for us, and I love you but I guess I'm just wondering how you feel about things, or if you think it's a legitimate possibility for you to be traded, and how that would work for you...and for us,"

I finish weakly. Jackson blinks and takes a moment to process my word vomit.

"Well, Jenny's right, sort of. Anyone could get traded prior to the trade deadline, technically." Jackson smiles when my eyes widen and hurriedly adds, "But seeing as the trade deadline was last week, it's not happening for me."

My shoulders sag and in the corner of our video call, I see the relief apparent in my own reflection. I didn't realize how stressed out I was about something that, unbeknownst to me, wasn't really possible at the moment. Jackson laughs gently. "Were you getting yourself worked up over this, Ames?" I nod, my cheeks flaming at my own stupidity. "You know you can always come to me with your concerns and I'll reassure you. You should have called or texted earlier. But in case you can't reach me and you're worried about trade rumors, I'll give you Sean's phone number. He usually finds out that stuff before me, even, and he'll shoot you straight. But Jenny is right; I don't have a say in whether or not I get traded. I just have to roll with it." I can feel a stress headache coming on. I was not prepared for how out of control I would feel just because I was dating someone in professional sports.

"Amy, I know it's hard, but try not to worry. It's not something that's going to happen this year, and I have three more years on my contract in Chicago. I'd like to spend all of them there, but if I get traded, then I'll have to leave, and we'll figure it out then. But in case you were worried about us, specifically, I'd want you to come with me. It'd be a lot to figure out, logistically, but I told you a long time ago, Ames, I'm all in on this. I'm all in on you. So we're going to make it work," he finishes definitively. I can't help the smile that creeps onto my face. "Anything else you're worried about, pretty girl?" I shake my head. "Good. Now tell me about your day."

Chapter Fifty-Two

Amy

I relish the pull against the muscles in my back body as I press into downward facing dog. I slowly pedal my feet, deepening the stretch against my calves and Achilles. Pushing up onto my tiptoes, I gently drop my feet and hips to one side, then the other. My low back crackles with delicious release.

I initially told Jackson I loved him a month ago, but I should have told him sooner. This last month has been nothing short of bliss, ever since I spoke those words into the atmosphere and the universe responded with so much warmth. STEM camp wrapped up nicely and the kids should be settling into the beginning of a new school year. My mind is buzzing with ideas for field trip programs. My brain is usually firing on all cylinders in the middle of my yoga classes. It usually flits from one topic to another, sometimes revisiting the same ideas multiple times in one class. But, without fail, by the time we reach savasana, the final resting pose, I'm relaxed and my brain is at ease. This is exactly why I practice. The only times my brain feels truly offline is at the end of a tough yoga class or in bed with Jackson.

Jackson returns home from a road trip late tonight. He already asked me to wait at his place for him—as if I had anywhere else I'd rather be. Earlier this week, my name was released as Jackson's girlfriend on the Foxy Fanatixxx website. I don't know how they figured out my first *and* last name, but that seems to be all the internet can figure out about me. Luckily, I keep my social media profiles private, and my name is relatively common, so I haven't felt unsafe or hounded, but I've avoided the Foxy Fanatixxx website and its comments section all the same. I'm finally in a place where I feel good about myself and my relationship with Jackson; no need to rock that boat with uninvited internet trolls.

On the way home from class, I stop by Caffeine Kingdom to grab a dirty chai. I'm planning on heading straight to Jackson's to wait for him and will need all the caffeine I can get. He's due to land around ten, which isn't that far off, but between a long day of work and a particularly grueling hot yoga class, I'll need help staying awake any longer than the few minutes after my shower typically allows. I've slowly moved my shower products to Jackson's house over the last month; he threatened to buy extras of everything if I didn't just leave them there when he caught me packing them up to bring home before one of his road trips.

I'm pleasantly surprised that my anxiety about our relationship and our future has quelled as much as it has over the last several weeks. Ultimately, I know it's because Jackson has proven over and over again that he has no plans to abandon me anytime soon and he is beyond worthy of my trust. I'm so wrapped up in my thoughts about the happy state of our relationship and how far we've come, I don't notice the footsteps behind me until they come up immediately next to me. I catch a glimpse of someone pulling up beside me on the sidewalk just prior to them grabbing my arm, squeezing tightly, and hissing into my ear.

"Keep walking, Amy Stone. Act natural and no one will get hurt."

CHAPTER FIFTY-THREE

Jackson

I lost the last round of Mario Kart to McClintock. I was in first place until he launched that goddamn blue shell at me at the last minute. I have to hand it to him, his timing was impeccable. That round should have been mine. Of course he had to destroy me in the last round, just as the wheels touched down at O'Hare and there was no more time left for another round.

I shove my Switch and headphones into my backpack, eager to deplane and get home to Amy. I turn my phone off airplane mode, mildly disappointed not to have received any messages from her while we were in the air. She often will send me cute little messages about how excited she is to see me, and to say I'm obsessed is an understatement. I know Amy was heading to an evening yoga class, but I was hoping she'd send me a quick text when she was done. Caleb grins, seeing my scowl as I refresh my texts.

"Everything okay?" he asks with an annoying smirk. "No texts from Amy?" I immediately regret sharing my girlfriend's cute little habits with my best friend. He's so annoying.

"It's fine," I say, rolling my eyes at Caleb. "She'll be at my place waiting for me. She's had a long day, so a hundred bucks says she's asleep in my bed right now, asshole."

"I can't wait to get back to Jenny. I'm going to wake her up and make love to her if she's feeling as good as she has been lately."

"Dude. Stop. I don't need to know about you *making love* to Jenny." I roll my eyes again, but I'm secretly happy for both Caleb and Jenny. Her health has been on an upward trend lately, and if she's feeling good enough to have sex with her fiance, then that's all I could ever want for the two of them.

Caleb climbs into his car, blowing me a kiss and yelling, "Bye, pretty boy. Say hi to Amy for me, if you can remove your tongue from her mouth long enough to form words."

I climb into my own car, flipping him off through the front windshield, but I can't stop the grin stretching across my face. Only a twenty minute commute stands between me and my girl, and I cannot wait.

When I finally roll up to my building, though, I immediately know something is wrong. Sitting on the front steps and under the glow of the porch lights, instead of safe and happy inside my condo unit, is Amy. She's sitting with someone, and her body language indicates she's not happy. Did she get locked out? She knows the code to the building, though, and can always grab the spare key from Lisa and Desiree, so I can't make sense of why she is waiting outside. As I pull in closer, Amy spots me and I see a brief flash of relief on her face, before I take in the woman standing next to her, gesticulating wildly. Amy is not alone.

Standing next to her, looking feral and unstable, is my mother.

CHAPTER FIFTY-FOUR

Jackson

I don't bother pulling into the parking garage beneath my building. I make it as far as the front drive, inside the security gate, before throwing the car in park and launching myself out of my vehicle.

"What the fuck are you doing here?" It comes out as a low growl. If I wasn't so panicked about Amy's well-being, I'd laugh at the realization that my voice sounds as wild as my mother looks at this moment.

"Jackson, baby! Is that any way to greet your mother?" I ignore her, sprinting towards Amy, who looks pale but unharmed. My mother steps between us and I easily sidestep her, moving around her to get to my girlfriend.

"Are you okay?" I ask quietly, taking Amy's shoulders and trying to complete a quick visual inspection. "Are you hurt?" Amy shakes her head right as my mother decides now is the best time to latch onto my arm.

"Jackie, baby, I need your help. I found your girlfriend and I knew she'd bring me to you. You weren't answering your phone! I'm in a bit of a situation, you see, and I knew if anyone could help, it'd be you, my beautiful boy," my mother rambles quickly, as if she knows if she doesn't get the words out fast enough, I'll cut her off like I'm about to. Instead, I ignore her. Her brown hair is dirty and stringy; my mother looks like she hasn't eaten a solid meal in days, maybe longer. Her eyes are wild and wide.

"Leave. Now." I spit at the woman who birthed me, shaking her off my arm. She seizes the opportunity to grab Amy's arm. Amy winces, and I see red. "You have one second to get your filthy hands off my girlfriend, Laurie."

My mother sputters. "Laurie? What happened to *Mom?*" she squawks, but releases her grip on Amy's arm.

"You haven't been my mother for more than twenty years," I reply, cold rage coursing through my blood. "Now leave. Do not contact us again, or I'll call the police."

"Jackie, my boy, listen to me. I'm in a tight situation and I just need you to listen. I just need your help."

I take Amy's hands, tugging her gently toward me. "Come on, Ames, we're leaving. Get in the car." My voice is lethally quiet; beneath Amy's thin veneer of stoicism, I can start to see her fear. I imagine she's at peak anxiety right now and I just need her in my arms. I need to make sure she's okay. My mother continues her unhinged ramblings and I'm only vaguely aware she's still talking.

"I didn't want to have to do this, you know! You're forcing my hand, Jacks!" Laurie's voice has reached a squeaky pitch, desperate and piercing. I turn to tell her to never call me that name when I catch a flash of silver.

I pull Amy behind me, my movements so quick and automatic, I know I've acted on instinct alone, placing myself between my girlfriend and the barrel of a gun.

CHAPTER FIFTY-FIVE

Amy

My head is swimming. My brain is processing everything in slow motion, like I'm trying to run through molasses. I can't form words, I can't form thoughts.

It's true what they say: fight or flight is a real fear response. When flight wasn't an option after Jackson's mother initially grabbed me and steered me toward his condo, anger and fight was my first response. How *dare* she seek out her son after all this time–after she abandoned him? My righteous anger had everything to do with her attempt at a sudden reappearance in Jackson's life and almost nothing to do with her assault on me in the middle of the sidewalk. I had no choice but to walk with her to Jackson's condo, but she didn't need to know that I had a key. There was no way I was letting that woman into his building, let alone his actual dwelling. I've seen enough true crime shows to know you don't go with a psycho to a second location; it's bad enough she forced me to the outside of Jackson's building. So we sat on the front steps, waiting for Jackson's return, while I tried to formulate a plan.

What I don't count on, however, is my total freeze response after Laurie pulls out the gun. Jackson becomes a man of action, throwing me behind him. His voice is calm, lethally so, and if I wasn't so terrified of Laurie Jeffers in this moment, I might be scared *for* her.

"Laurie, put the gun down." Jackson's stillness is almost alarming. I can't stop the shaking in my limbs, and I clutch the back of his shirt, desperately sucking in ragged breaths, trying to imbue some semblance of calm into my terror-stricken brain. He reaches slowly behind him, taking hold of my hand and squeezing gently. The pressure of his touch anchors me, and some of my trembling subsides.

"I am your *mother!*" Laurie screams. Her hand holding the gun shakes with her increasingly anguished cries, but her grip is white-knuckled and strong. "You're going to *listen* to me, Jackson!"

He holds up one placating palm, keeping a tight grip on mine with his other hand, never relinquishing his hold. "Okay, okay, I'm listening. Mom," he adds hastily. The addition of her title seems to mollify Laurie slightly. "Let's talk. Just put the gun down, Mom." Jackson seems to have picked up on Laurie's desperation to be addressed as his mother.

"No. No. I'm not going to do that," she repeats quietly. "We're beyond that. You're going to listen to me because I need your *help*, son."

I feel Jackson physically recoil when she calls him her son, but he says nothing, silently inviting her to get on with it.

"Ron and I are in trouble." Jackson's whole body tenses at the mention of Laurie's boyfriend. "We need money, and we need it now. And if you could *just* give us enough to pay off the interest on our loan, then we can work something out to pay back the rest." Jackson doesn't say anything. I start to worry that he's now frozen in fear, but Laurie doesn't seem to notice. She rambles on. "Ron is in a real bad way. He's sick, you know. He can't help it, he needs just a little more meth to balance him out. And if we don't get them the money, they'll hurt him."

Laurie is crying now, desperate sobs wracking her thin body. She's emotionally desperate, but otherwise physically put together, other than maybe needing a shower, so it doesn't seem like she's on drugs at this moment. But she's not making a lot of sense and I don't know who the *they* is that she's talking about. Still, Jackson is silent.

"How much money do you need?" I whisper, unsticking my tongue from the roof of my mouth. Jackson whips his head around to stare at me, eyes wide, as if he's terrified, or angry, that I'm trying to rationalize this situation.

"Two hundred and fifty thousand. For the interest," Laurie whispers back, gripping the handle of the gun tighter, steadying herself.

"Two hundred and fifty thousand?" Jackson roars. I want to remind him there is still a gun pointed at us, and now is not the time for indignation over money, not when a mentally unstable family member is wielding a weapon, but I can only rationalize with one person right now.

"It's the interest payment!" I'm not sure what point Laurie is trying to make, as if a quarter of a million dollars is somehow justifiable as interest alone. "Once we pay off the interest, we can talk about the rest of the payment plans. We borrowed money from this guy named Lucien, and I was able to make payments initially. Remember how good I am at poker, Jackie?"

Laurie's words come tumbling out of her mouth, faster than my mind can make sense of them. I shake my head, urging my brain to keep up, to somehow say or do something to fix this mess we've found ourselves in. I can practically feel the rage vibrating off Jackson at this point, but he never lets go of my hand. I'm grateful for that, as I'm not confident my legs will continue to hold me up for much longer. For a wild, brief moment, I wonder if I can slip my phone from my yoga bag without Laurie noticing, but I know there's not a chance in hell I can do that without drawing attention to myself.

"I'm so good at it, but I hit a tough streak, and we needed more money. I bet on the wrong horse, so to speak." She pauses to glare at Jackson, as if that was somehow his fault. "Remember that rough patch you had? I kept betting on you to break it, to go on a hitting streak, but it took you so long, and I couldn't keep waiting. And wouldn't you know it, as soon as I started betting against you, you got hot again." Laurie resumes her wild gesticulations, as if by explaining her situation, she is reliving the tension. "Jackie, we can fix this. *You* can fix this. I just need a little bit of money right now, and I'll bring it to Lucien myself. I won't let Ron do it this time. It wasn't his fault the last time, he needed the drugs." Laurie shakes her head and I wonder if she's trying to convince us or herself that Ron is innocent. "Once the interest is settled, I'll just need you to set up with me before each game how you're going to play it. I'll make my bets accordingly, and we'll be even."

My heart stops. Is Laurie actually asking her son to cheat, in order to help her win sports bets to pay off this debt? Laurie Jeffers is asking her son, the most trustworthy, honorable man I know, to destroy his reputation, his career, his *integrity*, in order to pay off some debt his deadbeat mother accrued? Jackson seems to come to this realization at the same time I do.

Thinking in this moment feels like swimming through slowly hardening concrete. I want to move, want to agree with Laurie, to say anything to get her to put the gun down and walk away. But I can't get my mouth to form the words. Luckily, Jackson speaks for me.

"Fuck. You."

Shit. Those were not the words I needed Jackson to say. We needed to be talking Laurie off the ledge, not pushing her closer to it.

Sirens sound in the distance, but I've lived in Chicago long enough to know they are probably not for us. There's enough crime in this city, albeit not as much in this exact area, for me not to be able to trust that someone is coming to save us.

"Laurie," I start. My voice comes out as a shaky whisper. I clear my throat and try again. This time, it's a little stronger, enough to break through Laurie's desperate ramblings. "Laurie. I can get you the money, okay? It might take me a little bit of time, but I can get it together. I have some savings, and I can go to the ATM tonight, okay?"

Jackson's hand tightens around mine, in warning or surprise, I'm not sure. But Laurie seems reassured by my words. I don't have nearly all the money she's looking for, but I'm hoping the few thousand I do have saved is enough to hold her over, long enough to get her to give up the gun, at least.

"I'll pay it," Jackson says quietly. "Let Amy go, and I'll do whatever you need." I gape at Jackson, although he can't see my face. There has to be another way to get out of this. I won't let Jackson destroy himself.

"See, I knew you'd help me, Jackie boy. Ron said you wouldn't, but I knew you'd see reason," Laurie gushes. The tension in her arms and the aim of her gun loosens slightly, but noticeably.

"I'll help you, and then you're out of my life forever. Sean's and Nate's, too." Laurie is nodding along, but I don't know if she's even listening anymore. She heard what she needed to.

"Go get the money, Jackson," she snaps, suddenly all business. I stare at her incredulously. Does she think Jackson just keeps a quarter of a million dollars lying around in his house? Jackson makes no move to leave, clearly uneasy about any movement while Laurie is still brandishing the gun.

The sirens screech to a deafening roar as three police vehicles careen onto the street, lights flashing and tires squealing. *They were coming for us*, I think, my knees almost buckling with relief. Two officers hop out of the first SUV, guns drawn, while another calls from the neighboring squad car through the megaphone.

"Put the gun down!"

Everything happens in slow motion.

Laurie turns her head. Her arms swing wide, and in one slow, fluid motion that will forever be seared into my brain, squeezes the trigger.

My world goes black as Jackson falls against me.

CHAPTER FIFTY-SIX

Amy

It takes me a long time to realize the screaming I'm hearing is coming from me.

Someone is shaking me, yet I can't feel it. I see a woman's face, swimming in and out of focus in my line of sight. She brings her face close to mine and moves her mouth. I can't hear her. I don't know what she's saying. But it's her who is shaking me. Still, I feel nothing. I'm looking without seeing. Hearing without understanding. All I know is my world has shattered around me and I can't be here.

I don't want to be here. Not without Jackson.

All I know, all I keep replaying in my mind, is the sound of a gunshot blast and the feel of Jackson's body slumping, falling against me, dragging us both to the hard concrete in front of his building.

This isn't how this was supposed to go. This isn't how Jackson and I are supposed to end. We're supposed to die together, curled up together, hunched and shriveled in our old age, having lived complete and fulfilling lives together.

This is not how it's supposed to be.

CHAPTER FIFTY-SEVEN
Jackson

They say when you almost die, your life flashes before your eyes. I'm not sure if that's true or not, never having almost died myself. But I have lived through an excruciating, potentially life-threatening situation, and I can honestly say that it wasn't my life that flashed before my eyes in those potential last moments.

It was the life that could have been. It was the life I should have had with Amy. I didn't contemplate my past. I didn't experience a movie highlight reel of the best or most memorable moments of my life. Instead, when that gun went off, all I could think of was surviving with Amy, thriving with Amy, living the life we should live. Undergoing some sort of alternate reality where Amy and I grow old together after experiencing all of the best parts of life.

Traveling. Making love. Laughing. Crying. Dancing and sitting and *being* with each other.

As the paramedic presses gauze and towels against my left bicep in a painful attempt to staunch the bleeding, I try to collect my bearings. I attempt to sit up, and two sets of hands push me back down.

"Sir, the bullet grazed your arm, you need to keep still."

"Amy! Amy! Where are you?" My pleas are desperate. I need to get to her. I need to know she's okay. My ears are ringing. *Where is Amy?* I can't hear anything over the sound of someone screaming. I widen my eyes in an attempt to see more, to take in more, so I can just *find* Amy. Finally, the woman to my right, bent over someone on the ground, moves slightly, and I catch sight of wild chocolate eyes and a tangle of blonde hair. "Amy," I choke out.

The screaming stops. It was coming from her. My beautiful, terrified, unharmed girl. I shake off the paramedics attempting to keep me seated and crawl over to her.

Amy is sobbing as she takes my face in her hands, frantically patting me across my cheeks, my neck, my shoulders. Checking to make sure I'm really here, safe, alive. I clock the exact moment she takes in my bloody arm; she instinctively reaches out to touch it, to press my tattered skin back together. The EMTs stop her, pressing more gauze into the wound. My movements cause more blood to gush out of my arm, but the surrounding emergency response personnel seem to understand that I need Amy in my arms more than medical intervention right now. I pull her close with my right arm and she fully collapses against me.

CHAPTER FIFTY-EIGHT

Amy

"Here, my love," I say, handing Jackson a mug of coffee. I would have gotten him his usual order from Caffeine Kingdom, but I'm still not ready to leave him alone, so drip coffee from his kitchen will have to suffice for now.

"Thanks, baby, but I could have gotten this myself, you know. Laurie shot my arm, not my leg." I roll my eyes, then instantly feel guilty and pounce on Jackson, peppering his face and neck with soft kisses. "Not that I'm complaining, but Amy, baby, you're going a little crazy. All this taking care of me is a bit of overkill, don't you think?"

"As a matter of fact, no, I don't think it's overkill." I glare at Jackson. "You almost died—"

"It was a bullet *graze*, Amy. And I'm *fine*. A little sore, but Dr. Adams said I can return to play in another week."

"Well *Dr. Adams* didn't see you get shot!" Tears well in my eyes. Admittedly, I've been a lot more emotional in the week since the shooting. I know in my heart that Jackson is okay, but I can't help doting on him. When the gun went off, Jackson flung his arm up to shield me further. I'm still processing that, that in the one moment when everything mattered, in a life and death situation, Jackson, subconsciously or not, chose to protect me. Connie, my therapist, says to embrace my need to care for Jackson, that taking care of him is allowing me to feel some semblance of control in a situation so far outside of my control, but Jackson isn't used to being taken care of so thoroughly.

We later learned that Desiree, concerned with the shouting occurring outside of the building, looked out her bedroom window to see Laurie holding us at gunpoint. She called the police and stayed on the line with them, reporting Laurie's every move until the police arrived. I admit that I may have gone a little overboard in my gratitude response to Desiree, baking cookies and dropping new batches off at her and Lisa's door every few hours until Lisa kindly but gently begged me to stop.

Immediately following the incident, paramedics packed Jackson and me up in the ambulance–there was not a chance in hell I was going to leave Jackson's side until he was firmly and securely in the hospital, where they pried me off his body to take him in back to stitch him up and fill him with antibiotics. They brought me to my own bay for a few hours to check me out, diagnosing me with a mild concussion from hitting my head when the force of Jackson falling against me knocked me to the ground. My mother, stepfather, and Connie all met me at the hospital. I was a little embarrassed by the scene they were causing, processing their emotions with me in the waiting room, until Jackson's brother came in and all hell broke loose.

Sean stormed into the hospital like he owned it, barked orders left and right, and for some reason, everyone listened. Instead of releasing Jackson after several hours like originally planned, Sean strong armed the doctors into keeping him overnight for observation. Sean then disappeared for several more hours, returning in the early hours of the morning to report what he had learned from the police.

Laurie was arrested, obviously, and suffered only minor injuries from her takedown by the police. She claimed the gun went off accidentally, and she dropped it immediately after it fired. I'm not sure whether I believe the shooting was accidental or not; I haven't allowed myself to truly process that part of the situation yet. Sean worked tirelessly to get a restraining order for Jackson and me set up immediately. Not that it really matters, as Laurie is being held without bail, but it offered us a modicum of reassurance anyway.

When news of Jackson's shooting broke, the city lost its collective mind. The Foxes front office was inundated with flowers, cards, and fruit baskets. Jackson just shook his head, uncomfortable with the outpouring of love directed his way for what he termed as a "minor injury."

The worst part of all of this, though, is not the physical injury to Jackson's arm. The doctors said as long as his stitches are healing appropriately and he avoids infection, he can return to play in two weeks. Major League Baseball, however, is not so optimistic.

Jacks is currently under investigation for sports gambling, based on his mother's allegations and betting history. The injustice of everything makes me want to scream. Jackson is trying to take everything in stride, saying MLB just needs to do its due diligence, but I know he's worried. He held a press conference a few days ago, Sean and me by his side, expressing his confidence that the investigation would clear him of any wrongdoing.

So now we just wait. That's what is killing me. Not knowing if Jackson's career is over is nothing short of torture. I've been on leave from work since "the incident," as we are now referring to it. I attend virtual therapy every other day with Connie, and I feel like it's helping. I'm still terrified to leave Jackson's side unless someone else is home with him, so I haven't left the house much. Cognitively, I know that isn't helping, but emotionally, it's hard to let go of the fear enough to trust Jacks will be okay without me.

There are perks to being home with Jackson, both of us taking time away from work for a bit. He tolerates my doting and I tolerate his grumbles about not needing to be doted upon. We make sweet slow love, careful not to put a lot of pressure on Jacks' arm and risk bursting the stitches. And every night, we curl up into each other, safe in the knowledge we are alive and together, if nothing else.

CHAPTER FIFTY-NINE

Jackson

The second week of recovery is easier to manage than the first. Amy has stopped looking at me with fear in her eyes, like I am going to whither and die in front of her. The pain in my arm is manageable and my guilt surrounding my fall on top of Amy, causing her concussion, is starting to subside a little, too. My guilt about the entire situation? That's a different story. I'm not sure why all the manipulative women in my life are coming out of the woodwork this year, but Carolyn and my mother top the list, so there shouldn't be any more "surprises."

I know Amy's working through her own shit as a result of my mother's antics, and it kills me to know I've put her through this, however inadvertent my role was. When I expressed sorrow about what Amy went through, however, she reassured me she'd do it all over again if it meant keeping me alive. I didn't know what to say to that, so I said nothing to anyone for several hours, simply processing Amy's devotion and willing the burning sensation behind my eyes to subside.

When Sean calls me, I answer with dread. He now calls every few hours to check up on me, but he inevitably has some tidbit of information to share with me, either regarding my mother's impending trial, the ongoing gambling investigation, or the whereabouts of the suddenly-impossible-to-find Ron. Sean hired a private investigator to look into his whereabouts, and I know the police are interested as well.

"Hey, Sean," I greet. "What's going on?"

"I just got a call from MLB. They want us to meet them at the Foxes' admin buildings. They're ready to present their findings, and, as you know, you have a right to hear the information before it goes public. I'll pick you up in twenty." He says nothing more before hanging up, leaving me to swallow the lump in my throat and attempt to hold down my vomit for the next twenty minutes.

Sean is staying at a hotel near the ballpark, across the street from the Foxes' administrative offices. As I understand it, he visits in person daily to get updates, even though Major League Baseball is conducting the investigation, and not the Foxes. I think he feels just as helpless as I do, so going in and pressuring the Foxes makes him feel like he's doing something, which is better than sitting and waiting and doing nothing. I understand the feeling.

Amy presses a soft, lingering kiss to my lips before I go.

"You know I love you, no matter what, right? And you and I know the truth. No matter the outcome, I'm by your side, and we'll figure it all out, okay?" I nod, my throat too tight to speak.

Nate has been in town since the incident, too, staying with Sean in his hotel room. He's coming to stay at my condo with Amy while Sean and I head in to hear the results. I'm glad Amy won't be alone, but I know she'll feed off Nate's nervous energy the entire time I'm gone. I hope for everyone's sake that the verdict is quick. Just rip the bandage off.

"JJ, Sean, thanks for coming in," MLB's commissioner says when we walk into the conference room the Foxes have reserved for us. The late summer sun streaming cheerfully through the windows feels incongruous to the dread I'm feeling. The commissioner, Kelvin Pomeroy, is a bit pompous, but he seems generally fair from everything I've heard about him. However, I can't help feeling a little alarmed that he's here in person to deliver the results of the investigation. Doesn't he have assistants or other people to do this for him?

"As you know," he continues, inviting us to sit, "the public is extremely interested in the outcome of this investigation. JJ, you've been through a terrible ordeal. How are you feeling?"

"I'm hanging in there. Excited to return to play," I say with a false sense of confidence. I don't want to partake in small talk; just tell me the results so I can get on with my life, one way or another.

Pomeroy smiles, but I don't know him well enough to tell if it's a pitying or indulgent smile. He claps his hands and gets started. "JJ, we've done a lot of digging into your baseball career. Your performance has been reviewed since you signed in the minor leagues. We've also dug into your contacts with your mother and attempted contacts with her associate, Ron Plank. We appreciate your forthcoming with all of the evidence we've requested of you."

I nod curtly, unable to speak when Pomeroy pauses. "Your agent, Sean, has been forthcoming with all available information and reporting to regulatory agencies promptly each time your mother has attempted to contact you since you went pro." Again, I nod. I don't know what else to say. Pomeroy stands, walking over to a stack of documents at the head of the table.

He lays out document after document on the conference room table. "Here are the records submitted by Mr. Jeffers," Pomeroy inclines his head toward Sean, "and you. Here is Ms. Jeffers' statement to the police."

Sean reaches forward, a grim look on his face. We haven't seen Laurie's statement to the police. We haven't exactly asked for it, but I assumed we'd be denied any information on our mother's case, considering it's an ongoing investigation. Sean skims the document far faster than I'd be able to, never having seen a criminal statement in my life. Still, the suspense is killing me and I wordlessly urge him to read faster. The statement is several pages long and I'm losing patience. Finally, after what seems like hours, Sean looks up.

"Alright. I know the evidence JJ and I provided MLB exonerates him. Laurie's statement," he gestures at the packet he placed back on the table, "also clearly indicates all attempts at contact prior to the shooting were unsuccessful. Laurie admits she never successfully got ahold of JJ to sway his performance one way or another."

Pomeroy nods slowly. "Yes, that's true. But you see, we had to ensure she did not have other ways of communicating with JJ." Suddenly, I hate Kelvin Pomeroy. I want to slap his smug smile off his slowly nodding head. "We needed to thoroughly investigate any factors that could have directly or indirectly impacted JJ's on-field performance."

Sean's eyes flash. "Cut to the chase, Pomeroy." As much as I want to smack Pomeroy, I'm not sure Sean's tone of thinly veiled disrespect is the best course of action when this man holds my future in his hands.

"After near round the clock review, interviews with staff and teammates, and an overall thorough investigation, I'm pleased to report JJ is cleared of any wrongdoing. He does not appear to have been influenced in any way by Ms. Jeffers or Mr. Plank—or anyone else, for that matter." He tacks on hastily. "Mr. Jeffers," Pomeroy turns toward me, "I'm happy to report your temporary suspension for the duration of this investigation is lifted. You are free to return to play as soon as you are medically cleared."

CHAPTER SIXTY

Amy

Jackson's been gone for more than an hour and a half. He shouldn't be gone this long. I can't help but think if he was cleared, he would have been back by now. The only reason I can fathom for him taking this long is to refute whatever evidence MLB thinks they have on him.

"Jacks is gonna be cleared, Ames," Nate reassures me with a gentle squeeze of my shoulder, correctly reading my thoughts. "I'm sure they'll be home any minute."

I start pacing Jackson's living room, at a loss for what to do with my nervous energy. Bruno watches from a corner of the couch, unsure what's going on, but clearly picking up on the collective mood of the household for the last several hours. He hasn't even tried to chew his toys. His ears perk up when he hears the drag of the key in the front door lock. I swear my heart stops, anticipating the worst.

Jackson walks through the door, looking haggard and exhausted. Behind him, Sean's face is inscrutable.

"Well?" I prompt impatiently. It comes out less supportive than I woul liked, but my anxiety is in the driver's seat right now. Jackson smiles, and it's one of the most beautiful things I've ever seen.

"Cleared. All cleared," he repeats as I rush forward, falling into his arms. We slide to the floor together, the stress, fear, and exhaustion of the last two weeks culminating in our shared sobs as we clutch each other, mindful of Jackson's still healing left arm.

Nate turns away, wiping at his eyes. "I knew you'd be cleared!" he sniffles. Nate claps Sean on the back before whispering to him, "Good job, bro." He walks swiftly to the fridge to pull out a bottle of champagne I never saw him put in there. At Sean's raised brow, Nate shrugs. "What? I knew he'd beat it."

Sean crosses the room and pulls out whiskey glasses (Jackson doesn't own champagne flutes), while Nate splashes a generous amount of champagne in each one, spilling on the counter as his hand shakes. Jackson stands and pulls both of his brothers into a long, crushing hug. No words are said, but Jackson's shoulders shake, Nate's arms tremble, and when they break away, Sean clears his throat and turns away, giving himself a moment to gather his composure.

These men have been through so much. Brothers who have had to rely on each other too soon, from too early of an age, but who never stopped believing in each other. My tears find new tracks down my cheeks as I think about all that Sean and Nate have done for my beautiful, strong, honorable man.

Tonight, when he and I finally curl up against each other, Jackson lets out a long, shuddering sigh.

"I didn't know if it was going to go my way today, Amy. I was so scared. I'm afraid of who I'd be if I had to leave baseball with my reputation in ruins." I pull Jackson tighter against me as a single tear tracks down toward the tip of his nose.

"I'm so proud of you, Jacks. I was scared, too, but now we can move forward. Together," I whisper back.

"Thanks for sticking by my side through all the garbage of this investigation. I was terrified I'd lose you when that gun went off, Amy, but I was equally afraid of losing your trust if the results of the investigation were different."

"I don't need an investigation to tell me that my man is trustworthy, honorable, and honest. You've had my trust since the beginning, when you steadfastly, quietly, and steadily held my hand every day. You patiently waited for me when I wasn't ready to face my own feelings. You loved me when I've been so hard to love. One little hiccup isn't going to change that. You'll always be a man with integrity; that's who you are, Jacks. It's in your bones. And I am so, so proud to know and love you."

CHAPTER SIXTY-ONE

Jackson

My return to Foxes Field is shaping up to be quite the homecoming. I have three separate press conferences scheduled prior to the game, in addition to my normal pregame activities. Fans have been camped outside the player parking lot overnight. It's over the top and a little embarrassing, but a part of me is grateful for the attention and the love. It's a unique feeling, knowing an entire city supports you.

I arrive at the stadium several hours early, not only due to my packed schedule, but because Stephen, one of the clubbies, had texted me late last night to let me know my "fan club" was setting up shop already outside the player lot. If the fans stake out a spot, choosing to sleep on the concrete overnight just to show their support for me, the least I can do is show up early and get some face time in. I sign autographs for about forty-five minutes before Benny sends Kennedy, our hitting coach, to come drag me inside, much to the moans of the fans. I only got to sign for about half of the crowd.

Benny requested I conduct my pregame warmup in the training room instead of on the field to allow my teammates to better focus. When I do finally step out onto the field for the national anthem, the roar of the crowd is deafening. I take my place next to Caleb on the foul line, choking up. He slings his arm around my shoulder and keeps it there for the duration of The Star Spangled Banner, squeezing me roughly when my emotions momentarily overwhelm me. However, by the time the last note sounds and the announcer cries, "Play ball!" I'm locked in and focused on the game.

My first at bat is one I'll remember my entire career. Sure, half the crowd is just excited they let me keep playing baseball following my mother's addiction nightmare. But the tips of the hat I get from the umpire crew and opposing team let me know it's more than that; I'm lucky to be alive, and the force of everyone's gratitude for me being *alive* hits me like a freight train.

I need another moment to collect my emotions. And when the pitch clock runs out and I still haven't stepped in the batter's box, everyone, including the opposing team, ignores the time violation. I swipe at my eyes with the sleeves of my jersey and, taking a deep, centering breath, finally step in and ready my stance.

CHAPTER SIXTY-TWO

Amy

My ears are still ringing from the concert last night. Jackson dragged me to a pop punk band reunion tour, claiming the music would change my life. They were good, admittedly great, but after drinking all night with Jackson, Caleb, and Jenny, my hangxiety is hitting me extra hard this morning. Jacks reassures me I didn't do anything embarrassing in my drunken state, passing me a bottle of water and some ibuprofen. I narrow my eyes at him, not fully believing him. Jackson's definition of embarrassing and mine are a little different. Still, he holds me all morning and orders me greasy breakfast delivery from Moonshadow Diner to appease me.

I scarf down my cheesy potatoes and eggs, starting to feel marginally better but still anxious as fuck. I feel a pang of guilt that Jackson is in a relationship with someone who he constantly has to reassure. He always sends me texts letting me know when he'll be late so I don't worry unnecessarily. He never tires of telling me he's still happy in our relationship when I ask. He checks in on my emotional state even more frequently after the incident with his mother.

Laurie ended up taking a plea deal, avoiding a long, drawn-out trial. It was probably the most selfless thing she ever did for Jackson. The media surrounding the case was already a circus; the scrutiny Jacks and I would have been subjected to, had the whole thing gone to trial, would have been nothing short of a nightmare. Sentencing alone was traumatic. Jackson declined to give a victim impact statement, insisting he had nothing left to say to or about his mother. I, however, needed a little more closure, and Jackson stood by my side, holding my hand, as I gave my victim impact statement immediately before Laurie was sentenced. I cried throughout my speech, reminding Laurie she should be ashamed of herself for the horrors she put me through and the unending trauma she inflicted on her poor boys. Throughout the reading of my statement, Laurie kept her eyes down, staring at the table in front of her. Then, when she was sentenced, I walked away and effectively closed that chapter of my life. It surprisingly hasn't been hard to keep that door closed, knowing no more good can come from spending mental energy on Laurie Jeffers.

Ron Plank's bloated body was eventually found a few months after Laurie's sentencing, floating to the surface of a lake in Austin. Apparently, Lucien found Ron before Sean's private detective or the police could. I find it hard to muster a lot of sympathy for him, given everything Jackson's told me about him.

Still, I can't help but grieve on behalf of Jackson for all he's been through. I still have my moments of low self-esteem, where

I wish Jackson didn't have to put up with my anxiety and my mental health challenges. He deserves someone with unshakeable confidence not only in his love for them, but in their own ability to be enough for him. Connie and I have been working on communicating my feelings honestly, so I share this with Jackson.

His face softens as he shakes his head, giving me a small smile. "Amy, if I have to remind you every second of every day that you are enough for me, that you are all I've ever wanted and needed, I will happily do that for you. Because those thoughts are already in my head and those feelings are already in here," he says, placing my hand over his chest. "I love you. That's not stopping because you need a little reassurance. Period. But if you need reminders of my love, then that's what you'll get. You're worth the effort."

Together, we learned to accept that everyone comes into a relationship–any relationship–with baggage. It's part of being human. You can either trip over each others' baggage or sit down and unpack it together. So we unpacked it together, and we continue to unpack it once we notice our bags starting to fill up again.

My anxiety took a pretty big hit in the aftermath of the incident and Laurie's sentencing, but it has improved a lot with therapy, yoga, and time. Work is still stressful, as funding challenges persist, and the next round of layoffs is coming next month, we're told, but I know that as long as Jackson is by my side, we'll figure it out.

Being with Jackson has smoothed the jagged edges of much of my anxiety. Don't get me wrong, I still have an anxiety disorder.

I still feel the spikes of worry more intensely than most others. But between Jackson's words, the strength of his arms as he holds me, and his steady, unwavering countenance, I feel those spikes of anxiety a little less intensely. He can read me like a book, too, so even in those moments where my GAD gets the best of me, his constant reassurance gets me over those hard days a little faster.

Epilogue
Jackson

Four Months Later

Amy leans against me in the elevator, pressing her back into my chest, as I snake my arms around her hips. It's after hours and I convinced Amy to take me to her favorite exhibit at the Humanities Museum. She thinks I'm scoping the space for a possible fundraising location for my new charity, Game of Hope. Sean helped me establish the charity, which partners with local organizations working toward preventing childhood neglect. The charity is real, and so is our upcoming event, but the reason for the museum tonight is a ruse.

The elevator dings, signaling our arrival on the third floor. The Humanities Museum is one of the taller Chicago museums, with four floors total. Amy's favorite exhibit, the human body, is tucked towards the back of the museum, but spans all four floors. The third floor, however, houses the location I've staked out for tonight's activity: the heart.

Amy walks around the ribcage, dirty chai from Caffeine Kingdom clutched in her hands. I brought her the coffee earlier, and she's been savoring it for the last twenty minutes. I opted for a decaf black coffee, forgoing my normal red eye. I'm jittery enough; caffeine would likely undermine the feeling of calm I'm trying to elicit here.

Oblivious to my inner nerves, Amy chirps with ideas about how to set up the fundraiser night around the exhibit. "If you set up the dinner tables on the main floor, you can have photography stations within the human body exhibit! Wouldn't it be so cool to see everyone dressed in their black tie attire, hanging out in the lungs, or holding hands in the heart?"

She couldn't have given me a better opening. "The heart? What does that look like?" I ask, feigning ignorance. I smile as Amy giddily pulls me toward the chambers of the heart. The replica cardiac system is large enough for two people to stand comfortably in either of the ventricles. We stand in the left one, and Amy presses a plastic button on the wall. Instantly, the sound of blood pumping fills the speakers. Amy's eyes light up like a child's; she's totally geeking out over this and I take a minute to drink her in, pure joy radiating from within her.

When Amy turns to press more buttons, this time lighting arrows to show the path of blood flow through the veins and arteries, I palm the small box and pull it from my pocket. I'm on my knee before she turns around.

When she does turn, confusion momentarily flits across her face. When she sees me on one knee in front of her, her face crumples and she begins sobbing. Not exactly the start I envisioned, but I plow forward nonetheless.

"Amy. You are the most incredible, selfless, generous woman I've ever met. I've been slowly falling in love with you since I met you. I don't know what I would have done if Bruno hadn't forced you into my life; I'd probably still be wandering Caffeine Kingdom, lost and alone." Amy laughs and I take it as a good sign to keep going. "Telling you 'I love you' will never be enough to describe what my soul feels for you. Taking a bullet for you was the easiest decision of my life. Because there is no life for me without you in it. Will you let me prove my devotion to you every day for the rest of our lives? Will you marry me?"

Amy's a sobbing mess, tears streaming down her face, cheeks red, as she sinks to her knees in front of me. She's never looked so beautiful. She pulls me to her, clasping my face between her palms as she kisses me with the reassuring enthusiasm I needed, seeing as she still hasn't answered my question.

"Amy, baby," I interrupt her kissing, pulling back slightly. "Does that mean yes?"

"Oh, shit, I didn't say yes! Yes, of course I'll marry you! Nothing would make me happier!" She flings her arms around me, sobbing and clutching me, and I have to make a mental note not to drop the ring. Amy pulls back to give me a deep, passionate kiss that tastes of her tears, but also tastes of her love.

"Did you want to see the ring? I don't think you even looked at it," I begin.

"I don't care what it looks like, as long as I'm with you." And fuck, if that isn't the best answer she could have given me.

A few weeks later we begin the actual wedding planning, which is far more involved than anything I could have anticipated. Who knew guest lists were so complicated? Amy is heading up the planning, because, as she reminded me, if it was left up to me, we'd just have a barbeque on the roof of my building. She's not wrong.

However, charging Amy with wedding planning has led to her inevitably overthinking everything, and thus my plan to keep Amy as stress free as possible throughout this process, and hopefully throughout our marriage, is falling apart.

By the fourth major overhaul of the guest list, I'm truly concerned for Amy's mental health. She's overthinking more than usual.

"Amy, your overthinking is getting out of control. Do I need to remind you that you're not supposed to be doing that?"

She scrunches her nose while she debates the merits of providing a bratty answer. She makes her decision as she looks at me through her fluttering lashes and just says, "Yes."

"Good girl." I kiss her forehead, then her nose. "Now turn around and get on your knees."

The End.

Acknowledgements

If an author writes and publishes a book, but no one reads it, is she really an author? There is no Meghan French, author, without you, my readers, and as such, you deserve the first spot of thanks in this section. Your time and headspace is valuable and I appreciate you choosing to spend yours with my work.

Mr. French, thank you for your unwavering belief in me and your never-ending support. I couldn't have done this without you. Thank you for talking it through with me when my brain gets too stuck or overwhelmed to figure out my own plot. To my dog, who was my constant writing companion throughout this entire process: I love you. You're the best, most loyal, most handsome pup in the world.

My alpha readers, Alexa, Aleshia, and Jill: your thoughtful insights (and sometimes speed-reading) was invaluable in developing this from brain to keyboard to book. I still can't believe you all agreed to join me on this wild ride. Thanks for still being friends with me, even when I send you insane, multi-page NDAs.

Speaking of insane NDAs, the logistics of self-publishing my very own book simply would not have happened if it wasn't for my uber-talented and incredibly selfless brother. You may have regretted that law degree at times when I texted you at all hours asking what things meant and if legal considerations applied to me, but you gave me your time and energy without complaint. Thanks for not judging me when I swore you to secrecy about my romance writing aspirations (attorney-client privilege for the win!).

To Christina: thank you for talking me off the ledge when logistics like trim sizes and marketing and the overall overwhelm of independent publishing becomes too much. Your reminders about breaks and balance were necessary more often than I'd like to admit.

To Madison Abigail, a random B&N employee I bombarded with publishing and marketing questions...I appreciate your patience, opinions, and willingness to share your experience.

To my cover designer, Neil. You've created a gorgeous cover and spine. Your patience with me as I navigated my first cover design experience is much appreciated, and your work is unparalleled.

Jimmy and James, never once have you judged me on this adventure. Instead, you tirelessly gave me advice, laughed with me at my writing gaffs, and designed my very first logo without hesitation. I don't know how I would have managed the business and marketing side of publishing my first book without you both. Only a true friend would develop a sixteen-page analysis of trim sizes to help me make book publishing decisions. I'm lucky to call you both my friends.

Finally, to all of the romance and non-romance writers out there who have inspired me to take my own leap of faith. From a young age, I've devoured a steady diet of book after book, and you all have inspired me in your own way. Thank you for creating beautiful works.

About the Author

Meghan French is a romance author who loves writing about strong female characters and the swoonworthy, dirty-talking men who love them. A self-professed foodie and yogini, she lives in Arizona with her husband and rescue pitbull. When she's not in a writing cave, she spends her time as a school psychologist, hiking, and reading all the romance novels she can get her hands on.

Want to join my Facebook group? Find it under Meghan's Francophiles!

Also by Meghan French

Casual Now

JJ and Amy's Story

Book 1 of the Chicago Foxes Series

I'll Look After You

Warner and Alicia's Story

Book 2 of the Chicago Foxes Series

(Coming Soon!)

The Way You Say Good Morning

Benny and Delaney's Story

Book 3 of the Chicago Foxes Series

(Coming Soon!)

Reckless Behavior

Asher and June's Story

Book 4 of the Chicago Foxes Series

(Coming Soon!)

www.ingramcontent.com/pod-product-compliance
Lightning Source LLC
Chambersburg PA
CBHW071735110726
47908CB00006B/1590